P9-CRH-597

# Also by Terry Spear

# JOY *to the* WOLVES

## TERRY SPEAR

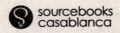

sourcebooks
casablanca

Published by Sourcebooks Casablanca, an imprint of Sourcebooks
P.O. Box 4410, Naperville, Illinois 60567-4410
(630) 961-3900
sourcebooks.com

Printed and bound in the United States of America.
OPM 10 9 8 7 6 5 4 3 2 1

*To Darla Taylor, who shares my love of gardening and birds and butterflies and Carolina anoles! Thanks for loving my stories and helping to catch the errors of my ways.*

# PROLOGUE

BROOKE CERISE couldn't believe it. She swore it was a family conspiracy!

She'd loved her parents with all her heart, but when they'd died in a head-on collision with a driver who was texting his girlfriend, they'd left a stipulation in the will that Brooke couldn't sell their antique and gift shop in Phoenix, Arizona, for three whole years. She was required to maintain it like they had, in the hopes that she'd carry on with the business long after that.

For three years, she'd kept the shop profitable so that when she could sell it, it would go for a decent price. She'd worked in her parents' shop forever before that, and she had a knack for knowing which items were real antiques and which were shams. Still, during all that time, she couldn't wait for the three years to end so she could get rid of the shop and do something else. *Anything* else. She had been too busy to think of what else she might do, but she couldn't have been happier when the time had come to sell. At least with all her hard work, she had made a good profit off the sale of the shop and its contents.

Then a couple of weeks after that, her beloved great-aunt, who owned an antique and gift shop in Portland, Oregon, died of a massive heart attack and left a similar stipulation in her will. For three whole years, Brooke had to run the shop herself to truly realize the value of the business. Brooke felt her parents and great-aunt had been in a conspiracy to make sure she would continue to do their bidding and finally realize that their dream to run a shop like this was her dream too.

She was devastated that she had lost her last living relative, but she couldn't believe she would have to manage Great-Aunt Ivy's antique shop now. However, since it had been her great-aunt's dying wish, Brooke would honor it with the same enthusiasm as she had her parents' request for their shop.

Her house sold, Brooke was finally leaving Phoenix for good and settling in Portland, where over the previous years, she had spent her summers helping her great-aunt manage her shop.

The only thing that made this will different from her parents' will was a cryptic note that had been attached: *Find a list of treasures, and you'll find your own destiny.* Her great-aunt had known how much Brooke loved treasure hunts, and Brooke cherished her beloved great-aunt for doing that for her one last time.

Before Brooke left Phoenix, she received an invitation to attend the estate sale of Randall Gulliver. She didn't need to buy anything more to sell in the shop. She knew her great-aunt's Victorian house-turned-shop was stacked to the gills. But Gulliver had come from money and was said to have collected valuable antiques, jewelry, sculptures, and paintings from around the world, and Brooke was curious why she would get a special invitation.

She got there before the auction started, and it didn't take her long to zero in on three bronze garden sculptures she wanted to buy for the courtyard that connected her great-aunt's Victorian home to the shop. *Despite* not planning to buy anything. But this was different. The wolf sculptures would be her keepsakes, and she'd take them with her once she sold the shop and moved somewhere else.

One was a wolf leaning up against a light pole, and she could picture decorating it for all seasons. Another was of a wolf drinking out of a fountain, a bird perched above it, watching him. The last was a statue of a couple of wolves sitting on a park bench. She knew Gulliver wasn't a wolf, though she'd heard he was called a ruthless wolf in his business dealings as a land developer. *She* was truly one, and she wanted the sculptures if the price was right. These were unique and nothing like anything she'd seen before.

She saw a black-haired woman, about thirty, dressed in high heels that made Brooke's arches ache just seeing them, skinny black jeans, and a sparkly black-and-silver sweater top that made her look like she was going to a New Year's Eve party. What had caught Brooke's attention more than anything was the woman giving an Asian gentleman grief before the auction began. Brooke recognized Mr. Lee from news photos she'd seen of him and Mr. Gulliver. Mr. Lee had been Gulliver's assistant in all things. He was about sixty, with graying temples, dark eyes, and an almost imperceptible smile as he saw Brooke watching the woman berating him. Then the woman stormed off, and Brooke continued to look over the three wolf sculptures.

Mr. Lee joined her, and she was surprised to smell that he was also a wolf. A gray wolf. She was a red wolf.

"Tibetan wolf," he offered. "I'm Mr. Lee, and you are Brooke Cerise. You're the daughter of the late Matt and Irene Cerise and the great-niece of the late Ivy Cerise. My heartfelt condolences for your losses. I knew your parents. Your mother located some Chinese porcelain for me to help fill in the pieces my sister owned and had lost. They were special serving dishes our parents had passed on to her, and she used them for all the holidays. You don't know how much it meant to her to find some in the same pattern. Your parents gave me a more than reasonable price on them. I am pleased to reciprocate. I sent you the invitation, believing you might be interested in the wolf sculptures. I'm sure you have a greater appreciation for them than others who might wish to buy them."

"I'd keep them," she quickly said.

He inclined his head. "Offer me two fifty apiece, and they're yours."

"But they're in the brochure." At nearly ten times the price, but she didn't want to mention it if he was willing to give them to her for so much less. What if he changed his mind?

"They should never have been placed in the brochure. They are not part of the estate but mine, so I can sell them for whatever price I see fit."

Her smile couldn't have stretched any bigger as they shook on it. "It's good seeing one of my kind here. I'll mark them as sold. You can pay at the register. I also have five boxes of stuff stacked over there. Nothing of real importance to most anyone else, but they're special to me, and since you still own an antique and gift shop, Ms. Cerise, you could probably easily make a little bit of money off the trinkets. They're mostly antique, but not considered valuable to the big buyer. They're yours for free."

"Special to you?" She frowned, not getting his meaning. This was Gulliver's estate sale.

"Yes. Now that I will no longer be working for Mr.

Gulliver, I need to get rid of some of my stuff I'd had at the estate, so I figured I'd do it here at the auction. The money will go to me, rest assured."

"Thanks." She was going to decline. The wolf statues were one thing. More boxes of junk? Brooke knew her aunt had plenty of those stacked in spare rooms in the shop.

"I would take them if I were you. You might find something that is valuable to *you*. You never know about these things until you take the time to discover the truth. I met your great-aunt when she visited. Ms. Cerise was a marvel, but she—how do I say this?—was a free spirit. I fear she might have dealt with some criminal element."

Brooke frowned at him. "What do you mean?"

"She's purchased things from all over the world for years, and those she dealt with… Well, she hadn't been as careful as she used to be. I had learned your great-aunt had a Tibetan urn I might be interested in. I was in the vicinity on business and traveled to Portland to see the urn, and it was just the item I was looking for to give my sister. Ms. Cerise also showed me a couple of antique Chinese vases, but they wouldn't have suited my sister's decor. Ms. Cerise confided in me at the time that she'd made a mistake in dealing with some people. She wouldn't say who for fear I could get in trouble. I was never to mention it to anyone, but since you may have inherited the trouble, I feel obligated to tell you. If anyone from Colombia contacts you to sell you pottery, don't deal with them."

"My great-aunt received illegal merchandise from them?"

"No. But since you've taken over the shop, they might try to deal with you next."

"Do you know the names of the people involved?"

"No."

"Thank you. I appreciate you telling me so I know what to watch out for." She couldn't imagine her great-aunt buying stuff from disreputable people. "What will you do after this?"

"Retire. My sister lives alone, and now that I'm no longer living at the estate here, I will move in with her and help her out."

"I'm sure she'll be grateful. If you ever need anything from me, you know where I'll be." At least for the next three years. She handed him her business card.

He accepted it and tucked it away.

"If you don't mind me asking, who was the woman who was so angry?" Brooke suspected it was one of Gulliver's disgruntled heirs. There were four of them, and instead of being grateful they had all received huge settlements, they were squabbling about the proceeds.

"Daisy Gulliver, Mr. Gulliver's daughter. She believes she is owed more of the estate. You are lucky, in a way, that there were no other heirs, either for your parents' or your great-aunt's estates."

"Well, I always wished I'd had a brother or sister, or both, but I understand what you mean." Brooke ran her hand over one of the wolf sculptures. "I will treasure these always."

"For us, that means for a very long time." He handed her his business card, bowed his head to her, and then walked off to speak to a man at the register, who looked back at her and smiled.

Now it was time to pay for her new purchases, hope Mr. Lee was right about her making some money on the items in the "junk" boxes, and drive to Portland and her new life. Unfortunately, her car was filled to the roof with all the last-minute stuff she had to pack, so the boxes—and the statues—would have to be shipped. Brooke couldn't wait to have the wolves in her garden. They were the bright spot in all this.

She just hoped Mr. Lee was wrong about her great-aunt dealing with bad sorts.

———————————

Before dawn at the Wilding Reindeer Ranch, located twenty minutes outside Portland, Oregon, Police Detective Josh Wilding was running as a red wolf with his brother, Maverick, who oversaw the reindeer ranch. They were glad to take a moment out of their busy day before they returned to the ranch house, shifted, dressed, and headed off to work.

Once they were home and dressed, Maverick fixed them cups of coffee. "Our pack leaders say the late Ms. Cerise must have left her estate to her great-niece, Brooke, who might be settling in at her great-aunt's Victorian house soon. Having another single she-wolf living in the area is always great news."

"Or she could be selling the place as soon as she can. She lives in Phoenix and might have no intention of moving here." No way did Josh want to get involved with a she-wolf who wasn't planning to stay in the territory.

"One of us needs to get over there and welcome her as soon as she arrives, even if she plans to sell the place. Maybe one of us can try to change her mind about leaving if she's of a mind to do so. And do it before the other bachelor males in the pack meet her."

"Why don't *you* go see her?" Josh shook his head. "Antique shops are not my thing. Unless she has a break-in, I don't see myself dropping in there anytime soon. We don't even know if she's coming here. She might just sell the place through a real estate agent."

He certainly wasn't going to run over to the shop to bother the she-wolf. Wouldn't their pack leaders have known if she was going to settle here?

Since they hadn't said anything to anyone, that probably meant it wasn't happening.

# CHAPTER 1

*Two weeks later, Portland, Oregon*

"WHAT MORE COULD GO WRONG TODAY?" BROOKE Cerise asked herself as "Jingle Bells" started playing on her radio, reminding her that it was time to rise. Except it *wasn't* the right time! It was an hour later than she always got up. She'd planned to wake even earlier this morning because she had a Christmas open house at her shop today.

At least her wolf statues had all arrived yesterday, and she couldn't be happier with them greeting her in her courtyard every day. She'd decorated them in bows and Christmas lights to help showcase them. The boxes of trinkets from the Gulliver estate still hadn't arrived. It could have taken some time to get everything boxed securely for shipment, and with the Christmas holiday package deliveries, the boxes must have been delayed. Brooke still hadn't been able to find the list of treasures her great-aunt had mentioned in the note. She felt like just closing the shop with a sign on the door stating: *In search of a treasure list that would fulfill my destiny. Be back when I find it!*

Brooke rushed to pull on her favorite green wool sweater and red-and-green-plaid wool skirt, leggings, and black suede boots. She was wearing a red lace bra and matching panties, making her feel Christmassy all the way to her bare skin—something her mother had always championed. Feel sexy just for yourself. She didn't need a mate to dress up for.

She was glad she'd taken a shower last night, or she'd be even later this morning. Hurrying to apply makeup, she wished she could just run as a wolf this morning and forget about the shop. She'd been meaning to check out Forest Park in Portland, which was only a few minutes away and one of the largest forested urban parks in America. After moving here, she'd been so busy getting everything ready for her opening that she really hadn't had the time.

She began making herself a thermos of lavender tea. "You know you could do this at the shop and at least be *in* the shop panicking," she told herself. Being a creature of habit, she'd already started heating the water, and she was still brushing out her unruly red hair.

Her store was full to bursting with boxes in the spare bedrooms of the Victorian house-turned-antique-shop. She wished she had said no to taking anything at Gulliver's estate, but she just couldn't have said no to Mr. Lee. He'd been too nice, though a little mysterious.

Finding treasure had been in Brooke's family's blood; her mother, father, great-aunt, and great-uncle were all treasure hunters. Which meant she was used to her family's obsession with finding valuable items discarded by those who couldn't discern the value of the collections. She was more interested in emptying the boxes stored in the rooms, properly sorting through the stuff, and cataloging it for sale. She envisioned emptying all the rooms and getting the place ready to sell—in three years.

Christmas was her favorite holiday, so she always served hot chocolate in addition to cranberry, cinnamon, and plain scones in the morning in the shop and wassail, Christmas tree—decorated chocolates, and caramel apple-cider cookies in the afternoon.

With her hot tea in a thermos in hand, Brooke set the house's security alarm, then headed for the back door. The courtyard garden connecting the two buildings was now decorated in Christmas ornaments for sale, the beautiful bronze wolf statues, and a fir tree covered in twinkling colored lights.

"Shoot." She needed to get the boxes out for recycling. And put on gloves and a hat. It was so much colder here at Christmastime than it was in Phoenix. *Brrr.*

She grabbed a red-plaid scarf and wrapped it around her neck, pulled on a soft, red knit hat, and slipped on some black kid-leather gloves, then opened the back door and stopped dead in her tracks. A young reindeer was standing under the eaves on her porch, head twisting around from where he'd been eating berries off Brooke's holly hedge, wide, warm-brown eyes staring back at Brooke. A thin leather strap of jingle bells jingled when the reindeer turned and walked over to join her.

"Ohmigod, where did you come from?" Brooke guessed the reindeer was about eight months old since he didn't have antlers yet, and reindeer calves were usually born in May or June. She'd learned all about them at the Grand Canyon Deer Farm in Williams, Arizona.

She saw that one of the gates to the four-foot-tall, wrought-iron decorative fence was standing open although she was sure she'd locked it last night. The problem was that the latch needed to be replaced, like a lot of things in the old Victorian houses. It had a habit of not staying shut. Even when she locked the gate, if the latch hadn't caught hold, a little wind could push it open.

Not wanting to scare the calf off but wanting to secure him so she could call someone to come get him, Brooke set her thermos of tea on the wrought-iron café table next to her and calmly talked to the young calf. "Hey, little guy. I'm going to take you into the shop, okay?" Not that Brooke had ever planned to have an animal in her shop, which made her think of a bull in a china shop if the poor little reindeer got scared. But Brooke had to open her shop, and her courtyard wasn't secure enough, even if she could reach the gate and close it before the reindeer ran off. What if the calf could jump over the short fence? White-tailed deer could bound over an eight-foot fence. Maybe a reindeer calf couldn't leap that high though.

Still, Brooke didn't want to chance losing him. She had to learn where the calf belonged and return him to his owner.

She continued to talk softly and reassuringly to the calf. The reindeer didn't bolt, thankfully. In fact, he seemed interested in meeting Brooke, who held out her hand, wishing she had some sort of treat. The reindeer sniffed her hand and seemed gentle and unafraid. She suspected he might be from a reindeer ranch and used to people petting him.

Taking hold of the reindeer's jingle-bell collar, Brooke walked him toward the shop. Once she and the reindeer were inside, she rushed to turn off her security alarm and turn on all the Christmas lights and the Christmas music, starting with the "Carol of the Bells," soothing her frazzled nerves. Already a few people were peering in her windows and beveled-glass door, probably wondering if she was ever going to open the shop. She knew what it was like to be standing outside in the cold, waiting for a shop to open on time.

As soon as Brooke opened the front door, the sleigh bells over the top jingled their merry tune, and she smiled brightly at her customers. "Welcome, come in."

Seven people had been waiting, more than usual, but it *was* her open house. Brooke supposed she should be grateful there weren't more customers so she could get things set up before a bigger crowd arrived.

"So sorry for the delay in opening." At least Brooke had a good excuse for opening fifteen minutes late. She still needed to warm up the scones and make the hot cocoa. She realized her thermos of tea was still sitting on the table on the porch.

She smiled and presented the reindeer. "I had an unexpected guest this morning."

"Oh my," the three ladies at the front of the gathered shoppers said when they saw the reindeer calf.

If anyone had been annoyed with Brooke for letting them into the shop late, that melted away the irritation.

"Oh, isn't he adorable," one of the women said, pulling out her phone and immediately taking pictures.

"Come in. Shop." The women were petting the reindeer when Brooke said, "I'll be right back with the food. In the meantime, if you don't mind helping, make sure he doesn't get outside."

"We'll watch him," one of the women said, her voice reassuring and cheerful.

Everyone was taking pictures of the calf. With his jingle-bell collar and the way he was standing next to a Christmas tree decorated in antique and antique-replica Christmas decorations and twinkling lights, the reindeer made for perfect Christmas-card pictures. With the Christmas music playing overhead, the scene was perfect for videos too.

Brooke hoped the reindeer didn't go to the bathroom in the shop. She would have to take him out on breaks until someone came to get him. Was he thirsty? Maybe.

She fetched an antique-replica washbowl and filled it with water. Then she checked on her phone to see what reindeer could eat. "Carrots!" She had some of those in the shop's kitchen. Probably a couple would be enough until someone claimed the calf. Brooke set the water next to the tree so the reindeer could drink when he was thirsty.

The calf lapped it up. Poor little thing. He was really thirsty.

Brooke gave the carrots to two of her first customers who were taking pictures of the reindeer. "If you'd like to feed him, they love carrots."

"Oh, sure, thanks," one of the women said, and in the spirit of Christmas, they broke the carrots into smaller pieces to offer to other customers to feed the reindeer.

The Christmas cinnamon potpourri scented the air, giving the whole shop a delightful Christmas fragrance. The hot cocoa and cinnamon, cranberry, and blueberry scones added to the festive scents. Brooke set the tray of food and drinks on the serving table in the dining room and was astonished to see the seven people now numbered about twenty, all wanting to see the reindeer calf. Before she had more of a mob scene, she hurried to call the police about him.

"Hi, I'm Brooke Cerise, and I found a reindeer calf in my courtyard this morning. I have him in my shop, Cerise's Antiques and Gifts. Has anyone reported a reindeer calf missing?"

"This is a joke, right? Call Santa. I'm sure he'll tell you all his reindeer are accounted for." The police officer hung up on her.

Brooke wanted to growl! Though she suspected it did sound funny, and the officer might be used to getting crank calls about Santa and his reindeer during the holidays. Still, she was *not* amused!

---

Josh Wilding had taken a long wolf run with his brother at the ranch that morning, the first time in a couple of weeks. They'd paused to play-fight before he had to get into work. For now, they were red wolves, snarling and growling, biting and barking and having a ball. They needed to experience the more primal side of their existence, their wolf roots, and enjoyed the bonding. Like playing games with each other, wolf style.

Then they'd howled, signaling an end to their wolf games, and raced each other back to the ranch house. Time to get on with work.

"Hey, I'll see you tonight," Josh said, dressing in his bedroom after taking a shower, his brother already in the kitchen getting coffee.

"Yeah, pizza tonight, right?"

"Sounds good to me." Josh left his bedroom, grabbed a cup of coffee and a Danish roll, and headed out to work. He hadn't even gotten there when his brother called him on the Bluetooth.

"Hey, I was just in the barn and saw that one of our reindeer calves has been stolen."

Hearing one of the reindeer making a honking noise and their hooves moving around on the ground, Josh could tell Maverick was in the barn with them right now. "Which one?"

"Jingles. I made sure he hadn't sneaked out of his stall, but he couldn't have. The latch was closed."

"None of the other ranch hands left it open by mistake?"

"No. And it was latched. I smelled an unknown male wolf. A human too maybe, but we have so many tours, it might have been someone here yesterday on a tour."

"Hell."

"I'll keep you posted. I'm checking the security videos next, but I wanted to let you know right away that he'd been stolen."

"Thanks."

A few minutes later, Maverick called Josh again. "Jingles is at Cerise's Antique and Gift Shop."

"You're kidding. The new owner has our calf?"

"Or someone else might have taken over the business. There are tons of messages going out on social media about a reindeer calf at the shop, and it is Jingles, from the pictures I saw of him."

"I'm on my way! I'll let you know what I discover." Josh turned his car in the direction of the shop, ready to question the new owner about why he, or she, had their calf there. He was glad Jingles was unharmed and being taken care of, but he had to find out who had stolen him in the first place. He wanted answers *now*.

# CHAPTER 2

BROOKE CALLED THE FIRST REINDEER RANCH she could find the number for while she hurried to leave the boxes outside for the recyclable trash. When she returned to the shop, someone from the ranch picked up the call.

"Hi, I'm Brooke Cerise, and a reindeer calf showed up—" She quit speaking when she saw a tall, dark, and handsome man walk into her shop wearing a suit, a parka, and a badge. He'd better not be the bozo at the police bureau who had hung up on her!

The man glanced at the reindeer calf and then moved through the customers taking pictures of him. He reached Brooke, his posture saying he was in charge and going to get to the bottom of this. "This deer belongs to Wilding Reindeer Ranch. Do you care to explain why he's in your shop?" He raised a dark brow. He had an Indiana Jones-type build—muscled enough to swing across caverns and climb tall peaks, nice broad shoulders, physically fit, not like he sat around in an office eating too many doughnuts. "This *is* your shop, correct?"

"Yes. I'm Brooke Cerise, the owner."

That was when she smelled the officer's scent and realized he was a red wolf like her. Wild, wolfish, and an Ivory fragrance. A red-wolf pack was located outside Portland, but on her visits to see her great-aunt, she hadn't had time to meet anyone. She hoped it wouldn't be a problem for her to move into the area without contacting the pack leaders first. Did he belong to the pack? Not that she could ask him in front of her human customers.

She said to the man on the phone, "Uh, sorry, it looks like I just found where the calf belongs."

"No problem. Thanks for calling and checking with us."

"You're welcome. Have a great day." She ended the call. "I called it in, but the officer I spoke to thought it was a crank call. The reindeer just walked into my courtyard."

"I'm Detective Wilding, an investigator with the Portland Police Bureau. I've called the ranch, and someone's coming to pick him up." He had a nice, manly voice, warm and sexy like one of her favorite narrators of the romance audiobooks that she enjoyed listening to. He took a deep breath of her scent too. She wondered if he'd known her great-aunt.

Brooke realized she was getting so much publicity that the police must have seen the news that the reindeer was at her open house and sent an investigator to investigate.

"I need to get your statement," he said, all official-like.

As if she were at fault for the reindeer calf being here! Hopefully, the other local wolves were a lot more welcoming than he was. That was all she needed though. To be considered a rogue wolf who committed crimes!

"By the way, you don't leave anything important in your trash, do you? Like credit-card or bank-account information without shredding it?"

"No, why?"

"Someone was looking at your boxes."

"Maybe to use for packing boxes?"

"Maybe."

More people crowded into her shop. Brooke sure hoped people were going to purchase something and not just come to see the reindeer. Though she had to admit the little fellow made for a great marketing tool with all the social network shares that were going on. It was putting her shop on the map. He was adorable, and he seemed to be enjoying all the company.

Several of the customers were still texting about the reindeer and posting about her shop, and a few people had migrated to the drinks and food and begun to enjoy them. Then a couple of customers brought items over to her checkout counter. *Yes!*

"Sorry, why don't you do your police-officer duty and take care of the reindeer? I'll give you a statement when things slow down, Officer," she told Detective Wilding. She didn't expect him to do anything with the reindeer, but she hoped he'd leave her alone while she was checking out her customers.

"Detective," he corrected her. He situated himself right next to the checkout counter, waiting for her to finish ringing up her sales.

How annoying!

The ladies thanked her and smiled at the detective, who smiled back at them with a little lift to one corner of his mouth, giving him a charmingly handsome appearance. The ladies took their packages and left. Brooke glanced in the direction of the other people in her shop, wishing a whole bunch of customers would inundate her with merchandise to ring up so she could ignore the detective further, but nope. That meant she was at the detective's mercy. Again. *Darn it.*

"Okay, give me your statement now." He stood there tall and imposing, his dark hair windswept, his dark-brown eyes capturing her gaze, powerful, demanding. There was no smile for her.

"He was eating holly berries off my shrub. Someone had left the gate open."

"Not you, of course."

"Of course not. I always close it." Brooke folded her arms across her chest. She knew that was a defensive posture when she had nothing to be defensive about. She had nothing to do with stealing the reindeer!

"But you didn't lock it."

"Usually, I do." She let out her breath. "I must have forgotten."

"But you didn't forget to close the gate."

He might be gorgeous to look at, but he was annoying her to pieces. She was a law-abiding citizen, and she wasn't in the market for a reindeer calf. How could he make her feel like she was guilty of a crime just because she must not have locked her gate last night?

"The latch needs to be replaced." She hated having to concede that to the detective.

"Faulty latch, hmm," he said, writing it down.

Oh, for heaven's sake. You'd think she'd committed the crime of the century!

Brooke got another two sales and thankfully could take a break from the inquisitor. Once her customers left with their packages, she figured she'd need to make more hot chocolate before manning the register again. She didn't bother telling the detective what she was going to do. It was none of his business. He needed to figure out how the reindeer had left the ranch and ended up at her place—not hassle her.

But his focus remained on her as he followed her into the kitchen. "Why don't you watch the customers and make sure no one takes off with anything of value? Since you're a police detective," she reminded him. She started making more hot chocolate. The fragrance of chocolate filled the kitchen. She added some peppermint to a mixture of coffee and hot chocolate in a mug for herself, and she was in heaven.

"I'm here about the stolen reindeer," the detective said.

She raised a brow, taking a sip of her peppermint mocha. She'd heard that peppermint could help lower blood pressure, and hers was on the rise because of his badgering. "I *didn't* steal it. He was standing on my patio when I left the house."

"You said he was in your courtyard."

"My house is behind the shop."

"Show me exactly where you found the calf."

The guy was *so* exasperating. "Don't you have anything better to do with your police time?" She pointed out the kitchen window. "There. See the holly bush by the back porch to my house? That's where he was. Standing there. Eating my holly berries."

"Hell, those wolf statues have to be worth a small fortune at the very least. You need to lock your gate."

Brooke wanted to growl at him, and she was sure she gave him her most growly look. Mostly because she knew he was right.

Someone rang the bell on her checkout counter.

"Coming!" she called out.

She carried the hot chocolate pot into the shop and set it on the trivet by the scones. Then she grabbed her peppermint mocha and went to ring up more sales. "Sorry. I had to set out more hot chocolate. Did you get some?" she asked the customer.

"Oh yes, thanks. It's great on a Christmassy cold day. And the reindeer is so cute."

"He is, and luckily we've found his home."

"Oh good. Merry Christmas," the lady said.

"Merry Christmas." Brooke had been so rattled from the events of the morning that she hadn't even been wishing anyone a happy holiday.

The police detective went over to pet the reindeer, thankfully, but then returned to stand by the counter again. "Where were you last night?" he asked.

"At the shop, getting ready for the open house. Later? At home, making dinner. Then I went to bed. No, wait. I took a shower first, brushed my teeth, and then went to bed."

The detective looked like he was fighting a smile. Then his expression turned stern again. "Does anyone else live with you who could verify your whereabouts? Or whether you closed the gate last night?"

This was too much. Brooke folded her arms. "Are you *really* a cop?" If he was going to hassle her, she was going to hassle him back, just a little. "You didn't show me your ID."

With a hint of a smirk, he handed his ID to her. "Police detective."

She gave it a long, hard look. Teach him to badger her.

A man hurried into the shop who didn't look like he was interested in shopping. He instantly went over to pet the reindeer and give it a hug. The owner? He looked a lot like the detective inquisitor, except that his eyes were more amber, not as dark a brown, and his hair was a lighter shade of brown and shaggier. But he had the same hard, square jaw and angular features and the same good looks. They had to be related.

After greeting the calf, the guy headed straight for her, smiling. "I'm with Wilding Reindeer Ranch. Maverick Wilding." He offered his hand to her. He took a deep breath and smiled appreciably.

Just like she was breathing in his wolfish scent. She wondered how many red wolves lived in the area. She smiled and shook his hand. Things were looking up. When she'd realized she was going to have to take over the shop for three years, Brooke had begun hoping to join the red pack.

"I'm Brooke Cerise, owner of the shop. I'm pleased to meet you."

"Likewise." Then Maverick frowned. "You're Ivy Cerise's great-niece, aren't you?"

"Yes."

"My condolences. So she left you the place in her will?"

"Yes. I visited her whenever I could in the summers. I lived in Arizona."

"We're so glad to have you here." Maverick smiled broadly.

She didn't think *everyone* was glad to see her here.

"You're staying here, right?"

"Uh, yes." At least for now. She smiled again.

"I'd still like to know how Jingles got into your fenced-in yard." The detective acted as though he still thought she was involved in the stolen reindeer caper, and he wasn't letting her off the hook, even though Maverick, the owner of the calf, didn't seem to believe she had anything to do with it.

"That makes two of us. You are brothers?"

"Yes, that's Josh. My twin brother, five minutes older than me," Maverick said. "He texted me to say you had Jingles."

"Ohh-kay. If you'll both excuse me, I need to bring out some more food for the customers."

"Thanks for taking care of Jingles," Maverick said.

"You're welcome." She gave Josh a disgruntled look. "At least one of you is nice enough to say so."

Josh smiled at her. That was the first true smile he'd offered her, and despite not wanting it to happen, she felt her insides melting under his observation.

She noticed the reindeer had finished off a good amount of his water and probably needed to go outside to relieve himself. "Hey, you might want to take Jingles out back in case he needs to…"

Too late.

"Uh, do you want to do something about that?" she asked Maverick.

"You're the one who brought him into the shop and got the publicity for it. We ought to charge you for the rental of our reindeer," Josh said.

She ground her teeth. "*Your* reindeer? I thought it was *his* reindeer." She motioned to Maverick.

"The reindeer ranch is family-owned and operated by the two of us. We may be brothers, but I'm the nice one. I'll handle it," Maverick said.

"Thanks." She served more scones, then returned to the checkout counter. Two news reporters and the local TV station reporter suddenly walked into the shop. Ohmigod, Brooke couldn't believe this. She was so thrilled she wanted to howl for joy.

Luckily, Maverick cleaned up the reindeer mess before the cameras got rolling.

"So how did the reindeer end up coming here?" a reporter asked Brooke as she was ringing up another customer's purchases.

"He loved my holly berries and came right into the courtyard to nibble on a few. He's been entertaining my customers ever since. Then the policeman and his brother showed up to take him home. I was glad to learn where the calf was from and that he'd be fine." Except that the police detective and his brother weren't leaving. She knew Maverick wanted to be friendly, while Josh wanted to question her some more.

Finally, Jingles curled up under the Christmas tree to sleep, and the reporters left. Maverick helped Brooke make more wassail that afternoon, while Josh dealt with crowd control. Brooke couldn't help but be amused that he finally had to do some real police work. Even though he was a "detective."

"What are you going to do about lunch?" Maverick asked Brooke.

Josh walked into the shop about that time and overheard Maverick's question. "I'll pick us up something. What do you want to eat?" he asked Brooke.

She was shocked. She wasn't sure if he was serious, but she was taking advantage of his offer. She always had her granola bar for a quick snack for lunch if nothing else. If she had a lull in customers, she could place an order for a sandwich at the bakery across the street and run and pick it up when it was ready. That was where she had gotten her delightful bakery goods for the shop.

"I'll have prime rib roast, mashed potatoes, gravy, candied carrots, and no drink. I can have tea here. Oh, and peppermint bark for dessert." Arms folded across her chest, she smiled.

Josh's jaw was hanging before he masked his expression, and he glanced at his brother. "You?"

Maverick was grinning. "I'll have the same, uh, but make the peppermint bark a fudge brownie."

Josh shook his head. "Whatever happened to hamburgers for lunch?" he said under his breath as he headed out of the shop.

Not only did the meal she asked for appeal, but she would have enough left over to have for dinner—and it would take the detective longer to get the order, so he wouldn't be underfoot for a while.

An hour and a half later, the detective showed up, carrying a sack of food from her favorite steak restaurant. Brooke was checking out a customer, and Maverick was returning from a trip outside with Jingles. At least the courtyard had a nice-sized patch of grass, something her great-aunt had maintained when she raised dogs over the years.

"I had to take care of a matter at the bureau," Josh told his brother, setting the food in the kitchen. "The things I do for you."

"Hey, since you offered and she wanted something special, I figured we might as well all go for it." Maverick smiled. "I thought you might just get a hamburger for yourself."

His brother gave him a get-real look as Brooke joined them in the kitchen when the last customer left the shop. Sometimes it was busy during lunch hour, and she couldn't get a bite to eat, but sometimes, like now? Perfect. She hurried to make ice water for everyone, then took her seat and began eating.

Maverick smiled. "She was hungry."

"If a customer comes in, I'll have to quit eating. I have to hurry."

"We can cover for you. We have ranch hands taking care of things back at the ranch." Maverick smiled at her.

"Thanks. Boy, this is sure delicious. I like eating a big lunch and then a light dinner, but it rarely works out that way except on my days off when the shop is closed."

Thankfully, they all had time to eat while Maverick talked about all the reindeer they had at the stables and Josh periodically studied her as if he was waiting for her to confess to the crime of stealing a reindeer calf. She finished half the meal and thanked him again for the food, then slipped the remainder in the fridge. As if on cue, her shop door opened, and five more women came inside to see the reindeer. Two of them purchased gift items for their families.

By the time it was six o'clock and Brooke could close the store, she was exhausted. The brothers still hadn't left. Though Josh had disappeared for a time, maybe doing some detective work.

She thought Maverick had wanted to keep the calf here to help her business. At the same time, he was handing out business cards, telling customers about the reindeer ranch and tours they conducted any time of the year. So it benefited them mutually.

"Do you want to have dinner with me?" Maverick asked, looking hopeful.

"Thanks, but I've got the other half of the meal I had at lunch. I'll have that tonight for dinner. I've got a ton of things to do before tomorrow gets here." Like restock the empty shelves. It looked like she'd had a going-out-of-business sale, because so many of the shelves were practically empty. Which was great.

"Be sure and lock your gate from now on," Josh said, giving her a stern look. "You've got a lot of merchandise in your courtyard that someone might want to steal."

"Thank you, Detective. I'll do that." She didn't need his advice. Though she thought she ought to thank him again for the great lunch. "Thanks for the prime rib lunch. That was great." Too bad her lunch companion had made her feel like squirming under his scrutiny. She suspected he didn't often eat meals—or pay for them out of his own pocket—with suspects on his most-wanted list. "It sure beat having a granola bar."

He inclined his head and left the shop.

She supposed she needed to make a to-do list for closing so she wouldn't forget to do any of the important stuff. Like locking her gate! Though it had worked out for the best, because the calf had ended up in her yard and he'd been safe.

Maverick began to take the reindeer out front. He'd periodically taken him out for bathroom breaks in the courtyard throughout the day, and luckily, they hadn't had any more accidents. He'd put straw down for Jingles and even cleaned up after him.

Brooke walked outside with Maverick as he took the reindeer calf out to his truck and placed him in a trailer, all the customers now gone. She noticed Josh was on his phone talking to someone. "Do you rent the reindeer calves for promotional purposes?"

Maverick locked the gate to the enclosed trailer. "Usually not the calves, but the adult ones, sure."

"Oh."

He smiled. "Everyone loves to see them for Christmas. We show them off at the ranch. Jingles seemed to enjoy all the attention he was getting here. It all worked out in the end."

"I was thinking about doing this again next year. I hadn't expected to have that much business, and having Jingles here really helped sales. I could rent one of the adults and have photo ops for anyone who came to the shop. The reindeer would be out in the courtyard, and I'd be better prepared the next time, make a big deal of it and promote it." Though it had worked out well this year, with all the press she'd received.

"We can do that. One of us is always here with the reindeer for the event, so that wouldn't be a problem at all," Maverick said. "I sure can arrange it."

"Thanks, and do you belong to the red wolf pack in the area?" she asked.

"Yeah, Leidolf and Cassie Wildhaven's red wolf pack. They live on a ranch with over thirty thousand acres of land. We all go down there when we want to run as wolves. There are other places, too, but with that much acreage, there's so much to see and explore that we never get tired of it. Best of all, it's safe. Though we also have four thousand acres on the reindeer ranch, and you're free to run there as a wolf anytime." Maverick gave her the pack leaders' phone numbers and his own. "Just call them. They'd love to meet you. If you'd ever like to have dinner, just call or text me."

"Thanks. As soon as I have time, I will." She might. Just not right away.

Josh said into his phone, "I'm on my way." He hurried off without saying goodbye, which suited her fine.

"Don't mind my brother. He's concerned the calf was stolen from our ranch. Then, for whatever reason, Jingles was dumped off at your place, or maybe some distance from here, and found his way into your courtyard and had his holly-berry breakfast. Josh doesn't really believe you took the calf."

"Thanks." Though Brooke didn't believe Josh had absolved her of the crime yet. She'd freely admitted she had benefited from the reindeer calf being here. Though if she'd been that devious, she would have planned things a little better. "Did you want me to pay for Jingles being here all day?"

"Absolutely not. We're just glad he was safely here with you. I need to get him home to the herd. We'll talk later."

"Thanks again." She returned to the shop and closed and locked the door. And smiled. Man, was that the best open house ever. Even better? She'd met two members of the wolf pack she wanted to be part of once she got a little more settled in. Maverick was super nice. Josh was...the one she couldn't quit thinking about. Arrogant, annoying, antagonistic!

Brooke hoped Josh could learn the truth about how the reindeer had ended up in her courtyard. She was ready to be off his suspect list.

# CHAPTER 3

Josh knew as soon as he joined his brother for dinner that night that Maverick would give him hell for even thinking the little red wolf had stolen their reindeer. But he was a police detective, and that was what he did. The person in possession of the stolen item was usually the one who stole it.

It seemed reasonable to him to believe she did it to get publicity for her open house. That certainly could be a motive. If someone had stolen the calf to keep or sell it, why leave it in her courtyard? Sounded suspect to him. Though she was a wolf, new to their territory, and probably interested in joining the pack. That made it seem unlikely she would want to do anything illegal, particularly when she could rent reindeer from them for special occasions. Except that she couldn't rent the calves.

When Josh arrived at the reindeer ranch, he parked his car and headed inside the sprawling ranch house to have pizza and beer with his brother.

"What was that all about?" Maverick frowned at him as he brought the pizza out of the oven.

Josh pulled a couple of beers out of the fridge, and they sat at the table to enjoy their cheese, pepperoni, hamburger, and sausage deep-dish pizza. "If you mean questioning the she-wolf at her shop for being in possession of Jingles, I was doing my job."

"She's a red wolf."

"I noticed." Josh pulled off a slice of pizza and took a bite.

"She wouldn't have done it."

"She had motive."

Maverick shook his head. "You know, when you're like this, it's because you're interested in the woman but you don't want to show that you are. How many years are going to go by before you give another she-wolf a chance?"

Josh frowned at him. "It's only been six months."

"I know. But it could be years the way you were so upset over Joy's death. Listen, you couldn't have done anything more for her. Joy was a rookie cop. She was too impulsive, too roguish. She wouldn't listen to you and was too ready to disobey your orders to prove she had what it took to be a good cop. And then she died. It wasn't your fault. She wouldn't have been the right one for you, even if she hadn't been secretly mated." Maverick shook his head. "You need to get on with your life. You didn't think of her every minute of the day. You were glad to have time away from her so you could breathe." He pointed a slice of pizza at Josh. "We have two new she-wolves who have joined the pack down at Leidolf and Cassie's ranch. I keep telling you we need to make time to see them."

"What about Miss Cerise?" Josh asked, surprised Maverick would mention seeing the other ladies when Brooke lived even closer by.

"Sure, but she already turned me down for dinner, so there might not be anything there. I was definitely my charming self. *You* certainly didn't interest her—you annoyed her the whole time you were there."

Josh finished his second slice of pizza. "She's a suspect until I learn otherwise. Man, does this pizza hit the spot."

He knew his brother was right about Joy, but he didn't want to get involved with another woman anytime soon. He was glad his brother didn't mention how, because of Joy's impulsiveness, Josh had been shot three times. He'd heard it enough for a lifetime.

"Thanks. We haven't had a pizza in a while, so I thought it was about time. So you checked our security videos and didn't find anything suspicious?"

"About that. The video was looped." Josh pulled loose another piece of pizza.

"Ah, hell. I didn't notice when I checked it out. Someone took the time to cover their tracks then. Someone who works for us?" Maverick shook his head before Josh answered him. "Everyone who works here is a wolf, and why would they do it?"

"It was an unknown wolf—and maybe a human male—who did it."

"I smelled the scents too." Maverick took another swig of beer. "It can't be Brooke. This was someone who knew what they were doing and probably had an accomplice or two."

"She could have."

"If you don't look for the real culprit, you might not find who did this. Then what? We have the same problem again? We need to know when—"

"Sometime last night between two and three."

"Who and why."

"She made a lot of money off sales today, all because Jingles was drawing the crowds to her shop. She had the best motive in the world. And she had possession of the stolen property." Because of those two things, she would remain Josh's number one suspect.

"Ahh, I see now."

"What?" Josh pulled off another slice of pizza.

"If she continues to be your one and only suspect, you can keep seeing her under the guise that this is just police business."

Josh gave a sarcastic laugh. "Since when do I get interested in dating suspects?"

"I'd say right about now."

"She just moved here. Is it someone she knows? Or someone who came with her? She didn't tell me if she lived alone or not. What do we know about her? Nothing. I need to question her further about who she knows in the area."

"She's not involved."

"You don't know how devious women can be. In the business I'm in, I'm used to it."

"You're wrong in this case, Brother." Maverick finished his last slice of pizza. "That's okay. I'll keep pursuing her then. Just don't mess up my chances with her by badgering her."

Josh had every intention of learning if she had any part in this or not.

---

Brooke went outside and was about to lock her gate before she did anything else when she noticed it had a bright, shiny new latch. She couldn't imagine anyone replacing it. Except for Maverick taking Jingles to have potty breaks outside, he'd been inside with her the whole time.

Had Mr. Detective done it? She couldn't even envision that.

She didn't want to have any more trouble just because she didn't lock her gate again. As much as she hated to admit it, the detective was right about someone being able to come in and steal her wolf statues. She sure didn't want that. At least the gate shut properly now, and it was locked.

She went back inside her shop and began cleaning the kitchen, washing the chocolate pot, the slow cooker she'd used to make the wassail, and the serving dishes. Once that was done, she brought out the boxes of gift items her great-aunt had purchased, figuring that was the fastest way to fill the shelves. Due to their wolf's enhanced longevity and their slow aging process, Ivy had accumulated lots of stuff that might not have been that valuable when she had purchased it but could be now.

Once Brooke hung a ton of ornaments on the tree, she filled shelves and straightened up her shop. She turned off all the main lights, leaving a few security lights on, and turned off her Christmas music. She was eager and hopeful she'd find some fun, saleable items in the attic next. With all the repairs she'd had to make to the house and the shop and getting ready to open it, she hadn't had time to see what was in the attic, and that was driving her crazy.

What she loved best was that she didn't have to drive anywhere to be home. And she could watch over her shop better, though she hadn't expected to have a young reindeer calf standing on her porch this morning.

During the spring, Brooke planned to fill the yard with garden ornaments to sell. She couldn't wait to smell the lavender and lilac and see the cherry blossoms in full bloom. Even though she intended to sell the place in three years, she might as well enjoy it as much as she could while she was stuck here.

She wiped down the new stove in the shop. The old one had gone out two days after she moved in, and the heat pump had quit working the day after that. As soon as she had time, she needed to renovate the kitchen in the house before anything else went out. She just hoped nothing more would go wrong. That was the problem with having two Victorian houses to maintain.

Brooke picked up the antique bowl by the Christmas tree that she'd used for a water bowl for the calf, cleaning it and setting it on the kitchen counter to dry. She was glad the little calf had come into her life, especially since she'd been able to meet some wolves from the local pack. She hoped Josh Wilding would seriously look at some other suspect and discover who had done such a thing to make sure it didn't happen again.

She glanced out the shop's kitchen window at the courtyard and frowned. How had the little reindeer made its way all the way here from the Wilding ranch?

Finally ready to check out the attic, Brooke climbed the stairs to the second floor, passing the three bedrooms and the bathroom on her way to the attic stairs at the end of the hall. She switched on the light to the attic and climbed the steps.

In the attic, two beautiful vintage steamer trunks sat near the windows along one wall. But they were locked. She'd have to hire someone to unlock them for her without breaking the locks, which could be worth something, too, as old as they looked.

The room had enough height for a full-grown man to

stand, and the windows would let in a nice amount of light during the day, if they were cleaned. Another project for when she had more time. The walls sloped down at both the front and back of the room. She noticed it was fully finished, with air-conditioning and heating ducts, unlike the average attic storage space. The attic had a thermostat, and she saw the temperature was the same as for the rest of the house. She assumed the room was also well insulated.

Boxes and crates of stuff filled most of the space, though her great-aunt had left room to walk around some of the crates and the trunks. Everything was covered in dust. Old spiderwebs, broken and dusty, hung from the ceiling. The dust and spiderwebs made the attic look more ready for Halloween than Christmas. It would take Brooke forever to go through all this stuff to see what might be valuable. Though on the two days her shop was closed, she'd make a concerted effort to do just that.

She noticed a shelf behind some of the crates filled with vinyl records—plastic sleeves protecting the records and plastic covers protecting the album covers. Her great-aunt had meticulously cared for the vinyl records, but why store them in the attic?

Brooke found a record player that looked in great shape in a box and carried it down to the second floor. Then she began to haul the vinyl records down the stairs, setting them in the hallway so she could carry them down to the first floor and out to the house. She needed to price each one, and there had to be around two hundred here.

She paused when she found a 1963 record, *The Freewheelin' Bob Dylan*, and hoped it was one of the album's mistake pressings where four songs were replaced with newly recorded tracks. In mint condition, the albums could be worth a small fortune—up to $35,000 each. The Beatles' *Please Please Me*? Oh yes! Well, if it was one of the early ones.

She left the record player in her office in the shop so customers could listen to the records if they were interested in them. She started hauling all the records to the house and saw her thermos filled with tea still sitting on the table where she'd left it when she found Jingles standing on her porch. She fished in her pocket to pull out her house keys, unlocked the door, dropped off the records, turned off the security alarm, and put the thermos of tea in the kitchen. Then she locked the back door.

She wondered what other treasures were hidden in the attic. She'd looked on and off for two weeks for her great-aunt's inventory sheet and still hadn't found it. For now, she'd spend the rest of the evening going through the records, learning the value of each, move some of the books off the living room shelves to make room for the records until she found buyers for the collectibles. She set the books on the floor behind the Christmas tree and would have to sort through them one of these days too.

By the time she went to bed, she realized what a fortune she could have just in vinyl records. Even at the low price of a few hundred dollars per record, she could have between $50,000 and $200,000. Her great-aunt had managed to collect a few first editions, and they were worth from several hundred dollars to $35,000 apiece.

Things were looking up.

Dressed in her red flannel pajamas covered in little reindeer—which made her think of Jingles—and lying in bed, Brooke placed her arms behind her head on her pillow, looked at the ceiling, and smiled. This had been one perfect open house, as crazy as the day had started out. She took a deep breath and thought about running in the woods as a wolf, the perfect way to end an already great day.

Her phone on the bedside table played a little of the "Carol of the Bells," and she frowned, wondering who would be calling her at eleven at night. When she looked at the caller ID, she saw it was Josh Wilding.

What now? He'd better not want to question her any further tonight about how Jingles had arrived in her court-yard this morning.

When she answered the phone, Josh asked, "Did you lock your gate tonight?"

"I'm in bed, trying to get to sleep. Some people need their sleep, you know. Oh, but I was surprised and pleased to find a new shiny latch on the gate."

He didn't say anything, so she figured he hadn't replaced the latch. She let out her breath. "I hope you find your real suspect soon." Then she hung up on him.

She really wanted to sock him! He had no business call-ing her at this time of night, making sure she did what he'd told her to do.

———————————

When Brooke Cerise hung up on Josh, he chuckled. She had a temper to go with the fiery-red hair. He could envi-sion her cheeks flushing, like they'd done earlier when he'd questioned her about Jingles. He meant to ask her about the unknown male wolf who'd been at their place, tampering with their security equipment. He wanted to know if she knew any other male wolves. If she'd heard anything the night before that would indicate someone had slipped into her courtyard where they'd left the reindeer. But the first words out of his mouth had been about her locking her gate—his main concern.

When he checked the gate to her courtyard earlier, he'd smelled the scent of the male wolf there too. In the courtyard. But not in the store. Would Josh smell him in her house?

Once he'd discovered her gate latch wasn't latching properly every time, Josh had run to the hardware store on the next block over and picked up a replacement, hoping that would keep the gate from opening on a whim. He was glad she had been pleased, but he hadn't even had time to say he did it before she hung up on him. He smiled again.

Then he ran his hands through his hair and looked out the window at the ranch and the barn where the reindeer were sleeping. He knew the thief couldn't have been from one of the reindeer ranch competitors. If he had been, the whole thing had backfired because, according to Maverick, they'd received more business than they'd had all season with all the media coverage. The chances a competitor would hire a wolf to do the sabotage would be practically nil. But it did make Josh think they'd made an enemy of a wolf. Someone they didn't know.

He kept thinking about Jingles and how happy he'd been in Miss Cerise's shop. How she'd taken him inside to keep an eye on him. Or hide him? Except if that had been her intent, it hadn't worked, because all her customers had shared on social media about the little lost reindeer. It had made for a great special-interest story for the news at Christmastime.

"Do you know where your reindeer is at this hour?" one woman had texted with a cute picture of Jingles sleeping underneath the Christmas tree in the shop. Another had said, "Have you hugged your reindeer today?" Then she'd had someone else take a picture of her hugging Jingles.

He found the store's Facebook page and read through the hundreds of comments. "I wish we had a reindeer ranch near us." "Aww, isn't he cute." "I want one for Christmas."

He smiled. At least having Jingles there had been good for business. Then he lost the smile. He had other cases to investigate tomorrow, but as soon as he had time, he was dropping by the antique shop to question the little red wolf some more. He had to know if she knew any other wolves in the area. And if she knew anything about working with security equipment. Or knew anyone who could work on security equipment. Her reaction should help him judge if she knew something about *their* video equipment.

That was one good thing about having the wolves' enhanced sense of smell. They could smell someone's anxiety, deception, depression, even interest. The wolves were lucky to be able to use more than just the visual cues a suspect would give up, something the police were trained to watch for.

Josh wanted to call Miss Cerise back in the worst way. He wanted this resolved before anyone else stole one of their reindeer.

The fragrance of cinnamon and cocoa and apple-cider wassail stuck with him, the Christmas music playing in her shop still replaying in his head, no matter how much he wanted to turn off the music and get some much-needed sleep. But as soon as he closed his eyes, in his mind's eye, he saw the feisty red wolf giving him grief, her sweetly annoyed voice telling him to provide security for her shop, to watch the calf, to do anything but bother her.

Her green eyes had flashed with annoyance when he'd continued to stick by her as if she were a criminal who might flee his interrogation at any minute. He told himself he'd stayed close because he wanted the truth from her. To resolve the case so he could get on with other police business.

And he'd question her again tomorrow for the same reason. He was always thorough when conducting criminal investigations.

# CHAPTER 4

THE DETECTIVE HAD PINNED HER WITH HIS INTIMIDATING *gaze, so why did Brooke want to be swallowed up by his dark-chocolate eyes? Her gaze broke free of his, and she studied his masculine lips as he asked her something. What? The words were spoken as if the audiobook narrator she loved was telling her he loved her, that he wanted to kiss her, that he wanted to get her naked in his bed and ravish her.*

*But then a word or two of what the detective was really saying came crashing through: Where were you last night? She frowned at the handsome face, annoyed with him for interrogating her again.*

Somewhere off in the distance, Brooke heard music. Christmas music.

Her alarm! She was instantly awake and scrambling to get out of bed.

"Police Detective Josh Wilding is a nightmare! Not a dream." Unfortunately. She hurried to dress in a green wool sweater and a green-and-blue-plaid wool skirt, leggings, and her dressy boots, along with green lace panties and bra this time, and skipped making tea at the house. She had enough time to make some peppermint mocha at the shop.

Brooke grabbed her bag of money for the cash register from the safe she'd installed in the house, set her security alarm, and closed and locked the door to her house, then turned to see Detective Wilding peering over her gate at her, startling her. This was *so* not the way she wanted to start her day. "It's locked, okay?"

"I see that. The new latch seems to work."

As much as she knew she needed to unlock the gate for customers, Brooke didn't want to unlock it for the detective. She let out her breath and stalked across the cobblestone walkway to the gate, pulled the chain of keys to the shop—locked cabinets, house key, and gate keys—out of her pocket, and unlocked the gate. "Did you put the new latch on? I mentioned it last night, but you didn't say you had done it."

"You hung up on me."

She smiled.

"Does anyone else have the key to unlock the gate?" the detective asked.

"Unless my great-aunt gave someone a key, no." She left the gate open, not sure if he wanted to enter the courtyard, but she had a lot to do to get ready to open her shop, and she wasn't standing there all day waiting to hear what he had to say. She headed down the path to the back door of her shop. The gate closed behind her.

She heard his footfalls on the garden path, heading in her direction. Apparently it was too much to hope that he had left.

Brooke unlocked the shop and entered it, wanting to shut the door in his face and lock him out. But she'd rather get this over with now so that he didn't harass her while she had customers in her shop.

Against her better judgment, she let him come inside and walked into the hallway to turn off her security alarm, then went to the kitchen to make some peppermint mocha for herself while he shut the door.

"Be sure and lock it." She didn't want customers coming in through the courtyard, thinking she was already open and slipping into the shop through the back door before she was ready.

He locked the door with a click. Suddenly, she felt vulnerable, alone, locked in with a wolf who believed her guilty of a crime.

He watched her make the peppermint mocha. "Got some more of that?"

Yeah, but not for him. She let out her breath and made him a mug. "I didn't steal the calf. I had no idea it would be here when I left my house yesterday morning." Then she pulled out her phone and looked up her legal rights. "By the way, the Fifth Amendment to the Constitution says I don't have to say anything to you in the off chance I might incriminate myself."

He'd just taken a sip of the hot drink and choked on it. *Good.*

She pointed to her phone. "In addition, I have a right to an attorney, according to the Sixth Amendment."

He continued to cough, trying to clear his throat. She almost felt sorry for him. *Almost.*

"And the Fourth Amendment gives me rights against unlawful searches and seizures." She took a sip of her hot peppermint mocha and swore the drink instantly made her feel better. Less aggravated with Hot and Sexy standing before her, tears in his eyes.

He cleared his gravelly throat, coughed, and cleared it again. "You know, when people start telling me their rights—"

"They're smart, right?" Brooke arched a brow, her backside leaning against the kitchen counter, mug in hand.

"It means they're guilty."

"Yep, that's what the police try to tell you."

His eyes widened. "You have a lot of experience with police interrogations?"

She scoffed. "I've been in a couple of car accidents over the years, neither of which were my fault. Somehow, the investigating officer always makes it seem like it's your fault. Once, I was accused of stealing a blouse from a store when I had paid for it. The real culprit got clean away, while the store cop made me return to the store and have the clerk identify me as the thief. You should have seen the look on the clerk's face. Of course it wasn't me. I had my bag and the receipt for the blouse and had just purchased it, so she recognized me as the one who had paid for the merchandise. The woman who hadn't? She was long gone."

"Did you plead your rights to the store cop based on all the amendments?" He sounded half-amused.

Brooke *wasn't* amused. "The clerk cleared me. *You*, on the other hand, *haven't*."

"Great cocoa," he said, "by the way."

"Peppermint mocha, and if you drink it down the right way, it is." She left the kitchen and began to turn on the Christmas music, store lights, and Christmas lights.

"Do you know any male wolves in the area? Besides me? Or my brother?" the detective asked, following her. "You didn't say whether you lived alone or not. Instead, you misdirected the conversation when you asked to see my ID."

She smiled, remembering the ploy and how it had worked. "I live alone, and no, I don't know any other male wolves. No female wolves either in the area." She paused to look at him, frowning. "By the way, do you have security cameras at your ranch?"

"We sure do." His dark eyes held her gaze.

"You didn't catch anyone stealing a calf from the ranch on the video?" She couldn't believe a police detective who had security cameras hadn't figured out who the real thief was from the outset.

"No. The video was tampered with."

"Oh wow. Now *that's* something I know nothing about."

"I considered you had an accomplice."

She cast him an annoyed look. Someone rang the doorbell at the front of the shop, and she went to get it. It was the mail carrier. She answered the door and smiled at him. He was an army veteran who had served in Iraq and could be a younger version of actor James Earl Jones. He didn't wear glasses, but he had the same neat mustache and the same infectious smile.

"It's just like Christmas every day," she said.

The mail carrier smiled back. "Speaking of Christmas, I heard about the reindeer at your shop. I wish I could have seen that and taken a picture for my kids."

She signed for the four boxes, astonished that she was still getting merchandise that her great-aunt had purchased before she died. She couldn't believe the boxes from Gulliver's estate hadn't arrived yet.

"Next year, I'll actually schedule to have a reindeer here. You can bring your kids and have them pet the reindeer and take pictures," she told him.

"Or you can always drop by and see the reindeer at the ranch. They love visitors." Josh gave him a business card.

Brooke was surprised the detective had business cards on him for the ranch.

"Thanks, I'll do both." The mail carrier said goodbye, and Brooke saw Sarah Burns, the owner of the bakery across the street, bringing her the baked goods she had on standing order while Josh carried the boxes inside.

Josh shook his head. "Man, if he didn't look like James Earl Jones."

"He's got a great voice too." Brooke smiled at Sarah. "Good morning, Sarah. Thanks so much for delivering the scones and cookies this morning."

Sarah's black hair was graying, her full cheeks red from the cold, and she was wearing an apron that had Sweet Treats, the name of her bakery, on it. She was just like her baked goods—as sweet as could be—and had welcomed Brooke with treats as soon as she took over and reopened the antique shop. Sarah had been so glad the shop had remained in business, because Brooke's customers often visited her bakery, and Brooke loved to buy baked goods from Sarah's shop.

"I had a moment and thought I'd run these over." Sarah glanced at Josh. A hot and sexy treat, but definitely not sweet.

Josh gave Sarah a big smile. Looks could be deceiving.

Sarah looked like she was waiting for an introduction, but Brooke needed to get ready to open the shop—and didn't Sarah have customers to take care of? She opened her shop earlier than Brooke did.

"Oh, you have some more customers," Brooke said, motioning to a car that had just parked in front of the bakery.

"Oh, so I do." Sarah smiled at Josh again and hurried off.

Brooke knew Sarah wanted to know if Josh was becoming an item in her life. No. Way. Sarah had asked about Brooke's status in the beginning, curious to know if she was engaged or married to anyone, and Brooke had to tell her no on both accounts.

"If you don't mind, we can carry the boxes into the office this way," Brooke told Josh as she relocked her front door. She might as well put him to work if he was going to bug her while she was trying to get ready to open the shop.

"Sure."

"It's something my great-aunt purchased." Brooke frowned. "These are from Colombia."

"Yeah?"

Brooke began opening one of the boxes. "I purchased some boxes of stuff at an estate sale in Phoenix. The assistant, a Mr. Lee, said my great-aunt was worried she'd purchased some things from someone in Colombia who wasn't reputable."

"Do you mind?" Josh motioned to the box.

"Go ahead." As soon as she opened a box, she gasped. "Ohmigod. There are remnants of white powder in the box. Do you think there are drugs inside the hand-decorated clay sculptures?" She pulled one of them out of the box to examine it.

Josh glanced into her box while he opened his. "Uh, yeah. Hell. I've smelled it before—courtesy of my heightened wolf sense of smell. Powder cocaine. Humans can't smell it, so I had to be careful not to let on I could tell from a whiff of it. There's a tiny bit of white powder in this box too. I'm sure your great-aunt wasn't selling it—"

"Which means someone will be coming for it."

"Exactly! I'll get ahold of the DEA special agent I work closely with." Josh immediately got on his phone. "Hey, it's me, Ethan. I'm at Cerise's Antique and Gift Shop, and we've got a situation." He explained what was going on. "Since Ivy Cerise was one of ours, she wouldn't have gotten into this with the intent to sell. We need to make sure the new owner—Ivy's great-niece, Brooke Cerise—isn't implicated in any wrongdoing. We also need to ensure that if the drug dealers come for their stash, we take them into custody and keep her safe."

Was Ethan a wolf too? He had to be if Josh was telling him her great-aunt was one of theirs. That would be good news.

Josh made another call, and when he ended that, he told Brooke, "DEA Special Agent Ethan Masterson is gathering all the necessary people to handle this. They'll want to catch these guys trying to take possession of the boxes."

"Is Ethan a wolf?"

"Another red wolf like us."

"Oh wow, that's great. So what are we going to do?"

"I suspect we'll have company as soon as you open the shop. Most likely the drug dealers have been watching for the delivery. They'd want to grab the boxes before you sold the clay figures to customers."

"What about my customers?" Brooke immediately worried about their safety and couldn't believe her great-aunt had mistakenly gotten involved in the shipment of illegal drugs.

"Everyone's safety is tantamount. The DEA will want to catch these guys and trace the shipments back to where they originated, but not at the expense of civilians. I'd send you home, but I don't want you to get into trouble on the way over there." Hell, Josh wasn't sure what to do. He sure didn't want Brooke in the cross fire. "Do you have an interior room with no windows where you can hide?"

Brooke folded her arms and looked cross with him. "I'd prefer turning into a wolf."

"Right. I know how you feel, but they'll be armed with guns and who knows what else. A wolf wouldn't stand a chance. Not to mention that we have law-enforcement agents coming who will be human." He got a call from Ethan.

"Hey, Josh, the house in back of the shop is Ms. Cerise's, right?"

"Yeah."

"The DEA wants to set up there. We've got agents moving into the area, but they don't want to spook the drug dealers."

"I'll make sure it's okay with Brooke and get the keys to the house." Josh relayed the request to her.

"Uh, yeah. I guess." She sounded like she wasn't happy with the prospect.

"The sooner we get this over with, the sooner you can get your shop open, as long as we don't have a major crime scene to deal with. I'll need the keys to the house."

Brooke fetched the keys and told him what the security code was.

"Don't let anyone into the shop. I'll be just a moment. Lock the door after me."

"I will."

"Don't let anyone see you inside the shop." That was one problem with having a glass door and big glass display windows. Josh left through the back door, waiting until she locked it after him.

He hurried to the house, unlocked the back door, and went inside, praying Brooke didn't get hurt while he was gone. After he turned off the security alarm, he unlocked the front door. The special agents hurried inside and questioned him about the layout of the shop.

Hell, he didn't know how it was laid out except for the kitchen, the main room where her checkout counter was, the office where they'd taken the boxes, and the bathroom on the first floor. He had no idea about the rest of the shop.

"You stay here, Detective," the man in charge said. "We've got this now."

"Hell, no. The shop's owner is in the store right now. I need to be there for her."

"You should have brought her over with you."

"And worry someone might be watching for her to leave the shop from the back? No way."

"You get her out of there and stay out of the way."

"Sure thing." Josh wanted to be involved. He *was* involved. He was the first law-enforcement official on the scene, but this was the DEA's case. He headed back over to the shop, and as soon as he found Brooke in the office, he said, "Come on. The DEA's taking over, and we need to return to your house."

Glass broke at the front door of the shop, and Brooke swore under her breath. "That glass is beveled and—"

"Go to the second floor and lock yourself into one of the rooms if you can."

"What about you?"

"I'll make sure they don't go up the stairs. Just...go."

She let out her breath and hurried for the stairs. The door opened to the shop while Josh was texting Ethan: Someone's breaking into the shop through the front door. Now!

Josh suspected the DEA agents were planning the operation, getting agents in place, trying to do this the safest way possible.

As soon as three men entered the shop, throwing the door open and rushing in Josh's direction, he slipped into the office and called Ethan. "Brooke is upstairs in a locked room. I'm downstairs in the office, to the right of the back door and down the hall. That's where the boxes of drugs are. Three men are entering the shop."

Josh hid behind the desk, his gun readied if the drug dealers came into the office to get their drugs, as all hell broke loose. Men were barging through the back door and front door of the shop shouting, "DEA agents! Get on the floor now!"

"Don't do it, man!" one of the agents shouted.

Then there was a scuffle. "Hands behind your back! Now!"

As soon as Ethan entered the office, Josh straightened. "Did you get them all?"

Ethan was wearing a bulletproof vest, his badge on the front and DEA printed on the back, with jeans, boots, and a black shirt. "I had to chase one outside and take him down, but the rest had entered the shop. These are the boxes of cocaine?" Ethan turned his attention to the boxes.

"Yeah."

The agent went to field-test the drugs while a police

officer read the arrested men their rights. Every one of them had been carrying guns.

Josh left the office to check on Brooke while the perps were being hauled off. He ran up the stairs and found the room where the door was locked and knocked. "Hey, Brooke, it's me, Josh."

She unlocked the door and threw her arms around him and hugged him hard. He was so surprised, it took him a moment to respond. He embraced her back, wanting to reassure her everything was fine. "It's okay. They got them. The drugs will be confiscated and taken to a DEA lab for testing."

"What if they think my great-aunt was involved in the drug-dealing business? That it wasn't just a mistake on her part? What if they confiscate any cash we have for the business?"

Josh looked down into Brooke's tearful green eyes and felt her pain. "They might take Ivy's computer if they think it might have any clues about the origin of the drugs or anything about the people who sold them to her."

"She didn't have one."

He smiled down at her. "Then not that. How much cash do you have on hand?"

"One hundred dollars. It's in the cash register."

He smiled again. "One hundred dollars is no problem. On the bust we made last month, a woman had $300,000 in cash. That's the kind of money they're looking for."

"No, nothing like that."

Someone started to tromp up the stairs. Ethan poked his head into the room. "We'll need a statement from you both…" He paused and smiled broadly at Brooke. "I'm

Special Agent Ethan Masterson." He shook her hand. "If there's anything you need"—he reached into his pocket and pulled out a business card and handed it to her—"don't hesitate to call me. I knew Ivy Cerise, and I know she wouldn't have distributed the drugs. Do you have any idea how she got in touch with these people?"

"No. Well, a Mr. Lee of Phoenix, Arizona—a Tibetan wolf—said he purchased a Tibetan urn from my great-aunt, and she told him she was afraid she might have dealt with the wrong people. She must have purchased the boxes of sculptures shortly before her death. He told me not to have anything to do with purchasing pottery from Colombia."

Ethan jotted down the information. "I'll check into it and see if he knows anything else. I'll be discreet."

"Thank you. My great-aunt didn't want Mr. Lee to tell anyone about it, but he worried the dealers might contact me about purchasing more stuff. Still, he didn't seem to know anything more than that, or I'm sure he would have told me."

"Thanks. We'll be clearing out. I've got to help take this stuff out of here. I'm afraid you won't get the clay sculptures back. They'll have to be broken to get to the contents."

"That's no problem. If it helps put these guys in jail and keeps this off the street, that's all that matters."

"We'll wrap up things here then." Ethan shook her hand, gave Josh an evil smile for being there first to protect the she-wolf, and headed down the stairs. "Let's get this wrapped up and get out of here," he said to his men.

"Are you ready to go downstairs?" Josh asked.

"Yeah. We need to lock up the house and set the alarm if everyone's vacated the place."

"Let's do that, and then we can open the shop for business. Are you going to be okay?" he asked her.

"Sure. I just hope that was the last of it and there aren't any more boxes of the stuff coming this way." She shook her head. "It's a good thing my great-aunt wasn't here to deal with this on her own. Thanks for being there for me. I'm not sure I would have handled it as well as you did. Even if I had called the police, I suspect they wouldn't have gotten here as fast as they did when you called them."

"With a potentially volatile situation on your hands and the promise of making a big drug bust, I'm sure they would have."

"If they'd thought I knew what I was talking about. You have more credibility."

Brooke and Josh checked over the house and found it was empty. She set her security alarm and locked it, and they returned to the shop.

Ethan had waited for them before he left, and Josh was glad about it, since glass had been broken out of one of the panels. "I knew Josh would get right on it when he had a moment, but in case he didn't have a chance, I called to have one of our people come out and replace the glass in your door," Ethan said. "He should be here within the hour, about the time you open the shop. I sent George a picture of the glass, and he said he'll match it the best he can."

"Thanks so much, Ethan."

He inclined his head, smiled at her, saluted Josh, then left the store.

"Do you have a broom and dustpan? I'll sweep up the glass," Josh offered. He thought Brooke seemed a little dazed.

"Thanks. I'll get them." She soon returned with the broom and dustpan and handed them to him.

In the meantime, he examined the door, but the only damage was to the glass panel the man had broken to reach in and unlock the door. Josh cleaned up the mess, and Brooke brought a tall kitchen wastebasket to empty the broken glass into.

"I'm going to wait until George gets here to replace the glass, and then I've got to do some investigating concerning Jingles's case, if you think you'll be all right."

"I will be." She took a deep breath. "I just need to get another cup of peppermint mocha."

# CHAPTER 5

JOSH NEEDED TO ASK THE BUSINESSES DOWN THE street about their security videos to see what he could learn about the stolen reindeer, though he'd hang around longer if Brooke needed him to. Luckily, he didn't have any more serious cases this morning, having cleared the last one before he dropped by to see Brooke. He was damn glad he had. He was worried about her and how she was feeling. She fixed him another mug of peppermint mocha, and they took a moment to relax before George arrived to replace the window.

When George Taylor arrived, Brooke smiled warmly at him and shook his hand. "Thanks so much for coming to do this so quickly."

"You're welcome. I'll have your door fixed in a jiffy."

"Thanks." Then she said to Josh, "Why don't you learn what happened to Jingles? I need to be cleared of that crime."

Josh smiled at her.

"Did you look at the videos for all the other shops?" she asked.

"That's what I'm about to do." He hadn't seen video security in her shop when he looked yesterday, but maybe he had missed it. "What about yours?"

"The security company is scheduled to come after the holidays."

"All right then. I'll let you know what I find, and I'll check on you and make sure you're okay."

"I'm okay, really."

"Here's my card if you think of anything further concerning Jingles."

Brooke looked heavenward, took the card, and slipped it into her pocket.

Josh headed across the street to the bakery and walked inside. The place smelled as sweet as Brooke's shop, only this one had lemon meringue and coconut pies and other baked goods. The older woman he'd met earlier greeted him with a smile. "Ohmigod, we saw all the commotion across the street. What was going on?"

"I can't really say. It's an ongoing investigation."

"Oh, sure. How may I help you?"

He showed her his badge and asked if she had video security he could take a look at. "I'm trying to solve the mystery of who stole the reindeer calf and left it at the antique shop."

"I'm Sarah Burns, the co-owner of the bakery. My husband is in the kitchen behind the shop baking. The morning before everything happened, Brooke's gate was closed, and then she opened it to let people wander around her courtyard and shop. She said she'll have plants and garden decorations in the spring, more than she does right now, but she has those heated birdbaths and more Christmassy kinds of garden items for sale. I bought one of her heated birdbaths the first week she opened."

"I'll have to get one too. Anything to help the wildlife make it through the winter."

"Right." Sarah pointed to her monitor. "See, she left the gate open. You can see her lights are on in the store late that night, so she must have been working. She's been doing that late every night. Then she turned off the lights, and she closed the gate to her courtyard."

On the screen, Josh saw a black pickup truck pull in front of Brooke's shop later that night, but he couldn't see what the driver and passenger were up to. The passenger door opened, the light coming on briefly, but the driver had a hood covering his head and was turned to watch the other person leave the truck so Josh couldn't see any of their features. The passenger closed the door, opened the back door, and then shut it. He disappeared for a few minutes, but then opened the passenger door, climbed back into the truck, and slammed the door. The driver sped off. From this angle, Josh couldn't see the license-plate number or what the man had been doing. Maybe the dress shop next to Brooke's would give a better picture.

"The gate was closed before the truck appeared. Then it parked in front of the gate so you can't see what's going on," she said.

Josh was amused she was guiding him through the scenes.

"The next morning, the gate was open. So I assumed she had already opened it for her customers."

"She said she had closed it the night before when she went home," Josh said.

"Right. You can see she did. Whoever that was, they opened her gate—and see how it looks like it's closed, but a bit of wind blew it open? There!" The woman excitedly pointed to a figure in the backyard. "That's the reindeer, don't you think?"

"Yeah." Though it wasn't a clear picture and it was shot from the shop across the street, Josh did believe it was Jingles moving toward Brooke's lighted back porch.

"So then Brooke finds the reindeer the next morning, and people are coming here to have baked goods and telling us the remarkable story about the reindeer. Everyone's joking about Santa missing one of them, and then you come along to question her," Sarah said.

"Right."

"But she didn't steal it. Whoever was in that black truck did."

Brooke was in the clear. Not that Josh really had doubts any longer.

They watched more of the video—featuring tons of townspeople, news reporters, and TV station crew who all showed up at Brooke's shop.

Her arms folded across her chest, the woman smiled. "That made the best business for us too. We can't have a reindeer over here, but I think the other shop owners in the area agree that we'll help Brooke rent the reindeer for next year, since we all did so much business from having so much traffic."

"Can I get a copy of the video?" Josh asked.

"Yes, sure." She emailed him a copy. "I hope you catch the person who did this."

"Thanks, I appreciate it." Josh headed to the dress store next to Brooke's shop to see if they had a security video that showed anything.

He walked inside the store, where a couple of women were perusing the sale racks, and spoke with a middle-aged woman who was making a sign behind her checkout counter. "Hi, I'm Detective Josh Wilding with the Portland Police Bureau." He showed her his badge. "Are you the manager or the owner?"

"The owner, Polly Whitmore. You've come about the reindeer calf? I saw the pictures of it once everyone started posting about him. He is adorable. If I'd had help that day, I would've gone over to take some pictures. Or"—her eyes widened—"are you here about that other business today? DEA all over the place. The SWAT team, even. What in the world was going on?"

"It's an ongoing investigation I can't talk about. I'm here to learn more about the reindeer theft."

"Okay. I couldn't sleep that night—insomnia, you know. I kept thinking about all the merchandise I wanted to tag, the stuff I wanted to put on the sale rack, the new posters I wanted to make. I have a home behind the shop like Brooke does, so I just walked across my garden and entered my shop. I have big picture windows, as you can see, and we have hardly any traffic at night because all the shops are closed early. I saw this truck drive past real slow. That grabbed my interest.

"He parked in front of Brooke's gate. Not like he would have done if he'd been visiting her store, but parallel parked.

"I heard a truck door open, and another open, then one slammed. I was watching the security monitor by then because I couldn't see what was happening out my windows. I had to run back to my office and check the security video. My camera is set to capture things that happen in front of my shop or at the gate, and that means it catches what's going on in the direction of Brooke's gate too. I thought they were going to steal something in her courtyard, but then the one guy returned to the truck, and he wasn't holding onto anything. He climbed into the truck, slammed the door, and the driver took off."

"You didn't see him moving something out of the truck and into the courtyard?"

"No. I had moved from the window to my office to see the security video. By then, he was returning to the truck empty-handed. So I figured the guy had been drinking and went to the bathroom in her courtyard. A guy did that in my courtyard once. I kept it locked after that. I didn't even think to check out what had happened earlier. People steal stuff. They don't usually leave stuff behind."

Josh immediately thought about discarding dead bodies, but he didn't mention that. "Did you catch the license-plate number?"

"Come into my office and watch the video. I couldn't make it out, but maybe you can."

When he reviewed the video, Josh couldn't make the license number out with the naked eye. He had high hopes the techs could. "If I could have a copy of this, I'd really appreciate it. I'll share it with some of our tech people and see if they can get anything more from it."

Then he got a call from the police bureau. An armed robbery had just taken place at a local jewelry store. Armed perp down. They needed Josh to investigate.

"Got to run, and thanks," he said to the shop owner. He got into his car and glanced at Brooke's shop.

She was smiling and talking to George while he replaced the glass in her door. Josh was glad she wasn't too upset about everything that had gone on earlier and seemed to be in relatively good spirits.

He sent the video to the police bureau so they could figure out the truck's license plate number. He hoped to talk to the owner of the truck and solve the case of the tampering with their security video and the theft of the reindeer calf.

So why was he thinking of making sure Brooke had something more than a granola bar for lunch today?

---

As soon as George finished replacing the glass in her window, Brooke had a few customers waiting to enter the shop. She paid George, thanking him for doing such a great job. "If I ever need to replace more windows, I'll be sure to call you."

The gray-haired man smiled at her. "Always good doing business with others like us. You look so much like Ivy that you must be her great-niece. She was always talking about how much fun she had with you when you stayed with her."

Brooke smiled. In Phoenix, they only had a small pack of wolves, and they didn't have so many wolves that had different skills to call on. She was glad she could get help from the wolves in the area. It was nice her great-aunt had a good reputation and Brooke was able to benefit from it.

She sure hoped Josh would solve the theft of the reindeer calf, she thought as she let potential customers into the shop to look around.

"Did a vandal do that?" one of her customers asked, motioning to the door.

"Someone who wanted to get into the shop before I was open for business."

"What is the world coming to?" the woman asked. "I wanted to see if you had any old-time Santas. The kind that have the long cloak, rather than the newer style of Santa costume."

"I do. Antique and replicas." Brooke took her to a cabinet full of Santas. "Is this what you're looking for?"

"Oh yes. My daughter collects the vintage ones."

"I'll let you look at them then. I need to warm the baked goods and fix a pot of hot chocolate while you're looking them over." Brooke headed for the kitchen and said to another customer, "Are you searching for anything special?"

"Just browsing, thanks."

"If you need anything, just let me know." Brooke set out the cinnamon rolls she'd bought from the bakery and the hot chocolate, finally having a moment to come to grips with what had happened to her that morning. She couldn't believe her great-aunt had bought several boxes of pottery filled with drugs! Brooke still felt a little shaky over the whole matter. She was grateful the DEA special agent in charge was one of their kind, because she was sure that would help keep her great-aunt's name in the clear. Although her great-aunt would most probably be in the news as an older woman duped into buying merchandise filled with drugs.

Brooke just hoped there wasn't any more of it on its way.

# CHAPTER 6

As soon as Josh arrived at the scene of the crime, he spoke to everyone at the jewelry store. He recognized the man who had been shot as a repeat offender—armed robbery being his specialty. His partner in crime had gotten away. The EMTs stabilized and loaded the wounded robber into the ambulance.

"Did he say anything?" Josh asked one of the first police officers who had arrived at the scene.

"He was mumbling about Ackerson always getting away and that he had all the luck."

"Ackerson," Josh said, writing the name down. "No first name?"

"No, sir. Once he mentioned his partner's name, he wouldn't say anything more about him as if he realized he shouldn't have said that much. I think he was pissed off and in so much pain it just slipped out."

"Did you get a description of the guy that got away?"

"The clerk said Ackerson had blue eyes and was wearing a black ski mask. The clerk said he saw a dark-brown mustache above the guy's lip. He was dressed in blue jeans, heavy black boots, black ski gloves, and a dark-gray parka."

"Thanks." Josh spoke with the store clerk, two customers, and the owner, took all their statements, and looked over the security video. The shop owner had only been defending himself when the two men broke into his shop and raised loaded guns at him. Ackerson shot the security camera and fired a round at the shop owner, but he missed, hitting the wall behind the man. The shop owner grabbed his 9mm hidden underneath the counter and fired back, hitting Ackerson's accomplice, a man named Curly Buckner, in the chest. At least Josh knew Ackerson's scent now, and he hoped they could find the robber in the database. And they knew he had a mustache, maybe a beard, and probably brown hair.

Josh went back to his office and filled out paperwork for the rest of the morning. He didn't find anything on the name Ackerson in the database though.

Adam Holmes, a red wolf and fellow police detective, Josh's partner, joined him. "Hey, if you're caught up, do you want to grab a bite to eat?"

"I can't. I'm still checking into the business with the stolen reindeer calf."

"I hope you get that resolved soon. If you need my help, just let me know. I had another call come in about the time the DEA agents stormed the shop, so I couldn't get there and help out or meet Brooke Cerise, but I checked later with Ethan, and he said you're already laying claim to the she-wolf."

Josh shook his head. "I was there questioning her further about the reindeer calf when the boxes were delivered from Colombia."

"Yeah, yeah. I've heard that story before. We can catch up later, man."

"Sure." Josh headed out to his car and called Brooke on Bluetooth.

"Did you learn who calf-napped Jingles so you can take me off your suspect list?" Brooke asked.

"Still working on it. Since I have to be in your area"—checking out more security videos, sure, but Josh had it in mind to have lunch with her—"what do you want me to bring you for lunch?" He assumed anything he brought her would be infinitely more satisfying than a granola bar.

"Do you think bribing me with food will convince me to confess all about the reindeer calf?"

He smiled at her tenacity. "What do you want?"

"Chicken marsala."

He headed toward the restaurant he had in mind that made the perfect chicken marsala. "I'll see you in a little bit."

Soon he arrived at the antique shop with the meals in a sack, hoping he could talk to Brooke about where he was at in the reindeer case, but she was busy taking care of customers, trying to find something one of the customers was looking for. He hadn't considered that part of the equation. She motioned to him to take the food into the kitchen. "Go ahead and eat."

That certainly wasn't the plan he had in mind. He really wanted to eat with and talk to her. Had she seen the black pickup truck parked in front of her garden gate before? Was there a reason the truck stopped at her place in particular?

He set the food out on the kitchen table, and Brooke hurried into the kitchen as the shop door closed. Then she smiled, and her smile stirred his loins. Hell. He was thinking about a kiss.

"I might have more customers anytime now."

"Take a seat and enjoy your meal then."

She grabbed a cup of water for each of them and sat down to eat. "Hmm. This smells so good. Thanks."

"I imagine it'll also be your dinner."

"Of course. Thanks for bringing me lunch and dinner today. What I want to know is, what will you bring me tomorrow?"

Josh chuckled. He hadn't expected that. He'd ended up getting the chicken marsala for himself, too, and started to cut into the chicken and mushrooms topped with cheese and wine sauce. "About the Jingles case…"

Brooke made a long-suffering sigh and scooped up some of her mashed potatoes covered in gravy. "I am still a suspect." She ate the mashed potatoes and pointed her fork at him. "You remember what I said about my rights."

He smiled and explained what he had learned.

She was about to spear a piece of chicken with her fork when he told her she had closed the gate to her courtyard that night. She pointed her empty fork at him again. "See? I told you the gate was closed!"

"It was. You were right."

"So?"

"I need to speak to the owner of the pickup to learn where he was when the truck was parked in front of your place and around the time the reindeer calf was stolen." Josh showed her the video of the truck. "Have you ever seen that truck before?"

"Are you kidding? As many black pickups as there are? No. I don't make it a habit of watching out the shop windows for black pickup trucks."

"Did you hear anything that night? A truck door slamming? Your gate opening?"

She sighed and began working on her meal again.

He supposed he should leave off with all the questions so she could eat before anyone else entered her shop.

"No," he said for her.

"I. Was. Sleeping. I think I already gave you my statement, Detective Wilding."

"Right, but I thought you might have forgotten something or heard something and just dismissed it as nothing important."

"Like a reindeer being dropped off in my courtyard."

"Uh, right."

"I'm not a heavy sleeper normally, but I must have been really tired and sound asleep about that time."

Maverick called Josh, who wondered what his brother needed now. "Yeah, Brother?" He put it on speakerphone.

"I've got to get more feed in town for the reindeer. Did you want to grab a hamburger with me?"

"You should have called earlier. I'm already having lunch."

Brooke said, "Tell Maverick I said hi."

"You're eating with Brooke at her store?"

"Yeah. I came by to tell her what I learned about the reindeer theft." Josh cut into his chicken.

"And question me some more." Brooke cut up one of her asparagus spears.

"You're there questioning her again?" Maverick sounded annoyed.

"I'll see you tonight, Maverick."

"What did you get her for lunch this time?"

Josh knew his brother would give him grief over questioning Brooke further when he went home for dinner. "Talk later." Josh didn't see himself as a pushover, but what could he say when Brooke wanted a special meal?

"You didn't tell him what we were having for lunch," Brooke said.

"I'll tell him tonight. If I didn't end the call, he would have continued to talk."

"About me."

Josh leaned back in his chair. "He didn't think you were guilty of stealing Jingles."

"But *you* did."

"From a police detective's point of view, I had to consider anyone who had motive, opportunity, and the stolen reindeer in possession as a possible suspect." He drank some of his water. "You have to admit things were looking bad for you."

She shook her head. "Have you ever run in Forest Park in Portland? It's supposed to be one of the largest urban forests in the United States, and I've never run there before. I was thinking of doing it tonight."

"Yep, with eighty miles of trails, fire lanes, and forested roads, the park stretches over seven miles. It's open from five in the morning until ten at night, so we could run tonight after it's closed. Fishing and hunting are prohibited, and no fires, camping, fireworks, or firearms are allowed, so we should be safe running as wolves. We might even see others there from the pack."

"We?"

He shrugged. "Think of me as your tour guide. My brother and I have run there for years, when we're not running on our ranch or Leidolf and Cassie's ranch."

"What about Maverick?"

"I'll ask him if he wants to go."

She was about to take another bite of her chicken when the front door opened with a jingle. She sighed again. "Thanks so much for lunch. It was delicious." She packed the rest of her meal in a microwave container. "This will be perfect for dinner. Feel free to enjoy the rest of yours. I've got to help my customers. I'll see you after ten tonight?"

"At the shop or the house?"

"House." She stuck her leftovers in the fridge and hurried off to greet the new people in her store.

Josh finished the rest of his meal, figuring it was better than just grabbing a burger and eating it on the run, even though he had wanted to visit more with Brooke. Then he got a call.

"Hey," Adam said, "we've got another case. Another robbery. Same MO: two guys wearing black ski masks, blue jeans, heavy boots, dark-gray parkas, black ski gloves—"

"Like Ackerson."

"Yep. I smelled his scent for sure. Either he picked up another partner or this guy was with him on the other case, too, but maybe the getaway driver that time. We have no description of a vehicle. They stole about $40,000 in jewelry, threatened the clerk with guns, and tore off before the clerk could call the police. They must have been parked somewhere else."

"Like the last time. Location?"

"Johnson's Jewelers. Five miles from the other store."

"I'm on my way." Josh couldn't believe the same man would rob another store so soon after the other one. Then again, there was really no rhyme or reason for what some thieves did. Maybe the thief was emboldened because he didn't get caught the last time. Maybe he was angry he didn't get anything out of the earlier attempted robbery and was determined to do so this time.

Josh hoped they'd catch him and his cohorts before they

hurt any innocents. Was Ackerson in charge of these jobs, or was someone else hiring him to do them?

Josh threw out his trash and put their cups in the dishwasher, then left the kitchen. He had the unfathomable urge to kiss Brooke before he left the shop—as if their lunch together had been a real date—but she was cheerily talking to a customer. He noticed she was standing underneath an archway, and above it, mistletoe was hanging. She waved goodbye and mouthed a thank-you to him. He thought if he could time it right later, he'd kiss her under the mistletoe. She couldn't object to that, could she?

Josh headed outside but hadn't gotten very far when a brown tabby wound its way around his legs. He petted the cat, checking out the collar. Her name was Muffy, and there was an address on a tag. The customer Brooke had been ringing up walked outside and smiled at him and the cat. He lifted Muffy into his arms before she ran away.

"Are you going to find the owner?" Brooke asked, poking her head outside of the shop.

"Uh, yeah. Her tag says she belongs to a place a couple of doors down from your shop."

"Good." Brooke gave him the wickedest smile and petted the cat's head. "I'm glad you didn't find her in my courtyard. No telling *what* you'd think."

"That you had a refuge for lost animals." He smiled. "See you tonight."

"See you then." She walked back inside her shop, and he went to the garden shop turned Christmas shop for the holidays to find Muffy's owner.

"Ohmigoodness, you silly cat. She always stays in the shop, but something outside must have caught her eye when a customer opened the door. Thanks so much." The woman took the cat from Josh's arms and thanked him again. "No more running off." She took Muffy to a back room and shut the door, while Josh left the shop to get on with the business of catching Ackerson and whoever else was running with him.

He brushed the cat fur off his clothes before he climbed into the vehicle. Then he thought about running with Brooke tonight as wolves. Instantly, all his crime concerns vanished, and he smiled. Then he lost the smile. He hoped his brother wouldn't tag along.

He called Maverick on Bluetooth on the way to the jewelry store. "Hey, Brother, Brooke wants to run with me in Forest Park tonight. I'm picking her up at ten. Did you want to run with us?"

"Man, oh man, I told you that you were chasing after the little she-wolf, and not just because of the case of the stolen reindeer calf."

"She asked me about running in Forest Park. What could I say? She needs a tour guide."

Maverick snorted. "You could have offered *my* services."

Josh knew he had to be kidding. "Do you want to come with us?"

"No. At least not this time. I know how I'd like it if I had a wolf date for a run and you came along to run with us. Later, but not for the first time."

"It's not a date. I'm just showing her the park."

"Just keep telling yourself that. Will I see you for dinner?"

"Yeah, she has leftovers from lunch to eat up tonight."

Maverick laughed. "Déjà vu. What did she ask for this time?"

Josh parked his car at Johnson's Jewelers. "Chicken marsala."

"When did you ask her if she wanted you to pick up something for her for lunch?"

"After I saw her about the reindeer."

"I told you that you were interested in her. See you tonight at dinner then."

Josh wasn't about to tell his brother Brooke had already mentioned him bringing lunch to her tomorrow.

───────────────

Brooke wished she and Josh could go running earlier, though she'd busied herself after she closed the shop for the four hours before he arrived. But she was tired! And ready to shower and call it a night, even though she really wanted to run as a wolf.

When Josh arrived at her house, she immediately went outside to get into his car so they could get started on their run.

"We'll go to Carver's house—his place is butted up against the park. He and his family are taking a vacation right now, but any of the wolves of the pack are welcome to park at his house and shift in a little shed out back so we can do it in privacy," Josh said.

"Oh, that's good. Even though this park is closed, I always worry about someone being in a city park illegally after hours and witnessing a shift."

"I agree. And if a park ranger found our clothes? We can leave the car in Carver's driveway without any difficulty."

"That's good. I haven't run in months. I might be…a little rusty."

"We'll have a nice run, explore, and let you work up to your full potential."

They parked at Carver's house and left the car, then headed around through the gate to the backyard. Brooke immediately saw the little garden shed with a red roof and windows with curtains. When Josh opened the door, he reached inside and turned on a light. They had benches and a trunk inside. How nice that the Carvers had set this up for other wolves in the pack.

"For anyone to change in so neighbors with their two-story houses don't see us getting naked, though the evergreen trees should shield us from prying eyes."

They went inside, removed their clothes, and then shifted. Brooke was trying hard not to look at his toned body, though she lost her balance when she tried to remove her panties, and his arm shot out to grab ahold of her. Heat spread through her whole body, despite them being in the cold storage shed. Their eyes locked for a second, his dark-brown ones capturing hers, and she felt as if she were frozen in time. She was way too impulsive when it came to dating wolves, and she had sworn she wouldn't turn a chance encounter into something deeper. Not right away. She always became disillusioned after the first few dates. And those wolves hadn't even accused her of committing a crime!

Josh released her, though his gaze had dropped to her lips, and he looked like he wanted to kiss her. Before she allowed him to, she shifted. His lustful look changed to a smile, and he shifted, too, the blurring of forms so quick that if anyone saw them shifting, they would believe they had imagined the whole thing.

He was a beautiful red wolf with a coat that had a distinctive copper color to it. She was more red, though she had a few gray and black guard hairs. The insides of her legs were white, her belly white, and her face partly white. His face was red, except for a little gray on his forehead, and he wore white boots. He was larger than her, a magnificent specimen of a red wolf.

They bolted out of the shed and headed for the gate and wolf door in Carver's back fence. Josh poked his nose through, making sure the coast was clear. Once everything looked safe, he moved out, and Brooke followed him into the park. Instead of staying on the path like humans were required to do, they ran freely through the forest like animals would, only crossing a path on occasion and then venturing back into the woods.

This was what she'd been missing. The wolf run, feeling the chilly wind in her fur, breathing in the scents of the firs and pines, the rabbits, squirrels, and birds now sleeping for the night. An owl hooted, and another passed on the warning farther away that wolves were on the prowl. Brooke ran through the woods, feeling invigorated and no longer tired. She knew she'd be sore tomorrow because she hadn't exercised as a wolf in forever, but she didn't care. She loved running as a wolf.

Not to mention that the male wolf behind her was making the run even more enjoyable. He bumped against her flank, telling her to move to her right. Then he was right beside her, guiding her to a Japanese tea garden. It was just precious: a waterfall cascading down rocks to a pond from above, bridges crossing the waterways, crane sculptures standing beside still waters, and koi swimming across the pond.

For some time, she and Josh walked through the tea garden, then he led her out of the garden to run some more.

They were running side by side when she turned and licked his face.

He woofed a little, and she swore he stood a little taller and prouder. She smiled and headed back toward Carver's house. She'd loved the run, but they had been out there for at least an hour, and Josh still had to drive home. And if she was going to wake on time in the morning, she'd have to get some sleep. She was hoping to do the wolf run on a regular basis. Not with poor Josh though. She didn't want him to have to come late at night, run with her, and then return home so much later that night. She could do it on her own, now that she knew to go to Carver's house and change and shift there.

The two of them raced each other back to the house, trading off the lead. They were nose to nose when they reached the gate and wolf door, and Josh waited for her to go through first.

After he followed her through the wolf door, they made their way to the shed and shifted, then hurried to dress. He was buff, looking like he lifted bales of hay at the reindeer ranch on his off-duty time from the police force. His backside was as hot as his front side. Seriously toned and delectable. Tearing her gaze away from him, Brooke hurried to pull on her lacy panties and then her bra.

"Anytime you'd like to do this again, just ask and I'll come and pick you up." He pulled his sweater over his hot abs, hiding them and making her sigh.

"But it's a drive for you to come in and then go home again." She pulled her sweater over her head.

"Just let me know. It's not too long a drive, and I truly enjoyed the run."

"I did too. Thanks for being such a great tour guide." Once they had finished dressing, they drove back to her house. The run had been a lovely way to end the day. "Just in case you're not busy and you want to bring me lunch tomorrow, beef Stroganoff would be great," Brooke said. "That's only if you're free. I always have a granola bar waiting for me."

He chuckled. "I will endeavor to bring you lunch."

When he dropped her off at her house, the Christmas lights sparkling on the roofline and the shrubs and the lighted wreath made her feel so perfectly Christmassy.

As to Josh, she reminded herself not to get too involved with him too fast, gave him a sweet peck on the cheek, and hurried inside. She needed to get a quick shower and go to bed, or she'd sleep through her alarm clock tomorrow.

Finally, she was in her pajamas in bed and trying to fall asleep. Instead of thinking about shop stuff like she usually did—watching for packages to arrive and sorting through all the stuff she already had—all she could envision was one hot wolf getting naked in a shed behind a pack mate's house before taking a jaunt in the woods with her as if they were a couple of wolves on an enjoyable date. And the rakish smile he'd offered her when he dropped her off at home and she'd hurried to give him a peck of a kiss and scurried out of the big, bad wolf's way. She suspected she wouldn't get away with that the next time. Nor would she want to.

# CHAPTER 7

"How was the run, Brother?" Maverick asked, getting a cup of milk as Josh headed into the kitchen to get some water before he went to bed.

"Perfect. No trouble at all. And Brooke had a good time."

"You know you could bring her out to the ranch, and you two could run out here."

"I will. The park is closed so late that she might like coming here right after she closes shop, and we can even have dinner."

"Once you stop making sure she has leftovers for dinner." Maverick put his empty cup in the dishwasher. "I knew you had something going on with Brooke. What's tomorrow's lunch going to be?"

"Beef Stroganoff, if I can swing it. You know how work goes. I never know if I'll be in the middle of an investigation when lunchtime rolls around."

"The best place for beef Stroganoff doesn't deliver. Let me know if you can't make it, and I'll pick up lunch for her. I'll tell her it was from you."

Josh didn't want that to happen. If he wasn't interested in the lady, why would it matter if his brother took her a meal? Despite that, since she would be expecting it, he would rather his brother pick up lunch for her if he couldn't make it. It really was an ingrained need to impress the she-wolf when he hadn't thought he'd be headed down that path again anytime soon. "Sure, I'll let you know."

"Good. That shows what a caring wolf you are, and I won't even have lunch with her. I'll just drop it off for her."

"If we can't get together and you take her meal to her, you get yourself some too. There's no sense in you going all the way into town to take her lunch and not have some yourself. I'm sure she'll enjoy your company in any event."

"I'll do that. I need to run a couple of errands afterward, so that will work. I could even get a meal for you, and you could reheat it in her microwave when you finally get through with your investigation. She might have more of a lull in her shop then and be able to sit down and take a break with you."

"I'll let you know."

"By the way, Ethan called and said he was coming out to the ranch to run with us tomorrow night. Have you told him we've met Brooke? I don't want to mention her if you're keeping her secret."

Josh cleared his throat. "I'm not keeping her secret. He knows about her. We had a situation at her shop this morning." He told his brother what had happened with the Colombian shipment.

Maverick sat down to hear all of it. "Hell, I would never have thought Ivy would get herself into that kind of trouble. Ethan said Brooke would be all right, correct? Leidolf will have a fit if the DEA thinks she was involved in any of it."

"Ethan assured me he'd handle it. You know he's got our backs. Brooke didn't know anything about it, and apparently her great-aunt must have had some clue something was wrong after placing the order."

"Poor Brooke. She must have been terrified."

"She seemed to be in good spirits when I had lunch with

her." Josh sighed. "I'm headed for bed. See you bright and early in the morning."

Josh couldn't stop thinking of Brooke and her funny comebacks about him questioning her concerning the calf. And all her requests for lunch. Normally when he went to bed at night, he thought over unsolved cases he was working on, trying to figure out who, what, when, and where.

Tonight, one beautiful red wolf stole all his attention. Much better than thinking about chasing down suspects.

Then he got a call he wasn't expecting from Ethan. "Brooke said she met with a Mr. Lee who told her that her great-aunt had been dealing with some disreputable people, which probably meant the shipment of cocaine, so I had a contact in Phoenix talk to the man."

From the tone of Ethan's voice, Josh knew what he had uncovered wasn't good.

"I need to talk to Brooke. I figure you'll be there with her tomorrow?"

"If I can be."

"I'd prefer if you were there at the same time since you've been there for her from the beginning. I'll let you know when I'm headed over to talk to her."

"Talk to you tomorrow." Josh sure hoped he'd be free to be there when Ethan dropped by.

---

Brooke was up early, looking forward to eating lunch with Josh and running in Forest Park tonight. He called her before she had finished dressing, and she was afraid he was going to tell her he couldn't make it for lunch. Not that she was surprised. He had an important job to do.

"Hey, hope you're up."

"I am. I'm getting dressed." She put the phone on speaker and pulled on her boots.

"I've got a lot going on with the job today, so I might not make it in time for lunch."

"Don't worry about it, Josh. I'll grab something quick to eat."

"No, Maverick will bring you your beef Stroganoff if I'm not able to make it."

"Oh, he doesn't need to."

"It's only if I can't make it, and he offered. He'll pick some up for himself too. Maybe also for me, and I can drop by later and warm it up in the microwave. But I wondered about picking you up after six and bringing you out to the ranch to see the reindeer. We can run out here. Then we don't have to wait until ten to go for a wolf run."

"Uh, sure."

"I'll let you know if I can make it or not."

"Thanks. See you tonight no matter what." She was glad Josh had called her to give her a heads-up. She thought it was sweet of him and his brother to bring her lunch even though she really hadn't needed them to. She suspected nothing would change their minds.

"Before I go, I just need to tell you one more thing. Ethan spoke with a contact he has in Phoenix and wants to talk to you about Mr. Lee. He wants me to be there when he does. I'm hoping I can take off from work to join the two of you as soon as he says he's dropping by."

"Why didn't he call *me*?"

"Since I've been there from the beginning, I think he feels I need to be there to hear what all's going on."

"Okay. Do you think it's good news?" She needed some about now.

"I think he needs to clear things up more."

She let her breath out on a heavy sigh. "Like you did with your Jingles case."

He chuckled. "Uh, yeah. Like that."

"As long as I'm not a suspect in this case. I've got to go. See you when I see you then."

"Sure."

All she needed was to have *Ethan* harassing her about a case now!

When she arrived at the shop and received a postal delivery, she thought it would be from the Gulliver estate. But it wasn't. It was another box for her great-aunt. Shivers ran up Brooke's spine, but the return label said the merchandise was from Michigan. She sighed with relief.

She thanked the substitute mail carrier and brought the box into the shop and locked the door. Then she took the box into her office, logged it in, and carried it up to the second floor. She stacked it on top of other boxes in the first of the bedrooms she used for storage. She really needed to go through these rooms and start unloading these boxes so she could sell the merchandise.

She went downstairs and checked her emails and found she had a potential buyer for some of her vinyl records. She was thrilled. The buyer would be dropping by in a couple of days to look at the records.

Then she got a call from Ethan. "I'm on my way over. I hoped to talk to you before you open the shop."

"Have you eaten yet? I'll make some hot cocoa, and I bought cinnamon rolls from the bakery across the street this morning."

"That sounds good. I called Josh, and he said he's headed over."

"Okay."

She expected Ethan to arrive first, but Josh did instead, and she was glad. She didn't know what to expect from Ethan. She unlocked the door for Josh and then locked it again. "Would you like a cinnamon roll and coffee or hot chocolate?"

"Yeah, coffee and a cinnamon roll. I'm surprised Ethan isn't here already."

"I thought he'd be here first too." She was pouring a cup of freshly brewed coffee for Josh when there was a ring at the shop's front door.

"I'll get it."

"Thanks," Brooke said. "I'll just warm the cinnamon rolls."

"Hey, man," Josh said to Ethan as the door jingled while he opened it. "Brooke's in the kitchen."

"Coffee or hot chocolate?" she called out.

"Coffee would be good." Ethan locked the door before he and Josh joined her in the kitchen.

"What did you learn when you spoke to Mr. Lee?" Brooke asked, dying to know. She set the cinnamon rolls out for the guys and brought over Christmas reindeer mugs of coffee. She smiled at the way Josh was eyeing them. "They're mine."

He chuckled. "Reindeer always catch my eye."

Everyone sat at the table, and Brooke ate some of her cinnamon roll.

"I had a friend with the FBI in Arizona check out Mr. Lee, but he was dead." Ethan drank some of his coffee and watched her reaction.

"No. How? When?" She couldn't believe he had died since she'd last spoken to him.

"He said it was before an auction they'd held at the estate where Mr. Lee worked."

"What? No. I know what Mr. Lee looks like." Brooke knew it had been him. "He gave me his card. I've seen him in the news."

"Do you have his business card?" Ethan asked.

"Somewhere. I've cleaned out my purse since I moved, and I'm not sure where I put the card. When I find it, I'll give it to you." She so did not want Mr. Lee to be a bad guy. Especially since he was a wolf and he'd been so nice to her.

"Did you know him by scent?" Ethan took a bite of his cinnamon roll.

Brooke opened her mouth to speak, but then closed her mouth. "No. I had never met him in person before."

"He was murdered, shot to death. My FBI friend went to see his body at the morgue, and it was confirmed that he was Mr. Lee."

"A wolf? Right?"

"He was a wolf."

"He knew my parents. He knew my great-aunt. He knew we were red wolves. He…he'd bought items from my parents and from my great-aunt for his sister, he said."

"Do you have any proof of that?" Ethan ate another bite of his roll.

"No. It might be somewhere in my parents' files for sales receipts, but I don't even know when he purchased the items. My parents were as bad as my great-aunt about keeping records on a computer."

"It's possible he never met your parents or your great-aunt and never even purchased anything from them. The man you met wasn't Mr. Gulliver's assistant. Mr. Gulliver's son Ralph was."

"That doesn't make any sense." She couldn't believe any of this! "A Daisy Gulliver was giving Mr. Lee a hard time at the estate sale. And then Mr. Lee spoke with the guy manning the cash register. I paid for the wolf statues. Mr. Lee gave me the five boxes of stuff free. If he wasn't in charge or didn't have some authority there, why would the cashier have taken orders from him? Mr. Gulliver's daughter undoubtedly knew Mr. Lee, or she wouldn't have been berating him the way she was. He came over and spoke to me afterward, so it wasn't like she'd told a trespasser to leave the auction site. Unless the woman wasn't Gulliver's daughter."

"Maybe the man you spoke to worked for Mr. Gulliver in some other capacity and so the cashier knew him. Maybe he pretended to be Mr. Lee, and everyone thought he was the same man because he looked similar. Mr. Lee's body was discovered in his home the day after the auction, but he'd died the day before, according to forensics." Ethan drank some of his coffee.

"What if Mr. Lee, being a wolf, had a twin brother?" Not for one second did Brooke believe Mr. Lee wasn't who he said he was. She was as wary a wolf as any other, and she would have smelled the deception.

"I checked to see if there was another Mr. Lee working for the estate. There was not." Ethan ate the rest of his cinnamon roll. "Your Mr. Lee lied about being Mr. Gulliver's assistant."

"It's in all the news stories. That's how I knew Mr. Lee was Mr. Gulliver's assistant. Mr. Lee didn't tell me that."

Ethan nodded. "So the son took over once the real Mr. Lee was murdered."

"Mr. Gulliver was already dead, so why would the son suddenly be his assistant?" she asked.

"You have a point. Did your Mr. Lee lie about his name? About buying things from your family, knowing of your wolf heritage, and sending you the invitation to attend the auction because of the friendship he had with your family? Do you have the invitation, by the way? We could try to lift fingerprints off the document," Ethan said.

She didn't know what to think. "No. I threw the invitation out. I never thought I'd need to save it as evidence and turn it over to the DEA. Did your friend talk to the man who was cashiering?"

"Yeah, but he said he didn't know anything about you."

"What?" No way. Unless there were so many customers at the auction he forgot. "I bought the wolf sculptures from him." Then she wondered about the five boxes of mystery stuff that hadn't arrived yet. What if they never arrived? What if they were never meant to arrive? At least she had the wolf statues. That was what was really worth something to her. "He was a blond guy? Midforties? Brown eyes."

"No. The man in charge of taking the money was dark-haired, wore glasses, and had blue eyes. Late fifties. My friend took a picture of him to show you." Ethan pulled out his phone and found the picture and showed it to her.

She frowned. "That's not him." She could envision the

whole scene before her. Mr. Lee talking to the blond guy and him glancing back at her, smiling and nodding. "Did the man you spoke with say the wolf statues were stolen, if I didn't pay the right man for them? Mr. Lee said they weren't part of the estate. What if they really had been?" She couldn't believe the man called Mr. Lee had cheated the estate out of the money.

"The man serving as the cashier didn't say anything about it, and my friend didn't mention it. I didn't want you to get in trouble for something that might have been illegal."

"If he wasn't Mr. Gulliver's assistant, and he wasn't Mr. Lee, and the guy who took my money wasn't the cashier, then wouldn't someone have been suspicious?" She didn't believe some unknown person could do that without arousing suspicion. Plus, the woman who had been berating him had known him. Unless…the woman wasn't Gulliver's daughter. "Did you talk to Gulliver's daughter?"

"She's in Paris and hadn't been at the auction," Ethan said.

Brooke's jaw dropped. "So all of it was a lie."

"How did you pay for the merchandise?" Josh took hold of her hand and squeezed, reassuring her none of this was her fault.

"I used a credit card. I hadn't planned to buy anything. I was just curious why I would get a special invite to the auction."

"Did the charge come up on your account?" Ethan asked.

"I don't know." She pulled out her phone and logged into her bank account online. "No. There wasn't any charge for it."

"Maybe Mr. Lee wanted you to have the wolves for free," Josh said.

"But why?"

"That's what we have to find out," Ethan said. "And who he really is. Thanks so much for the coffee and the roll. I've got to run. I'll let you know once I learn anything more."

"Thanks, Ethan." She let him out the door.

Josh took her hand. "Are you going to be okay after learning all this, Brooke?"

"Uh, sure." Then she smiled and kissed him. She meant for it to only be gentle, nonintrusive, but he pulled her into his arms and kissed her soundly, like he'd wanted to do this to her in the beginning. She parted her lips for him, and he took advantage, sweeping his tongue over hers, when they saw movement in the glass door. "Hmm, Josh, now that's a nice way to start the day."

He sighed and rubbed her shoulders. "I planned to do that with you under the mistletoe."

She smiled. "Hopefully we'll be able to get together later today."

"I sure hope so." But Josh sounded skeptical.

# CHAPTER 8

BROOKE UNLOCKED THE DOOR AND LET HER CUSTOMERS into the shop while Josh took off in his car to get on with his own work.

Traffic was slow in the shop for the first couple of hours, and all she could think about was what Ethan had told her concerning Mr. Lee. She wanted to find his business card tonight and give him a call to learn what she could, if he'd tell her the truth about anything.

Her last paying customer left the shop, and then Josh called to say he was busy on a case. "Maverick's on his way to bring lunch. I'll join you when I can."

"That works. Who wouldn't want two dashing wolf lunch mates?"

"No customers?"

"No, I'm not as busy as you. I keep working on stuff. I have a ton of boxes of my great-aunt's inventory to go through." Brooke had sold off everything in the Phoenix shop.

"All right then. See you later."

Maverick arrived a half hour later, just as she was checking out a customer. "I'll join you in a moment," Brooke told him. "Just take it in the kitchen, if you would."

She wished the customer a Merry Christmas and waited until the shopper left before joining Maverick in the kitchen. She served up glasses of water, then sat at the kitchen table to eat with him. "Thanks for bringing lunch."

"It was all Josh's idea. He's busy with a couple of robbery cases. I, uh, got you the lunch portion, per Josh's orders. I think he wanted to have dinner with you tonight."

"Okay. Does he talk to you about his cases?" She was enjoying her beef Stroganoff and Maverick's company and was curious about Josh's work.

"When he wants to bounce ideas off me. Though people in law enforcement shouldn't discuss cases, we're wolves, family, pack members. We keep the secrets to ourselves."

She wanted to ask what the cases were about when the door to the shop opened. She sighed. "I'll be right back. I have to assist a customer."

Because she had so many customers after that, Maverick came and relieved her at the cash register once he was done so she could finish her lunch. Then she relieved Maverick of his job.

"Thanks so much, Maverick, for lunch."

"You're welcome. I'll see you tonight at the ranch." He didn't mention a wolf run because Brooke still had customers in the shop.

"Sounds good."

Maverick left the shop, and Brooke received another delivery.

A man hurried up about that time, and when she signed for the item, he offered to carry the box inside for her. He didn't look like her usual kind of customer.

He was wearing a heavy black sweatshirt with a hoodie, blue jeans, and heavy black boots. His hair, mustache, and beard were dark brown, and his blue eyes kept glancing down at the box in his arms.

"Thanks so much," she told him and had him set it in

her office. She'd check it in on her laptop later. "Were you looking for anything in particular?"

"Something for my mother. I'll look around and see if I can find anything."

"Call on me if you need anything." She checked out another lady and had several more customers after that. She realized she'd never seen the sweatshirt dude leave the store. It was time for closing as she checked out her last customer, then started to look through the whole shop, hoping the guy wasn't still here. No one was in the bedrooms or bathroom on the second floor, or the bathroom and other rooms on the first floor. From the scent he'd left behind, she found he had wandered all over the shop, though, used the bathroom, and even went up the stairs to look in each of the bedrooms used as storage rooms. Snooping? Looking to steal something? She smelled his scent only by the boxes most recently stacked in the room, the ones up front. Chills raced across her skin, making the hair on her arms stand on end.

She checked the attic door, but it was still locked. The man must have left when she got busy.

Then she got a call from Josh. "Hey, I know it's about time for me to pick you up for dinner and a wolf run, but I've got a murder case I'm looking into that just came up, so I'm going to have to work late."

"I'm so sorry, Josh. Did you get some lunch at least?"

"I picked up a hamburger. How was your beef Stroganoff?"

"Delicious. We'll run another time."

"Tomorrow, if I don't get hung up on another case or I'm busy with this one," he promised.

"That sounds good."

"What did you want for lunch tomorrow?"

"I'll figure out something. Don't worry about it. We'll get together when you have some time off." She didn't want Maverick to have to pick up lunch for her if Josh couldn't make it. She really could just make a sandwich or microwave a meal.

"We'll try to run tomorrow night," Josh said.

"Sure." If he couldn't, she was running at Forest Park herself. In fact, that was what she could do tonight. First, she wanted to see what other treasures were up in her attic. She'd have to wait until nearly ten tonight anyway to run, so she might as well get some work in. She slipped her phone in her pocket, unlocked the attic door, and stepped inside to go on yet another dusty treasure hunt.

---

After ten, Josh finally got home to find the house all lit in Christmas lights, welcoming him, and the Christmas tree covered in reindeer ornaments and sparkling with colored lights. He was making a grilled cheese sandwich for himself when Maverick asked, "So what happened on the murder case?"

"After a few hours, the husband broke under interrogation and confessed to murdering his wife. I wish the bastard had done that earlier so I could have brought Brooke out here for dinner and a wolf run."

"It's a good thing you got him to confess though. We had a little bit of excitement. A two-year-old ran into the corral with the reindeer calves, but he wasn't hurt. He wanted to pet the big doggies."

Josh chuckled. "More fun than my day."

"Yeah, luckily—"

Josh got a call. "Hold that thought." He pulled out his phone and frowned at the caller ID.

"Is something wrong?"

"My favorite former suspect in the stolen Jingles case is calling." Josh answered the phone. "Hey, it's Josh. What's up?" He wondered if Brooke was checking to see if he was home and wanted to run as wolves tonight.

"There's someone in my shop." Brooke's voice was breathless, worried, hushed. "I'm hiding in the attic. I—" The phone went dead.

"Hell." Josh was out of his seat, grabbing his gun out of the safe and racing for the door in the next instant. Brooke's voice had been low, fraught with fear, and it made him sick to think she was in trouble. He wished he'd never given her grief about Jingles. What if she didn't survive the encounter with the intruders? He'd never forgive himself if he didn't reach her in time.

"What's wrong?" Maverick was off his chair in a second, waiting for guidance.

"Brooke says someone broke into her shop." Josh yanked open the door. He hoped it wasn't someone looking for the cocaine they'd confiscated who hadn't gotten the word that the DEA had all of it.

"I'm going with you." Maverick grabbed a rifle from the gun cabinet, then locked the cabinet back up. "Why didn't she call someone else on the police force or 911?"

Josh hurried to his car, and Maverick was right behind him. "I'm a wolf? She felt she could trust me?"

"She hung up on you?"

"She might have been afraid the person was going to hear her talking on the phone." Just thinking about it gave Josh chills. "What if she got another box of that damn cocaine?"

"Hell. She's in the shop?"

"Yeah. Hiding in the attic with no way to get out safely." Josh's blood was pumping hard, the adrenaline running high, his heart racing as much as his brother's was. He secured the light to the top of the car and tore off from the ranch, siren blaring, praying they'd get there in time.

"Should you call a unit to respond that could be closer by?" Maverick asked, rifle in hand, ready to shoot the intruder as soon as they reached the shop.

"I'm calling Ethan." But he couldn't get ahold of him. "We're getting close. There has to be a reason she called me and no one else. What if it has to do with her turning into a wolf? We can't get the human police involved." Josh called Adam and told him to get to Cerise's Antique and Gift Shop as fast as he could. "There's a break-in in progress, and the shop owner is hiding in the attic. I'm ten minutes from there." Adam was the only other red wolf in law enforcement who might be close enough to help.

"I'm on my way, but I'm a lot farther out than you are now," Adam said.

"Just get there as quickly as you can." Josh ended the call.

"What if whoever it is kills her before we can get there?" Maverick sounded as angry as Josh was.

"We'll get there, damn it." At least Josh sure as hell hoped so. He wanted desperately to call her back. To ensure she was all right. But he knew that could be a fatal mistake if she was hiding in the attic and he alerted the intruder that she was there.

"Drive faster, Josh," Maverick said.

"I'm going as fast as the car will go, damn it." Now Josh wished he hadn't had to deal with the murder case and could have taken Brooke for a wolf run like they'd planned and kept her out of harm's way.

"She's got to be turning into her wolf," Maverick said.

"That's what I was thinking too."

They were finally in town and getting closer to her shop. Josh slowed his car down, but he didn't stop the sirens from blaring. He'd rather scare off the intruder than give him the false sense of security that he was safe and had time to harm Brooke.

---

Brooke sure didn't expect somebody to break into her shop tonight. When she heard two men's muffled voices as they looked for something and heavy footsteps moving around the shop and into her office and the storage room on the first floor, she was thinking she should have left *all* the lights on and the Christmas music too. Since she moved here, she hadn't had any problems, and the Realtor had assured her the area was safe—no bars on the windows or doors, no breaks-ins or thefts. Her great-aunt had never mentioned having any trouble here. Not until Ivy had ordered merchandise from the wrong people.

The shops were fairly safe from crime since most of the quaint little shops had homes behind or above their businesses. That meant somebody was usually at home at night when the shops were closed.

Had Brooke left her front door unlocked? She hadn't

thought so. She was trying to do too many things at once. Maybe she had. *Damn it.* How could she claim someone broke into her shop if she'd left the door unlocked? Had she even left the Closed sign in the window? Now she couldn't remember.

Worse, the guy who was installing her security cameras wasn't coming until *after* Christmas because all the security services were too booked up! Or she could have caught the intruders on video.

It didn't matter now. Whoever was rummaging around in her shop must be looking for something they could sell. Back in Phoenix, Brooke was careful to have antiques appraised that might be valuable and then keep them secure, but she hadn't found any records that indicated her great-aunt had done so for her merchandise. Worse, what if the intruders were some of the drug dealers looking for more cocaine? Of course they could be hunting for something that was only of value to the person looking for it— not drugs but something else.

Brooke was afraid to move around on the creaking wooden floor to search for something she could use as a weapon, concerned she'd alert the intruders that she was right above them in the attic, so she started to strip off her clothes. She wanted desperately to turn off the attic light, but she was afraid that would catch someone's attention. Not to mention she'd have to walk across the creaking floorboards to do it. She hoped they'd believe she forgot to turn off the light in the attic, not that she was up there hiding.

At least as a wolf, she could protect herself better. Which was why she called Josh to come to her aid and not 911, when a police officer on duty might have been closer. She finished pulling off her panties and bra. In a flash, she shifted into her wolf.

Hopefully, Josh wouldn't call other police officers to the site to protect her if she had to fight the intruders in her wolf coat. With any luck, the intruders wouldn't bother checking the attic.

She heard things crashing downstairs, glass breaking, and she wanted to kill the men!

"I don't see the boxes down here," the one man said. "You think they're upstairs maybe?"

Her skin prickled with fresh awareness. At least she learned one thing: the guy's comment meant they hadn't just randomly broken into the shop for stuff to steal. They were looking for something specific. Now, if only they would tell her what they planned to take. The news had reported that the DEA had confiscated over $25,000,000 in cocaine, so she'd hoped anyone else associated with those drugs would realize the boxes were no longer in her shop. Unless there were more to come.

"Yeah, or the house," the one guy said. "We'll check here first. We can break into the house when she's at the shop during the day. At least she has no security cameras anywhere."

Which irritated Brooke again when she thought of how she wouldn't get the cameras in any sooner. It would have been great to have gotten a video recording of the guys, though she guessed they would have destroyed her cameras, if she had them.

The two intruders tromped up the stairs. Maybe they wouldn't go into the attic. Three other rooms and a bathroom were below her on the second floor. Her great-aunt, like her parents, had the estate sale/garage sale/thrift store sale obsession. They told themselves it was because they needed to keep their shops well stocked. Brooke knew deep down it had been more than that. They were treasure hunters, and they figured one of those days, they'd find the treasure of a lifetime. And then? They'd look for another.

She thought about making some noise to warn the men she was here. Maybe she'd spook them, and they'd leave. But she was afraid it was too late for that. There were no guarantees that she could scare them off if they really wanted the item they were searching for.

There was no lock on the attic door from the inside of the room, so she had no way to keep them out. The door was standing wide open, inviting them right in. She suspected if she'd managed to lock it, they would have just kicked in the old door anyway. As a wolf, she moved soundlessly toward two large trunks, one a Victorian leather-covered humpback trunk and the other a wall steamer trunk covered in embossed metal and metal bands to strengthen the frame and add a decorative touch. That one she recognized as a Louis Vuitton trunk, and it still had labels from the ships the traveler sailed on. She quickly reached the trunks and crouched behind them.

*You may arrive anytime now, Detective Wilding!* She hoped she hadn't made a mistake in calling him and not just dialing 911.

Brooke prayed he'd get here, sirens blaring, and these men would run off. Maybe he'd catch them. But mostly she hoped they'd leave before she had to deal with them.

She realized the problem she now faced. If she killed the men, what would she do with them? If she only bit them, she might turn them. That was a total no-no. Then she was back to having to kill them.

They were rummaging around in two of the three rooms below her. "Shit," the one man said. "She's got so much damn stuff in here. We'll never find it."

Good. Though it could be safer for her if they found whatever they were hunting and left. Not that she wanted them to steal from her. What if it was the treasure her parents and her great-aunt and great-uncle had always hoped to find?

"Check the other storage room. I'm going to see what's up those stairs. The light's on and the door's open, unlike earlier when I checked the place out."

Ohmigod, he was the man who had carried the box into the shop for her earlier when the mail carrier delivered it. She should have recognized his voice from earlier!

"We should have checked there first." The man climbed up the stairs to the attic door, every footstep making the stairs creak, causing Brooke's heart to beat even faster. When he reached the landing, he paused. She envisioned him surveying the boxes and trunks, maybe looking to see if someone was hiding in the room.

"Anything up there?" the other guy asked.

"More damn boxes and junk." The floorboards creaked, and he went straight for one of the trunks.

The other guy came up the stairs. *Just great.* He started to walk across the floor headed for the other trunk—the bigger of the two that she was crouched behind.

Angry they had broken in and no longer afraid, maybe because she was wearing her wolf coat, Brooke curbed the urge to growl and come out and bite them. She had to keep her wits about her and let the police detective—if he ever got here!—handle matters.

The first of the men swore. "The damn thing has a lock on it I can't open."

"Same with this one."

She smiled with some satisfaction.

"Shoot them off," the one man said.

Then her phone lit up. She'd turned the sound off, but someone was trying to call her. She prayed that the men wouldn't see the light go off where her clothes were, close by her.

"What the hell," the one guy said and began to move around the steamer trunk.

She was a dead wolf if she didn't take him down first. The floor creaked where he was walking toward her, and both men took the safeties off their guns. She readied herself to lunge.

# CHAPTER 9

WHEN JOSH PULLED UP IN FRONT OF THE ANTIQUE shop, his sirens still going, he heard the distinctive sound of shots being fired, coming from the attic. Cold chills ran up his spine. That was where Brooke was supposed to be. He envisioned her wearing her red wolf coat and dodging bullets, damn it.

His heart doing double time, he jumped out of the car, pulling his gun out, and yelled to his brother, "Head around back so they can't get away that way. Watch yourself. They're armed and dangerous."

"Hell, yeah."

The front door to the shop was shut, but when Josh tried the knob, it was unlocked. His first thought was that Brooke hadn't locked the door, just like she hadn't locked the gate to her courtyard the other night. Not that he blamed her. She had a lot on her mind—lots to do and no one to help her do it—and it was easy to forget things. He threw the door open, and it banged against the wall.

Right now, all that mattered was that the two people firing shots in her attic hadn't ceased, even with his siren wailing. They had to be concentrating so hard on shooting at her that they hadn't heard his siren. He couldn't imagine she would have survived the onslaught, and that made his stomach knot with tension.

"Police officers! Come down with your hands up!" Josh was certain someone else living nearby would have heard the shots and called the police. He just had to protect Brooke if she was in her wolf form.

He headed up the stairs, the darn steps creaking with his weight, warning them he was on his way. Neither of the men responded, and he worried they might try to take him out before he reached the attic. He had no cover here, but he had to reach Brooke as quickly as he could.

A couple more shots were fired. *God damn it.*

Josh was running up the stairs when he heard a banging noise and then glass breaking. He reached the landing and peered into the attic room. The front window was broken. The men were gone.

Someone was running up the stairs behind him, and Josh whirled around to see his red-faced brother, just as angry as he was, rifle in hand.

"They got away out front. Brooke?" Josh called out, afraid she might not be able to respond, not wanting to consider the worst-case scenario. He was searching behind the antique trunks and stacked boxes, but he hadn't located her. "It's me, Josh Wilding, and my brother."

Wearing her red wolf coat, Brooke came out from behind a bunch of boxes full of bullet holes. She was limping, bloodied, her tail down. She managed a small tail wag when she saw them.

Josh was so glad to see her alive. He quickly looked her over to make sure she wasn't wounded anywhere that could be life-threatening. She licked his cheek, and he gave her a small hug. "Was there more cocaine in a box?" he quickly asked, thinking he needed to call Ethan back. Ethan would have a DEA team over here in a heartbeat.

She shook her head.

Maverick was trying to get around him in the narrow space to see the damage too.

"It looks like two flesh wounds, one to her right hind leg and one to her right foreleg. Take care of her, will you, Maverick? More police are bound to be on their way. I need to try to find these guys so they can't return and hurt her or anyone else."

"I've got this."

Josh went back to grab her clothes from behind one of the bigger antique trunks, found the sexy lace underwear she'd stripped out of, and returned to shove the clothes at his brother. "Get her dressed before anyone else arrives." Then he bolted for the stairs, determined to catch the bastards and learn what was so valuable that they'd broken into her shop to find it. What made him see red was that they'd shot her. He just prayed her wounds were superficial like he thought they were. And he hoped she hadn't bitten one or both of the men and turned them.

His primary goal as a sworn police detective was to take down the criminals. Well, taking care of Brooke's injuries first if his brother hadn't been there to do so. But damn if he didn't want to be the one checking on her injuries and helping her to dress before the police officers arrived. He didn't want to admit it was more than just a need to make sure everything was done right before the other officers got there. He wanted to be the one ministering to her needs and protecting her.

---

"Can you shift?" Maverick asked Brooke.

Hurting horribly, which was why she seemed to be

doing things in slow motion when she should have shifted already and dressed, she nodded and shifted. She wasn't embarrassed to be seen naked in front of one of her kind. She was used to stripping and shifting to run as a wolf with a pack. Maverick wasn't part of the pack she'd belonged to, but it still didn't bother her.

What bothered her was that Josh had run off on his own to take down the shooters and could get himself killed! Maybe they wouldn't shoot at an officer of the law. Maybe only at what they had probably thought was a guard dog. Still, she couldn't help worrying about him.

When she tried to dress, she needed Maverick's assistance. She hated not being able to do things on her own, especially something as simple as dressing herself. But she was shaking, hurting, and unbelievably wobbly. She couldn't pull on her panties without falling over, and she absolutely couldn't fasten her bra in back.

Desperate to hurry before human police officers arrived who wouldn't understand why she'd been naked in the attic, Brooke knew she had to rush, which was only making things worse. Maverick was fumbling around, not used to dressing women, she suspected. At least she was glad she only had a couple of flesh wounds, but it was going to be hard to explain why she was naked when she got shot since there were no bullet holes in her clothes. Unless they didn't mention it, which would make the case—and the men— seem less dangerous.

"I need to stop the bleeding," Maverick said as he pulled on her socks.

"Later. I need to finish getting dressed."

"Do you have a first aid kit in the shop?"

"In the bathroom on the second floor under the sink."

"I'll be right back."

"I need to get dressed! What will the police think?"

Maverick glanced around the attic room. "That rack of vintage clothes! You were about to try one of the gowns on when you heard the men coming up the stairs. You didn't have time to grab your sweater and skirt. You just had time to grab your phone and hide and call Josh."

"That sounds suspicious."

"Better than that you were wearing your fur coat when you were shot."

Then she heard more sirens headed their way. And cars squealing to a stop. Doors slammed, and a rush of people headed into her shop.

"Shoot. We need to have your injuries documented," Maverick said.

"I don't like it."

"We have to do it. They have to be charged with attempted murder."

They heard people moving through the shop on the first floor.

"I was a wolf," she whispered.

"I know, but they have to be charged with shooting you," Maverick insisted.

One of the officers dashed up the stairs to the second floor.

Maverick called out, "The shop owner, Miss Cerise, is up here. She's safe. We need an EMT. Two bullets grazed her. Detective Josh Wilding ran after the two men."

The police officer ran up the stairs to the attic and entered the room. He had his gun out and was wearing blue jeans and a shirt and parka. He was a fair-haired man, his green eyes narrowed. He hollered to the EMTs, and two more men ran up the stairs.

"Adam. Am I glad to see you," Maverick said.

"Josh is trying to chase down two men who shot up my whole attic," Brooke said. "Go after him and help him. He needs backup."

"He called it in, Miss Cerise. I'm Detective Adam Holmes. I'm Josh's partner, and I'm here to investigate the crime scene. Some of our men are in pursuit of the two men. The others are downstairs, making sure no one else is here that shouldn't be. It was just you here and no one else?" He moved in closer to take her hand.

Breathing in her scent, he raised his eyebrows. "You were wounded as a wolf. I smell blood, just yours." Then his frown deepened. "Unless you bit the men."

"It's my blood. The bullets just grazed me, but I can't let anyone know because—"

"You were wearing your wolf coat. It doesn't matter. We need to have your wounds documented."

A policeman with a camera joined them and photographed her wounds and then began photographing the attic. The EMTs hurried into the attic and took care of her wounds.

Then Maverick pulled her sweater over her head while the EMTs left the attic.

"Do you have security cameras?" Adam asked.

"No. The man was installing them next week."

"We'll have it done pronto," Adam said.

"Thanks."

Maverick lifted her leggings off the floor, but she shook her head. "Just my skirt and boots, thanks."

"Do you know what the intruders were after?" the detective asked her.

"I have no idea. I just inherited the store and house. All the contents came with it. One of the men mentioned they were searching for boxes. So not just breaking in to steal stuff in general."

"What about a description of the men?" the detective asked.

Maverick helped her into her skirt and then had her sit on one of the trunks while he pulled her boots on for her. "She needs to catch her breath."

"No, it's okay if it helps us catch them. I don't want them returning anytime soon. One was blond-haired, and the other had dark-brown hair. Both had blue eyes, and whiskers like they hadn't shaved for a few days. They were wearing black ski hats, but no masks. They were tall, maybe six feet. They were of average weight, wearing jeans, boots, and bulky, dark-gray parkas. Oh, and black gloves. One of the men had been here earlier. He helped carry in a box the mail carrier had delivered. The man didn't buy anything, but he wandered throughout the shop, even where he shouldn't have been."

The police photographer headed down the stairs to the first floor to take more photographs.

"Thanks. It sounds to me like he was casing the shop," the detective said. "So exactly what do we say about how we found you dressed?"

"She had stripped down to her panties and bra and was going to try on one of those vintage dresses"—Maverick pointed at the rack of them in the corner of the attic—"when she heard the shooters in the shop. She grabbed her phone and hid behind a trunk while she called Josh. She didn't have time to reach her clothes."

Adam smiled at Maverick. "Thank you, Maverick. Is that how you want to describe your actions prior to being shot, Brooke?"

"Yes. The floor creaks. I didn't want to walk across the floor to grab my clothes and give myself away. I think it works. Don't you?"

Adam glanced around the room. "Yeah. Where were you hiding when they began shooting?"

She pointed behind the trunk.

"Then you showed your wolf self?" Adam asked quietly.

"Yes. They were going to shoot off the locks. I'd turned the sound off on my phone, but the darn thing lit up with a call, and one of the men noticed it. He started to come around the trunk and saw me, but I knocked him down before they started shooting. And I hid back there." She pointed to the crates where she'd hidden. "Then they broke the window and escaped right before Josh arrived."

"That works. When you can, I'd like to have you give a description of the men to our sketch artist. We'll be able to recognize the men by scent, but we need a visual sent out to everyone. I'll have the artist come to your house. Why don't you go there and take it easy."

"Thanks."

"We'll see you later," Maverick said to Adam.

A couple of men were coming up the stairs, and Brooke and Maverick had to wait until they reached the attic and moved out of their way.

Adam told them who she was, but everyone knew Josh's brother. Then she started down the stairs while Adam gave orders to the policemen. Other police officers were checking out the mess downstairs. In disbelief, Brooke stared at the breakage and was totally disheartened, wanting to cry and scream out in frustration. Though the passing thought crossed her mind that tearing into them as a wolf would make her feel even better. The intruders had thrown everything everywhere, glass and pottery broken all over the floor. Despite being angry and not wanting to show how bad she felt, she couldn't help it when her eyes puddled up with tears.

"What are you doing here, Maverick?" one of the officers asked. *He* wasn't a wolf.

Brooke recognized his voice. He was the officer who had hung up on her at the police station when she had reported she had a reindeer calf at her shop.

"I'm just here helping a friend."

She wanted to tell the guy off, but then again, she didn't want to cause trouble for herself later, in case he decided to hassle her.

Brows raised, the officer snapped his fingers. "You're the woman who called about the reindeer calf in the shop. I remember the name of the shop now."

"You're the officer who dismissed me as a crank caller and hung up on me." Oh well, he'd brought it up, and she was feeling too much pain and not in the best mood to deal with someone like him.

The man's face turned a little red.

Maverick said, "The calf was one of ours. We're still trying to figure out how it ended up at Miss Cerise's shop."

"Uh, sorry, ma'am. You wouldn't *believe* how many crank calls we get about Santa and his reindeer around Christmastime," the officer said, sounding truly apologetic.

She was grateful the officer had told her the reason for his rudeness and had apologized. "I was just glad I found where he belonged."

"Josh and Maverick are good friends of mine, and I had no idea."

"No problem."

"Any word on Detective Wilding?" she asked the officer, worried about Josh.

"He said he's headed back to the store. He lost sight of the men about a mile from here."

That was bad news. If the thieves didn't get what they were coming for, they'd surely be back again. But she was glad they hadn't shot Josh too.

"Adam told me to escort Miss Cerise to her home so she can take it easy for a bit," Maverick said. "She's feeling pretty shaky."

"All right."

She and Maverick left the shop as she tried not to limp too much, but the wound on her leg was hurting like crazy. Her arm too, but as long as she didn't have to use it, it wasn't as bad. Maverick held onto her good arm, keeping her from stumbling. At least the intruders hadn't shot bullets through the fabric of her sweater and skirt, which would have ruined them.

She fished out her keys and unlocked the door of her house, then hurried inside to turn off her security alarm. "Would you mind starting a fire in the fireplace and turning on the Christmas lights on the tree?" She wanted the cheerfulness to help block out what she'd gone through. "I'm going to put on something else."

"Right on it." Maverick locked the door after her. "Did you need my help to change?"

"I'm good." Once she was in her bedroom, trying to pull off her sweater, she hurt way too much. She could kill the men for breaking into her place, breaking her things, and shooting her! Worse, she was certain they would return for whatever they'd been looking for.

# CHAPTER 10

HIS BLOOD HOT WITH ANGER, JOSH RACED AFTER THE two intruders who slipped down a side street. He berated himself for not having gone after the men sooner, yet he wouldn't have forgiven himself if Brooke had been injured worse and he hadn't ensured she lived. It didn't matter that his brother had been there. As a police detective and the older brother, Josh felt it was his responsibility to make sure she was okay.

He couldn't catch up to the men, no matter how hard he tried. They had way too much of a lead on him. If he'd been in his wolf coat, they would never have escaped him. He yanked out his phone and alerted Adam that he was in hot pursuit of the two shooters, but it didn't look like he was going to catch up to them on foot. "One of them is bleeding. I thought it would slow him down, but it doesn't seem to be."

"I'm sending men after you. I'm pulling into the parking lot of the store now."

"Good. Brooke's going to be fine. We have to get these guys."

"We will." Adam was running up the stairs in the shop, his footsteps heavy on the wooden floor.

"I'm turning onto Fern Street, headed north."

Adam directed men on a radio to meet up with Josh. "They're on the way."

"All right. Talk later."

Sirens sounded in Josh's direction, and he knew the officers would at least be chasing the shooters down in cars. When he reached Fern Street, he heard a car peeling off around the corner of Fern and Oak, headed away from him, so he couldn't see the vehicle. He was certain the shooters were driving off in the vehicle. He rounded the corner, and three patrol cars rushed to meet up with him. The car was gone. No sign of the men. Josh listened for running footsteps, looked for more drops of blood like a bread-crumb trail, but they stopped right where he imagined the car had torn off.

*Damn it!*

Then he realized the one man's scent seemed familiar. He remembered he'd been concerned when he'd first met Brooke that she had set out boxes to be recycled and a man had been looking over them. Later, the boxes were gone, but the trash collector might have picked them up by then. Still, the fact that one of the men who shot up her attic had been looking over her boxes earlier made Josh suspect the man had been looking for something of hers.

One of the officers gave Josh a lift back to the shop, while the other patrol cars searched for the vehicle.

He glanced up at the full moon hanging in the night sky, and he prayed to God Brooke hadn't bitten the man and that was why he was losing blood! He could just imagine the bitten man turning and then him biting the other man. They'd have two brand-new *lupus garous* on the loose in Portland. And not the kind of men they'd want in the pack either.

———————————

Someone was knocking at the door when Brooke managed to get the sweater sleeve off her good arm, and she was silently swearing as she struggled to pull off the other sleeve.

She hoped the person at the door wasn't the police sketch artist.

Maverick called out to Brooke, "It's just Josh." He unlocked the door. "Hey, Brother, we were worried about you."

"I'm fine." Josh sounded disgruntled.

She was glad Josh had made it back all right and hadn't been injured.

"Did you get them?" Maverick asked.

"Hell, no. They had a ride before I could reach the street where they took off. Patrol cars are still out looking for them. I wanted to get back here and make sure Brooke's okay. How's our patient?"

"Struggling to get out of my clothes." Brooke figured Josh was asking his brother the question, not her. Before she knew it, Josh was entering her bedroom.

"Here, I'll help you. Maverick is making the fire."

Like Maverick wouldn't have offered to assist her and *then* return to finish making the fire.

"Did the EMTs see to you?"

"They did, and a policeman took pictures of the injuries, but I want to get into something more comfortable. I can't get out of my things."

Josh was gentle with her, while Maverick had been rushed while attempting to get her dressed in the attic. Josh slid the sweater off her injured arm, then unbuttoned her skirt while she held onto his shoulders to keep her balance.

He sat her down on her chair and pulled off her boots and socks. "What do you want to wear?"

"I was going to put on something soft and warm for bed." She wanted to go to bed.

"Which drawer?"

"Top left drawer of the tall chest."

"Got it." Josh crossed the room to the tall chest and pulled open the drawer. He didn't ask which one of her nightclothes she wanted to wear. He just sorted through them and then pulled out a blue pajama set with white owls flying across the soft, warm flannel fabric. He set them on the bed and removed her bra first, then pulled on her flannel top and buttoned it for her. Then he helped her out of her panties and pulled on her pajama bottoms. "Socks? Slippers?"

"Slippers. Wolf. In the closet on the shoe shelf."

He went into the closet and came out smiling, looking them over. "These are cool."

"I know they're kind of silly, but they're nice and warm."

"I think they're great." After he slipped them on her feet, he helped her up. "Can you walk?"

"Since I was little."

Josh cast her an elusive smile. "You should be sitting down, taking the weight off your leg. We heal faster than humans, but not instantaneously. Besides, you look pale." He assisted her into the living room. "Did you want to talk about what happened?"

"Sure. Adam said a sketch artist will be coming."

"That would be Sierra Redding. She'll get you through it painlessly." Josh helped Brooke sit in her favorite recliner. "I'll be giving her a description too. Adam told me how much of a description you gave of the intruders. I was surprised you could notice that much detail, considering they were shooting at you."

"I got a good look at them before they started shooting." She told him about the man who had come to the shop earlier.

Josh told her about the man who had been looking at the boxes she'd set out for the trash earlier.

"So one of them was looking at where the boxes were from maybe." She shivered.

"How bad are your wounds?"

"Thankfully, they're flesh wounds. With our enhanced healing abilities, they'll heal up in a few days."

Josh said, "Even so, keep checking them to make sure they don't become infected."

"I will. Thanks to both of you for coming to my rescue." Even though the fire was going and the heater was on, she was feeling chilled and wished she'd thought about getting a robe before she left the bedroom. She realized how much she was still getting over the shock of the shoot-out and her injuries and let out her breath. "I'll be right back. I'm going to get a robe."

Josh offered, "I'll get it for you. Where is it?"

"The white fluffy one, hanging near the closet door inside the closet."

"I'll be right back."

Josh was certainly accommodating with her, now that he wasn't grilling her about the stolen reindeer calf.

He soon returned with her robe and helped her into it. The brothers were smiling at her as she resettled on the recliner.

"What?" she asked.

"You look like a sheep among wolves," Maverick said.

"I'm a wolf in sheep's clothing," she said.

"You sure are. Did you want something warm to drink? Hot cocoa?" Josh asked.

"That would be great. Beers are in the fridge if you guys would like them." She knew the questioning would begin. Not from Maverick but from his detective brother. She didn't mind since he was trying to learn what these guys were after, but she was just so tired. She explained the story she and Maverick had made up about her being in her underwear in the attic. "Adam thought the story worked."

"Sounds good to me. " Josh made her a hot cocoa while Maverick brought out a couple of beers.

When the cocoa was ready, he handed it to her, and he and Maverick sat down on the sofa and waited to hear her story.

"Did you bite either of the men?" Josh asked her.

"No, I didn't bite either of the men. Before I shifted, I realized it could be a problem if I turned one of them. Or both. I couldn't defend myself against them as a helpless human. I thought I might be able to scare them off if they saw a big, ferocious-looking 'dog' in the attic, but I was trying to remain hidden behind the antique trunks at first. They were going to shoot off the locks on the trunks, but then my cell phone lit up. One man came around the trunk, and I knew I had to react or get shot."

"I don't blame you. The antique trunks. What's in them?" Josh asked.

"I have no idea. I inherited everything—the store, house, all the furnishings intact. I've been having so much repair work done and trying to get the shop open that I haven't started looking at the stuff in the attic. I went up to see if there was anything more I could sell in the shop."

"We need to open those trunks and find out what's in them," Maverick said.

She hadn't expected him to propose that, but she was glad the brothers wanted to help. Then again, if it could help their police investigation, that was tantamount.

"If something important or valuable is in them, why did these men come just now to steal from the shop? Why not do it before I took over the property? They could have stolen from the shop at any time after my great-aunt died, while the shop wasn't open, and no one would have been the wiser."

"Maybe what they're looking for is something you purchased more recently," Josh said.

"Not me. I've just been trying to unload stuff." Brooke rubbed her forehead. "Like my parents, my great-aunt would buy from estate sales from time to time. Sometimes, they just bought mystery boxes of stuff. Sometimes, there were real finds, and they made back what they'd paid for the boxes with just one item and the rest was pure profit. They always broke even, but they usually made money. They never knew exactly what was in the boxes, just a general inventory.

"Other than that, they would sometimes buy from garage sales. People sell off stuff they've inherited and don't think it's worth anything. Often it isn't worth anything except to a person collecting that kind of item. They also bought new replicas of antiques. Some want the old-time look or memorabilia but at a cheaper price. They don't really care about having true antiques, but I can't imagine anyone breaking into the shop for any of those."

"What about lists your great-aunt made of the merchandise she had in the shop?" Josh asked.

"I haven't located any yet. I can't imagine she didn't keep track of her purchases for tax purposes. In the will, she said she left me a list of treasures, but I haven't located it yet either."

"A list of treasures?" Josh's brow rose.

"Yeah."

"You're sure you didn't bite anyone?" Josh asked.

She knew why Josh was concerned about that. "I have no blood staining my teeth and no blood on my lips. I don't smell like I have anyone else's blood on me. I didn't bite anyone. I jumped on the one man, knocking him down. The other guy looked horrified and started firing as soon as his friend was clear. I dodged behind the trunk. I sneaked around to the other side, worried that with all the bullets he was discharging, I was going to get hit for sure. It hadn't registered that I'd been already hit—twice."

"The adrenaline will keep you from feeling the pain initially," Josh said.

"Right. I finally managed to hide behind a stack of boxes and wooden crates, hoping the men wouldn't come around them to shoot me. They were all shook up, and I think that's the reason they didn't come looking for me."

"They probably thought you were a guard dog," Josh said.

"Why do you keep asking me if I bit the men?" She wondered if Josh thought she was afraid to tell him the truth!

"I smelled blood and saw drops of it trailing all the way down the sidewalks."

"Oh good." She hoped one or both men had shot themselves! "But you didn't smell the man's blood in the shop." She suspected Josh must not have because none of the rest of them had smelled anyone else's blood but hers.

"No, not there. Just on the sidewalks and the streets when they crossed them. Maybe one of them cut himself on the glass from the window when they broke it or while climbing out," Josh said. "The glass fell outside the window. The bloody shards of glass would be down below in the shrubs in front of the shop. We wouldn't have smelled the blood in the shop."

"If one of them cut himself badly from the glass, maybe he'll have to be seen in an urgent-care facility, but nobody would know he was involved in a crime." Brooke would have nightmares about them shooting her. Even now, she could envision the guy who'd been in her shop earlier, his blue eyes catching her gaze. He'd seemed out of place there, but not dangerous. He hadn't smelled of fear, as if he was worried about being caught. "We need to gather the evidence then."

"Adam would make sure they did. He'll alert hospitals in the area to be on the lookout for someone who cut himself badly on a broken glass window," Josh said, "if that's what the injury was from."

"They tried to open the window, but it was jammed."

"I wondered about that," Josh said.

"It was an old window and probably hasn't been opened in a millennium. The frame had been painted over several times too. They were panicking, and finally one of them took a brass lamp and smashed the window, and it broke."

"A brass lamp. Too bad the one who grabbed it didn't leave fingerprints." Josh said.

"They were wearing gloves."

"Right. I'd seen them wearing them outside the shop, so I guess they didn't remove them when they were looking for whatever the item was." Josh took another drink of his beer. "They sound like they know somewhat what they're doing, but they should have been listening for the sirens."

"I'm sure the wolf had their full attention." She finished her cocoa. "I need to make some calls. Someone has to board up the attic window until I can replace it—George, I guess—and I have to clean up the shop once the police are done with it. I need to lock it and set the security alarm too."

"I'll get with Adam and board up the window tonight," Maverick said. "I suspect my brother, being the police detective first called to the scene, wants to stay here and serve and protect."

"If that's all right with you," Josh said to Brooke.

"Thanks, Josh. And thanks, Maverick, for taking care of the window. Tell Adam thanks too."

"I will. What's the security code? We'll set the alarm after we lock up. And we'll need the keys," Maverick said.

"They're on the kitchen counter." She gave him the security code.

"Got it." Maverick headed out the back door, and Josh locked up.

The adrenaline rush had completely whooshed out of every cell in Brooke's body, and she was suddenly very tired. She left the recliner and headed into the kitchen. Josh joined her in a heartbeat.

"Is there something I can get for you?"

"Some more hot cocoa? It really appeals."

"Sure. Did you eat dinner?"

"Uh, I was going to fix something after I refilled the shelves in the shop and checked out the attic. But I never got to it." Her eyes filled with annoying tears, and Josh quickly put the container of cocoa down and led her to the barstool.

"Hey, I know what you're going through. The adrenaline rush has probably dissipated, and you're upset about the mess in your shop when you'd worked so hard to get it ready for tomorrow. The fear of being shot to death, the worry the men will return, and the shock of being shot all take a toll. Even if the wounds were nothing major, it's still a trauma to your system. Are you going to be okay?" He handed her a tissue from a box on the bar.

She wiped away the tears. "Yeah. It was a good sales day, and then tonight was a total nightmare."

He made more cocoa for her and brought over the mug. "What can I fix you for dinner? Or do you want me to call for takeout?"

"Takeout. I don't want to have to deal with a messy kitchen too. And I think the stove might be going out."

"I'll fix dinner."

She didn't want Josh to have to make a meal for them. She pointed to a bunch of takeout menus sitting in a pile on the other end of the counter. "Just pick something for me. I can't think straight. I keep trying to figure out what the intruders were after. Oh, and they said if they couldn't find it there, they were going to search my house while I was at the shop."

"Hell." He brought over the stack of menus. "Pizza? Chinese? Sandwiches?"

She closed her eyes and touched one of the menus. She opened her eyes. She'd pointed at the sandwich shop and knew just what she wanted without having to go through the menu. "Grilled ham-and-cheese sandwich, pickles, fries, and a hot fudge sundae."

He chuckled. "I thought you couldn't decide what to have and you were cold."

"That's my favorite from the restaurant. You can make me a mug of hot chocolate again after I eat the sundae. Chocolate takes the edge off."

"Works for me." Josh placed the order for her and ordered a hot fudge sundae for himself. "About tonight—"

"I'll be all right. The men said they'd come here when I wasn't here."

"I wouldn't rely on that. My brother runs the reindeer ranch, so he's needed back there tomorrow. I'm off work for the next two days, so I'll stay close, help you get the shop back in order, and we can inventory those trunks in the morning. We can also start checking the boxes of stuff you think might contain something of value."

"Before the shop opens at ten."

"Correct."

She chewed on her bottom lip. "Okay. I know I wouldn't sleep a wink tonight, both from worry about getting the shop ready to open all over again and from concern those men will try to return there or come here. So thanks. I appreciate it."

"You are sure you don't have any idea what could be so important to those thieves?"

She let out her breath in exasperation. "Look, I have no idea what they were looking for. If suddenly something pops into my head that I think might be important, I'll let you know. Seriously."

"A simple no would have sufficed."

"I seriously doubt it."

He smiled.

Thirty minutes later, the front doorbell rang, and he went to check it. "Hot fudge sundae delivery, and all the rest." He paid the guy at the door, then closed and locked it.

"Oh, I should have gotten some money for you," she said.

"I took care of it. We're good." He was bringing the food over to the bar when there was a knock at the back door. "I'll get it."

"You're handy to have around." Especially since she was feeling so wiped out, and every time she walked, her leg hurt.

"You need someone to help you until you're feeling better." Josh saw that it was his brother and opened the door. "You guys get it done?"

"We did," Maverick said, entering the house. "Adam wanted to know how come the two of us had to replace the window, with George's help—but you got the girl."

Brooke was taking a bite of her sandwich. She put her finger up in the air and finished chewing, then said, "He didn't get the girl."

"Who's staying overnight to protect you?" Maverick asked.

"I am," Josh said without hesitation.

"I rest my case," Maverick said. He frowned at the meal Brooke was eating. "Don't tell me you're having dinner with Brooke too."

"Dessert with her. I had dinner at the house with you, remember?"

"Where's mine?"

Josh handed him the menu. "They can bring you something in a jiff."

"Since you're staying the night, do you want me to run to the store and pick up a couple things for you?" Maverick asked Josh.

"Sure, thanks. I've got my emergency kit with my toiletries and one change of clothes in the car, but I'll be staying a couple of days."

"Be right back with my very own dessert. Oh, and Adam said if it's all right with you, Brooke, he'd stay at the shop tonight until we can get the security cameras installed, just in case someone tries to break in. First, he's taking me home though."

"Maverick, that would be great," Brooke said. "There's a Napoleon-replica bed in one of the rooms that Adam can sleep on. I'll grab some sheets for it for when you return."

"I'll let him know." Maverick left the house, then returned before Josh could lock the door. "Keys to your car? I rode with you."

Josh fished out his keys. "Thanks, Maverick."

"No problem." Maverick headed through the courtyard, and Josh locked the door again.

"The house has two guest bedrooms and a foldout couch, so it's your choice where you want to sleep tonight," Brooke said to Josh.

"Thanks." He sat down at the bar and scooped up some of his ice cream. "So about the front door of the shop. Had you locked it before the men entered it while you were in the attic?"

# CHAPTER 11

JOSH HAD TO ASK BROOKE WHETHER THE DOOR TO her shop had been unlocked or not. It wasn't just because he was a police detective. He couldn't quit wondering how the intruders had gotten in. He knew she was perturbed with him for asking her questions about the break-in, but until it was resolved, like the issue with the stolen reindeer, he couldn't let it go. Particularly if she was in some danger because of it. True, the would-be thieves had been shooting at a wolf and not a human woman, but he had to assume if they wanted something desperately enough, they would have shot her, too, if they'd found her in the attic in her human form. No witnesses left behind.

"I'm certain I flipped the sign from Open to Closed on the door, and I'm sure I locked it out of habit. But I had so many things I wanted to do—clean up the dishes from making the hot cocoa and the wassail, and then restocking my shelves and being concerned that my great-aunt had ordered more boxes of stuff from Colombia—that I can't be completely positive."

"The door lock didn't appear to be tampered with."

"Great."

"I intend to help you sort through whatever you need help with," Josh said again. He had the time off, and what better use of it than to help a wolf in need?

"Thanks." She sounded weary, and he was ready to put her to bed, but he was waiting for his brother to return with his dessert before he turned in.

Then a knock sounded on the front door, and he went to answer it. He looked through the peephole and saw Maverick standing on the doorstep, sacks in hand.

Josh opened the door for his brother and locked it after him. "Thanks, Brother. What dessert did you get for yourself?"

"Chocolate brownie smothered in ice cream and topped with hot fudge."

"Did you bring me one too?" Brooke asked.

Maverick looked a little bummed that he hadn't. "Did you want mine?"

She laughed. "No. I was just teasing. I already had my sundae."

Someone knocked on the door again, and Josh went to get it. "Our sketch artist is here."

Brooke looked done in, but she knew the importance of doing this.

"This is Sierra Redding," Josh said, introducing the ladies. "And, Sierra, this is Brooke Cerise."

"Oh, oh, a wolf. I'm so glad to meet you," Sierra said. "Adam should have mentioned it. I'm so sorry I didn't get here sooner. Criminals are keeping me busy. Let's get this done. You look like you could use some rest."

"Thanks." Brooke was all smiles, and Josh was glad Sierra had finally arrived and the two she-wolves had met each other.

"I'm looking forward to shopping in your store. I love antiques." Sierra pulled out her sketch pad.

"Oh, that would be great."

"Is someone staying with you tonight?" Sierra asked Brooke.

"I am." Josh hadn't meant to say that so quickly, as if he was afraid someone else would step in to volunteer. His brother chuckled.

"I'll have to scratch *you* off my list of eligible bachelors, I see." Sierra gave him an evil smile.

Everyone knew Josh wasn't dating anyone. He handed Brooke another mug of hot cocoa to warm her up after having the sundae. "Would you like one, Sierra?"

"No, thanks, I'm good."

"How long have you been doing this?" Brooke asked Sierra.

"For about a year now. I was a finance officer and retired from the army, then joined my brother and the pack about two years ago. I was working in the pack as a preschool teacher, but my true love is art, and I was sketching a lot of pictures for people—kids, families, wolves and humans— while also teaching art to the little ones. Then Josh and Adam asked if I might be interested in being a police sketch artist. As the bureau's sketch artist, I love helping to catch the bad guys, but I still teach art to the kids, and adults who want lessons, in the pack."

"Oh, how wonderful."

"I love it." Pencil raised, Sierra said, "Start by telling me everything you can remember."

Josh hovered over Sierra's shoulder to give his input.

"You know, Josh, you could give me your own descriptions. Separately. So the two of you don't influence each other. That's how we're supposed to do this." Sierra tilted her chin down as she looked up at him, giving him the *look*.

Josh thought she'd be perfect as a mate for his brother. She seemed more like a sisterly type to him. "Brooke's got most of it right. She saw a lot more than I did. I saw mostly the backs of their heads except for a couple of times when they looked back to see if I was still following them. She was much closer to them than I ever got. I saw the one man leaning over a bunch of boxes Brooke had out for trash earlier though."

Sierra nodded. "Is there anything else you can think of?" she asked Brooke after she'd given Sierra all the details she could remember.

"Thanks, no. That's it."

"What about you, Josh?"

Arms folded across his chest, he shook his head.

"We'll get the composites out right away. By the way, did you ever learn who stole your reindeer calf?" Sierra asked Josh.

"No, but I'm hoping we can wrap that case up fairly quickly while looking into the other situation."

"What's the world coming to when someone will steal a reindeer calf so close to Christmas? Nice to meet you, Brooke. We'll have to get together for lunch or dinner and shopping, whenever we're both free," Sierra said.

"I'd love that."

"You take care. You look like you're fading. Adam told me you were shot."

"I was, but luckily they didn't hit anything vital. The bullets just grazed me."

"That's good." Sierra said her goodbyes and eyed Maverick's brownie crumbs on his plate. "You didn't save any for me?" Then she laughed and was out of there.

"She seems really nice," Brooke said as Maverick locked the door after Sierra.

"She is. But none of us have had a chance at dating her yet," Maverick said.

"Why not?" Brooke got up from the recliner, and Josh was right there helping her.

"She's been dating some wolf from out of state."

"Is she going to mate him?" Brooke held onto Josh's arm, her eyes half-lidded, looking exhausted.

"Most of the bachelors figure if the guy doesn't live here and she didn't stay where he was, she's not that interested in him. But she hasn't gone on any dates either. So it's a toss-up," Maverick said.

Brooke managed a smile. "I'm exhausted. If you don't mind, I'm going to bed."

"Go ahead. We're going to talk until Adam returns to pick up Maverick. We'll try to keep our voices low so you can sleep."

"Thanks, guys, for everything." She yawned. "Good night." She padded down the hallway to the master bedroom. Then she padded back to the living room with some sheets, a blanket, and a towel. "Sorry. Tell Josh what the cost of the window and the labor were, and I'll pay him in the morning. He can give the money to you and Adam and George, Maverick. These are for Adam to use on the Napoleon bed at the shop tonight. There's no sense in him staying up all night when he can probably just sleep. The store was once a house, so there's a bathroom with a shower on the second floor he can use. The kitchen has lots of stuff he can snack on if he gets hungry."

"I'll tell him," Maverick said.

"Thanks." She headed back down the hall to the master bedroom.

"Was the door locked to the shop?" Maverick asked Josh.

"She doesn't remember. I looked at the lock, but it didn't look like anyone had tampered with it."

"Adam and I swept up all the glass and porcelain and dumped it in the dumpster. We put stuff on the shelves, though we didn't know where everything went," Maverick said.

"Thanks. I'm sure she'll really appreciate returning to the store in the morning and not seeing the wreckage all over again."

Maverick frowned. "Did you need me to stay the night, too, or do you think the two of you will be fine? I can stay until I need to return early in the morning to feed the reindeer. Or I can reschedule one of our ranch hands to be in charge."

"We should be good. She said the thieves didn't intend to come here until she was at the shop. I'm going to ask Adam if he could stay at the house tomorrow while I'm at the shop with her since it's his day off."

His brother smiled. "You know what Adam's going to say."

"That I could stay here while he watches over her." Josh smiled.

"Let me know if you learn anything, and if you want to bring her out to the ranch to have a meal together, just call. I figure she'll want to stick close to home until this is resolved now though." Maverick pulled his phone out and texted someone.

"Thanks, Maverick. I will."

"Adam is coming to pick me up. I texted him on the way

to the sandwich shop." Maverick got another text message and responded to it. "If you haven't mentioned to him about staying in her house when she's at the shop tomorrow, I'll ask him."

"Go ahead."

Maverick texted Adam. He received another text. "Tell Brooke not to worry about the window. The pack takes care of its own, even if she's not officially one of us yet," Maverick told Josh.

"I will. I wasn't going to make her pay for it. I would have paid for it myself," Josh said.

Maverick smiled.

"It doesn't mean anything."

Adam called Josh on Bluetooth. "Hey, I thought you were not planning to date another wolf for at least six months."

"I'm not. It's all about trust. Brooke trusts me. What can I say?" Josh said.

Adam laughed. "You sure have her bamboozled. I just pulled into her driveway."

"Adam's here," Josh told Maverick.

"Gotta go," Maverick said.

"Thanks for everything, Maverick." Josh walked with his brother out to Adam's Hummer.

Adam was shaking his head. "If you were being honest with yourself, *I'd* be staying with the she-wolf."

"Actually, I was thinking about that. I'll need to be back at work in a couple of days, and we'll need to have someone watching out for her." They would until they caught these bastards.

"I'll see if I can take off some time from work."

"If not, I'll check with Leidolf and Cassie and see if they have anyone else who can be here for her."

Adam laughed. "You'll have all the bachelor males breaking down her door."

"Hey, I'll get someone to take over at the ranch, and I'll do it," Maverick said.

"We can figure it out in a couple of days." So why did Josh want to insist only mated wolves watch over her? "Thanks for planning to return tomorrow to watch her house until we close the shop for the night."

"No problem," Adam said. "I'm off anyway. I'm glad I could help."

"Did you find blood on the broken window? I smelled blood while I was trying to chase down those guys," Josh said.

"Yeah. Someone must have cut himself good on the glass. We're testing it for DNA to see if the injured guy is in the system."

"I sure hope he is. See you tomorrow then." Josh waved goodbye, then pulled his bag out of his car, headed back into the house, and locked up. He turned off the Christmas tree lights, put out the fire, then took the bag of items Maverick had picked up for him and his own and headed for the guest bedroom closest to the master bedroom.

He had planned to volunteer to work at the White Wolf Sanctuary on one of his days off during the month, but Brooke took priority. He certainly hadn't thought he'd be trying to track down one of their reindeer calves, then aiding a she-wolf in need.

Josh finally settled down to sleep, though he'd be on alert if anyone tried to break into Brooke's place tonight.

He closed his eyes, but he couldn't sleep. All he could think of was seeing the men running through the town, the one dribbling blood along the way. Josh had wanted to kill the bastards for hurting Brooke. And making her feel unsafe. Not to mention he was afraid they'd return for whatever they were after.

He kept envisioning her coming out from behind a crate as a red wolf, her front leg and hind leg bleeding, her tail wagging slightly to show she'd been glad to see them.

He turned on his side and stared into the dark room, finally seeing a little red wolf sitting on her rump in the guest bedroom, watching him.

Surprised to see her but glad she'd come to him, he smiled at her and patted the mattress. "Do you want to join me?" He suspected she was feeling anxious, safer in her fur coat, and like him, unable to sleep. Before she could jump onto the bed, he said, "Wait, I'll help you." He suspected jumping on the bed might aggravate her injuries. Though he was afraid he might do the same when he lifted her onto the bed. He normally would have slept in the raw, but he was wearing boxer briefs in case he had to grab his gun and protect Brooke. He pulled aside the covers and got out of bed.

He gently lifted her onto the mattress and climbed back under the covers, and she curled up next to him. If he wasn't planning to protect her using his gun, he would have snuggled with her as a wolf. He was glad she'd come to him and not tried to brave it out by herself if she was feeling anxious.

He checked her wounds to make sure she wasn't still bleeding. She wasn't, which was a good thing since she wasn't wearing bandages any longer.

He wrapped his arm around her, and she laid her head on his chest. He had no intention of courting her, but this sure felt nice.

# CHAPTER 12

BEFORE FULLY WAKING THAT MORNING, JOSH FELT A warm human body snuggling with him under the covers, and he quickly opened his eyes to see Brooke in his arms. When the hell had that happened? And how had he slept through it? Not that this was unwelcome, just that he was supposed to be protecting her, damn it. Not sleeping through everything.

He hoped Brooke knew she'd shifted and wouldn't be shocked when she woke. He wrapped his arms around her and closed his eyes, trying not to think of having the beautiful she-wolf in his embrace, but it wasn't working. With her hot little body resting naked against his, her sweet cinnamon scent and her warm breath against his naked chest were waking parts of his body that needed to go back to sleep.

She was warm and soft and cuddly. Trying to put the feel of her out of his thoughts, Josh somehow managed to fall asleep for another hour, waking to an alarm going off in the master bedroom. For the first time in a long time, he wanted to just stay in bed and sleep the morning away…with the she-wolf in his arms.

Brooke lifted her head and groaned. He sighed. He was afraid she was going to regret having joined him in bed. He was glad she'd slept through the night and they hadn't had any disturbances.

"Uh, sorry about that." She quickly kissed his cheek and

just as quickly climbed off the bed and hurried out of the room.

He smiled. "It was all good. You kept me warm when I was getting a little chilly," he called after her, wishing he had caught her before she ran away and had given her a more… meaningful kiss. It was probably just as well because she might not be ready for that when she was naked in bed with him.

"Ha!" she called out from the other bedroom.

"You *did*."

"You stole the covers last night, and I was trying to get them back."

He chuckled. "I just wanted you to stay close."

She laughed.

Josh got out of bed, took a shower in the guest bathroom, and dressed in the change of clothes he had in his emergency pack. His brother had bought him a red sweater? Hell. He guessed his brother thought he should be dressed for Christmas if he was going to work in Brooke's antique shop for the holidays. Josh never wore red or Christmas sweaters. Thankfully, Maverick had picked up a couple of pairs of regular jeans for him. Josh put on the boots he'd been wearing, glad they hid the red socks Maverick had bought him. *The turkey.* Josh had used his socks from his emergency kit and had forgotten to put a fresh pair in his bag.

He was glad his brother had bought him a couple extra pairs of black boxer briefs—not red underwear, which he probably couldn't find—in case Brooke caught sight of them. Josh headed to the kitchen on a quest for coffee.

Brooke walked into the kitchen while Josh was making the coffee. "Hope you don't mind."

"No, go right ahead." She was wearing a red sweater dress that caressed all her curves, reminding him just how curvy she was when he woke to find her naked, sleeping against him like she belonged there with him.

Not that he should go there. He couldn't help thinking about it though. She was a she-wolf in need, unattached, the right age, and totally appealing.

"Adam's meeting us here to house-sit in case the intruders show up while we're at the shop," Josh said.

"Oh good. I worried about that. I'd hate to come home to find my house was ransacked next."

"Right. What did you want me to do?" he asked.

"Could you make the lavender tea for me for my thermos?" She set it on the counter. "And if you'd like"—she brought out another thermos—"you can make yourself some coffee to go. We can get more at the shop since I have a kitchen there, but I get so busy, I often don't have time to make it. When I do have time for the kitchen, it's to make cocoa and wassail for customers. So it's easier to take a thermos."

"Sure. Though while I'm at the shop, I can help you out with anything you need."

"Thanks. Does French toast and bacon for breakfast sound good?" she asked.

"That sounds great."

They sat down to eat at the kitchen table in the little nook where her bow windows looked onto a garden. Evergreen shrubs bordered her property, and she had a couple of fir trees so her front yard didn't look barren like it might otherwise in winter.

"I don't remember ending up in the wrong bed last

night." She lifted a piece of bacon in her fingers and took a bite.

"You came in as a wolf. I figured you were cold." Not really. He assumed she was worried about an intruder showing up.

"I guess I was having a nightmare and I instinctively knew you would be hero material and protect me. I don't usually shift into my wolf in the middle of the night without knowing I'm doing it. I'm a royal, so I can shift anytime I want."

"Me too. I was glad you joined me, and I hoped I could make you feel better and you could sleep."

"You really didn't mind? Here you're taking care of me and I offer you a guest bed, and the next thing you know, I'm making you share it with a virtual stranger."

"We're not exactly strangers any longer. Besides, I couldn't sleep until you joined me. I was worried about someone breaking in and you being by yourself in the other room. It really worked out for the best when you came in to share the bed with me. If you don't remember, you very politely waited until I saw you and told you to join me."

"Vaguely. It was like I had been dreaming. Including the part about snuggling up to you as a human. I never do that with my guests. *Ever.* I just wanted you to know that."

He laughed and finished up his breakfast. "I'm glad to hear it. You were a welcome companion. You were tired though. I checked the house about four times during the night, looking to see if anyone was observing it and making sure everything was fine, and you never once stirred."

"I was having trouble sleeping well at first because I was still hurting. Then I must have finally fallen asleep. Thanks for being so understanding."

"You're welcome. It's what we do for each other."

Josh suspected the word hadn't gotten out to the rest of the pack about her yet, or some of the other bachelor males would have been here already, offering to help.

She finished the rest of her French toast, carried the dishes to the kitchen, and placed them in the dishwasher. "As soon as Adam comes over from the shop, we need to hurry over there to get it ready so we have some time before I need to open it."

Just then, Adam arrived, a tall cup of coffee and a sack of doughnuts in hand. Perfect timing. Brooke thanked him for everything, including coming to stay there today to watch over things.

"Tomorrow, if you stay the night, you can have breakfast with us. I should have offered last night."

"Thanks. Uh, you didn't tell me the Napoleon bed was barely bigger than a child's bed."

She smiled. "You could have turned wolf and curled up on it."

"I did. It was nice and comfortable otherwise."

She laughed. "Well, some people were smaller back then."

"We picked up security equipment, the best we could get," Adam said. "A couple of the guys are coming here to install it first thing this morning, both on your house and the shop, inside and out, if that's acceptable."

"Oh, thanks so much. With all the trouble I seem to be having, I need the cameras. How much do I owe for the security equipment and the labor?" she asked.

"Leidolf and Cassie said it was on them—anything to protect a new she-wolf to the pack."

Brooke smiled broadly. "That's wonderful. I should have moved here a long time ago. I hope they don't believe taking me into the pack will be a mistake after all the difficulties I've had."

"Not at all. As long as you're not a rogue wolf, he and Cassie and, well, the rest of us are delighted. The guys with the security equipment should be here soon to start installing it. Maybe I can order something to eat for us when it's time for lunch." Adam set his thermos and sack of doughnuts on the kitchen table.

"I have to stay at the shop," Brooke reminded them.

"I'm sure we can work something out." Josh knew Adam was trying to come up with a way to have lunch with Brooke and hopefully get to know her better. He didn't blame him. Adam *had* done a lot for her already. "I take it you didn't have any problems over there."

"No, it was really quiet. Same at the house?" Adam asked.

"Yeah," Sierra said.

Josh took a sip from his mug of coffee. "It was a perfect night." Especially the part about sharing it with Brooke.

A blush rose on Brooke's cheeks, her gaze turning to Josh's. Josh smiled at her.

Adam cleared his throat and raised a brow. "Just call me if you have any trouble."

"Same with us. If these guys show up at the house, don't play the hero. Let me know, because I'll be your closest backup," Josh said.

"Right. What appeals for lunch?" Adam asked Brooke.

"Pizza. I haven't had any in ages." Brooke motioned to the bathroom. "Bathroom is that way. Feel free to eat or drink anything you want. Make yourself at home."

"Thanks. I will," Adam said. "See you at lunch then."

Brooke and Josh left the house, thermoses in hand. Even though he and his brother had pizzas recently, he didn't mind eating one again.

"You said you were able to sleep finally. How are your injuries this morning?" Josh asked her.

"They're much better. They hurt some, but not like yesterday."

"Do you want me to check them? I thought you might have groaned a little at one point when you were in bed with me, but then you didn't do it again, and I didn't want to wake you to see if you were hurting. I should have asked you first thing this morning."

"I groaned because you pulled the covers off me."

He chuckled.

"Really, my injuries are fine."

Wanting to be sure, he transferred the second thermos into his other hand and placed his free hand against her forehead. He was glad to feel she wasn't too warm. "No fever."

"No, the EMTs did a good job of disinfecting the wounds. I'm sure I'll be fine, but thanks for being concerned."

"You tell me if you start feeling poorly."

---

With apprehension, Brooke unlocked the door to her shop and opened it. She couldn't believe her eyes. She'd envisioned seeing broken glass, porcelain, and merchandise scattered all over the floor. But everything—that wasn't broken—was neatly stacked on the shelves again, and there wasn't a shard of breakage on the floor anywhere.

Tears filled her eyes. "They did this? Adam and Maverick? They cleaned everything up?" She hurried into the shop to turn off her security alarm.

"They did so you'd be all set when you returned to the shop."

"Ohmigod, I'll have to have all of you over for dinner one night to thank you. You don't know how much all this means to me."

"We'd love that. Since they were looking for something specific, we figure they did damage like some thieves looking for random stuff would do to throw us off the case. Do you have a list of the merchandise you've bought recently in case there's something among the items that those guys were after?"

"No. I haven't purchased anything since I've been here. All the stuff that's still coming in are things my great-aunt purchased. Well, except for the five boxes I have coming from Gulliver's estate, but I haven't received them yet. The things my aunt purchased were preordered or handmade— like the Colombian pottery stuffed with cocaine—so they weren't shipped right away."

"I wondered about that."

"I thought we could unlock those trunks. I don't even want to see the condition of them after those bastards shot so many bullets all over the attic last night. I had figured I might be able to sell the trunks. There may be nothing salvageable inside them, but the trunks themselves would probably have sold."

"I'm sure we can find someone in the pack who can restore the trunks." Josh pulled out a set of lockpicks.

She eyed his lockpicks. "What would I do without you?"

"Call a locksmith?"

She smiled and then set the thermoses in the kitchen.

"Why don't you wait here, and I'll check everything out first, even though Adam was just here. He did run to the doughnut shop, and that took him a little while." Josh pulled out his gun and headed into the other rooms of the shop.

Brooke pulled a knife from a kitchen drawer for protection, realizing she hadn't even thought of the possibility that the intruders from last night had gotten into her shop while Adam was out. She was glad Josh was here with her. She imagined if he hadn't come with her, she would have been feeling horribly spooked, afraid the thieves would be waiting in the shop for her to arrive or could show up at any time tonight after she closed the shop. In fact, she probably would feel unnerved when Josh couldn't be here with her a couple of days from now, if Adam or someone else couldn't stay with her. She hated feeling like that. At least until they caught the bastards who had broken in.

Tension filling her while she waited in the kitchen, she listened to Josh moving about the rest of the shop, praying he wouldn't run into any trouble. She heard jingle bells ringing in one of the rooms, then growing closer to the kitchen. She frowned, wondering what Josh was up to.

He walked into the kitchen holding antique leather sleigh bells and an antique Alaskan dairy postcard featuring Alaskans milking a reindeer. "I know the shop isn't open yet for business, but I'll take these. I'll settle up after I check out the rest of the shop."

She was amused to see him "shopping" as if he were a customer and not her police protection. "Are you kidding? After all you've done for me? They're yours."

"Thanks, but—"

"No buts, they're yours." No way was she making him pay for them after all he'd done for her.

"Thanks."

She took them from him and set them in her office so no one would think they were for sale.

Josh began climbing the stairs to the attic, the steps creaking, and then he walked around the large attic room and finally called down, "All clear."

"Coming!" She was glad no one had been in the shop, waiting for her to open. She turned on all her Christmas lights and her Christmas music, then hurried to the stairs and heard the clicking of keys—or in this case, lockpicks—opening a lock on one of the antique trunks.

She entered the attic room and found Josh with a padlock in hand, heading for the other trunk to unlock it. She hated seeing where the bullets had clipped the metal bands and sunk into the metal. Maybe someone in the pack *could* restore the trunks and she could sell them.

Light was filtering through the big windows in the attic, and she was glad the guys had replaced her window. And it was perfectly clean! Which meant she needed to clean the others too. She looked around the room. It was huge, and it would be perfect for fixing up and using as an additional salesroom—something whimsical and fun. A German-crafted goat pull toy was standing in one corner, peeking over a box. Made of goat skin and real goat hair, it would fetch around $600.

Brooke hoped she'd find a treasure trove of valuable objects that would help make up for the ordeal she'd suffered. She was determined to go through all this stuff to sell it, but even now, she was trembling a little, the scene flashing through her mind, remembering the deafening sound of bullets being fired and hitting wood, cardboard, and metal. And the bite of the bullets as they sliced through her skin and fur.

Trying to shake loose the raw memories, she waited for Josh to finish so they could see what was in the trunks at the same time. Then she pulled her phone out of her pocket to document the contents before they began rifling through them.

She lifted the lid of the steamer trunk first. Everything smelled musty, like the trunk hadn't been opened in years. The men had obviously only thought that since the trunks were locked, something valuable had to be inside. Something that they were looking for.

"Did you want me to remove the items since you appear ready to catalog them with your phone?" Josh asked.

"That would be great. Thanks, Josh. I bet you never expected to be helping with something like this on your days off."

"No, but this is more in line with what I normally do— police work—so it works for me." He brought out each item from the steamer trunk and the other.

She took pictures and added notes. "I still can't believe anyone would wait this long to look for the items if they knew that something valuable was inside the trunks."

"What if they only just found out your great-aunt had something of value in the shop? Or the house? And now they're searching for it."

"That could be. Though they did mention boxes, and that makes me think they were waiting for something to arrive here that had been shipped."

"Like more cocaine?"

"Maybe." She didn't want to admit she had considered there might be more boxes of cocaine coming and she could still be in a world of danger. Anyone who was helping her out would be too.

Josh pulled out an old Santa suit and a little girl's hat and muff and coat that appeared to be from the 1930s. Oh, how cute!

"Anything of value in there?" he asked.

"These are lovely, well preserved, like they'd been worn only a few times and then put away. They should sell pretty well once I get rid of the musty smell."

"What do you think? Someone your great-aunt knew played Santa? Your great-uncle, maybe?"

She shrugged. "Maybe. Why else would she have it in this trunk?" She sorted through the old costume jewelry. "Some of these have real diamonds. They could be worth some money. A couple of old Chinese vases. I'll have to check on all these things to see if they're truly valuable or just pretty decorator pieces."

Then they began searching around in the attic. She found a whole bunch of old paintings leaning against one of the walls, a floor-length mirror, and boxes and crates of stuff she'd need to sort out later. Thankfully, the mirror and the paintings hadn't been hit by gunfire.

She didn't have time to look through everything right this minute. She was thinking she needed to hire someone to run the shop while she sorted, cataloged, determined values, and then priced the items for sale. Not to mention she needed to update her website where she listed all the major merchandise.

Josh peeked through a bunch of dishes he found in one crate, each one wrapped in newspaper.

"I haven't inventoried the boxes of merchandise my great-aunt has stacked in all the rooms. I haven't had time to go through them. Any of the new merchandise she bought should have inventory lists packed in the boxes. For the past two weeks, I made some headway on listing items she already had out for sale, so they're now on a website people can search through. If they want an item, they can claim it and then come in within forty-eight hours to pay for the item and it's theirs."

"You need to have it where they can pay online."

"Yes, next job to do. Oh, and be careful with the newspapers wrapped around objects. They can be sold also, depending on the shape they're in, what the news was, and the age of the newspaper."

He looked over one. "1911? Does that mean these dishes have been wrapped up in this paper since then?"

"Probably. And that's great. The dishes and the newspaper might be worth something. Depending on the quality and the name brand of the dishes, they could bring in some money. Though only collectors want stuff like that. Most everyone wants microwavable dishes nowadays. Which is why so many people get rid of their old dinnerware now."

"That makes sense. I know that's all Maverick and I use. We didn't have any hand-me-down dishware though."

"You don't use paper plates?"

He smiled. "We have a dishwasher."

"The last guy I dated used paper plates and cups for everything."

"No dishwasher?"

She chuckled. "No dishwasher soap."

"I have him beat there. What about the rest of the items in the chest?"

"Tintype photos, which can be worth a little. A wedding gown, a beautiful red ball gown. They can be used for displays and sold."

He looked over the red gown. "It looks like it would fit you."

"It would be pretty to wear for New Year's, once I clean it. Oh, also, I'll be closing early on Christmas Eve. I usually close early because I don't have many sales after about two. At least that was the case in Phoenix. At that point in the day, everyone goes to the mall and the big-box stores for their last-minute shopping."

"We also have a pack party. You could wear it to that."

Was he inviting her to the Christmas party as his date?

"It might be a little dressy for it. Let's leave this for later. I can lock the attic so no one gets in here, hopefully, but I'll take the jewelry with us, just in case it's valuable," she said. "I had a built-in safe installed in the house. It's the first thing I did when I moved in."

"Good idea. Do you want me to take anything downstairs?"

"Grab the vases, if you don't mind. We'll put them in the office in the safe I had installed, and I'll check the value of them later."

Then they left the attic, and she locked the attic door. She should have done it last night, but with all the police there and being injured, she hadn't thought of it.

"Do you always lock it?" Josh followed her down the stairs.

"Yes, except last night."

The doorbell rang. She glanced at the Felix the Cat clock. "It must be the mail carrier with another package. It's not time to open yet."

"Or it's the guys coming to install the security equipment. I'll go with you, or I can handle it."

"You can come with me. I can't be afraid of answering the door every time someone is there. And you can't always be here."

"I'll make other arrangements with pack members to be here until we catch these bastards. If whatever you have is valuable enough, I'm sure they'll be back."

"I just wish I knew what it was."

And she really wanted to know if Josh wanted to take her to the pack Christmas party.

# CHAPTER 13

IN HER OFFICE, BROOKE OPENED THE SAFE. SHE PUT the Chinese vases in there and locked them up, then opened her laptop. "Here are all the lists of merchandise I've added to the website with the prices my great-aunt had them listed for, but I don't know what they cost." She pulled some papers from a file. "These are the invoices for the new vintage-looking merchandise she bought from wholesalers that I put out on the shelves last night."

He looked at the four-drawer oak file cabinet. "Yours or hers?"

"Mine. She has one, too, but her filing system isn't like the way I set things up, so I'm having a hard time finding anything. When I came here during the summers, she wouldn't let me touch her filing system."

He smiled. "Sounds like my brother and me. He keeps track of all the costs and revenues and keeps all the records. I'd do it in a totally different way, though it wouldn't mean I'd do it any better than him. Just that it would work better for me. Since he usually handles all of it, I let him deal with it."

"I can imagine. That's how it was with my great-aunt and me. I keep paper copies of all my records, but I also list them on the computer for easy reference. I have to have the original cost of the items so I can determine how much profit I make for tax purposes. I've had a few things I've paid a couple dollars for that brought in thousands."

"That's not a bad return on investment." Josh could see

where this could be a fun business, when he hadn't thought it would be. It would be like Christmas—getting a gift that turned out to be something valuable. Or like winning the lottery.

"I agree on the return on investment. That's what I always hope for. Even the trunks could sell for $300 to $1,000 apiece. As long as I can refurbish them without having to pay a lot for someone else to do it." She glanced at the grandfather clock in the corner. "If you want to go through the items listed on the website, I'm going to heat the cinnamon rolls and then open the door for the customers."

"I can do that." And he'd see if he could find her great-aunt's inventory lists.

Brooke set the cinnamon rolls in the microwave and started it.

Josh texted his brother: Bring Jingles and Cinnamon to the shop.

It was a last-minute idea he'd had. He really wanted to help Brooke with her sales before the big reindeer season was over and do something to make her feel better after what had happened to her last night.

She returned to the office and handed Josh a mug of peppermint mocha. "I miss Jingles. That will be one Christmas open house I'll never forget. If I sold as much as I did that day every day, between the breakage last night and brisker sales, I'd be bought out though."

"That's a good thing, isn't it?" Josh didn't believe she would be sold out. Not with all the boxes of stuff she had stacked everywhere in the attic and the other rooms on the second floor. But it would save having to have massive sales after Christmas.

She laughed. The microwave dinged, and she returned to the kitchen and pulled out the cinnamon rolls. "Off to unlock the door."

Josh jumped up from the desk chair. "I'll go with you." He hoped she wouldn't be upset that they were going to have two calves here today, but she'd had so much fun with Jingles being here, and her customers had loved him, and her business was so brisk that he thought having the two reindeer visit might lift her spirits a bit. It wasn't that she seemed down, exactly, but disquieted. He hoped she'd appreciate the surprise.

She sighed. "Thanks for looking out for me. I keep forgetting I might have unwelcome customers."

"Hazard of the business I'm in. Everyone, yourself excluded, is suspect."

She turned her sign from Closed to Open. "You still think I stole Jingles."

"Maybe so you could meet me."

She laughed out loud. "In your dreams."

Maverick finally texted Josh back about bringing the reindeer calves to the shop: Man, are you making a play for the she-wolf!

Josh texted: Just have someone bring the calves. And bring the reindeer sign.

Maverick texted: Will do, but you owe me.

Josh smiled and pocketed his phone.

When Brooke opened the shop, three people came inside, and a trickle of customers continued to come in after that.

Adam texted Josh: The guys are over here installing the security cameras. They'll be over there in a couple of hours.

Josh texted back: I'll let Brooke know. She just opened the door for her customers.

Josh was watching everyone who turned up at the shop, smiling and greeting them as if he were part owner of the establishment. They were all women shoppers so far. He suspected the thieves wouldn't show up when the store was open, but still, he would be vigilant, just in case.

He was planning to go over Brooke's inventory lists in more detail, though he wasn't sure what to look for except high-dollar items. But while she was at the register or talking to customers, he continued to oversee things. Then he heard Maverick's truck pull up. He headed outside to help his brother with the reindeer.

Before Josh, his brother, and the reindeer reached the shop, Brooke was getting the door for a customer who was leaving with packages in hand. As soon as Brooke saw the two reindeer, she smiled the brightest smile, and Josh knew he'd done the right thing. He was glad she was happy to see them.

"Ohmigosh, two reindeer calves this time? How fun. So that's Jingles and…?" Brooke said, hurrying to pet them.

"This is Cinnamon. They're best friends," Maverick said. "We figured these two could keep each other company. I'll get the reindeer sign and put it out front."

"Since there are two of them, we could take them out back and have them on that section of grass in the courtyard," Josh said. "We have the sign to put out front that says Santa's reindeer are here, but we usually have an adult reindeer for that, so that's what is pictured on the sign. I'll post about it on social media."

"Oh, me too," Brooke said. "This is so much fun. I'll go get my phone."

The lady who was leaving with her packages deposited them in her car, then returned to take pictures before Josh could move the reindeer calves to the courtyard.

"Thanks so much for bringing the reindeer," Brooke said to Maverick as she brought out her phone and took some pictures of the sign and the calves in front of her shop, then posted them.

"You're welcome. I would like to take credit for thinking of it, but it was all Josh's idea."

She smiled at Josh. "Really? Thanks so much, Josh."

"I hoped you wouldn't think they were underfoot too much," Josh said. "I should have asked, but I wanted it to be a surprise."

"I love surprises like this. I'm thrilled to have them here, and it will be really nice for them to keep each other company."

"I agree. I'll stick around and watch the reindeer while Josh is in the shop helping you. When he wants to swap places, I'm available." At least Maverick was all bundled up in a parka, gloves, hat, and scarf.

"For bathroom breaks and when you need to warm up, we can switch off," Josh said.

"I'll spell you so I can pet the reindeer," Brooke said.

Josh and his brother laughed. "Adam said the guys were installing the security cameras at your place and they'll be over here next." Josh glanced at the heated birdbaths and remembered he needed to buy one. "And we want to buy one of your heated birdbaths."

Brooke frowned at him. "Seriously?"

Maverick was smiling at Josh.

"Which of you is a birder?" She sounded as though she didn't believe either of them were.

Maverick waited for Josh to answer her.

"We both are," Josh said.

She laughed. "Sure. For all your help, pick out any you'd like and it's yours."

"I meant to buy it."

"After all you've both done for me, no way."

Then Josh took the reindeer back to the courtyard, and Maverick hauled food back there for them while Brooke returned to the shop.

"How long will they be here?" a lady asked Josh, following him out to the courtyard with two other ladies in tow who were waiting to hear what he had to say.

"Until six, closing time," Josh said.

"Thank you. I'll be back with my daughter and my grandkids in a little while," the one lady said.

"That will be great." Josh hoped it would mean more sales for Brooke and not just more traffic. Like the customers who had been here the other day, these women were taking pictures and sharing the images, bringing even more people to the shop. Josh slapped his brother on the back. "Thanks for bringing the reindeer. I think Brooke needed a bright spot in her life today."

Maverick was setting out bowls for fresh water for the reindeer. "In all seriousness, I'm glad you're here for her. She needs to feel safe, and it doesn't hurt for you to enjoy the time with her while you're getting over your last ordeal."

"Don't mention it."

"It's not the same thing as last time. Brooke is staying here. And *she's* not mated. And she's not going to get you shot like the other one did."

Josh raised his brows.

Maverick shook his head. "You could be in the line of fire in this case, too, but not for the same reason. Not because she's foolhardy. She's just a victim of circumstances."

"Right. I'm going inside to help and watch over her. Come inside to warm up whenever you need to."

"I will."

Josh returned to the shop and saw Brooke smiling and greeting her customers with enthusiasm and directing them outside to see the calves. He was glad she seemed cheered to have the reindeer here today.

It took about an hour for word to reach people and the crowds to show up. A lot of them were interested in seeing the reindeer calves. Josh took charge of making another pot of hot chocolate and grabbing some blueberry scones and set them out. He glanced out the kitchen window and saw his brother having a ball talking it up with a bunch of kids about the reindeer.

This was what made it fun for them to raise the reindeer on the ranch: seeing how everyone loved them and educating people about them.

Brooke joined him in the kitchen, ran her hand over his arm, and peered out the window at the reindeer. "Maverick's having fun, isn't he?"

"He is. So is everyone else. I'm glad you're okay with having them here."

"I'm really thrilled. They're drawing a crowd."

"How are sales going?"

"Well, you know I said I wouldn't have any more merchandise if we had big crowds today. I really didn't believe that."

"But?" He hadn't checked the shelves to see how sales had been doing.

"I need some more ornaments on the tree and some more merchandise on the shelves." She glanced back to see a customer at her checkout counter. "Oh, I've got to help another customer."

"I'll get the stuff."

"Thanks! In the room down the hall, there are boxes of new vintage-like merchandise." She hurried off to check out the customer.

In the supply room, Josh started digging through boxes that Ivy had purchased through wholesalers, then realized nothing had price tags. He started setting merchandise out on a table and then headed for the checkout counter.

"Hey, why don't we swap places, and you can put price tags on the merchandise." Josh moved behind the counter.

"Oh sure, thanks. I didn't think of that. Can you manage the cash register?" Brooke asked.

"I work at the gift shop sometimes at the White Wolf Sanctuary and sometimes at the reindeer ranch. I've got this. If you'll bring me the price tags, I can get them ready when I'm not busy."

"Sure thing." She brought a box of Christmas tree ornaments and set them on the counter. "Two fifty on each of these. They came in really late, so that price is the sale price."

"Gotcha." He rang up the customer while she looked over the Christmas decorations, then added ten to her order.

"These will make perfect stocking stuffers," the woman said.

The lady behind her agreed and picked out another six. Heck, he didn't need to put price tags on them. Once the ladies had their purchases in hand and were leaving the store, he made up a sign: SALE—BRAND NEW! 50% OFF! $2.50 EACH.

Then he set them in a box so customers could rummage through them.

Brooke was busy setting out more items on the shelves so they didn't look so bare.

Maverick came to the door and poked his head in. "Can someone watch the reindeer while I take a restroom break?"

"I'll do it." Brooke grabbed her hat and coat, headed outdoors, and closed the door behind her.

"Looks like she loves the reindeer," Maverick said, walking to the bathroom.

"She does." Which was a good sign. Not everyone loved them. Josh was eager to show her the rest of reindeer at the ranch when her shop was closed. The sign on the door said she was closed on Sunday and Monday, so he'd have to take her then—when he had off—if she'd like to do that. He also still meant to run with her as a wolf after hours.

When Maverick came out of the bathroom, Josh said, "Why don't you stay here and warm up, and I'll go out and watch the reindeer."

"That's a deal. What do I need to do?"

Josh handed him another box of ornaments. "When the box is empty, fill it up again."

———————————————

Brooke wished they could bring the reindeer inside the shop so no one had to stay outside with them, but there wasn't enough room for the two calves. She loved having them here, and like before, they really brought in the business.

Some of her customers who had come in yesterday came again just to see the two calves. And take pictures. And buy some new things she'd brought out to sell. She could see having this set up next year with a Santa Claus, the reindeer, picture taking, and red-and-white lighted candy canes lining the way to her courtyard.

Even a school had gone through all kinds of hoops to get permission to bring a group of five- to seven-year-olds to her shop, but thankfully the teachers took the kids out to the courtyard through one of the gates and not through the shop. Brooke carried a tray of hot chocolate and cookies out to them. A little goodwill never hurt anyone.

She thought the world of Josh for having his brother bring the reindeer. Her phone rang, and the call was from Adam. "Are you having trouble?" she asked, though he probably would have called Josh, not her, if he was.

"Nope, everything's quiet here. What kind of toppings do you want on your pizza? I saw Maverick brought a couple of calves to showcase."

"Josh suggested it. They've been a lot of fun." She paused. "On the pizza? Anything but pineapple is good for me. Do you want me to ask the brothers what they'd like?"

"No. I already know what they like. I'll order a couple of large pizzas. With the four of us here, everyone can take turns eating. Oh, and the guys are headed over to install your security cameras at the shop."

"That sounds great." She would feel a lot more secure with that done.

It wasn't long before Maverick was watching the store and Brooke and Josh were eating at the house while Adam stayed with the reindeer. Maverick called Brooke and said,

"The guys are here at the shop installing your security cameras."

"Oh good. Tell them thanks."

Then Josh took over reindeer watch while Brooke returned to the shop and Adam and Maverick ate at her house.

It was a whirlwind of sales after that.

"The Christmas party is Sunday. That's when your shop is closed, right? I could take you," Josh said.

She planned to get her shop ready for the next open day during her days off, but she would need a break and would love to meet the pack. "Sure. I'd like that. What's the dress code?"

"Anything you feel like wearing. It's casual. A lot of people wear something red or green or both, but it's not necessary. They have a big barn at the pack's ranch for dances, parties, celebrations, dinners. Anything they need the building for, especially in inclement weather. Maverick and the ranch hands will be bringing some reindeer, and someone will be Santa and hand out presents to the kids."

"Oh, how fun. Sure. What time?"

"It starts about four. I'll pick you up about three."

"Thanks." She smiled. So he *was* going to take her to the party! She was glad. Even though she felt comfortable around Josh and his brother and Adam, she'd prefer going with Josh rather than just showing up to a pack event where she didn't know anyone else. "Oh, except for one thing… No one will be at the shop or at the house to watch the security videos."

"You can watch them anywhere, and we can turn on music, lights, and whatever else we can come up with to make it sound as though someone is at the shop and the house. We'll leave a vehicle out front of each place too. Maybe a couple of people can carpool. We have some who live close by."

"That's good."

Business was slowing down, the last customer leaving the shop, while others were outside getting last-minute pictures with the reindeer calves.

Josh said, "I was thinking we could put some more merchandise out, and then after the shop closes, we can start going through some boxes of merchandise from estate sales."

"Sure." She was amused at how much Josh was taking over the restocking of her shelves. He had a good head for merchandising, and he seemed to enjoy it. "We could carry some boxes from the shop to the house tonight and start going through them. I wanted to start checking the prices on the items we found in the attic, too, so I can get some of this stuff out to sell."

"We can do that. Don't you need some extra help? You have to work in the shop all day and then have to do all this other work afterward," Josh said.

"I've thought of it, and I'd love to hire one of our kind to work here. It would be fun to have another woman working with me." Sure, having the extra muscle of a male wolf would be welcome, and if she had trouble with theft, a male might be more of a deterrent, but she'd rather work with a woman to avoid the hassle of a bachelor male wanting to work for her just with the intention of dating her.

"You can mention it to Leidolf or Cassie, and they'll spread the word. Just be sure to tell them you're interested in a female employee, or you'll have a ton of bachelor males signing up to do the job."

She laughed. "Are there that many bachelor males with the pack?" Since she only knew of Josh, his brother, and Adam—oh, and the DEA special agent, Ethan—and no other wolves had shown up to check her out, she thought Josh might be pulling her leg.

"Oh yeah. Guaranteed."

"You know, I'd hire you in a heartbeat since you've done a great job as my assistant all day. The problem is you already have a job."

He sighed. "I do."

"Too bad. You'd be a shoo-in. I'm going to tag some more merchandise." She glanced at the box that had the Christmas ornaments in it. "They're all gone. Did you price them and hang the rest on the tree?"

"No. I kept telling everyone they were on sale, to add them to Christmas stockings, brand-new merchandise showed up too late, and they all sold."

"See? You'd be perfect for the job. Having the reindeer here, sales pitches at the counter, helping me with the merchandise, and serving as store security? Perfect."

He smiled at her. "Do you have anything else you want me to sell while I'm waiting on last-minute customers?"

"Yeah, I'll be right back." She rushed to get another box for him. Free labor was much appreciated. She figured she'd fix him a steak for dinner for all the help he'd been. She returned with a box filled with more decorations. "Sell them for the same price. I'd like to get rid of them all so I can buy new Christmas decorations next year."

"Speaking of Christmas, what are you doing for it this year?"

"Um, cleaning out the shop, getting ready for the new

year, crying while I watch *It's a Wonderful Life*, eating a turkey. I get one of those small-breasted turkeys so it doesn't take me long to finish up."

"Why don't you come and have Christmas lunch with Maverick and me? We can play games, watch your movie, and cry with you—"

She laughed.

"Just have some fun."

"I'd love that." Though she figured she'd feel guilty about all the work she had to do if she goofed off all day at their ranch.

"I thought you might like to come out and see all the reindeer at the ranch on your day off."

"I'd love to, but I don't want to be gone too often until I know what's going on with these guys who tried to steal from me."

"We certainly could wait until then. We could have Christmas at your place."

"That would work if we still don't know what's going on."

Another couple of customers came in, and they had to see the reindeer, but after that, it got quiet at the shop. Maverick came in and said, "Hey, the last two ladies just left. I'm going to take Jingles and Cinnamon home now, if that's all right with you."

"Sounds great. I want to thank the three of you for doing all this for me," Brooke said.

"It's been fun. I don't know if Josh told you, but we do stuff like this with the reindeer all the time around Christmas. The gigs help to pay for the reindeer's upkeep. And they love all the attention," Maverick said.

"But I've had the reindeer here for two days and haven't

paid for them. I bet they're only at these other locations for a short while, not all day either."

"We have twenty reindeer, so no problem. These little guys wouldn't have been out anyway. Just the adults. They've had fun. And we've had a lot of new requests for reindeer visits. It's all because of the publicity with the news station and publications that carried the story about us being here. Their stay here has made more than enough money to make up for you not paying anything," Maverick said. "I bet the owners of the other two reindeer ranches are wishing they'd thought of it."

Brooke chuckled. "*Now* the truth comes out. You all staged the theft of the reindeer and left him here so I could ensure he had lots of publicity." She gave Maverick a hug. "Thanks so much to you both. The calves are adorable."

Maverick winked at Josh. "I'm off."

"I'll go help him out with the reindeer and the food and all," Josh said.

"Okay. We'll be closing in about fifteen minutes." She looked out the window. "No customers. I'll get some stuff together to work on at the house tonight."

"I'll help you carry it all over there," Josh said.

The brothers went out to the truck and loaded the reindeer and supplies into the trailer while Brooke moved some of the boxes to the back door. Josh soon rejoined her, and they began carrying the boxes into the house and setting them up in the living room.

"Hey, let me help with that." Adam headed to the shop to carry more boxes over. "That was the last of the boxes by the door. Did you need anything else?"

"No, thanks. I'll just go lock up. Nobody else is out

there, and it's time. Did you want to have dinner with us?" Brooke said.

"I've got a…um, date." Adam smiled at her.

Smiling, she raised her brows.

"One of the new ladies in the pack."

"Wow, that's great."

"First date, and she's a live wire. No telling what will happen."

Brooke laughed. "I can't wait to meet her. Will she be at the Christmas party?"

"Yes. But she warned me she's dating everyone in the pack who asks her."

"Oh." She laughed. "That's not a bad idea."

Josh smiled.

Adam laughed. "What about having someone watch the shop tonight?"

"I have a security alarm I need to set. And now with the security cameras, we should be good," Brooke said.

"Josh, you're hanging around, right?"

"I'll be here with Brooke."

"I guess I'll see you at the Christmas party too."

"Thanks, Adam. Josh is picking me up. And good luck on your date."

"Thanks. I'm hoping it goes well." Adam said goodbye and left the house.

"Let's set that security alarm at the shop," Josh said to Brooke, "and we can leave more lights on if you'd like."

"Hopefully, all this will be a deterrent this time." Most of all, she hoped they could catch the would-be thieves, learn what they were after, and keep whatever it was from falling into their hands.

# CHAPTER 14

"What do you need me to do first tonight? Help with the cooking? Work on the boxes?" Josh asked.

Brooke turned on the Christmas tree lights. The outdoor lights came on and shut off automatically. "If you don't mind, go ahead and start laying some of the merchandise out on the table." Brooke began broiling the steaks and frying the potatoes and Brussels sprouts.

Josh started to unload one of the boxes. "You have a lot of items listed online. What if it was something you have listed on your website that someone wants to steal? Maybe something that has a higher value than you have it listed for, but they don't want to pay your price anyway, and then they'll resell it. That's why they know you have the item."

"They were looking for some boxes though." She turned the potatoes and Brussels sprout halves over in the frying pan.

"True. It must be something that's valuable to a particular person."

"Like a document they need to keep secret. Or a murder weapon. Or a will that, if revealed, would mean they wouldn't inherit." Brooke filled up glasses of water.

While the meal was cooking, she brought her laptop to the end of the dining room table. Taking the jewelry she'd found in the trunk out of the box, she set it on the table. She sat down and began looking up the value of the items on her laptop. "Most of this is costume jewelry, but vintage, so it's worth twenty to fifty dollars. But these…" She got up from the table and pulled a jeweler's magnifying tool out of a drawer in a bureau. "Oh, here's the business card from Mr. Lee." She pulled it out of the drawer.

"Ethan confirmed Mr. Lee was dead. So did the man claiming he was Mr. Lee give you one of the now-deceased Mr. Lee's cards?"

"I hadn't considered that." She called the number. There was no answer and no voicemail.

Josh was watching her in anticipation.

"No answer. No answering machine. I'll try again later." She sat back down and looked at some of the jewelry using the jeweler's magnifying glass. "Now these are diamonds and emeralds. Some of these pieces could be worth about $300 to $750. I'll list them on the website. Sometimes I can get more traffic for goods online than I do in the store."

"That's a good deal."

She took pictures of the items and then began listing them on her website. A short while later, the timer went off in the kitchen. "The meal's done."

Brooke went into the kitchen to serve up dinner.

Josh joined her and carried the plates to the table while she brought glasses of water.

"It could be something that my great-aunt ordered but that hasn't arrived yet. Some unusual tapestries my parents bought came from Russia, and they took twelve weeks to arrive in Phoenix. Then there are the shipments from China that take forever. Even Australia. I keep thinking that it's something delayed in shipment and the thieves are trying to grab it. Though why would they want to look in the trunks?"

"Maybe they thought you'd already had something

delivered and had locked it up there for safekeeping. The trunks were locked. Those intruders wouldn't know that you hadn't locked something in there recently. You haven't had any trouble before this?"

"No. Everything's been fine."

"Has anything unusual happened? Has anyone made an inquiry about anything lately?" Josh served glasses of red burgundy, then took his seat across from her at the table.

"I've got a list of inquiries for different items that have been made since I opened the shop. Most of the items have been sold and collected. I'm certain whoever is involved in this wouldn't want to leave a paper trail."

Josh cut up some more of his steak. "The T-bone and the rest of the meal is delicious, by the way."

"Thank you. You deserve a good meal after all the work you've done for me."

"It was my pleasure." He wondered about the sleeping arrangements tonight. Then again, she might tell him she didn't need him to stay the night, now that she had the security cameras in place, just as she'd told Adam he didn't need to stay.

It was her choice, but Josh still would worry about her, and he hoped she would decide she wanted him to stay.

Then he got a call and saw it was from one of the guys at the police bureau. He hoped nobody wanted to call him in tonight if Brooke wanted him to stay with her for the evening. "Yeah, Jefferson?"

"Hey, we have an update on the case concerning Cerise's Antique and Gift Shop. At least one of the men won't be bothering Miss Cerise any longer. He was found in an alley where he'd bled to death, covered in newspapers. Someone stole his boots, and he wasn't wearing a jacket or gloves. The coroner said she'd get right on it. We have no more details than that, but I wanted you to know one of the men is dead."

"It was verified that he was one of the men?"

"Yeah. Same description Miss Cerise gave the sketch artist, right down to his knobby nose, the scar over his left eye, and a piece of the glass was still imbedded in the man's arm—same as the old glass from the window we had as evidence. Adam verified it was him too."

"Good show. At least that's one fewer to hunt down."

"Right. There was no ID on him. Naturally. I would guess he'd been bleeding all the way from the shop, and the other man dumped him before he actually died."

"Which means the injured perp bled all over the vehicle before he was dumped."

"Most likely."

Now they just had to find the vehicle. "Thanks for the update."

"You're welcome. I thought you'd want to know right away."

"I did. Thanks, Jefferson. Catch you later." Josh set his phone on the table. "Well, that was partially good news. One of the intruders in your shop died from the broken-window cut he'd received."

"That's good. But the other one is at large, and the dead man wasn't carrying any ID?"

"Right. They'll still be trying to learn the dead man's identity from his DNA, if he's in the system."

"I'm glad at least one of them is no longer among the living. Too bad the other guy didn't have just as bad of an injury. I suspect whoever was after the item sent these men, so he'll just hire someone else."

"That's what I'm afraid of too."

After dinner, they cleaned the dishes, then sat down to work on the merchandise. Brooke was going over more of the jewelry, so Josh began making up envelopes for the items and adding the prices.

"I don't keep expensive jewelry in the shop. I just post it online. If someone wants to see it, they can let me know, and I'll bring it to the shop that day."

"Do you want me to put these in the safe after we finish tagging them?"

"The expensive ones, yes. The vintage faux jewels can go in the shop. I put them on jewelry racks on the counter or inside the locked display cabinet if they're more valuable."

"Good idea."

Once she was done with that, he brought over a box and began setting the merchandise out on the dining room table. "How about I take pictures of the items while you look for what they're worth?" Josh figured that might speed things up.

"Sure, we can do that." She spent about an hour working on the merchandise, then once he finished tagging the items with price tags, he brought over another box and began unloading the contents.

She smiled up at him.

"What?"

"I have to hire you. Seriously. I've gotten more work done in just a couple of hours than I ever do."

"I can see where it would help to have a couple of people working on this at the same time." He began taking pictures, and she sent inquiries on a couple of items and sent off the pictures.

"It really does." She sighed. "I'll try to stay out of your bed tonight," she finally said, pausing to look at him.

He was thrilled she wanted him to stay with her again. He focused on another teacup and saucer and took a picture. "Don't do it on my account."

"What would the other bachelor males think if they knew I was sleeping with you?"

"That the would-be thieves had shot you and you needed to feel safe." He sure wanted to be the one to make her feel protected. He eyed her, waiting for her to respond. He thought she was considering staying with him. He hoped she was. "Even though I'll be on duty again after tomorrow, I can return after work and stay here with you. It's closer to my job than the reindeer ranch is." He didn't want her to be alone, and he sure as hell didn't want any of the other bachelor males staying with her.

"Won't your brother miss you?"

Josh smiled. "He'll know it's important for your safety and welfare."

"If it hurts your chances of courting another she-wolf…" She began looking for prices again.

"Did my brother tell you I had been dating a she-wolf about six months ago?"

"Uh, no. Was it a bad ending?"

"Yeah. The worst."

"What happened, if you don't mind talking about it?"

"She was a rookie cop, a gray wolf, and we were dating. We had lunch, and she wanted to pick up a watch she'd needed to have repaired. When we walked into the jewelry store, we saw right away a robbery was in progress. I indicated to her we needed to get the hell out of there and call for backup. She wanted to make a name for herself. She pulled out her gun and yelled, 'Police officers!'"

"Ohmigod, no."

"I knew it would end badly. The two robbers turned and started shooting. I tried to protect her and took three bullets. She died right away, and I nearly died. Then at the funeral, I learned she had a mate." He hated telling anyone he had dated a mated wolf, even though he hadn't known it.

"I'm so sorry she died," Brooke said. "And that you were wounded so badly! Why would she be mated and hide the fact from you? Was she nuts?"

"She lived in Arizona, but she got hired on here to be a cop. I didn't know it at the time. I gave her a ticket for speeding, and she—"

"Tried to talk you out of it."

"Yeah. We went on a few dates. I was at the funeral when her mate showed up, furious that I'd been seeing her. He'd seen the news article about her death. He hadn't even known where she was. Hell, we mate for life. I never thought I would have to ask her if she was mated already."

"I'm not." Brooke went back to searching prices for items.

"Good thing to know, because I've already slept with you."

"Right. Good thing."

"You don't have a family, a brother, or a father who might give me trouble, do you?"

She shook her head. "You're safe there. No family." Then she frowned. "Where was she from in Arizona?"

"Near Phoenix."

"What was her name?"

"Joy Greyling."

"Ohmigod, that woman is...was such a bitch. I could have told you that. Though I'm sorry she died."

"You knew her?" Josh couldn't hide his surprise if he'd wanted to.

"She stole my boyfriend."

"Mr. Paper Plates and Cups?"

"No great loss. They were mated shortly after that. I swear it was to prove she could steal him from me." Brooke continued to check prices on more teacups.

"I didn't sleep with her."

Brooke didn't look at him but smiled.

He attached a price tag to another teacup. "Where do you want me to put these so we can have more room for the next box?"

She motioned to the kitchen table. "In there, if you don't mind. We can haul them over in the morning."

He carried the teacups to the kitchen table and returned for some more teacups and saucers.

She looked into a box of old Christmas ornaments. "Wow."

Josh checked out the pear-shaped glass ornaments, which looked stained and not in the least bit interesting. "Good, huh?" He couldn't imagine they were worth much. Just a bunch of old ornaments that had seen better days. He was certain he would have tossed them and picked up new ones to replace them.

She looked them up on the computer and pointed to a page. "German-made kugel, hand-blown glass, made between 1840 and the early 1900s."

Josh's attention focused on the price tag of one that had sold for $18,000. Brooke had an antique box of a dozen. She had a veritable mint gathering dust in her shop. It showed what he knew about old things.

"Collector societies exist for just about everything," she said.

"You need to talk to the pack about this. Some of our wolves who have lived forever might have things stuffed away that could be valuable. You have the contacts. You could help get their items appraised and assist them in finding buyers for a commission."

"Or for free, as goodwill for the wolves of the pack."

"They won't go along with that. You'll help them do 'spring cleaning' and get some cash back for them at the same time. More than they could ever hope to get if they tried to sell their valuable antiques on their own. You'll be doing them a big service. Hell, now Maverick and I will have to go through our attic and a couple of old storage buildings."

She laughed. "I'll help you, once we get this situation with the would-be robbers resolved. Ooh, look, Halloween postcards made in the Victorian era, pre-World War I."

"Oh, my great-grandmother had a bunch of Victorian postcards. She loved stuff like that. We have them in a box somewhere."

"Great. Those sell. The Valentine ones? Christmas ones? They all do. If you have a big reindeer collection, some might be valuable too."

Josh shook his head. "We collect the reindeer ones and have a shop where we display the items. They're valuable—to us."

She laughed. "See? You are a collector in your own right. We've finished with the stuff from the boxes. Let's look at the paintings." She brought up a site that showed some of the items people had found in the trash, thrift stores, garage sales, and attics. "Here's a painting that turned out to be an original oil painting by the Renaissance artist Caravaggio, collecting dust in an attic filled with clothing, toys, and clocks. Who would have known? A woman bought a faux diamond ring for thirteen dollars—and wore it for thirty years—but it turned out to be a 26-carat diamond worth over $800,000. I can't imagine wearing something that valuable all those years, thinking it was pretend."

"It was a good thing it looked as fake as she thought it was."

"Exactly. The gilded frames on these oil paintings are worth a lot," Brooke said. "This is an A. F. Tait painting of birds, circa 1865, worth about $10,000 to $25,000. The oil painting of the fox is by William H. Beard, around 1874 and worth about $15,000. This one is a John Haberle painting of the cat and bird in the cage, circa 1885, worth around $23,000. Kittens in a trunk by Charles van den Eycken, nineteenth century, worth around $29,000. That's the high end."

"I'll have to see if we have any old paintings we didn't think were worth anything that are sitting in storage."

"You never know. I'll have to have these cleaned, but I'll store them in the spare bedroom closet for now. It's getting late, and we've finished all we had to do. Are you ready for bed?" She glanced at Mr. Lee's business card and picked it up and tried ringing his number again.

"Sure. I'll help you move these paintings into the bedroom."

"Thanks. No answer." Brooke grabbed two of the paintings and carried them into the guest bedroom.

Josh carried the other two into the guest room, and they carefully set them in the empty closet.

She retired to her bedroom and pulled out a pair of pajamas.

Josh followed her into her room. He wasn't sure she wanted him to sleep in there. "I'll just take my shower then." He motioned to the guest bathroom down the hall.

"I'll take mine in here. Then you'll join me so I don't have to jump into the guest bed in the middle of the night?"

He smiled. "You bet." He was glad she wanted him to join her there.

It didn't take him long to return to the master bedroom soapy clean, wearing a fresh pair of boxer briefs, and join her under the covers.

She was wearing a pair of tiger pajamas and smelled of the delightful scent of vanilla. She sighed and snuggled against him. "If you thought I was guilty of stealing the calf and had an accomplice, that means the cop is now sleeping with the crook."

"You're vindicated."

"But you haven't caught the real culprit yet."

"I had considered it was a prank. Once I discovered the security video had been tampered with, I didn't believe so. I just can't figure out why anyone would do that and then drop the calf off at your place."

"Unless they were about to get caught so they dumped the calf. Maybe they even planned to come back for it, but something happened, and they couldn't." She frowned. "You haven't heard back about the pickup's tag number?"

"They haven't been able to discern what the tag number was."

"Tomorrow, while I'm at the shop, why don't you check with the stores about their video security and see if you can learn about the men who shot me. You shouldn't have to worry about me now that I have the security cameras. You can monitor them while you're off on your quest to learn the truth. If I have any trouble, I'll call you. You'll be close by and can be back to my shop in a heartbeat. Besides, I doubt the other intruder will return during the day."

"You call me if anything seems amiss. *Anything.*"

"I will. Can you run an announcement about it too? Telling the public that the police are actively investigating the theft of a reindeer calf. Mention animal endangerment. Maybe someone will know something about it and report it."

"I can. Because he was found safe and sound, it's not a case that anyone else on the police force is looking into."

"What about any of the people you employ?"

"All wolves."

"Did you fire anyone recently?"

"No." Josh rubbed his chin. "Come to think of it, we did have a disgruntled customer a few days ago. He felt we over-charged him for time on a couple of our reindeer he rented. We had another job lined up right after his, and we needed to get them to the next location. We have built-in time for issues like that, but we charge for it too. Our contract spells out that if the customer delays us, we have to be reimbursed for the time. Otherwise, we'd have issues with a fair number of customers. You know, one last picture. Ten pictures later, one more picture."

"Which is totally reasonable on your part."

"True, though I can't imagine him going to all the effort to steal a reindeer calf because of it, but he's the only customer we've had issue with recently. Everyone else has had a great time with the reindeer visits."

"What's his business?"

"He's in charge of a security systems company."

Brooke frowned. "So he could have the know-how for tampering with your surveillance video equipment."

"Right. But he's more of a businessman. He was having a big Christmas party for his staff, Santa and the like. It doesn't sound like he would stoop that low."

Brooke scoffed. "You had a perfectly great suspect with the capability to do it and the motive—revenge—and you picked on me?"

Josh smiled and kissed her forehead. "Maybe I just wanted to see more of you."

# CHAPTER 15

BROOKE COULDN'T BELIEVE SHE'D CLIMBED ONTO THE guest bed to be with Josh and now she had asked him to join her in her own bed. Yet this seemed so right. Better than right. Amazing. She felt secure and happier than she'd ever thought she would. His body was snuggled against hers, his thigh between her legs, pinning her against the mattress—so different from when they'd snuggled before. It had been sweet then and sexy, sure, but this was...hotter, more intense, with a deeper purpose. His hand caressed her face, his gaze focused on hers.

She couldn't help but question her sanity. Was she ready for even this much of a commitment to the wolf she'd only just met? Would she feel any differently about him if he hadn't been there to protect her?

Her heart said that the way he had been there for her—from questioning her innocence to charming the pants off her—had endeared him to her.

"I never thought I'd be in bed with a tantalizing tiger." Josh's rough voice broke into her thoughts. He ran his hands over her tiger pajama top, the soft, stretchy fabric rubbing against her nipples, making them erect and sensitive and needy. His chocolate-brown eyes darkened, his expression hungry, almost predatory.

"I never thought I'd be wearing my tiger pajamas in bed with a male wolf." But not just any male wolf. One who had fascinated her from the beginning and made her feel hot and eager to have his hands running all over her.

His darkly captivating expression turned her on, and she wanted more of his touching her, just as much as she wanted to run her hands over every muscular part of him. She pressed her breasts against his large capable hands, loving the feel of his stroking her. His thumbs caressed her taut nipples, and then he turned them so his thumbnails gently scraped over her shirt-covered nipples, and she moaned.

Her scent was aroused and titillated every bit as much as his was. She ran her hands over his face, hard angles and stubbornness personified when he wanted things his way, hot and pliable when he was giving in to her caressing touch and she was having *her* way.

She could become addicted to this. To him.

He slid his hands up her top and cupped her naked breasts, and then massaged them again, only this time with the palms of his hands, the friction heating her skin. Relishing the feel, she ran the planes of her hands over his nipples, soliciting a deep moan. She loved sliding her hands over the back of his boxer briefs too. It wasn't enough to feel his toned buttocks beneath the fabric though. She wanted… needed more—the skin-to-skin contact between them. Slipping her hands inside his boxer briefs, she squeezed his firm ass.

He groaned and captured the bottom of her top, his fingers making her skin sizzle on contact. He slid the top up her body, exposing her breasts, the cool air making her skin tingle with sweet awareness. His warm, slightly fuzzy face nuzzled each of her breasts, tickling her before he pulled her top off over her head. Then he began kissing her mouth, her neck, her breasts. Every kiss made the area between her legs just a little wetter. She was so ready to have him claim her, as she would claim the wolf for her own. Though she knew they couldn't go that far, not just yet.

Then she seized the waistband of his boxer briefs and slid them down his hips. He pulled them off the rest of the way and tossed them aside. His arousal freed, his erection poked her belly. If they'd been ready for a mating, she would have welcomed his cock thrusting deep inside her. She loved how she could make him hard with wanting.

He rocked his steel-hard erection against her, showing just what he had for her, rubbing his aroused scent on her. The slow, seductive moves were meant to stir her need for completion, his cock rubbing against her mons. She softly moaned while experiencing the delectable sensation.

"Man, oh man," he murmured against her neck, nuzzling and licking her skin, making her shiver with need.

He slid his fingers down her pajama bottoms, through her curly hairs, moving so slowly she was throbbing with anticipation. And then his fingers touched the center of her, feeling her wetness, and he smiled. Yeah, he did that to her. He grabbed the waistband of her tiger pajama bottoms and pulled them down until she could kick them off the rest of the way.

Brooke's body thrummed with sexual need as she pulled Josh closer, her eyes and mouth pleading with him for another kiss. To take a chance. To prove this wasn't rebound for him and it wouldn't be just another case of a disappointing relationship for her.

His dark eyes were already swimming with lust when he leaned over and kissed her mouth again, his breathing heavy, his heartbeat—and hers—pounding away. The kiss morphed from gentle to hot and passionate within seconds.

She wet her lips, touched her tongue to his, and he devoured her. Their mouths melded, an intimate contact that made her even wetter with want.

His beautiful eyes closed, his lashes thick and black, he turned his head slightly so he could kiss her cheek and then the other. Then he was kissing her mouth again, parting her lips with his tongue, dueling with her. He tasted of pinot noir grape, not heavy or strong, but of cherry and dark fruits, crisp and lush. His masculine heat warmed her as he pressed his body against hers, rubbing his arousal against her mound, stirring the craving to come.

He groaned, the sound deep and guttural, telling her how much this was killing him too. The wanting, the waiting, the seeking of fulfillment between two wolves of a similar mind. She wanted his full cock thrusting deep inside her. And to be wrapped up in his arms like she enfolded him in hers. To have their naked skin sliding against each other, the friction upping the sexual tension. To feel the heat escalate from sizzling to an inferno.

The exquisite pleasure she felt in being with him was like no other time she'd been with anyone else.

His hand trailed along her breastbone, moving to a breast, cupping it, molding his large, capable hand over it, and gently massaging. She absorbed the feel of his comforting and sensual touch while she stroked his sides, enjoying the hard muscle and the silkiness of his skin. His animal magnetism drew her in, bumping up her pheromones. Hers kicked his into a tailspin.

Their hearts were beating hard, their breathing shallow as he leaned down to lick the nipple of the other breast.

She sucked in her breath when his warm, wet tongue

touched her sensitive, peaked nipple. Reveling in the feel of his strokes on her nipple, she arched against his cock. He switched the attention of his tongue and mouth to hers. Leaving a trail of heat in their wake, his fingers swept down her waist, targeting her nubbin as he moved to the side of her.

She hated losing the heat and weight of him pressing against her body when he moved off her. Until he began stroking her between her legs.

And then she was lost in the magic of his touch, the feel of his mouth against hers, his tongue plunging between her lips, and his fingers plying her feminine nub with strokes meant to bring her to climax. The peaks of the mountains were calling to her—the climb well worth the sweet tension drawing her forth. And then she gave in to the feelings sweeping over her. The sensory assault pushed her to the edge. And over.

She cried out with exultation, feeling spent and glorious, basking in his warmth and wonderful ministrations. For the longest time, it seemed to her, she lay there, glorying in his touch while he continued to caress her skin, her tummy, her breasts, her arms as if he loved every blessed inch of her and couldn't get enough of touching her, just as she couldn't stop touching him.

Smiling up at him, she reached for him, pulled him close, and kissed his mouth. He rubbed his cock against her and kissed her mouth just as greedily.

She pushed him onto his back, straddled his legs, and took hold of his cock. Now it was her turn to make him cry out with pleasure. Or…maybe groan or growl a little.

Josh couldn't believe how finding the stolen reindeer calf at an antique shop had brought him to Brooke and now her bed. Though he wished the other reason he was in her bed didn't have anything to do with the men shooting her in her shop.

He was hoping this would not be the end but the beginning of something beautiful and long-term.

Her skin was like satin, the scent of her arousal like an aphrodisiac. Their pheromones were playing tag, and now she was kissing him before she finally roused from her satiated state to push him onto his back. He hoped she'd never been pleasured so thoroughly, though he didn't want to stop. He wanted to take it all the way with her. He'd never felt that way about another she-wolf before.

He watched her expression as she straddled his legs, her gaze and hand on his cock, stroking while he ran his hands over her soft, warm thighs. He was lost in her touch, her strokes bringing him close to the end, though he was trying to hold off releasing too quickly.

She leaned over and ran her free hand over his abs. "Glorious," she whispered.

She was the one who was glorious, every bit of her from her shiny red hair to her creamy skin, blushing nipples, and curly red hairs. Every splendid stroke of her hand on his arousal brought him that much closer to heaven. She moved off him, never letting go of him, leaning over his chest to kiss his mouth. His hands framing her face, he pushed his tongue into her mouth and caressed her tongue with his while she kept up her strokes on his cock.

He felt the end was near. His skin sizzling from her touch, he tried to hold on to the sensation building longer, but he couldn't. He exploded and growled, wanting to howl his pleasure, but he bit back the inclination.

She released him and kissed his mouth. Then he wrapped her in his arms and held her tight. For several minutes, they hugged each other. But then she said in a sleepy voice, "We'd better clean up before we fall asleep like this. The bathroom's in there."

"I shall return." He left the bed to take a quick shower, soaping up his body, thinking about her touches and kisses only moments before, and already he was becoming hard again.

He heard her taking a shower in the other bathroom. They could have shared.

Maybe she wasn't quite ready for more of a commitment. Hell, he knew he was.

---

The next morning, Josh woke to find Brooke sprawled all over him. Smiling, he stroked her back, her skin silky soft. He liked sleeping with her, cuddling in the middle of the night, waking to find her claiming his body with her own. Yeah, he could sure get used to being with her like this.

She let out her breath and ran her hand over his chest in a gentle caress. "I guess we have to get up."

"Or we could put a sign on the door of your shop that says: 'Family emergency, closed today and tomorrow.'"

She smiled. "Tempting. You don't know how much. But I don't think so."

Then she and Josh dressed. In the kitchen, they fixed ham and cheese omelets and ate, then cleaned up.

At the shop, Brooke turned off the security alarm and turned on the Christmas lights and music.

They brought over several loads of the merchandise that they'd priced last night. She still couldn't believe how much she could get done with Josh's help.

She set the alarm on her house. Josh walked through the shop to make sure no one had entered it or tampered with the security cameras while they'd been in the house, then checked to see if anyone had been around the shop or courtyard during the night.

"Did you see anything?" She began placing the new merchandise on the display shelves.

"No. It looks like no one approached the shop last night. They may wait until they believe things have died down a bit."

"Maybe they decided it wasn't worth it."

"That could be. There's an article in the online paper about the break-in." Josh handed her his phone.

"Great." She scanned through it. "No mention of the wolf in the attic." She handed the phone back to him.

"No, but there *is* a mention of them shooting up the place and wounding you. The police's official statement is that the two men are armed and dangerous. Sierra delivered the sketches to the police station, and they've sent them out everywhere so everyone will be on the lookout for the other man. Not only that, but a photo of the dead guy has been circulated, asking if anyone can identify who he was. That might be quicker than getting the DNA evidence back."

"That makes sense. If the man who's still alive is reading

it, I hope he's scared and doesn't try breaking in again. Are you going to check on the other shops' security videos?"

"Yeah. You call me about anything that doesn't feel right while I'm down the street. I mean it."

She smiled at him and wrapped her arms around his neck. "I don't know. You're a cop, sure, but you seem to be taking this awfully personally."

"A detective." He wrapped his arms around her waist and kissed her. "And I *am* taking this personally."

She kissed him back, taking advantage of the kiss and caressing his tongue with hers.

When the kiss ended, both of them panting and wanting more, she sighed, and they went to the kitchen where Josh offered to make the cocoa while she warmed up the scones.

Once they were done, she said, "Thanks for helping, Josh. I've got to open the door for the customers."

"I'll go with you." He kissed her mouth again and waited while she flipped her sign from Closed to Open. Then he left the shop while she let her customers in.

"Are the reindeer here today?" one of the ladies asked.

Josh smiled and headed across the street.

---

Heading first to the bakery, Josh figured checking out the other shops' security videos wouldn't take too long, and he was glad the shop owners were all too eager to help catch the man who shot up Brooke's attic.

"When we heard all the shooting, my husband and I were worried because the light was on in the attic and we were afraid she was up there," Sarah said. "We learned about the breakage inside her shop later. Our home is behind the bakery, so we didn't hear any of that. But the gunshots? Yes. We called the police right away. Melvin wanted to go help her, but he's got a bum leg from fighting in Iraq. I told him he'd just get shot anyway. It was horrible that she was hurt."

"It was. I'm glad you left it to the police, ma'am," Josh said, watching the security video. He was afraid any confrontation with the intruders might have turned tragic if Mr. Burns had tried to stop them.

"Do you think the two things are connected? The robbers and the day when the DEA and the SWAT team showed up?" she asked.

"Might or might not be."

"Maybe she is just having a week of bad luck. My grandmother used to say we had to throw a pinch of salt over our shoulder to blind the devil and then good luck would follow."

Josh smiled. He was half listening to her but mostly concentrating on the video showing the people hanging around Brooke's shop all that day. Most of her customers had been women while he was there, a few men, but he saw only the one suspect who arrived to carry the box into the shop for Brooke earlier. Which seemed off to him. If he'd been looking for a box being shipped to her place, maybe that was why he hurried to carry the one in for her that had just been delivered. To see if it was the one they'd wanted.

"I heard you were staying with her. As her police detail?"

"Uh, yeah. Since she's on her own and the man who's still alive might come back."

"Oh no. I sure hope you catch him. It was just fortunate

the other one cut himself on the window and died. Served him right."

"Yes, ma'am." Josh left the bakery with a copy of the video and called Brooke on the way to the next shop he wanted to visit. "Is everything all right over there?"

"Yeah. How's it going there?"

"I talked to the owner of the bakery across the street. I'm headed to the Christmas shop next since the men ran that direction. I was hoping we could get some facial recognition shots of the men to see if we missed anything. Are you sure you're okay?"

"Busy, but everything's fine."

"Good. I'll keep reviewing the shops' security videos then and check back in with you as I go."

"I'll be fine."

He sure as hell hoped so. He walked to the Christmas shop a few doors down from hers and asked the owner if he could see the shop's security video.

The owner thanked him again for returning her cat. "I guess you're Brooke's police protection. I've noticed you've been here a lot during the day and at night. I'm glad for that. Lucky girl. You sure can look at the security video. I'm so sorry about what happened to her. It's made all of us nervous, believe you me. And for her to have so much trouble this week…" The woman shuddered.

One of her customers waved a Christmas elf in the air and said, "This doesn't have a price tag on it. How much is it?"

"I've got to assist my customers," the owner said to Josh. "I'll see you before you leave."

"Thanks." Josh watched the grainy video. It was dark

when Brooke turned off the lights in the store. He could see her windows on the side of the store, but the attic didn't have windows on that end. Then he saw the two men approach the door. They'd come from the same direction in which they'd fled, talking to each other, hunched over, like darkly clothed thieves in the night. He was certain they went straight to where their vehicle was parked after they escaped out of Brooke's attic window. He needed to check the security videos along that street to where they had parked their vehicle. If he was lucky, the license plate number was captured on one of them and would be perfectly identifiable.

He'd spend the rest of the day doing that, if Brooke felt safe enough.

Josh thanked the Christmas shop owner and left with a copy of her security video. He planned to go next to the shops down the street near where the men must have driven off, but he wanted to see Brooke before he went that far away. Besides, everything that involved her interested him. He wanted to see her doing well with sales, wanted her to be successful, not just so she could support herself but so she would be happy here.

He pushed open the door and saw her talking away to her customers, showing them the teacups and saucers they'd tagged last night. He was glad he'd helped her with those. She seemed to be in good spirits.

"I need the blue ones. It doesn't matter about the brand name. I just collect blue and white," one woman said.

"Me? I love lavender, any shade of purple. If you get any more in, let me know and I'll buy them." The other woman gave Brooke her name and number.

"I sure will. I'll keep on the lookout for them." Brooke

glanced in Josh's direction, and her whole expression brightened, as if she'd seen her best friend arrive.

Or maybe a lover? That was what he felt like, without the consummated sex. A lover who was sitting on the sidelines, enjoying the way she visited with her customers, cheerful like she should always be. Not apprehensive and fearful because of the bastards who had shot her.

After she wrapped up the teacups and saucers for the two customers, she took their payments, and they left the shop.

"Slow day?" he asked, coming around the counter and running his hands up her arms.

"No, business has been brisk. Some have wanted to see the reindeer calf as if he lives here now." She put her hand on Josh's shirt and pulled him closer.

Josh smiled.

"Any more news?" she asked.

He told her what he'd found out, then leaned over and kissed her.

"Hmm, good thing I don't have any customers at the moment." She wrapped her arms around him and kissed him back.

"I'll canvass the other shops near where I think they picked up a ride, but I wanted to see how you're doing."

"Oh, really good. Thanks for dropping by, giving me a heads-up, and making sure I'm okay. A lot of people have been dropping in to get last-minute Christmas gifts. Some are just buying things for themselves."

"Sounds like it was a good idea to put more stuff out on the shelves this morning." He ran his hands over her shoulders.

"I'll say. You know what this means?" She raised a brow.

"We'll be working on more of the boxes tonight."

"Yes, and every night that you stay with me."

He chuckled. "I'm only too glad to help. I'll be back around noon, if not before then, to spell you for lunch."

"I'm feeling…Chinese. I'd love some beef and broccoli."

"I'll pick up an order later. What are you going to do in the meantime?"

"I'll work on some more boxes. The break from customers helps. Though selling the merchandise does, too, so I have more room to put out the rest of the stuff. Good luck."

"I might need it." He kissed her before he left, and he knew this was becoming a habit he didn't want to give up. She seemed to enjoy it just as much as she deepened the kiss. They didn't have to stand under the mistletoe to get into the spirit of things.

Then her shop door opened, the jingle bells jingling, and she pulled away from Josh. They both smiled and greeted the two women who entered the shop. After that, Josh took off to check out the other store videos, hoping he'd get what he needed to locate the second intruder.

# CHAPTER 16

BROOKE WAS EXCITED TO GET SO MUCH DONE AND STILL sell lots as she checked out her next customers. She was even happier that Josh had barged into her life. What a strange twist of events. He had enriched her life already, just through her getting to know him and enjoying his company. If she hadn't met him and his brother, Adam, and Ethan, she wouldn't have known what to do about all the trouble she was having. She was certain she would have been more at risk.

After one of her customers bought a couple of oil paintings and left, since no one else was in the shop, Brooke brought her laptop out on the counter. Then she retrieved the old Chinese vases she'd found in the trunk from the office safe, which had her thinking about Chinese food and fortune cookies. She was already getting hungry, feeling great about the finds they'd already identified in her great-aunt's attic, and she was ready to discover more treasures!

That made her wonder again where the treasure list her great-aunt had left for her was hidden. She told herself she might as well enjoy what she had to do for the next three years while keeping her great-aunt's shop going, but she had to admit this was like opening Christmas packages and finding some real treasures.

When she was low on inventory, she'd have to go on some garage sale and estate sale hunts. And truthfully, she was looking forward to it. She suspected some of her change of heart was due to finding a hunky wolf to date.

She began to examine the first of the vases and saw it was decorated with images of deer and cranes, beautifully painted, and it appeared to be from the Qianlong period—an imperial vase made for Emperor Qianlong during the Qing dynasty. It couldn't be. It was probably a replica. Yet it looked old, eighteenth-century, and perfectly preserved. She looked at the base of the vase and took a deep breath. The family rose was marked on it, which meant it would have gone to one of the emperor's palaces.

Her heart was already beating faster, her hands shaky as she put the vase down on the counter. She kept telling herself it was probably a replica that could be worth a couple thousand dollars. Not bad. Yet the rose on the bottom of the vase made her believe it wasn't. That it was the real deal. She could have in her possession millions of dollars in that one little vase. And her great-aunt hadn't even put either of the vases in a safe! Knowing her great-aunt, though, Brooke thought Ivy had probably put them in the trunk years ago, maybe when the vases weren't fetching as much of a price, and had forgotten about them. Maybe she never knew they were that valuable. As far as Brooke knew, the value for the emperor's china had only gone up in the last decade or so.

She glanced at the other vase. Different painting, yet it was very similar in age and artwork. And on the bottom of the vase, the Chinese emperor Kangxi's family rose. She couldn't wait to tell Josh, even if it wasn't for sure. That was something she hadn't had for a long time—someone to share something important with.

She took numerous pictures of the details.

Her door opened, the bells jingling, and having been engrossed in the business of the vases, Brooke jumped, startled. "Hi, welcome to Cerise's Antiques and Gift Shop. Let me know if you need anything."

The two women smiled, nodded, and began browsing the merchandise on the shelves.

"We hadn't known about your cute little shop until we saw the news about the reindeer and just had to check it out," one of them said.

"That's great. I have hot cocoa and scones in there if you'd like some." She was thrilled the reindeer had helped to spread the word about the shop.

"Thanks," both women said.

Brooke carefully took one of the vases and set it in a box filled with packing peanuts behind the counter, and then did the same with the other. Her skin prickled with excitement. What if they were the real deal? She would be in heaven. But she wasn't about to start counting her chickens yet. Though she did need to secure the vases in the safe if they turned out to be the genuine item.

She texted an appraiser she trusted to give her an accurate idea of the value and sent him the pictures.

Only a few minutes later, he texted back: If they're not replicas, you've got a mint on your hands. They could be worth up to $35 million—or more!—apiece if they're authentic.

That was just what she'd hoped! It would be the find of a lifetime, and if so, she suspected her great-aunt had listed them on the treasure list. She would love to know where her great-aunt had picked them up. Brooke had been looking for Ivy's diaries but hadn't found them yet.

Brooke's phone rang, and she about jumped out of her skin. She had to get her jumpiness under control. It was just Josh. "Hey, did you learn anything?" she asked.

"I've finally got the license plate for the black truck involved in the reindeer case. The tech department just figured out what it was from another shop's security video I sent them."

"That's wonderful! I'm going to need to put a couple of items in the safe," she said, feeling a little anxious with the Chinese vases sitting behind the counter with her.

"High dollar value?" Josh asked.

"If they're authentic. *Yes. Really* high dollar value."

"Could they be what the men were looking for?" Josh sounded concerned.

"I really don't think so. They were in the trunk."

"The vases?"

"Yeah. I'll tell you more about it later," she said.

A couple more women entered her shop, and Brooke greeted them.

"More customers in the shop?" Josh asked.

"Yeah. I could use a security detail. Truly."

"I'm your man."

She smiled. "I was hoping you'd say that."

"I'm on my way back."

They ended the call, and one of the ladies came to the counter with a couple of chocolate pots. "I saw some jingle bells in another part of the store the other day, but I couldn't find them. It pays to get the item you want right then and there and not waffle about it. Did they sell?"

Brooke smiled, glad Josh had her set the antique ones aside when he found them. "Yes, those sold. I do have the set hanging on the door if you'd like it. It's a replica of antique sleigh bells." She liked having her jingle bells on the door for the holidays, but she could always order another set for next year.

"Yes, I'll take them."

Brooke grabbed her footstool and carried it to the door. She was about to pull down the sleigh bells when Josh filled the door with his tall presence. She smiled and pulled the footstool back. He was tall enough to get the sleigh bells without using it.

He came in out of the cold and said, "What did you need?"

"The sleigh bells for a customer."

He smiled. "Good. You didn't sell mine."

"I wouldn't dare. I still need police protection."

"You'd get it anyway." He handed her the sleigh bells.

"Thanks." She took them and hurried back to the checkout counter and finished the sale.

When the customer left, Brooke whispered to Josh, "The two vases could be imperial porcelain worth millions of dollars."

His jaw dropped.

She laughed.

"Seriously?"

"Yeah. That's if they're authentic." She sure hoped they were. She didn't even want to speculate further about the price they might fetch.

"Hot damn."

The other customer came out of another room with a handful of merchandise.

"Here, let me help you with that." Brooke carried the merchandise to the counter. "Are you all set for Christmas?"

"Oh, never. It will be here whether I'm ready or not," the customer said, laughing.

"I hear you." Then Brooke wished her a Merry

Christmas, and when the shop was empty, she showed the vases to Josh again.

He looked them over and shook his head. "I can't believe it. The emperor's fine china."

"Yes."

"Speaking of Chinese, I ordered our meals for lunch."

"Oh good. I can't wait to see what my fortune cookie has to say."

---

Josh couldn't believe Brooke could be in possession of vases worth that much money. Here he thought all this stuff was just a bunch of junk worth only something to a collector, but never that much. He was thrilled for her and hoped it was true. "Where did they come from?"

"My great-aunt had been collecting things forever. She always had a nose for knowing when something could be valuable. I can't believe she hadn't sold any of this stuff yet though."

"They might not have been as valuable years ago."

"That's true." Brooke smiled and hugged him. "I couldn't wait to tell you. They still might not be the real thing."

"Do you want me to take them over and put them in your safe at the house?"

"Yes. Just don't drop them."

He laughed. "That would be a good way to ruin a day."

She gave him the safe combination, security code, and the keys to her house.

"I'll be right back." He made sure the vases had enough packing peanuts to protect them, sealed the boxes, and then carried them to the back door.

She opened it for him, and he walked through to the court-yard. She had some more customers who picked up several items and wanted to pay for their purchases. She was trying not to feel excited about the prospect of selling the vases for all that money, but she couldn't help it. She was thinking of all the renovations she could do to the shop, the kitchen, bathroom, other rooms. The attic. And the house too. She couldn't imagine having that much money or what to do with it.

Knowing the vases would be in the safe, particularly after the brutish intruders had broken so much of her glass-ware and porcelain, she felt relieved.

She assisted some of her customers and then found the regular bells her great-aunt had put up over the door when it wasn't the Christmas season and went to hang them up. Brooke wanted to hear the tinkling sound of the bells when people were coming and going, and she hated when she only heard the squeak of the door alerting her that custom-ers had arrived. She needed to oil that door.

She was hanging the bells when the food came, and she paid for it. A couple of her customers came to the checkout counter, and Brooke said, "I'll be right back." She carried the Chinese takeout into the kitchen, then returned and waited on them.

Josh returned. "I smell the food. I was going to pay for it."

"You planned that perfectly," she teased him. "Why don't you eat, and once I'm done here, I'll join you."

After her customers left, she joined Josh in the kitchen,

where he was sitting at the table enjoying his Hunan chicken.

Then he got a call. "Yeah? Roger Thornton? Thank you." He ended the call. "That was the name of the man who owns the black pickup truck that was parked in front of your place, Brooke."

"Is that the man who rented the reindeer from you and was upset about paying more?"

"No. I still wonder if it doesn't have to do with him. I need to speak to the owner of the truck though."

"Are you going to do it while the shop is open?"

"Yeah. His business is only about five miles from here. Will you be okay if I go check it out?"

"Yeah. You won't be that far away."

"I won't be long, and I'll see what he has to say. How's your beef and broccoli?"

"Great. How's your Hunan chicken?"

"Perfect."

She thought Josh was going to eat and run, but he waited while she finished eating.

"I'll stay and assist customers until you finish eating."

She smiled. "Thanks. Open your fortune cookie and see what your fortune says."

He cracked open his fortune cookie and flattened the strip of paper. "'A golden egg of opportunity falls into your lap this month.'"

"That sounds like a good fortune." She finally finished her meal and opened her fortune cookie. "Mine says, 'In the end, all things will be known.' I was hoping it would be as vast a fortune as yours."

He laughed. "I get the golden egg."

"Then I'm going to have to stick with you." The door jingled. "That's my cue. Back to work."

"I'm heading out."

"Good luck getting the truth out of the guy."

"I sure hope it's going to be that simple," Josh said.

"What will you do then?"

"It depends on the answers I get. If this is related to the man who rented the reindeer, I'll talk to him. I might not press charges, but we'll see."

"Be safe."

"You too, Brooke." He gave her a kiss, then headed back out.

She went to greet her customers with a cheery smile and a welcome.

"Are the reindeer here today?" one of the ladies with two kids in tow asked.

----

Josh had already sent the information to Adam about the black pickup truck and the owner. Adam was on his way to the guy's house. After checking to see if Roger Thornton had a son who might have stolen the reindeer, since Josh still thought it could be a teen prank, he discovered Roger had one sixteen-year-old son named Lucas. Josh drove to Roger's place of business. The company was owned by the man who had hired the reindeer for the Christmas party. Coincidence? Josh didn't believe in coincidences.

He parked at the brick-and-glass building and got out, then walked inside and said to the receptionist, "I'm here to see Roger Thornton."

"Do you have an appointment, Mister…?"

"Detective Wilding." Josh pulled out his badge, showed it to her, and then tucked it away.

"What's this about?" she asked, her hand on the phone.

"This is between Mr. Thornton and me."

She pushed a button and said into the phone, "A Detective Wilding is here to see you, sir." She glanced up at Josh. "He wouldn't say what it was about, sir… Right away." She hung up the phone and motioned to the door near her. "Go right on in."

"Thank you." Josh opened the door, stepped inside, and shut the door behind him. He noted the man behind the desk—fortyish, temples slightly graying, dark sandy hair, glasses, and soft gray eyes—as he rose to greet Josh from behind his mahogany desk, the leather chair swiveling slightly.

Josh expected hostility or genuine disbelief, which would mean he truly had nothing to do with it. One other scenario came to mind—the suspect would be surprised, yet a hint of recognition would appear—just as he realized who the guilty party really was.

Mr. Thornton offered his hand, and Josh shook it. Then he motioned to one of the leather chairs while remaining behind his desk as if the furniture shielded him from an arrest. "What can I do for you, Detective Wilding?"

Josh preferred to stand, but he took a seat. "I have surveillance footage of your truck parked in front of Cerise's Gift and Antique Shop after it was closed."

At first, Mr. Thornton's demeanor was apprehensive, but when Josh mentioned the truck, Mr. Thornton frowned, looking puzzled, but then it was as if the light dawned. He clearly knew who the driver was, but he didn't say.

Mr. Thornton cocked a brow. "And?"

Josh sat against the leather seat back. "We have a good shot of the license plate from a nearby shop's surveillance video."

"What's the crime in that?"

"A reindeer calf was stolen."

Mr. Thornton's jaw dropped.

"Your parent company had rented reindeer from the same ranch for your Christmas party. Two days later, someone driving your truck drops the reindeer calf off at the antique shop and places him in the courtyard but doesn't properly shut the gate."

"The calf's alive, isn't it?"

"Found and cared for and returned to the reindeer ranch, yes."

Mr. Thornton relaxed a little, either relieved the reindeer hadn't come to harm or relieved his son, if that was who had used the truck, wasn't in even more trouble.

"Still, it's theft and animal endangerment. Not only that, but the security video had been tampered with at the reindeer ranch."

Again, a hint of worry flickered in the man's eyes.

"Who was driving the truck that night? You didn't report it stolen, so we have to assume you, or someone in your family, was driving that night," Josh said.

"Do I need to call my lawyer?"

"My brother and I own the ranch. We can make a deal. Yes, the calf was safe, thankfully. The gate wasn't shut properly, and the calf could have left the courtyard and been hit by a car. Breaking into a security system is also a crime. I don't mind offering community service for the crimes, but I need some straight answers."

Mr. Thornton smiled. "You're fishing. You don't have any proof of anything. You want my alibi for the night in question?"

"No. I suspect you weren't driving the truck, but your son was. So I'll need *his* alibi. I'll be in touch." Josh rose from his seat and handed Mr. Thornton his card. "If you want to talk to me about it, feel free to call at any time."

Josh walked out of the office and shut the door, then pulled out his pen and notepad as if he had to write down notes of their conversation. Instead, he was listening at the door, the receptionist watching him. He assumed Mr. Thornton would call his son and chew him out about the incident. Josh loved his wolf hearing at times like this.

He noticed a button on the phone on the receptionist's desk light up, indicating Mr. Thornton was calling someone. "Lucas, did you have anything to do with tampering with the security video at the Wilding Reindeer Ranch and a stolen calf? Don't lie to me. The police have got surveillance video of the truck... Who else was with you?" Another pause. "Whose stupid-ass idea was it?" The chair squeaked in the office. "You and the others better come up with some airtight alibis ASAP in case the cop comes looking for you. And clean the damn truck." The receiver slammed down, and the button's light on the phone went out on the receptionist's desk.

Josh left the building and immediately called Roy Greycroft, a Portland judge who was a gray wolf and helped the wolves out when they needed it. "Sir, the truck used to transport a stolen reindeer calf is going to be cleaned, and we need a warrant to search the vehicle before that happens and we lose the evidence of the theft."

"Adam already called me to get a search warrant for the truck. He's getting the reindeer hair from the interior as we speak," Judge Greycroft said.

"Good. Thanks."

"We can't have them stealing Santa's future reindeer and not paying for the crime, now can we?"

"You're right. And there's a little issue of tampering with our security video out at the ranch. The dad's playing hardball, but I told him we'd be willing to just make a deal if he'd come clean."

"If Lucas hadn't committed a crime before."

"The boy's been brought before you already?" Josh asked the judge, damned surprised, though he shouldn't be. Criminals often committed a lot more crimes than they got caught for.

"Yep. Same stuff—as a hacker. It was a couple of months ago, before he turned sixteen. Nothing like the reindeer theft, though, unless they just didn't get caught. He had help, too, didn't he?"

"Yes, sir. Someone was driving the truck, and someone else got out to remove the reindeer."

"I'd place my bet on Ty Henson, if I were a betting man. He's Lucas's best friend. The two of them were involved in the other hacking job. They did community service that time too. The problem is they're both smart, but they need to direct that to worthwhile causes, not to crime."

"Thanks, Judge." Josh still felt that the boys could benefit from community service. Working at the reindeer ranch might give them some sense of caring for the animals, for one thing. For another, he and Maverick could have the teens look at their security video and tell them how they hacked in and maybe how to safeguard against it. After ending the call with the judge, Josh called Adam. "Did you get the evidence you need?"

"Getting it now. Plenty of Jingles's fur is in the truck. We can smell Jingles, so no trouble identifying it. I need to tell you something else though. When I went to his parents' home so I could give them the search warrant to search the truck, Lucas answered the door. He is one of us."

"What?" Josh thought he'd misunderstood what Adam had told him.

"I take it his dad isn't?" Adam asked.

"Hell, no. He's strictly human. Then Lucas is adopted?" Or maybe fostered, Josh thought.

"He must be. Or turned? Which would be bad news if he can't control his shifting. The other scents in the car are all human. So his friends aren't like us either. Lucas appeared shocked to smell my scent."

Josh couldn't believe it. "How long has he been living in the area?"

"He told me he and his parents moved here only three months ago."

"And he got into trouble just a month after he'd been here. Unless he'd been up to mischief before that but just hadn't been caught. He must not have met any of our wolves, or Leidolf and Cassie would have made sure he became part of our wolf community."

"That's what I figured," Adam said. "I asked him if he'd smelled wolf scents when he was tampering with the security video. His eyes widened, and I think he realized our kind work there. I think he would have talked if his dad hadn't called. I gave Lucas your number, too, since you're part owner of the reindeer ranch and would probably let him work with the reindeer for community service. I told him we can't tolerate criminal acts by our kind. That we can't go to prison."

"Okay. We need to get him on the right path then. He might even be able to date some of the teen girls in our pack," Josh said.

"Only if he cleans up his act. The judge said Ty Henson is his best friend," Adam said.

"He told me that too."

"Did you want to talk to Ty?" Adam asked.

"I can head on over to his home," Josh said.

"I was talking to Luke about his whereabouts that night. He said he was seeing Sandy Hicks, his girlfriend, at the park."

"Right. Maybe she was sitting in the back seat with Jingles."

"It could be. A female's scent is in the back seat, though it could be from another time. Then Luke got a call from his dad. It must have been after you talked to him, and the next thing we know, the boy is lawyering up. I gave him my card and told him if he wants to talk to me about anything, not just about the crime but anything, he could call me. I thought he looked like he was dying to know more about us. I would have told him what we do to our kind who won't toe the line, but his mother came out and told him to go into the house, glowering at me for talking to him. She isn't one of us either."

"Maybe something good can come from this."

"I was thinking of giving him hard labor, once the judge said he and his buddy had already been hacking computers. Hell, the kids were only fifteen at the time."

Josh laughed.

"Since he's one of us, that wouldn't do. The way he's going, he'll end up in jail, and we can't have that. Is Brooke still all right?"

"Yeah, but I'll give her a call to let her know what's happening." Josh was dying to talk to the kid. They needed to convince him of the error of his ways and learn if he was a royal like them, a wolf with roots so far back, he didn't have any issues with shifting. "Do you have an address for Ty?"

Adam gave the address to him.

"I'm on my way there," Josh said, glad they were getting somewhere with that case at least.

# CHAPTER 17

As soon as two men walked into her shop, Brooke immediately recognized them from having been here the day Jingles and Cinnamon were in the courtyard. She'd thought the men looked suspicious the first time too. They didn't look like her usual customers, though she'd had a lot of traffic because of the reindeer calves that she probably wouldn't have had otherwise. Josh had been outside with the calves, and Adam and Maverick had been having lunch at the house at the time.

The one man had shaggy brown hair, scraggy facial hair, and brown eyes; the other was a blue-eyed blond and wore a beard. Both were dressed in well-worn jeans and open hoodies revealing worn sweatshirts that looked like they'd seen better days. When they'd come that day, they'd said it was to see the reindeer calves everyone was talking about. They'd walked through her entire shop, making her feel they were going to steal something, and had not really been interested in seeing the reindeer. Most of the people who only intended to see the reindeer had gone around through the courtyard gate as a courtesy to those who were interested in buying or at least looking through Brooke's inventory. She should have asked Josh if the men had gone out to see the reindeer. She'd completely forgotten about it because she'd been swamped with sales.

These guys made her skin crawl. She was placing a price tag on a cast-iron frying pan when the last of her customers left the shop. Alone with these men, she felt even warier. One was lifting things off a shelf, checking prices, and placing the items back on the shelf. He didn't look like he was truly interested in buying anything. The other sauntered over to her counter, his mouth lifting slightly. The smile didn't appear genuine in the least.

"Where do you get your stuff from?" the blue-eyed guy asked, leaning against her counter. His unwashed body odor nearly made her gag. It was bad enough that probably any human could smell him, but for a wolf, the scent was really bad.

"All over. Did you need something in particular?" She desperately wanted to call Josh.

The guy gave her a one-shoulder shrug. "Five boxes from an estate sale? A thumb drive, really. You know a Mr. Lee, don't you?"

Her skin suddenly prickled with unease. Were these guys in cahoots with the others who had broken into her shop?

She was trying to keep her voice steady and pretend she wasn't worried about why they were here. What had Mr. Lee gotten her involved in?

"I have boxes I haven't even had time to sort through yet."

"From Gulliver's estate," the blond said as if she were confused.

Mr. Lee had encouraged her to take the boxes. If there was a thumb drive in one of them, what did it have on it that would be worth sending all these goons for, presuming the previous robbers had wanted the same thing?

"Mr. Lee said we could have the boxes. We paid for them," the guy said.

She didn't believe him.

"It was mostly just junk, but our aunt has an antique store, and the price was so reasonable for the boxes of stuff that she wanted us to get them for her. We put the thumb drive in one of the boxes and planned to haul them off to the pickup truck. But we needed to move it closer to where they were located. When we returned for them, they were gone."

At least now Brooke knew what the men wanted, but she hadn't received anything from the estate yet but the wolf statues. Would they even believe her if she said the other merchandise hadn't arrived? If so, they'd already revealed who they were and what they wanted, so she was afraid she wasn't going to get out of this situation unscathed.

The other man approached the counter and propped his arms on it. As soon as he did, she saw the grip of a gun in a shoulder holster underneath his jacket. "We need to see the boxes."

"I just moved here, and I've got stacks of boxes all over." She glanced at the clock on the wall. It was three o'clock, but Josh would probably need until closing to finish all the investigating he needed to do.

"Come on. You've got to have some idea where the boxes are," the darker-haired man said.

"Look it up on your computer," the other guy said.

She woke up her computer and desperately wanted to email Josh, but she didn't even know his email address! She wasn't sure what to do, but her first idea was to stall them.

Her cell phone was on the counter and so was her shop phone, neither of which she could use to call for help. The heavy cast-iron skillet was sitting on the counter, the price tag on it. If she had to, she could use it as a weapon. But there were two men, not just one. The other would eliminate her next if she managed to take out the first one with the frying pan.

At least one of the men was armed. She suspected the other one was too. She needed to bluff her way through this. Worried they would kill her if she said she knew where the boxes they wanted were and then they weren't there, she had to prolong the pretense that she was looking for them. What if she told them the boxes hadn't come in yet? Would they hold her hostage until they arrived?

If these guys were in league with the other two men who had shot her, at least she knew they weren't after anything her great-aunt had owned. Like the Chinese vases that could be worth millions.

"Well?" the darker-haired guy asked.

Thank God neither had moved around the counter to see what she was doing on the laptop. She knew she wouldn't have a prayer to crack one in the skull with the frying pan if one or both of them joined her.

"I'm looking through all the deliveries. They're not listed by estate sale. I had to look up when the estate sale took place and then try to search the records showing deliveries made from Phoenix. I actually purchased stuff from three different estate sales there that month"—she lied, hoping that would give her more precious time to come up with a plan to get herself out of this—"and sometimes after a sale, the items arrive late. Especially with all the Christmas deliveries that are being made right now."

"Just hurry it up."

"I am." Her shop phone rang, and Brooke saw Josh's

name on the caller ID. Before they could stop her, she quickly answered it, hoping they wouldn't shoot her.

Her skin chilled, she was glad she might have a chance to get word to Josh that she was in trouble. Again.

If she had to protect herself, she would use the frying pan on at least one of them.

---

On the way to Ty's house, Josh got a call from Jefferson at the bureau. "Hey, got some more news for you. The dead guy who was cut up by the window in the antique shop? His name was Pinky Struthers. He's been in and out of lockups for years. Mostly for armed robbery."

"Good work. Thanks, Jefferson."

Josh called Brooke next to check on her. "Hey, Brooke, I'm making some headway in the Jingles case. Is everything going well there?"

"No. I don't have any more sleigh bells in stock right now. I'm sorry."

She sounded worried, and he immediately suspected the worst. She was in trouble. If she wasn't and he was rushing to protect her when she didn't need him to, they'd have a good laugh about it later. But he wasn't taking the chance.

Josh spun his car around and headed back to Brooke's shop. "How many are there?"

"Two. I had two in stock. Correct."

"Males?" He wanted to kill them.

"Yes. Just the two."

"Is the man who shot you there?" His heartbeat accelerating, he had to reach her in time before they could hurt her.

"No. They were brand new."

"Armed?" He wondered if the other guy was out of the picture along with his dead partner.

"At least one."

"Is anyone else in the shop?" He was hoping there were no other people in harm's way.

"No."

"Good. I'm on my way."

"Thanks. Maybe I'll have some in a couple of days. Bye." She hung up on Josh.

He hated that she had to break the connection, but he knew the men would make her end the call before long, and he didn't want them to believe she was giving the caller clues. He also hated that he hadn't been there for her. *Damn it.*

His heart beating triple time, he floored the gas pedal, racing down the street while calling Adam. "Brooke's got trouble at the shop. Two armed men. Not the same men who shot her. There's no one else in the shop. No sirens. Unless I'm mistaken about this, but I don't think so, she's in trouble."

"Better to be safe than sorry. I'm on my way."

"I'll meet you there." Josh ground his teeth, his knuckles white as he gripped the steering wheel. He tried calling Ethan too. Because Ethan was DEA, he wasn't involved in matters like this, but they were friends. All Josh got was his voicemail, which meant Ethan could be in a situation of his own right now.

Josh called the bureau for further backup, at the same time thinking of the best way to handle this. He damn well didn't want the armed men to hurt Brooke. He was going to have to stay with her day and night. Were these men in league with the ones who had shot her? Or some random thugs looking to steal cash?

It seemed to take forever to reach the shop, and Adam drove up right behind him. Josh motioned for Adam to head around to the back door of the shop through the courtyard, then waited for him to have enough time to get there. Josh intended to be the distraction. He'd open the door to the shop that would jingle, while Adam opening the back door wouldn't make a sound.

He had to give Adam time enough to jump the men while Josh got their attention. Then he worried the men had locked the front door. He carefully tried it. Not locked. Someone drove into the parking lot, and he turned to see if it was other police. It was. Good. But he still didn't want Brooke in the line of fire.

If the armed men had really been on the ball, they would have put the Closed sign on the door and locked it. Josh opened the door, the bells jingling, and the two armed men turned to see who it was. Thankfully, Brooke was behind the counter, so she had a little protection if the shooting started.

Adam lunged forward and got the drop on one of the men. The other raised his weapon to fire at Josh. Before Josh shot him, Brooke grabbed a cast-iron skillet sitting on the countertop and bashed the gunman in the side of the head with a heavy *thunk*. He collapsed on the floor like a sack of rocks.

Adam was wrestling with the first man, trying to confine him. Josh dashed across the floor to help him, yanking the gun from the armed perp and sliding the weapon across the floor. Three other policemen rushed into the shop to help.

While Adam secured the one man, Josh tied up the other. EMTs were called to check on the injured man who was just coming to. Josh hurried around the counter to see to Brooke, who was looking pale and visibly shaking.

"How are you holding up?"

"I have to…to wash the blood off the…the frying pan." Tears filled her eyes, but she managed a quirky smile.

Josh hugged her. "Come on. Why don't you sit in the kitchen and have some water?"

"Sure."

Josh took her into the kitchen and helped her to sit down, then brought her a glass of water. "What did they want?"

"A thumb drive in one of the five boxes from Gulliver's estate sale in Phoenix. The one man said that Mr. Lee sold the boxes to them for their aunt's antique shop, but I don't believe them." She explained the rest of what he'd told her.

"I take it they didn't have a sales receipt for the boxes, nor did they give you the name of their aunt or her antique shop."

"Nope."

"Then these men are in league with the other ones who shot you?"

"I'm thinking they were. They didn't mention them, but since those men didn't find whatever they're after and made a mess of things, whoever is sending them must have hired these two. Instead of breaking in during the night and shooting up the place, these guys were being civil. I caught a glimpse of the one guy's gun in a shoulder holster and knew they had to be bad news. They didn't know you were a police detective and my savior who was calling to check on me."

Josh kissed her. "I'm so sorry. I'm sticking with you from now until we catch the one responsible, but when I interrogate these men, I'll make sure you're well protected."

"I never thought to check to see if the man who left the estate had died of natural causes. I just assumed he had. I was so busy getting ready to leave Phoenix that I wasn't paying any attention to the news," she said.

"You said it was a Gulliver?" Josh asked, doing a search on his phone.

"Randall Gulliver, Phoenix, Arizona."

"Murdered. Hell, what's going on?"

Brooke's jaw dropped. "Oh wow. Where did he die? And how?"

"At his home. He'd had a break-in. They don't know who murdered him, but he was shot to death."

"Were things stolen in Mr. Gulliver's home?"

"Yeah. Jewelry, a coin collection, and a stamp collection. The place was trashed. So the motive was listed as a robbery."

"Why would the thumb drive be so important to them? And why would they have dropped it in one of the boxes Mr. Lee gave me?" Brooke asked.

"I suspect they didn't put the thumb drive in the box. Someone else did. And they have to get it for whoever hired them to do the job," Josh said.

"If we consider it has something to do with the murder of Gulliver, who had the most to gain from it?"

"Four surviving grown children: Pattie, Daisy, Ralph, and Nat Gulliver," Josh said. "Often, family or someone the victim knew is the murderer. It's more unusual if it's a perfect stranger."

"Hmm, I wonder if the children received a life insurance payout." She sipped some of her water. "It would be a good motivation for murder, as wealthy as he was."

"Exactly."

"Do you think Mr. Lee put the thumb drive in one of the boxes?" she asked.

"If he did, he put you at risk."

"Can you bring me the skillet?" she asked.

"I'm afraid it will be in evidence for a while."

She sighed. "Years."

"It'll be worth even more when you get it back. I need to learn what I can about these guys and then I'll return. Are you going to be okay?" He hated to leave her for even a moment, but he had to know what was going on if he was going to stop it.

"Sure."

Adam was checking the armed thugs' pockets for IDs. Josh already recognized the man Adam had taken down by both sight and smell. Dishwater blond with a grungy beard and pale-blue eyes narrowed at him. "This one's been in jail any number of times for possession and armed robbery. Lonnie Matson. How the hell he keeps getting out is beyond me."

"Same with the other one, Howie Carpenter. I don't think I've ever seen them together on a job. Maybe they hooked up in jail." Adam looked over their ID. "Their ID still shows they're from Phoenix though."

"What happened to him?" one of the EMTs asked, coming in treat the injured man.

"He was going to shoot me. Brooke Cerise, the owner of the shop, protected me," Josh said.

"I heard you were dating her. I'd sure be careful about making her mad," one of the officers said.

The other policemen there chuckled, Josh and Adam smiled, and then the two would-be thieves were hauled off.

Once all the other policemen and the EMTs left the shop, Josh figured Brooke needed to close the shop now instead of in two hours like usual. She came out of the kitchen with a mug of hot lavender tea. "Do you mind staying with me until the shop closes?"

Josh was going to mention closing now, but then a couple of ladies came into the shop and a fortyish man too. Josh eyed him with wariness. "You bet."

"Me too," Adam said.

"Good, and thank you both."

"You're welcome," Josh and Adam said.

"I'll be on the phone in the office to learn what I can and direct another couple of our men to check out Lucas's girlfriend's story. Apparently, she's Lucas's alibi for the night that the black truck was picked up on video outside your shop," Adam said.

"But...?" Brooke asked.

"Reindeer hair was left in the truck."

She smiled. "So we've caught them in the lie."

"Yes. They've lawyered up, but we'll get them."

Josh agreed with Adam.

"Talk later." Adam took off for the office.

The female customers started to look at the merchandise in the shop, but the man headed straight for Brooke.

Josh put his hand on his holstered gun.

Brooke smiled at the man and said, "May I help you?"

He glanced at Josh and then frowned at Brooke. "Are you the one I talked to about the vinyl records for sale?"

"Oh yes." Brooke snapped her fingers. "You're here to look them over."

"Buy them, if they're in as mint condition as you say they are."

Brooke took him into the office. "There's the record player. The records are right there. Enjoy listening to them. I'll be in the shop working."

Adam smiled at the guy. "You're a collector?"

"Yeah. I got hooked on them some time ago. I always had them, but now I'm more into collecting the real rare records." He shook Adam's hand.

They began talking about the records while the sound of Beatles music mixed with the Christmas music overhead. "Do you want me to turn off the Christmas music for now?" Brooke asked.

"For now. Thanks," the customer said.

Brooke did and then returned to the checkout counter.

Josh took Brooke's hand and pulled her into his arms and kissed her. "I'm so sorry I wasn't here for you earlier."

"You needed to do your investigative work to catch these guys. We didn't think they would come here during the day again. I never believed two different men would show up, but I had seen them before. They supposedly came to see Jingles and Cinnamon. They'd been perusing the shop and made me nervous then too. I certainly didn't believe there was a connection between them and the other men though. Once they came back today, I wanted to call you, but I couldn't. After you and I talked on the phone, I was glad you were able to realize what was going on."

"Right away. I couldn't get here fast enough. It won't happen again. I'm assigned to your care, and I'm sticking like glue. When those boxes from that estate sale arrive, we're going to have an army of wolves watching over them."

"Thank you, Josh. I so appreciate you and Adam. Oh, and I don't even have your email. Though I guess that wouldn't have helped while you were driving." Then she noticed a couple of ladies heading to the counter, and she went to check them out.

Josh was still feeling shaken from the situation. He didn't remember a time when he was involved in shoot-outs or apprehending dangerous criminals that he'd felt that unsettled. Not until now when Brooke's life was in danger. Well, and when the rookie cop he'd dated put both his and her life in danger. "I'm texting you my email address."

She texted hers to him.

About a half hour later, while hearing the vintage songs playing in the background, Josh saw the customer who was interested in the records come out with a whole stack of them. It looked like Brooke had done well with some sales.

"I'll be back after the new year once I get my tax refund, and I'll listen to some of the other records you have," the man said. "I'd take all of them if they were in this good condition, but I have to watch my bank account."

She chuckled. "I totally understand."

With his armful of paid-for records, the customer left the shop, and she turned on her Christmas music again.

"Good haul?"

"For both of us. I gave him a deal, but I still made a bundle."

"That's good. Maverick and I might have a bunch of old stuff we could sell."

"You never know. How long have you had the reindeer ranch?"

"Forever. Our grandparents started the ranch. The ranch house is only ten years old, but there's an old house way off on the property that was abandoned about a hundred years ago. We never tore down the old homestead because it reminds us of our heritage."

"Hmm, what if it contains some treasures?"

He smiled. "Does everything remind you of treasure?"

"You bet."

When the ladies took their purchases and left the shop, Josh asked Brooke, "Which boxes did you want me to take to the house that we can work on tonight?"

"Any of them."

"Why don't I get them, and you can continue to watch Brooke," Adam said.

Josh appreciated it. "How'd it go with your date?"

Smiling, Adam shook his head. "I told you. She's dating every eligible wolf just once. Then she'll decide who she wants to see further."

Brooke smiled. "I really need to do that."

Josh chuckled. "You're not getting rid of me that easily."

"I guess I'll be sleeping on that child's bed for the next few nights," Adam said, tromping up to one of the second-floor rooms.

"You said when you were a wolf, there was no problem with it," Brooke said.

"Yeah. If anyone comes in the shop in the middle of the night, I might forget I don't want to kill them as a wolf."

"I'd really like to know who's behind all this." Josh was glad he was sharing Brooke's bed and not a child-sized one.

"When we figure out what he's after and tell the world, that will be the end of it." Brooke began working on a poster.

Josh came over to see what she was doing. A New Year's Eve sign. He wanted to be ringing in the new year with her. He just hoped they could catch whoever was responsible for this before anyone got hurt again.

Adam returned to the shop. "We need to get hold of some muscle to stay with Brooke while we question the two armed men we just arrested."

Josh agreed.

"If you two can learn what is going on, then do it. If you have someone else who can come and protect me, that will work. No one else can question these men like the two of you can," Brooke said, sounding afraid Josh might not go with his partner to learn the truth.

Josh got on his phone and called Maverick. "Hey. I need you to come and protect Brooke." He explained what was going on. "I'll call Sierra's brother, Brad Redding, to be here too."

# CHAPTER 18

"Maverick and Brad Redding, Sierra's mated brother, a former Navy SEAL, are coming to watch over you for a bit while Adam and I go to the bureau and question these men then, if you're sure you'll be all right," Josh said to her as she closed up shop.

"I will be," Brooke assured him.

An hour later, Maverick and Brad came to the door of the shop while Brooke and Josh were still straightening things up. Brad smiled and shook Brooke's hand. "Sierra told me you gave her the best description of a perp she's ever had to sketch."

"I enjoyed meeting her. We'll all have to get together sometime."

"We will."

"Good to see you again," Maverick said to Brooke, "but I wish the circumstances were less dire."

"I agree with you there."

"We're on our way to the bureau." Josh gave her a hug and a kiss, and then he said to Adam as they were leaving, "Hopefully between the two of us, we'll get what we need from these guys."

———————————

At the bureau, Howie Carpenter was brought to the interview room for questioning, his shaggy brown hair tangled, his dark-brown eyes narrowed. Howie was wearing a fresh shiner. Josh wondered if he'd fought with a prisoner or a guard.

"Howie, what were you supposed to find for the guy who hired you to rob the antique store?" Josh asked as he and Adam took seats opposite Howie. Josh knew it was a thumb drive, but he had to ask the suspect to state for the record why he'd been at the shop.

Howie shrugged.

"You asked for the boxes from the Gulliver estate. You have to know what you were supposed to get, just like the other two men did. You and your buddy are repeat offenders. Trying to shoot a police detective will put you in for a long damn time," Josh added.

"So what? If I tell you what it was, you'll let me go? You and I both know it's not happening, dude."

"Did you know Pinky Struthers, the guy who died?" Adam asked.

"You already know he was a former cellmate, so why ask?" Howie said.

"Did he tell you he had this job to do?"

"Yeah, man. He did. He and some other guy I didn't know. Ackerson, he said his name was."

Hell, the same guy who had been involved in the other two armed robberies Josh and Adam had been investigating? Josh and Adam exchanged glances.

"First name?" Josh asked, hoping they'd get lucky.

"You're lucky I knew his last name. He's done some prison time too. I asked Pinky why he didn't hook up with me next to do the job. He said the woman—"

Both Josh and Adam perked up to hear that a woman was involved.

"Uh…she already knew Ackerson, and he picked Pinky to help him do the job because he knew him from the joint. Pinky told her I was available for other jobs, in case she needed someone for something else. Anyway, so Pinky and Ackerson botched the job, and then I got called to do it. I knew Matson, so I called him, and he needed the money and agreed to come in on the job. Hell, who knew I'd get smacked upside the head with a cast-iron frying pan. The doc said if she'd hit me any harder, I would've been dead, but she had to strike from behind the counter, and that meant she couldn't deal enough force. We had no idea she had a boyfriend who was a cop staying with her."

"What's the name of the woman who hired you?" Josh asked, glad Brooke hadn't killed the scum so they could learn something more about the case.

Howie slumped in his chair. "Daisy Fern. At least that's what she said her name was."

Adam was on his phone, looking for someone by that name.

"What is she after?" Josh asked.

"Some thumb drive. She said someone slipped it into one of the boxes at the auction that was being shipped to the antique shop here. The person who was supposed to grab the box didn't get it in time."

"Someone? Who?"

"I don't know."

"Was the thumb drive slipped into the box on purpose or by accident?" Josh asked.

"I didn't ask. She didn't say."

"Why didn't she just ask the owner of the antique shop if she'd received a thumb drive by mistake? If it belonged to this Daisy Fern, why hire ex-convicts, armed to the teeth, to steal it?" Josh asked.

"Hell, she didn't tell me, man. How should I know? I was hired to get the thumb drive, no questions asked. If you ask me, I'd say it had some damning information on it."

Josh leaned back in his chair. "Not something valuable?"

"Maybe." Howie folded his arms. "You'd have to ask her."

"Do you have her phone number?" Adam asked.

Howie smiled. "Yeah. What does it get me?"

"If the information leads to an arrest and conviction, we'll put in a good word for you with the DA's office. We want the person behind the robberies before this turns deadly," Josh said.

Howie pulled up his sleeve and gave the number penned on his arm to Adam.

"Why didn't you guys lock the front door of the shop when you first entered it?" Adam asked.

"We had to wait for all the customers to leave. Then Matson was supposed to lock the door. And really, if the woman had just handed over the thumb drive, everything would have been cool. Imagine my surprise when you walked into the shop, your gun in your hands, ready to shoot me. I thought you were just a customer."

"The other guys who botched the robbery were trying to do the job without anyone being the wiser. You two weren't wearing masks or attempting to disguise yourselves in any way. What did you plan to do with your one and only witness?" That was what really bothered Josh. He was certain they hadn't planned to allow Brooke to live once she had told them what they wanted to know.

"I wasn't going to shoot her, okay? Matson bragged to

me so many times about how many people he'd offed, and no one ever was the wiser, so that's why I hired him. He was supposed to finish the job. Not me. I never killed nobody."

That they knew of, Josh thought. Howie could have killed any number of people himself, but he'd never been charged with the crime.

"Did you meet with Daisy Fern?"

"No. She just called."

"The area code for the phone number is Phoenix, Arizona," Adam said.

"No shit." Howie waved his hand at Adam. "I told you that was her number."

Adam tried the number and frowned. "The number is no longer in service."

"Hell, I can't help that. You should have called the number sooner," Howie said.

"How come no one tried to break into the shop again?" Josh figured someone would have tried before now, unless Daisy was afraid too many police were staking out Brooke's home and shop.

Howie lifted a shoulder. "I don't know."

"Take a wild guess," Josh said.

"She called me, asked me what I learned, and I told her. That the shop owner didn't have what Daisy was looking for. That it hadn't come in yet. So maybe Daisy, or someone she hired, is waiting for the mail carrier to show up with more boxes."

"So she has eyes on the shop?" Josh had wondered.

"I'm just guessing. All I know is I won't be doing the job for her."

"You don't think Daisy will try to order a hit on you and

Matson to tie up loose ends or because you botched the job?" Josh asked.

Howie frowned. "She's not getting me."

"You wanna bet? You think she would have let you live, had you retrieved the thumb drive for her?" Adam asked. "I'd sure watch your back."

Howie rubbed the back of his neck, looking down at the tabletop, then raised his head and slouched further against his chair. "I got burned the last time I did a job for someone because I didn't know anything about who was hiring me. The guy turned out to be a liar and a thief. Almost got me killed. So I asked Pinky what they knew about the woman. He said Ackerson used to handle problem people for her. He knew her from way back, and she always paid good money to deal with the issue. I trusted them. Hell, can't trust anyone in this business."

"No honor among thieves," Josh said.

Howie shook his head. "No kidding."

"Ackerson and Pinky are from Phoenix," Adam said. "So are you and Matson."

"I coulda told you that." Howie shrugged. "That's all I know."

"We'll look into this and see about talking to the DA because you've been cooperating with us." Josh would do anything to ensure this woman was caught so no harm would come to Brooke.

After Howie was removed from the interview room, Matson was brought in to interrogate. He had a longer face, his hair as shaggy as Howie's but longer, and his eyes a pale-blue, just as narrowed.

"Your friend Howie said you were to be the hit man and

kill the owner of the antique shop once you had the merchandise your boss hired you for," Josh said, eager to get as much as they could out of Matson and then return to check on Brooke. He knew she was in good hands, but he still wanted to be there for her.

"That stinking, lying rat. He was going to kill her. I was just there as backup. I'll kill him."

"He said you've killed a ton of people already, and that's why you were hired to do the job," Josh said.

"How do I know you're telling the truth? You could be playing me."

They let him listen to the part of the recording where Howie had said Matson was the hit man.

"Son of a... He's the one who offed Mike Landers last year. Bragged about it in our cell even."

"And you didn't tell anyone about it?" Adam asked.

"I ain't no stoolie, but all bets are off now."

Adam was looking up the man's name. "Mike Landers, killed by an armed assailant. Thought to have been the job of a hired hit man."

"Right. Howie did it. He said a woman named Daisy Fern hired him to kill Mike because he was becoming a problem for her," Matson said. "There were others too."

So Howie had known Daisy beforehand.

"Who hired the two of you to get the thumb drive?" Josh asked.

"Howie called and asked me about doing the job. I don't know the name of the person who hired him."

So Howie had played Josh and Adam. "What did he tell you?"

"That a guy hired him to get a thumb drive. No big deal.

And it was at an old antique shop. A woman owned it, and that was it. I didn't hear about the other two guys trying to break in before us until after we were arrested. Some cop questioned me about knowing the other men. I didn't know either of them. Just Howie."

"Okay." Josh wondered now if the woman Howie was calling Daisy Fern had really hired him for this job. Or maybe he was trying to disguise the fact that a woman had hired him, so he told Matson a guy had hired him.

They didn't get any further with Matson and finally left.

"Let's return to the house," Josh told Adam.

"We'll get whoever it is," Adam said as they drove back to the shop.

# CHAPTER 19

JOSH AND ADAM ARRIVED AT THE SHOP JUST AS BROOKE was getting ready to leave for the house, having finished what she'd wanted to do.

"Thanks so much for protecting me," Brooke said, Josh and Adam echoing the sentiment, and then Brad and Maverick took off in their vehicles.

Before Brooke, Josh, and Adam left the shop to have dinner, Adam got a call and glanced at Josh. "Yeah. Sure. We can talk. Just come to Cerise's Antique and Gift Shop. Yes, where you dropped off the reindeer. I'm here right now, and one of the owners of the reindeer ranch is here. He and the owner of the antique shop are both wolves, too, so you'll be in good company. See you soon." He ended the call and smiled at Brooke and Josh. "That was Lucas. He's coming to talk to us."

"He admitted to stealing the reindeer?" Brooke asked, surprised.

"No. But coming to see us about being wolves is a start. He might come clean about the reindeer. In any event, he needs to know about the pack. I finally got the security videos from two of the shops you hadn't managed to check out yet, Josh. We got the license tag, but the vehicle had been stolen just down the street from the shop. Not totally surprising," Adam said. "The pickup was abandoned at a mall. We checked the videos there and saw one of the men getting into the car and driving off. It was so far out in the parking lot that we couldn't really see what he looked like. So that was a dead end, no fingerprints left behind. Just a lot of blood in the truck matching the dead robber's blood."

"We'll find the other robber," Josh said.

They had to. She just hoped it would be soon.

About twenty minutes later, a black truck parked in front of the shop. Lucas got out of the driver's seat, shaggy black hair framing his tanned face, blue eyes glued to the entrance of the shop, hands shoved in his jeans pockets. He twisted his head, looking one way and then the other as if he was making sure no one saw him coming to a secret meeting of the wolves.

He reached the shop door, and Adam opened it. "Thanks for coming to see us. Believe me, we're as surprised to learn about you as I'm sure you were to learn about us."

"How many are there of you?" Lucas asked, his hands still shoved in his pockets, his shoulders slumped a little, as they locked the shop. He looked like he was in trouble with a pack of wolves.

"Thirty-one wolves in all," Josh said. "We're scattered around the area, but we all belong to the pack an hour south of here."

Lucas's eyes widened; then he smiled, the tension seeming to ease out of his posture.

"We'll go to my house and talk. I just want to grab a couple of things." Brooke figured Lucas would be more comfortable talking at the house, and she could make dinner for them.

She returned to the office and picked up Josh's sleigh bells and postcard and was about to leave the room when she glanced at the antique cabinet sitting against one of the walls. Her great-aunt had had that cabinet since Brooke was a child. A vague memory of finding a secret hiding place when she was about ten suddenly came to her.

Brooke set the sleigh bells and postcard down on the desk and ran her hands over the cabinet, trying to recall where the hidden compartment was. She opened a drawer, nothing. She pulled out the drawer, and up above it was a narrow shelf full of papers. They had to be something important, or her great-aunt wouldn't have hidden them there.

Josh joined her in the office. "I worried about you. Is everything okay?"

She spread the papers out on the desk and smiled. "Yes! Here are the authentication papers on the Chinese vases, paintings, and other valuable items in the shop. They're all for real! And"—she read over a handwritten sheaf of papers—"a list of where my great-aunt had 'hidden' her treasures." Excited about the prospect of finding the other items, Brooke couldn't wait to get started. "A note from her also to me." That saddened her, making her wish she could have spent more time with her great-aunt before she died.

Brooke read the note out loud. "'You were the daughter I always wished I'd had. The months you spent here with me in the shop during the summers were some of my fondest memories. You were always helping me with the shop, always so good with the customers, and well read on antiques.'" Brooke's eyes filled with tears. They'd butted heads so much on how to set up shop in a better way that she hadn't thought her great-aunt had appreciated all Brooke's hard work.

"'Your father and I didn't always see eye to eye, which is

why we didn't live in the same place. But you were always my bright spot. Knowing how much you loved treasure hunts, I have left a list of treasures for you to find. It's cryptic, should the list and this note find their way into the wrong hands. Many of the items are now truly valuable. I had no need to find buyers for them as I lived comfortably with what I made on the usual sales in the shop. Nor did I want to deal with selling them through auctions that would have cut into the profits too much. I know with your computer genius, you will find buyers through your own resources. Your dad said you were the one who always found the collectors who would pay top dollar. And I wanted this to be your legacy. I have every faith you will find the treasures and dispose of them and the proceeds in a way that will make you happy. Love you with all my heart, my little wolf. Love, Your Great-Aunt Ivy.'"

Brooke wiped away tears and hastily pulled a tissue from the box of tissues on her desk. She sighed heavily. "She always set up a treasure hunt for me in the shop. Part of it was finding stuff she'd lost track off, which I loved doing for her too."

Josh took Brooke into his arms and gave her a big hug.

"She and I butted heads. But I always loved the time I spent with her. Sometimes, she'd give me clues to find something I collected myself. Sometimes, it was to locate something valuable out of a box of items, just to see if I could. She always made it fun for me. At night after the store closed, we'd straighten up, put more merchandise out, and then head to the house for a meal we both planned."

"So what did you collect?"

"Marbles, at the time. I had some vintage ones worth a

lot of money. One opaque Lutz marble that had a lot of pink in it sold at auction for $25,000. I have one similar. I have some onionskin marbles, galaxy pattern marbles, painted sulfide marbles, pontil birdcage marbles, just a whole lot of different ones my great-aunt picked up eons ago and gave to me on my treasure hunts." She couldn't believe her great-aunt had left her a treasure list. "We should go to the house, have dinner, and talk to Lucas."

Josh released her and looked over the list, smiling. "Man, as long as this list is, you may have hit pay dirt."

"If we can find all this stuff, it's in good condition, and I can sell it."

"True. I suspect you can, and she knew you could."

"But the real fun is in finding it."

With the rest of the papers in hand, Brooke walked out with Josh to the house. He carried the sleigh bells and postcard, and Adam set the security alarm on the shop and locked the door. Lucas and Adam followed behind them as they walked through Brooke's courtyard to her house.

"My parents don't know I've come to see you," Lucas warned.

Brooke and the others glanced at him, and she was sure they were all thinking the same thing. "Hopefully, that won't get you into more hot water with them." She unlocked the door to the house and turned off the security alarm. "Does spaghetti sound good to everyone?" She turned on her Christmas tree lights, and they sparkled, illuminating the predominantly blue and gold balls and the vintage-style ornaments she had collected over the years.

A resounding yes came from all the guys.

"Not surprising that you didn't tell them about coming

here. They've lawyered up," Josh said. "They're not going to want you to see us until this is over with."

"Yeah, because my parents made me do it. You smelled me and you smelled the reindeer in the truck, didn't you?" Lucas took a seat in the living room with Adam while Brooke went into the kitchen, pulled out hamburger from the fridge, and placed it in a frying pan.

Josh joined her to help out and filled a saucepan with water to boil the noodles. "Yes, Lucas. We bagged the reindeer hair for proof you stole the reindeer for the benefit of those who need something more substantial than just our ability to smell scents."

"I only borrowed the reindeer."

"'Borrowed' means you planned to return it. You didn't. He could have been lost to us forever," Josh said.

"We thought the police were following us. Sandy wanted us to drop the reindeer off in the shop's courtyard and we'd come back for it. But my dad found out I was out driving around, and he wanted me to drop off my friends at their homes and then return home. We figured the reindeer was okay for the night. I was going to return to the shop and get it before anyone woke up that morning."

"But you didn't," Josh said.

"My dad was angry with me because I was out so late and took the keys to the truck. He said I couldn't use the truck the next day. Then I saw on the news that the woman who owned the shop was taking care of the reindeer and the owner had come to get him."

"Why in the world did you steal the calf in the first place?" Josh asked. "That's what I don't get."

"Ty's uncle owns the company that rented your reindeer

for their Christmas party. He's a powerful man, and he didn't like that he had to pay more for the rental because people took longer to take more pictures with the reindeer. Ty told us we'd borrow a reindeer to make up for the extra rental cost, not telling his uncle. But really, Ty just wanted to show him off to Sandy. He planned for us to take pictures with the reindeer."

"I thought Sandy was *your* girlfriend," Josh said.

"She was. But she and Ty have something going on." Lucas shrugged. "She wasn't really the right person for me. Not when I'm a wolf and she's not."

Everyone looked a little incredulous at him. Brooke couldn't believe he wouldn't be more upset about it than that. Not when Ty was his best friend.

"I know. I was mad when I first figured it out. Then I was like, why? She wouldn't be the right one for me. She never would have been. Anyway, we didn't get the pictures of us with the reindeer. We hadn't thought anyone would see the photos if we took them, since we were going to share them privately with friends."

"You know what happens when that's done?" Josh asked.

"Uh, yeah, but we really hadn't thought that much about it. As soon as Sandy saw we had the calf, she was angry with both of us and worried he could be hurt. She wasn't involved in any of it. After we showed it to her, she went with us in the truck because she didn't trust us to take the reindeer home."

"She was right," Josh said.

"*She's* the one who got scared when we thought a police car was following us. She told us to stop and put him in the courtyard and we'd come back for him later."

Josh shook his head. "What about the hacking of our security video?"

"It's just something I learned how to do."

"Adam already told you we can't have our kind committing crimes."

"Yeah."

Josh smelled his scent. "You're a gray wolf. A *lupus garou*."

"A black wolf," Lucas told him.

"That's the color of your fur, but you're a gray timber wolf," Josh said. "All the rest of us are red wolves. Arctic wolves exist too."

"Red is the color of your fur," Lucas said.

"We're red wolves, but the color of our fur has a lot of red. What do you know about your parents?" Josh asked.

"They died in a rockslide when I was seven. I didn't have any other family to take me in. We didn't belong to a wolf pack, and I didn't think there was one here. I knew about our kind, but what could I do? I couldn't tell anyone. I've had to run as a wolf in secret."

"Not any longer." Josh told him about the leaders of the red pack at the ranch south of there.

"Over thirty thousand acres?" The boy's eyes brightened.

"Yep," Adam said. "You can go there any time to run as a wolf."

"Are there girls?"

Brooke smiled as she began to serve the spaghetti. Josh poured wine for the adults and then set the bowl of salad on the table. Adam served water for everyone and brought over the plate of garlic bread.

They all sat down at the dining table to eat.

"A few teen she-wolves. Males, too, that you can make friends with," Adam said.

"See? I didn't need Sandy after all. Can we go running?"

Lucas asked. "I mean, close by. Forest Park? That's where I sneaked off to when I could get away with it. I haven't run with wolves since I did with my parents."

Brooke felt bad for him. She would have really felt isolated if she hadn't had a family to run with when she'd been younger.

"Can you control your shifting?" Josh asked.

Lucas nodded. "Yeah. I never have any trouble with it."

"We can go running," Adam said.

Lucas glanced at Brooke. "Sure, I'll go. I haven't shifted since the day I was shot," she said.

"Hell, I hadn't thought of that. Will you be all right?" Josh sounded like he was afraid that if she turned wolf, she might feel the terror all over again. "I've been there. I had three escaped convicts corralled, except they were all armed with semiautomatics."

"Oh wow, Josh, why didn't you tell me about that?" Brooke asked, reaching over to hold his hand.

Josh squeezed her hand. "Rookie mistake. Anyway, I was shot twice, and I was lucky Adam was on the scene first. He took a hit, but he saved my ass."

Brooke's eyes widened. "Adam, you too?"

"We're like wolf brothers. If one gets shot, the other has to take a hit so we can commiserate. Anyway, after we were both operated on, Leidolf managed to get us out of there before our injuries healed up too quickly. We stayed at Leidolf's ranch until we could be cleared for duty. We both got a medal for it. We captured the murdering bastards and kept the city safe."

"So you still have issues with being shot," Brooke said.

"The last time happened six months ago, but it gets

better with time. I can't tell you how many times I've wanted to hit the floor when I've heard the sound of gunfire," Josh said.

"Even when those men were shooting at me?" she asked.

"No. When you were in trouble, that's all I thought about."

"What about you, Adam?"

"Yeah, it doesn't matter how many times you get shot, that memory can be triggered by all kinds of sounds," Adam said.

"There's only one way to know how I'll feel, and that's by shifting and running," she said.

Josh said, "Do you think the house and shop will be all right while we're gone?"

Brooke scoffed. "We've got the security videos, and we won't be gone that long." At this point, she wanted to run as a wolf. She needed to run, to get rid of the pent-up sense of frustration she was feeling. To deal with the frightening prospect that these men were going to continue to come after whatever it was, armed to the teeth.

Josh reached over and took her hand and squeezed, his expression one of understanding. "We run. You're right."

Brooke smiled at him, glad he understood how she was feeling. "It was a good thing that we discovered who you were, Lucas," she said, changing the subject. "If you don't have any trouble shifting and can do it during the new moon, you have to be a royal. We still don't want any of our kind going to prison, because you never know what could happen."

"She doesn't mean we'd protect you," Adam warned. "We terminate rogue wolves. We can't have any of our kind outing us."

"And we don't turn humans," Josh said. "You need to find a girlfriend among our own kind."

"That's why I knew Sandy wasn't right for me."

"In rare cases, humans have been turned, but it's not something you really want to do." Brooke didn't know how much he had learned before his parents died or even had remembered. "You have to think of the human's family, how it would impact everyone, not just the girlfriend. And not everyone who is turned can deal with it. It changes their lives considerably. Some people can't handle it. They wouldn't be like you. Like us—royals, who can control when we shift at any time during the month." Brooke sprinkled parmesan cheese on her spaghetti.

"You must have been adopted, or are you fostered?" Josh asked Lucas.

"Fostered. No one wanted a kid as old as me when we couldn't find any other family I belonged to."

"You need to live with your own kind and learn more about our ways. I'm sure your parents, your wolf parents, were able to talk to you about some things, but at your youthful age, maybe not everything," Adam said. "You need to socialize with your own kind. Play-fight with juveniles, learn what it means to be a part-time wolf."

"How do you feel about all this?" Brooke asked Lucas.

"Relieved. I knew there were others of our kind somewhere, but no one advertises what they are. Dad had a good-paying job where we were in Medford, Oregon, and he didn't want to move from there to be around others of our kind. Mom kept saying I needed to meet others that were my age. They had disagreements about it a lot. They were going to see an opera and got a babysitter for me. Then the rockslide happened. A couple of other cars were caught beneath it too. No one survived. I thought because we healed more quickly than humans, my parents might make it, but they didn't."

"I'm so sorry," Brooke said.

Everyone else agreed.

"How do you feel about a judge 'finding' some of your family?" Josh asked him.

Lucas's eyes grew big.

"He's a gray wolf. He'd make sure you could be adopted, not just fostered, by an honest-to-goodness wolf family. Maybe not grays like yourself, but you'll be part of a real wolf family. They'll probably be at the pack's ranch, so you can be yourself and run as a wolf anytime you have free time," Josh said. "We homeschool our wolves, so no more regular school for you."

Lucas paused with a forkful of spaghetti raised to his mouth, evidently surprised at the news. "Cool."

"What about the Thorntons, who have taken care of you all these years?" Brooke asked. It wasn't as simple as just moving in with a wolf family who would adopt him. They could make it happen, but Lucas had to do what made him happy too.

"Uh, yeah," Josh said, as if he'd made a mistake in not taking that into consideration. "How do you feel about it?"

"They're wealthy and get foster-care money for me, but I pay for everything out of the inheritance I received from my parents. They didn't want to adopt me in case it didn't work out." Lucas smiled at Brooke. "*You* could foster me, and you wouldn't have to support me. I could work in your shop and help you with your website, promotions, whatever."

"She's not mated," Josh said.

"I figured that. That's even better," Lucas said.

Brooke smiled. Adam chuckled.

"You need to be with a family. One that has some other teens," Josh said with conviction.

"You're just afraid I'll get your girl."

Brooke thought Lucas was cute. He fit right in with the rest of the wolves.

"Josh is right. I'll take you up on hiring you to update my online store. I could really use some help with it." Brooke figured he would be perfect for the job. "But you'd have to wait to start working until I don't have any more trouble here."

"Like getting shot? Why is that happening?" Lucas served up a third helping of spaghetti.

"Someone is trying to steal something from my shop. He's sending armed thugs, so I don't want anyone else getting hurt."

"I could work out of your house, if that would be all right with you. I could probably work out of the home I'm going to move to," Lucas offered.

"You still need to do some community work for the reindeer ranch," Josh said.

"You can't prove I stole the reindeer. Not based on your sense of smell," Lucas said, cocky. He sprinkled more parmesan cheese on his spaghetti.

"You don't even want to go there." Adam set his fork on his empty plate and folded his arms across his chest.

Lucas laughed. "You're playing the bad cop, right?"

Adam only smiled.

Once they finished dinner, they cleaned the kitchen,

and then they visited for a while longer. When it was time to go to the park, they took Adam's Hummer.

"Are you sure your folks will be all right with you being gone this long?" Brooke asked, thinking she should have mentioned it earlier.

"They went to a Christmas party. They won't be in until after midnight."

Brooke looked forward to a run, though she couldn't help but think of what might happen while they were gone. Sure, she had security cameras up now, but her phone would be in the shed behind Carver's house if she was alerted to a break-in.

# CHAPTER 20

JOSH WAS GLAD LUCAS COULD RUN WITH THEM AS A wolf, but he was concerned Brooke would be upset if either her house or her shop were broken into and she hadn't been near the phone to call it in. He called to have a couple of patrolmen park in front of the house and shop for an hour, just in case. No sense in tempting fate.

He was glad she wanted to run with the boy. Josh should have been more sensitive to the way she must be feeling after all the trouble she'd been having. He was trained to deal with armed assailants. She was not. He got the distinct impression she really needed this run, and he was glad to do anything to make her feel better.

Adam and Lucas had waited for Josh and Brooke to undress and shift first in the shed at Carver's house, while Lucas told Adam, "I'm not shy. I don't mind if we all strip off our clothes at the same time."

Josh smiled at Brooke, thinking if he'd been Lucas, he would have been saying the same thing.

"They're courting. We need to give them their privacy," Adam said.

They all had to remember that Lucas had lived for so long among humans that he probably had no idea what the protocols were for this sort of thing. It wasn't that they couldn't all strip and shift at the same time in front of each other. Often that was the easiest. That was something the wolves in the pack would need to talk to Lucas about, since he hadn't learned all the nuances of being with other wolves all these years.

At first, they all stuck together, running through the woods. Then Lucas ran off like a racehorse, as if he needed to run as fast and as far as he could. Adam stuck with him, his companion on this new adventure and to keep him out of trouble, while Brooke played with Josh. He'd expected a quiet run with her, exploring the woods, enjoying the time together as courting wolves, though they hadn't exactly said that was what they were. As far as he was concerned, they were.

So when she started to play with him, he was all for it. He had the passing thought that Lucas would benefit from seeing a male and female wolf playing together. Josh quickly dismissed the notion when she nipped at his ear. Before he could retaliate with a lick to her cheek, she swung around and nipped at his tail. He growled in a fun way, and she tore off. The chase was on. Forget showing Lucas all about wolf courtship. Josh was too busy trying to catch up to his she-wolf to give any more thought to teaching a teen wolf what it was all about.

Josh had lost sight of Brooke, but he was smelling her scent. He hadn't played hide-and-seek as a wolf since he and his brother were younger. Playing the game with a wolf he was courting? It couldn't get any more fun than this.

He barely heard something moving behind him, whipped around, and saw Brooke sneaking up on him before she attacked. He wanted to laugh out loud, and he would have if he'd been in his human form.

She growled and plowed into him, snarling, biting, all in fun, and he attacked back, only much gentler, not wanting to injure her. Wouldn't that be a good way to ruin the court-ship right off the bat?

Then he raced off to reciprocate, her turn to find him. Except she never let him out of her sight, and he wanted to laugh about that too. She was cute, and he knew without a doubt he loved her. She was the one for him—if she felt the same way about him. They ran for several minutes, then heard movement and both paused.

Adam came out of the shrubs, panting. But where was Lucas? Hell, he'd better not have gotten himself lost. All they'd need would be to spend half the night looking for him.

Adam shifted. "I lost sight of him. I've been searching for him. Maybe he backtracked to Carver's house."

Josh shifted. "Why don't we go there first." Then he shifted back. He didn't want to waste time looking for Lucas if he was already back at Carver's house. Howling wasn't something they would normally do because it would alert anyone living in the homes bordering the park to their presence.

Then they heard a howl coming from the direction of Carver's house. That was another thing they needed to dis-cuss with him. At least Lucas had enough sense to return to the house when he'd lost Adam.

Josh was dying to know how Adam had lost him. Then again, he didn't want to say how Brooke had turned the tables on him while playing hide-and-seek either.

The three wolves ran for Carver's house, and when they went through the wolf door in the fence, they found Lucas sitting on a chair, reading his text messages on his phone. He immediately rose to his feet, looking like he was in trouble for losing Adam. But Lucas had done the right thing in returning to Carver's place.

Josh and Brooke quickly shifted inside the shed and dressed. She was smiling at Josh. "You should have seen the look on your face when I was sneaking up behind you."

"Surprise?" He pulled her into his arms and kissed her. "You're a surprise. My kind of surprise." He sighed. They needed to leave the shed so Adam could shift and dress.

When she and Josh left the storage building, Josh said to Lucas, "Quick thinking about coming here when you lost Adam."

"I thought of sitting next to a tree. You know, like hugging a tree if I'd been in my human form until someone found me? I figured returning to Carver's house would be better. I...I figure I'm not supposed to howl, but I knew you'd probably hear me and then you'd find me and wouldn't be searching for me all night."

"I lost your trail," Adam said, leaving the building. "I assumed you'd backtracked to the house, but it all worked out fine."

"But I shouldn't have howled." Lucas was waiting for confirmation.

"One little howl won't hurt us, and it let us all know where you were," Adam said.

Lucas glanced at Brooke to see her take on it, as if he were afraid the guys were being easy on him.

She shrugged. "You saved us from having to look for you half the night. What I want to know is how Adam lost you."

Adam laughed. "I do too. The kid is damn fast."

Lucas beamed with pride.

"Let's get you back to Brooke's house so you can head on home," Adam said.

When they reached her house and all piled out of Adam's Hummer, Lucas's cell phone rang. He saw the caller ID and frowned. "Damn, it's my dad."

"Go ahead and answer it," Josh said. Then he talked to the patrolman near the house and called the one out front of the shop, and everyone else walked inside the house and began removing coats and hats and gloves.

———————————

Brooke wished they'd had time to prompt Lucas on what to say and not to say, but it was too late for that. Josh soon joined them.

"Okay." Lucas answered the call. "Hey, Dad, before you get mad at me for taking the truck out without asking"—Josh and Adam both shared looks and shook their heads—"a family's adopting me out at a ranch. I'll be doing community service at the reindeer ranch for stealing the calf. And I've got a job at the antique shop where I dropped the calf off… No, I don't need your permission to be adopted." Lucas let out his breath. "Yes. I'll return the truck. But everything in my room I paid for." He hung up on him.

In a hurry, Josh was on his phone calling the judge, and Adam was calling the pack leaders to find a home for Lucas.

Brooke just smiled at Lucas when he set his phone on the table and looked up at her, appearing a little guilty that he hadn't discussed this with the rest of them. "He was pissed off at me," Lucas said.

"Judge, this is about Lucas, fostered by the Thorntons.

He's one of us, a gray wolf, and we need to get adoption papers pushed through for one of our wolf families to adopt him, pronto," Josh said. "Yep." He handed his phone to Lucas.

The teen might pretend to be all macho, but his hand was shaking when he took the phone. "Yes, sir?" He smiled. "Yes, sir. Yes, sir. Yes…uh, yes, I will. Okay. Yes, sir. Thanks." He handed the phone back to Josh. "He wants to talk to you again."

"Adam's talking to our pack leaders as we're speaking. He'll let you know as soon as we learn which family he'll be staying with. Trial period? I'll tell him. Thanks, sir." Josh laughed. "You've got that right. Thanks. Bye."

Adam said, "Thanks, Cassie. I'll let him know. Josh has talked to the judge, and he wants there to be a trial period, right, Josh?"

"Yeah."

"Thanks." Adam got off the phone and said, "All right. You have four families to visit with. This is as much a choice for them as it is for you. We'll need to drop off the truck at your foster parents' house, since it's in your foster dad's name and he doesn't want you to have it. We'll pick up whatever you need from your home and drive down to the ranch, meet with the pack leaders, and visit with the families. You can stay with the pack leaders or with one of the families on a trial basis. You can move around, decide where you really want to stay for good, and go from there."

"Four families?" Lucas sounded astonished, but Brooke was glad that so many wanted to take him in. He'd surely find a family he wanted to live with. "I can't believe the judge is a wolf too. I never was close enough to smell him. When do I have to start working for you?" Lucas asked Josh.

"As soon as you're settled in with your new family. There isn't any rush."

"If you can work on the website for me from your new home, I'd be grateful, and you can start earning some money from that." Brooke was afraid she was already going to lose her new hire if he lived too far away, and she needed the assistance. Plus she wanted to help him to feel like he was a needed member of their wolf society so he wouldn't continue to get himself into trouble.

"I can do that. I have a computer. I paid for it, so I get to keep it. But...it's time for me to live free as a wolf too."

"Good. This isn't about avoiding human contact but embracing your wolf side. Are you two going to be all right while I'm gone?" Adam asked Josh and Brooke.

"We'll be fine," Josh said. "Brooke?"

"Yes."

"If Lucas is ready, we're on our way," Adam said.

While Adam took Lucas home, Brooke was on her phone, taking a picture of the authentication paperwork on the Chinese vases and then texting someone. "I want to do this one thing before we go to bed. I've wanted to do it ever since I learned I had the papers showing the vases are authentic." Then she turned to Josh. "I know Lucas needs to be with our kind, but do you think it's a good idea to take him away from the family who has raised him for several years without giving him more time to think about it? Kids can be so impulsive, and I believe he should have taken a couple of days to think on it first. I worry he'll change his mind about staying with a wolf pack and miss his human friends and his foster parents, but the Thorntons won't want to take him back at that point."

She sent another text message.

"If he's good with staying with them, yes. Mainly because he's getting into trouble, something our kind can ill afford. It seems to me he needs to be with our kind to keep him on the right path," Josh said, thinking of the trouble Lucas could cause. He guessed he was thinking with his detective badge. He also believed Lucas needed to have friends his age who were just like him. Josh couldn't imagine living as a wolf among humans on his own as a teen. Not only because of the issues of reining in his wolf tendencies if he got aggravated but because he needed to learn to be a wolf among wolves. The ranch would be perfect for learning to take care of animals and horseback riding, if Lucas didn't know how. Even having a girlfriend could be a real boon. As long as he and the other male teens didn't fight over them.

Brooke sent another text message and let out her breath on a heavy sigh. "It's almost Christmas. Maybe we should have done this for the new year, not right this minute."

Brooke was thinking about Christmas, something Josh hadn't considered. She was right. What if his foster parents had bought Lucas all kinds of presents and they had a nice Christmas family gathering planned? Maybe it was a surprise even.

"I'll call Lucas and see what he thinks." Wishing they'd thought of it before, Josh called Lucas's number, then said, "Hey, Lucas, I'm putting this on speakerphone so Brooke can listen in. She is concerned you didn't have enough time to really think this over. That you might have needed more time to make a decision of this magnitude. We are so eager to have you in the pack, but we should have considered the impact this would have on you. It's nearly Christmas and—"

"My foster dad said if I messed up one more time, he *wasn't* going to have his lawyer take my case. He was going to let me take responsibility for what I've done. That's what I'm doing now. Taking responsibility. I think I've been…I don't know…missing out on what our kind do. And kinda acting out because of it. I mean, I know there's no excuse for it, but maybe this is what I need. As a kid, I remember running as a wolf with my parents, getting into trouble back then, too, but it was as a wolf, exploring. Got skunked once. Never again. Got lost when I chased after a rabbit. You know. Wolf pup stuff.

"My parents and I could talk about anything to do with wolves. For nine years, I've had to keep this secret. You know how hard that is? I can't tell you how many times I've wanted to howl my frustration. I won't be missing Christmas with my foster parents. They're going on a cruise, and I told them I didn't want to go. I was staying home alone. They were glad to have a honeymoon away from me. And you know what that means."

"Getting yourself into more trouble," Josh said.

"Yeah. Most likely. Though I didn't really have anything in mind. Tell Brooke thanks for thinking of me."

"You're welcome," Brooke said. "I was afraid you'd change your mind later and it would be too late. Everyone was so eager to have you join the pack and—well, I thought you might have needed more time to decide such a thing."

"I think my foster dad is really eager to get rid of me. He doesn't want my bad behavior to impact his work or his good name. He's told me before he believes I'll only get worse. He talked about sending me to a camp for juvenile delinquents next summer."

Josh glanced at Brooke. She shook her head in disbelief. "What else have you done that we don't know about?"

Lucas laughed. "Nothing illegal."

"Good, then you'll have a family that will teach you the way of the wolf, and that means staying out of trouble," Josh said.

"What about your foster mom?" Brooke asked.

"His first wife divorced him when I was ten, and I stayed with him. Then he remarried a year later. The other woman liked me, but this one just tolerates me. I'm sure it's a mutual dislike. She wanted him all to herself. I'm just a foster kid, not his real kid, and she had just married him, so she wasn't in agreement about fostering a kid. She's talked to him a number of times about sending me back."

"If I'm not mistaken, I believe you were reaching out to us," Josh said. "I figure you knew we'd catch on to you once you found out wolves were at the reindeer ranch."

"Maybe," Lucas said.

"That cinches the deal then. If the woman who's your foster mother doesn't even want you at home, there's no sense in staying there." Brooke was on her phone, typing away.

Josh wondered what she was doing now.

"That's what I figured. I think it will be an adjustment for them, just like it will be for me, but I really believe we'll all be happier. If things don't work out with any of the families at the ranch, I could always move in with you," Lucas said.

Brooke laughed. Josh didn't.

"I'm sure you'll like one of the families," Brooke said.

"You'll be just in time for the Christmas party the pack

is holding." Josh was glad Lucas would be able to attend the party with the pack soon. "Lots of food and fun."

"Adam was telling me about it. I can't wait. We're here at my foster parents' home. Adam said he'd call you if I have any trouble with them."

"Okay. See you soon. At the party at the latest." Josh ended the call and said to Brooke, "Sorry. I should have thought about the issue with Christmas and the family."

"I was thinking about how it would have been if I'd done that to my own family, which isn't the same at all. It sounds to me like he's going just where he needs to be. There will be ups and downs. Everyone has to go through that. He would have, had his own parents still been alive."

"That's so true. I hope he settles down with the new family. I'm working the investigation here for the next two weeks while this business with the armed robbers is unresolved, by the way."

"I really appreciate that, Josh."

Josh opened one of the boxes they'd hauled over from the shop earlier. "All the guys at the station are ribbing me over it. Adam especially."

"You sound like you're enjoying it."

"You bet."

Brooke smiled. "It's getting late. Let's go to bed."

"I haven't ever felt this way about another woman," Josh said as he and Brooke headed for her bedroom. In the room, he pulled her into his arms. "You are the one for me. We can date for a few weeks if you need more time, or we can—"

"Mate?" she asked, running her hands up his red-and-black-plaid shirt, her brows raising, an almost imperceptible smile playing on her lips.

"If you feel the same way about me."

"As in I love you?"

He smiled. She wasn't making this easy for him. "Like I love you. I'm seriously ready to give up everything to be with you."

Her lips parted in a look of surprise. And then she gave him a more impish smile. "Seriously?"

"Yeah."

"You mean you intend to give up your job? So you can help me unpack boxes and tag merchandise and help sell to customers? So you can—"

"Go on treasure hunts and provide personal protection and security for the store."

"Hmm." She pulled his shirt up, and he finished removing it. "It's tempting."

"But more. Hell. I'm not doing this right. I want to enjoy the time with you while you're working, we're working together. Take in estate sales on our days off. You won't have to spend all your free time managing the store because I'll be helping you sort out everything. We can keep Lucas on as our web designer. We can hire someone else to help out with the shop so we can—"

"Spend more time with each other?" Brooke ran her hands up his chest, her palms sliding over his nipples, making them erect and sensitive to her sensuous touch.

"Yeah. The nights will be ours. Running as wolves in the park or at the ranch, spending time like this." He pulled her soft red sweater over her head and dropped it on the floor. "And on the two days the store is closed too." He helped her sit down on the bed, then pulled off her boots. Then he sat down beside her and pulled off his shoes.

"But your job? I wouldn't want you to quit it unless you really were ready to. You had to have worked hard to get where you are. You must enjoy what you do." She knelt down before him and removed his socks.

"I did work hard to make detective. But I can retire at any time. With our longevity, I only look like I'm around thirty-five—like Adam and Ethan do—because of our slower aging process. We've all put in our twenty years. It's time to retire. It's time to do what I want to really do. Settle down with a she-wolf—not *any* she-wolf," he quickly added, "but you. Hell, I haven't had time to rehearse what I wanted to say to convince you I want to be your mate and love you always." He rose to his feet and reached under her skirt to pull off her black leggings. Once he had stripped her out of them, he kissed her mouth.

"I feel the same way about you." She kissed his bare chest. "That first day you walked into my shop, I knew I shouldn't have been falling for the detective who was accusing me of stealing his reindeer, but I couldn't help myself. You were so annoyingly frustrating and yet—"

"Lovable?"

She laughed and tweaked one of his nipples gently. "Hot and sexy. And you were so concerned about me, so protective, when I totally needed the protection. And helpful. I meant what I said about all the assistance you gave me. I was able to get so much more done with us working together. Most of all, you are the only wolf who has ever sent my pheromones reeling. Yes, I want you for my mated wolf, to love and to cherish and to enjoy the time we have to spend with each other—both as wolves and in our human forms. I love you. But—"

"There are conditions." He gave a dramatic sigh, even though he was ready to meet any conditions she set for him.

"I want you to stay on the force until you can help Adam learn who is responsible for the armed men coming to the shop so you'll still be able to question people about the case. I know Adam would tell us what is going on, but I think that having both of you working this investigation will help get results faster."

"I was going to say I wanted to stay until this case was done, though we'll have to wait to marry. I don't want anyone taking me off the case because I'm involved personally with the shop's owner."

She smiled. "I'm sure they already think that."

"True. But I don't want to make it official in a human way. They know we're seeing each other, but we're saying it's for your protection."

"Then mate me and make an honest wolf out of me." She smiled up at him. "That's as official as we need as wolves. We can have a ceremony later."

"After the holidays."

"After we resolve this case."

"Sure." He didn't want to consider the possibility that it could be a very long time before they could resolve the case. He was certain she was just as aware of it. All that mattered for now was they were going to mate. He kissed her forehead, then their lips melded with pent-up passion. "I want to be there for you. That's what I want to do too."

"I want you," she whispered in his ear, her hands sliding up his bare chest, "any way I can have you. You are the only one for me. Especially when you found the real culprits in the theft of Jingles."

His arms wrapped around her waist, he chuckled. "You will never let me live that down."

"You had what it took to get my attention."

"I'm sure glad I did something right."

"Hmm, you sure did." She pulled his face down to kiss him, their lips merging.

# CHAPTER 21

BROOKE WAS EAGER TO MAKE LOVE TO JOSH AND become mated wolves. She swept her hands down his delectable chest, her fingers reaching her mission, and began to tug to unfasten his belt. While she was struggling with that, he angled his head so he could kiss her earlobe and then her neck and her shoulder, taking her red bra strap in his teeth and pulling it off her shoulder.

Feeling sexy, playful, and loved, she smiled. "You are such a wolf," she whispered, licking his chest.

He growled in a hungry, fun way. She chuckled. She loved her wolf.

He caressed her skin with his mouth until he reached the other bra strap and grabbed it with his teeth and pulled it down. Then he nuzzled his face in her cleavage, and she giggled when his whiskers tickled her. He smiled, and she moved her hands down to his trousers zipper and gave a smart tug, then pulled them down.

He reached behind her and unfastened her bra, his chest pressed against her breasts as if he wanted to hug her at the same time. Her hands slipping to his backside, she pressed his growing arousal against her thigh and wiggled a little.

"Hmm, I like this kind of dancing," he said, his voice low but rough against her ear as he pulled her bra loose.

She did, too, and rocked her hips some more. They didn't need any music to make their own dance steps. Then he was back to business and sliding his hands down her waist until he reached her skirt. Once he'd unbuttoned the wool plaid skirt, he slid it down her legs and helped her out of it.

She worked on removing his trousers so that he was only wearing a pair of boxer briefs, straining with his aroused package, and she was wearing just her red panties. Sliding his hands down the backside of her panties, he cupped her naked bottom. She reciprocated, slipping her hands beneath his waistband and squeezing his muscular ass. She sure wished she could be that firm.

He was kissing her, his hands still on her ass, and she was kissing him back, his erection straining in his boxer briefs against her waist as they moved against each other, and then they were on the bed, her on her back, him between her legs, ready to make love to each other—all the way.

He kneaded her shoulders, his mouth on hers, the warmth spreading through her muscles, through her body. His hands and lips felt heavenly on her. She couldn't have found a better mate for herself than him.

She ran her fingers through his hair, loving the silky texture, breathed in his heavenly scent, the scent of male and wolf and her orange citrus body wash.

It felt natural being with him like this. His mouth again on hers, kissing, making her light-headed, her pulse sounding in her ears. She kissed him back, hot, tantalizing, pure chemistry. He was the meaning of life for her, the treasure she hadn't been searching for but had found. The only one she truly needed.

She realized once he had come into her life that she was no longer thinking of selling the shop in three years. She wanted to do this with him, as long as he wanted to. She wanted to find the treasures on her great-aunt's treasure list—and share in the fun *with him*.

And this? This was all part of the fun. Being with him, glorying in the passion between them. She slipped her tongue inside his mouth, and they kissed again, their tongues dancing together, the sensory assault melting her all the way to the tips of her toes.

With a roughened voice, Josh said, "I love you." He nuzzled her neck with his mouth in a seductive way, the tease of his warm lips stirring her blood.

"I love you back, you hunk of a wolf." Her voice was just as rough and needy, and she kissed his stubbly chin.

She loved the flex of his muscles against her as he moved his mouth to her breasts. He was such a wolf. Hot need filled her with urgency. Raw passion. Wolfish possessiveness.

He slid his hand down her belly, down through her curly hairs, and separated her feminine lips, then began to stroke her nub. His mouth recaptured hers, and she eagerly met his kiss.

She moaned with his strokes and arched her back. "Oh yes," she let out in a husky whisper.

He picked up the strokes, slid a finger and then a second one inside her, and caressed and twisted, making her want to scream out in ecstasy. Then the climax hit her, the ripples running through her. "Oh God, yes. You are the wolf for me."

He smiled and removed his fingers, licked her mouth, and spread her legs further. Then he entered her, his hard, full length filling her. Her body welcomed him, received him as part of her, just like she was part of him. Wolves mated for all time.

She couldn't have been happier than to enjoy the joining with her mate, the love between them just the beginning.

He continued to thrust, his arms resting on the bed beside her, his hands cupping her head, his eyes filled with lust as he leaned in to kiss her again. She loved him.

———————————

Beautiful, mysterious, tantalizing, and all his, Josh thought as he plunged his cock into Brooke, glorying in her wet heat, their pheromones dancing with each other. She arched her sweet, curvy body against him, propelling him deeper, brought her legs up around his hips and bucked. She squeezed his ass, sending another volley of heat straight through him. He thrust faster and harder. He slid his hands under her buttocks and pulled her tighter. He gave her a hard-fast kiss before he resumed his thrusts.

Then she gasped, and he felt her second orgasm hit hard, caressing his cock. He continued to kiss her, to thrust, to hold off the inevitable, wanting to treasure the moment as long as he could. But there was no way he could last, and he came. He rocked into her until he was spent. And this time, he howled. Being with her, being mated to Brooke, that was something to howl about, and he couldn't be happier that she'd chosen him for her mate when there were so many other male wolves she could have chosen. She was the only one for him.

———————————

When they woke the next morning, Brooke kissed Josh, then hurried out of bed to the bathroom.

He folded his arms behind his head and sighed. "You

know the shop is closed today, so there's no rush to do anything." He could have snuggled with her and made love to her all morning.

"The shop isn't closed today."

Hell, he must have his days mixed up since he was off from work. "Gotcha." He jumped out of bed and joined her in the shower, but she smiled, kissed him, and got out.

"I've got to do something this morning before we open the shop." She toweled herself off in a hurry and dressed.

"Maybe we should have waited to mate until we had two days off," he said, hurrying to soap up in the shower.

"No. Way."

He smiled. "It's going to kill me to have to wait until the shop is closed to have my way with you again. Do you want me to fix breakfast while you're working on the 'something'?"

"That would be great. You don't know how wonderful it is having you here. Though if you hadn't been here, I would have gotten up earlier." She finished applying her makeup and brushing out her hair and hurried out of the bathroom.

"I made it worthwhile to stay in bed a little longer, right?" He got out of the shower and dried off.

She laughed. "I was thinking we might start running as wolves in the morning before Forest Park opens to the public."

He dressed and joined her in the dining room. "They open at five."

"Right."

He'd rather sleep with her and make love to her.

"Or we'll have to wait until ten at night."

"Or we could head over to the reindeer ranch after the

shop closes at six, have dinner with Maverick, and go running." He massaged her shoulders as she was typing something on her laptop.

"Right."

"What are you doing?"

"While you were chasing down leads on the bad guys, I contacted three antiquity collectors who are collecting period pieces like I have. The Chinese art market is big right now. I was just texting them the certificates of authenticity and insuring the vases. I have the same insurance company my great-aunt had, so it was easy to insure all the contents and the house, shop, and car with them, and it shouldn't be a problem."

"That's good to know. Did you want pumpkin spice waffles for breakfast?"

"Sure, if I've got the ingredients for them."

"I'll check." He looked in the pantry and the fridge and began pulling ingredients out. "Cinnamon, ginger, cloves, light brown sugar, can of pumpkin, buttermilk, eggs, flour, baking powder and soda," he said, looking in her pantry and fridge. "You've got it."

"Good. Thanks. Sounds delicious."

"So the contacts you checked with… Did you have any interest in the vases?" He began to whip up the egg whites and set them aside. Then he mixed the egg yolks, buttermilk, pumpkin, and butter, beating the mixture until it was smooth. Then he added the rest of the ingredients, whisking them until the batter was ready.

"Yes. As to the potential buyers for the Chinese vases, one is interested in purchasing them for $10 million together, if they're authentic, which I now have proof they are. I told him they wouldn't go for less than $35 million each—since the other appraiser had said that's what they're worth—and that the collector was the first I had contacted. I didn't tell him I'd already sent word to two others who will be sure to outbid him for the collection. He knows I will, and he *was* the first I notified."

Josh's jaw dropped. "That's $35 million for one?" He warmed up slices of ham.

"Yeah. My great-aunt left me a real treasure. Well, now it's my mate's treasure too. But that's only if we can get top dollar for them."

"It's a good thing you didn't leave it to me to handle the auction. I would have jumped at the chance to have a million bucks for the *two* vases. Hell, I would have thought I'd won the lottery if I'd sold them for a couple thousand." He smiled at her.

She chuckled. "You'll learn the value of things soon enough."

Josh made up some lavender tea for her and a cup of coffee for himself, then brought the Christmas mugs to the table. It didn't take long for him to serve the waffles after that, with maple syrup and butter. Then he served the ham.

Brooke got another text and sipped from her mug. "From the other potential buyer. He's offering $12 million each."

"I suppose you'd say no and hold firm." Josh sat down at the table and buttered his waffles and then poured maple syrup over them.

"Yes. I tried to get hold of another private buyer, but he hasn't responded yet. One of these vases sold for $70 million, another for $80 million. So yeah, I'm holding firm. Wait, here's from potential buyer number one. Now he's offering $10 million each. I'm texting him back that I've contacted two other potential buyers, and one of them has outbid him. They're always the same art collectors for this kind of art, so he'll know his competition." She cut into a slice of ham.

"Are you telling him by how much the other guy outbid him?"

"No, I'm going to wait and see where it goes." She got another text. "This text is from the Chinese American who hadn't responded earlier. I really want as much as I can get, but I hope the buyer would be of Chinese origin, which was why I only contacted these three collectors. I don't know how my aunt ended up owning them, but these collectors often loan their treasures to museums to share with the world, which would be great."

He glanced at her laptop. She texted the Chinese American buyer: $35 million apiece. We have three bidders.

"They all can afford it, financiers who are worth billions. But they will all try to get the best bargain they can for the royal china."

He appreciated that she was including him in the business. He still hadn't quite begun to think of himself as part owner of her estate, just as she was now part owner of the reindeer ranch.

She texted the first two bidders back: A third bidder has stepped up to the plate.

Josh was fascinated by her business acumen as she let the bidding war go on.

"Woo-hoo! The first buyer just bought the vases for $40 million apiece. I figured he would outbid the others, which was why I contacted him first."

Josh was thrilled for her. She whooped for joy again and did a little dance. He gave her a hug.

"Man, this calls for a celebration," Josh said. "How do we get the vases to him?"

"He'll send his men to pick them up. A couple of men will guard the vases—one to hand over the money and take possession and another who is an antiquities dealer in China who will again authenticate the vases. I've sold one royal Chinese bowl worth half a million to the collector. It was a great find, but not as big as this, and I was able to pay off my house, car, and college loans with the profit, after taxes. That's how he handles purchases of this magnitude."

Josh glanced at the date on her laptop. "Wait. The shop is closed today."

She glanced at the date. And smiled. "Good. That means we can do some more work, take a nap, and this afternoon celebrate the sale of the vases and our mating with Adam and your brother."

That sounded like a plan to him. For now, he secured the two vases in the safe before they did anything else.

---

Much later, after they'd tagged merchandise from several more boxes and filled some of the shelves at the shop, taken a nap, and made love, Josh called Adam and put the call on speakerphone. "How did things go with Lucas last night?"

"I dropped off Lucas with the pack at the ranch last night, and he was thrilled to see the overwhelming welcome everyone gave him when he arrived. Poor kid was moved to tears. I packed a bag for my overnight stays at the shop. I thought I'd come over and help you go through a bunch of the boxes and help with tagging the merchandise like Josh was doing. I'll be there in about an hour."

"Good. Come over to the house," Brooke said. "We're going to celebrate the biggest antique sale I've ever made. I'll tell you about it when you get here."

"That sounds good to me. Did you need me to bring anything?"

"No, I have champagne, and I'll make us steaks for lunch. We should be good." She really had wanted to do this for Josh, Adam, and Maverick for all the help they'd been anyway. She still couldn't believe the amount of money they were getting for the vases, though she felt she couldn't plan what to do with the money until she handed over the vases and received payment for them.

"I'll be there as soon as I can."

"We just need Maverick to come," Brooke said to Josh when he ended the call with Adam.

"I'll call him."

"He deserves to be part of this, with all the help he's been."

"I agree." Josh called his brother. "Brooke's having an impromptu celebration for selling a couple of royal Chinese vases. Adam dropped off Lucas with the pack, and one of the families will take him in for now. We want to have you join us too. Lucas is the one who helped mess with our security video and stole the reindeer along with his friends. We found out he's a wolf. That's why we smelled a wolf around our security equipment... Well, there's one other kid who was involved. We'll still have to bring him up on charges so he can serve community service time. He's not a wolf though..."

Okay, good. We'll see you when you get here." Josh set his phone on the table. "Maverick wants to help with tagging stuff too. He thinks you might find some more high-dollar antiques that would be the cause for more celebrations."

"He may be right. My great-aunt knew what she was doing when she collected some of this stuff."

Josh pulled Brooke into his arms. "You didn't tell Adam about the mating, so I didn't mention it to my brother."

"I figured we'd tell them when they got here."

"I was afraid you might want to wait. I'm ready to shout it out to the rest of the wolves."

She laughed, rubbing his arms and then kissing him. "Don't worry. We'll let all the bachelor males know right away. There's no reason to wait." She went back over the treasure list her great-aunt had made. "The first on her list says 'Travel to Imperial China for double the treasure.' The two Chinese vases were in the steamer with Chinese ship-destination stickers. So that must have been the clue to them. I never would have guessed that they had been an emperor's treasure and valued at so much."

"I agree with you. It sounds like we have a party game for this afternoon." Josh looked at the next item on the list. "'You'll have to go to the *Miracle on 34th Street* and then you'll believe.'"

"The Santa suit we found in the trunk! Don't you think?" she asked.

"Yeah. It's all about believing in Santa, right?" Josh said.

"And it's about the commercialization of Christmas, even back in 1947." Brooke snapped her fingers. "A sticker for New York City was on the steamer trunk. Thirty-Fourth Street in New York City."

"This is great."

"I agree." She looked up information about one of her favorite Christmas movies. "Did you know that Edmund Gwenn, the actor who played Santa, actually was in the Macy's parade in 1946 and that's where they shot the film? It was bitterly cold too."

"No, I hadn't known that."

"Gwenn's cousin Cecil Kellaway rejected the role, and Gwenn grabbed it. To think his cousin missed out on the opportunity of a lifetime to play in a movie that has become a Christmas classic. It says here that Valentine Davies was inspired to write the story while standing in a long line waiting to buy his gifts at a department store," she said.

"I hadn't known that, but it's sure relevant today too. Though online shopping has helped considerably. But why would the Santa suit be valuable?" Josh asked.

"I'm not sure. What about the next clue: 'To believe, you have to dress the part. Especially in New York City.'"

"Both are about believing. Wait, both are about the movie?" Josh asked.

"Ohmigod, what if the little girl's coat and hat and Santa's costume actually *were* from *Miracle on 34th Street*?" Brooke went to find her colorized version of the movie and brought it out to show Josh. "That's it. The outfit that Natalie Wood wore as an eight-year-old in the movie. The Santa suit looks just like Santa's costume."

"How much would it be worth?"

"I have no idea, but maybe we can take them to the Christmas party for show-and-tell."

"That sounds great."

A knock sounded on the back door, and Josh went to get it. "It's Adam." Josh let him in.

"What are we celebrating exactly?" Adam had brought a pecan pie.

"Oh, thanks for the pecan pie. I love them," Brooke said.

"We're celebrating the sale of two Chinese vases owned by the emperor himself," Josh said.

"Really. So how much are they selling for these days?" Adam asked, setting the pie on the table.

"Forty million United States dollars each," Josh said before she could. "Hell, when the first potential buyer offered ten million for each of the vases, I would have sold them to him right then and there. Good thing I'm not helping with that part of the business."

Adam laughed. "Hell, I can't believe it. Did I see them?"

"Probably not. Once I thought they might be the real deal, Josh put them in the safe in the house. When Maverick arrives, Josh can open the safe and show them to you. No touching though."

The guys laughed.

"She's got a great game to play. Her great-aunt made up a list of valuable items and where they were located," Josh said. Then a knock sounded on the front door, and Josh went to get it. "Maverick's here. He brought a holiday cheese ball covered in fresh green chives and crackers. Hey, you're in time to help us figure out the clues."

Adam opened the bottle of champagne while Brooke fetched the champagne glasses.

Maverick set the food on the table. "So what are we celebrating?"

This time, Brooke shared about the sale of the vases, and

then with champagne glasses in hand, they went in to show off the vintage artwork, because the vases would soon be collected from Brooke and out of here for good.

"Wow," Maverick said. "Who would have ever believed a couple of vases would be that valuable."

"And even better—you're looking at two mated wolves," Brooke said.

Adam and Maverick looked shocked at first, glancing at a grinning Josh as if to see if it was for real.

"Ah, hell," Adam said.

Maverick laughed. "My sentiment too. Welcome to the family." He gave Brooke a hug.

"Just consider me part of the family. Both Josh and Maverick do." Adam gave her a hug. "Congratulations to both of you."

They hugged Josh too.

"So where's the list of clues?" Maverick asked.

Brooke brought out plates so everyone could grab some munchies, and then they sat in the living room while Josh made a fire. She returned with the list of clues and explained what they thought the first three items were.

"Sounds reasonable to me," Adam said. "We might not be able to help with these though. You've been unloading the trunks and boxes and have seen some of the merchandise."

"That's true." Maverick placed a couple of crackers on his plate and sliced off some of the cheese ball.

Brooke began fixing lunch, putting on the steaks, then boiling potatoes and frying up some asparagus.

"The next clue is: 'You need to vet the barn to make sure it isn't worthless.' What would that be?" Adam asked. "Wait, the next clue says 'You have to pickup the barn to use it to its fullest.' 'Pickup' is written as one word."

"So a pickup truck? What would be the value in that?" Brooke asked.

"If it's vintage, it could be worth something," Maverick said.

"Another clue: 'Luxuriate in Italy whether you're a sports fan or not, but you have to get out of the barn to do it.'"

"A luxury Italian car?" Maverick said. "Man, I'm in the market."

"I'm sure Brooke will give it to you for a Christmas gift," Josh said, smiling. "What if the clues are all referring to vehicles? A luxury Italian car could be a Ferrari, Alfa Romeo, Fiat. Maybe a Maserati or Lamborghini. They're all Italian luxury cars that could be classics."

"Which would you love to have?" Brooke asked.

"Man, oh man. If I could, I'd keep them all," Josh said.

She chuckled. "You're like my great-uncle, if these are vintage cars in the barn. He's been gone thirty years, so they'd have to be vintage. I can't imagine my great-aunt buying cars and hiding them in a barn."

"I wouldn't have them sitting in a barn collecting dust," Josh said.

"You'd be showing them off," Brooke said.

"Yeah. That's what they're for." Josh smiled. He couldn't imagine having something that grand to drive.

"If they're what we think they could be, maybe the 'vet' is a Corvette," Adam said.

"But there are no barns here on the property." Josh set out the plates and silverware.

"The other items she mentioned as far as travel had to do with the steamer trunk. But I think you're right. She has a parcel of a thousand acres of land that I inherited. Maybe something's hidden in an old barn on the acreage," Brooke said.

"Do you have the deed?" Adam asked.

"I'll get it." She went to her office and pulled it out of her file cabinet and returned to the living room. She looked it over while Maverick and Josh peered over her shoulders.

"This land borders ours," Maverick said. "I vaguely remember our grandparents mentioning that William, your great-uncle, purchased the land next to ours and built a home, and then they ended up later moving into town to buy two Victorian homes joined by a courtyard and turned one into the gift shop."

"That's great news. So we've been neighbors all along." Brooke returned to the kitchen and served the meal. "Time to eat."

Adam brought glasses of water to the table for everyone. "Who's going to look for a barn on the property after lunch?"

"Who's going to protect the house and shop?" Brooke asked.

The guys all joined her at the table to eat lunch, but they also looked eager to find rare vehicles in the barn—and forget about the house and the shop!

# CHAPTER 22

"SOMEONE CAN STAY AND SAFEGUARD YOUR HOUSE AND shop," Josh said to Brooke, his brother, and Adam. Josh wouldn't leave her behind though. He'd be worried about her safety if she was all alone. "We need to have someone stay here with Brooke while the others look for the barn."

"I'm going with one of you. We only need one person to stay at the house if I'm not here," Brooke said.

"Who's staying?"

Adam held up his hand. "I will, since I'm a police detective and can handle a crisis if someone tries to break in to either the house or the shop."

"I guess we'll take separate cars so that I can be home after we look for the barn," Maverick said.

"Good idea," Josh said.

They finished lunch and helped Brooke clean up afterward.

"Let's go," Josh said, eager to go. "We'll keep you informed about what we find, Adam." Josh got the car door for Brooke when they were outside, and she climbed in. "If we have this figured right, I don't understand why your great-aunt would have all these cars hidden in an old barn."

"If we're right, they were probably my great-uncle's and she didn't want to sell them off because they reminded her of him. She knew he wouldn't have wanted to part with them."

"Thirty years in an old barn that might or might not be where he'd put them that many years ago." Josh shook his head.

"Would they be that valuable?" Brooke asked. "I mean, if they're old and rusty and all."

"Oh yeah. They could still be valuable. I'm going to give Leidolf a call and tell him we're mated, if that's all right with you."

"It sure is."

Josh reached over and squeezed her hand. "I couldn't be happier, you know."

"Me either."

Josh called Leidolf and gave him the good news. Cassie got on the phone, too, and congratulated the two of them.

Cassie said, "You know we only just found out you had moved here to take over your great-aunt's shop and home. The bachelor males said Josh didn't play fair. Not that I blame him at all."

Leidolf added, "We can't wait to meet you."

"I guess you know I want to be part of the pack," Brooke told them.

"Yes, and we're happy to have you," Cassie said. "Will we see you at the Christmas party?"

"Yes. I look forward to meeting everyone."

"See you then. And congratulations to both of you," Cassie said.

Then they ended the call, and Brooke let out her breath. "My great-aunt might not have made the time to do pack events, but now that you can help me manage things, I sure want to."

"We'll certainly do that. I haven't been able to make a

lot of the events either because of the work I do, but it'll be different now. Well, once I retire."

"This will be good for both of us then."

They followed Maverick as he drove past a sign for the reindeer ranch. He finally pulled off the main road onto a rutted, paved road that weeds and grass had partly taken over. Trees encroaching on the one-lane road made it even narrower.

Maverick finally parked his truck at a gate and got out of his vehicle. He checked out the gate while they waited.

"It's probably locked," Josh said.

"Does Maverick have lockpicks?"

"Sure, but if it's a combination type, we'll have to cut off the lock. He's got a bolt cutter in his truck for emergencies."

"I might have a key for it, if it's a key lock. I found tons of keys in Ivy's desk but had no clue what they were for."

Maverick turned and smiled at them, jiggling his lockpicks in one hand, the key lock in the other.

"Yes!" Brooke said.

Maverick tried to open the gate. Josh saw him struggling and left the car to help him. Brooke soon joined them to help too.

"We'll have to cut back some of this brush later," Josh said. They finally managed to pull the gate open, and they piled into Maverick's truck because it could navigate the road better.

"Wow, I've never been here before," Brooke said as they continued to bump along the road. "It's beautiful with the creek and forest."

The creek that ran through Josh and Maverick's property also ran through hers. "We never had a fence between our properties because we're all wolves, though we never trespass beyond our own borders." Now that this was all theirs, they could start using the land too.

"This is wonderful. Maybe with some of the money from the vases, we could build a retreat. Cabins, hiking trails, fishing in the creek. Maybe a timber play-fort for the kids. We could have hot tubs, a swimming pool even. It could be rented out to wolves from all over. We could hire someone from the pack to manage the place," Brooke said. "And I want to donate some money to the wolf reserve south of here."

"I like the idea," Josh said, Maverick agreeing.

"Look over there at the paved road that's in mint condition, not like the beginning of this one from the gate," she said.

"Somebody's repaved it but didn't maintain the beginning of the drive, as if wanting it to look uninhabited," Josh said.

"There's the house," she said excitedly.

The two-story brick home didn't look to be in too bad shape. It needed some fresh paint on the trim work, but the brickwork looked good. It could probably use a new roof too. The road would have to be repaved and widened.

"Depending on the condition of the house, we could renovate it and have it as lodging too. Or the wolf who runs the cabins could live there," Josh said.

"Now that's an excellent idea. So he and his family, if he has one, would live there free and keep up the place. I want to see inside the house, if you can use your lockpicks to get inside. But over there"—she motioned to a big red barn—"we've got to check out the barn first."

Maverick parked the truck at the house, and they all got out to make their way through the tangle of shrubs that had grown all over the yard and finally reached the barn. It was in great shape, better than the house even.

"It looks like someone's been coming out here and maintaining the barn," Maverick said.

"Maybe my great-aunt hired someone to care for the vintage cars and the barn in memory of my great-uncle. It would make sense that if she had them, she wouldn't just leave them to rust in an abandoned barn."

"That would be good news." Josh reached the barn first, his lockpicks out, eager to see if the vehicles were inside.

When he opened the door, there they were. Beautifully polished, looking ready to take a spin. "That one's a '57 red-and-white Corvette."

Brooke quickly looked up the price. "It's valued at between $80,000 and $140,000, according to auction sites."

"Yes!" Maverick said, sounding as thrilled as Josh felt.

"And it's in great condition," Josh said, opening the driver's door.

"Wow, I just can't believe it. I can't believe my great-aunt never told me about it. I never knew my great-uncle."

"Now that's a Ferrari," Maverick said, opening the door and climbing into the car. "A 1966 Ferrari 275 GTB/2 with sports alloy wheels and blue vinyl interior with only 13,000 miles on the speedometer."

"That's great. I can't believe it!" Brooke was looking up something else on her phone. "Wow, for a 1966 Ferrari being auctioned off in Monterey, California, the price tag is $2,900,000 to $3,500,000."

"You have a mint here," Josh said.

Deeper in the barn, they saw a pickup truck. "That's a 1940 blue Chevy pickup truck," Maverick said.

"Worth"—Brooke was on her phone searching for a price—"between $35,000 and $40,000."

"They're all in mint condition. The barn is well sealed. Not like normal barns," Josh said.

"So what do you want for Christmas?" she asked as Josh and Maverick switched cars and took turns sitting in the driver's seats.

Josh smiled.

"One of the cars? It's yours."

He chuckled. "I got what I wanted for Christmas already. You."

"You're so sweet. Thanks."

"What would you like?" Josh asked her.

"Hmm, anything is good for me. You're my Christmas present too. I really couldn't ask for more." Brooke said to Josh. "No Christmas presents for us."

"Wait, I'm getting one of the cars, right?"

Brooke and Maverick laughed. "Yes. What about for Maverick? I'll give you guys the truck for the ranch, but you can have the other vintage car."

"Hot damn. I'm thrilled. You are definitely my favorite sister-in-law."

"I'm your *only* sister-in-law."

"And the best one ever. I'll take the Ferrari if it's all right by you," Josh said to Brooke, letting her sit in the car next. He supposed he should have allowed her to try it out first.

She smiled at him. "It's yours."

"Then I get the Corvette," Maverick said, looking like he was a kid in a toy store.

She left the Ferrari, and Josh gave her a hug and a kiss. Then he had to try out the Corvette.

"Somebody—in the pack, probably—is maintaining the cars and the truck. Would the pack leaders know?" she asked.

"They might. I don't think word has spread yet that you've taken over the shop. When I told Leidolf and Cassie we were mated, the pack members might have gotten word. We can ask at the Christmas party," Josh said, hands on the steering wheel in the Corvette, envisioning driving with his mate down Route 66, top down, wind in their hair.

Maverick went over and gave her a hug, tears in his eyes. "This is the best Christmas ever, since you came into our lives. And not just because of the cars and the pickup."

———————

Brooke hugged Maverick back. "You and your brother made it the same for me."

The guys moved on to check out the truck. She sat in the driver's seat of the Corvette and reached up for the visor. She didn't expect to find anything, but all the movies showed people putting car keys up on their visors, so why not try it? As soon as she pulled the visor down, the keys dropped onto her lap.

Well, *that* was a surprise. She wondered if the car would even start. Most likely not. But when she tried the keys in the ignition, it started. She pressed the gas pedal, and it vroomed. "Ohmigod, it runs."

Both the brothers hurried back to her and the car. They opened the hood and checked the engine. She smiled. She could imagine walking naked in front of them and they wouldn't see a thing but the beautiful vintage car they were drooling over.

"They're all gassed up, engines clean," Josh said, checking out the Ferrari. He found keys on the visor for it too.

Maverick went to check the truck and found the keys on the visor for it. "Well, hot damn."

"I bet whoever has been maintaining the vehicles has been driving them around on the property," Josh said.

"On the newer paved part of the road." Brooke took pictures of each of the vehicles to show Adam when they returned home.

"We can haul them out of here with the truck. I just need to get a trailer so they'll be more secure," Maverick said. "We have a double-car garage attached to the house and another garage that we use for storage and work vehicles. But we'll have room for the vehicles. We shouldn't drive them any distance until we have a mechanic look them over and make sure they're safe."

"We can check out the house in the meantime while you get the trailer," Brooke said.

"See you in a bit." Maverick drove off in his pickup, and Josh used his lockpick to unlock the house.

The door creaked when he opened it, and the first thing Brooke thought of was oiling the hinges. Inside, the house was dusty and cobwebby, but there was no furniture. She was glad for that because she figured it might need to be replaced anyway.

"It's in good shape," Josh said, checking the windows, his voice echoing off the walls. "We need to get some new locks for the house."

"Right. It looks like it mostly just needs lots of cleaning. It could probably use a fresh coat of paint. Floors look good." They walked into the kitchen. "Hmm, it could use some updating." She thought the same of the bathrooms. After checking out the four-bedroom, three-bath home, they sat on a window seat and were doing a Google search for cabin styles they could put up on the property when they heard a pickup arrive. Only it wasn't Maverick's pickup. It was somebody else's.

"It's Randy Winters," Josh said. "I bet you anything he's the one who's been taking care of the cars."

Josh and Brooke headed outside, and a redheaded guy with a beard and a big smile greeted them. "So this is the little lady who's got the whole pack in an uproar, slipping into Ivy's place, and you've been spending all this time with her and never let the rest of the pack know."

Josh laughed and shook his hand.

Randy looked old enough to be Brooke's father. He gave her a hug. "Welcome to the pack. And congratulations, you two. I've been taking care of the vintage cars and truck since William passed away. Ms. Ivy hired me to look after them since I was always up here tinkering on them with William."

"Brooke has given the vehicles to me and my brother, but we'll want to keep you on as our mechanic."

"That sounds good to me."

Maverick drove up, pulling the trailer, and the men all helped to load up the Ferrari.

"I'll go with you to help you park that baby in her new home," Randy said and went with Maverick to drop off the car.

After they finished moving the vehicles, Brooke and

Josh arrived home in time to relieve Adam of his duty so he could go to the pack Christmas party too. Before Adam left the house, Brooke handed him her phone to show him the pictures of the Corvette, the Ferrari, and the truck.

"Those are real treasures." Adam finished a cup of coffee he'd been drinking. "Did we get through all the items on Ivy's list then?"

Josh chuckled. "Have you got the treasure hunting bug?"

Adam smiled. "Hell yeah, when the treasure is worth this much."

Brooke shook her head. "I'm going to get dressed for the party." She hurried off to her bedroom.

Adam put the empty coffee mug in the dishwasher. "See you tonight before I start my night-shift guard duty."

"See you at the party, Adam," Josh said.

When Brooke came out of her bedroom wearing a soft, red sweater dress, Josh looked like he wanted to hug all that softness, but she directed him to the bedroom. "Go get ready."

He soon came out of the bedroom wearing a red sweater and jeans, and she smiled. "I love that on you. So nice and Christmassy for the party."

"Thanks. Maverick got it for me. I figured he wanted me to look more festive."

"Well, we look like a couple."

He smiled. "That's just why I wore it." He gave her a big hug and a kiss, and the way he groaned with the contact between her body and his, she figured he wanted to take her straight to bed instead of taking her anywhere else.

She wouldn't have minded, but she did need to meet the pack, and the Christmas party provided the perfect opportunity. She smiled up at him, her arms around his neck, her body pressed against his. "I need to meet the pack. Heck, I've mated you. I need to let the rest of the bachelor males know I'm with you."

Josh agreed. "Let's go."

She knew he'd have fun with her there, and this party would be different from all the others he'd attended, now that she was his mate. She couldn't have been more pleased with the way things had turned out. She was excited about seeing everyone and having some Christmas fun, but she still worried about someone breaking into her shop or house.

"A couple of patrolmen are going to keep an eye on both your places," Josh told her. "They're not wolves, so they won't be missing the party."

"Oh good. You are such an angel."

He chuckled. "My brother would wholly disagree with that statement."

She smiled. "I'll have to ask him about it then."

"I prefer my version of the stories."

She laughed and then saw the policeman parking outside her house.

Josh got out of his car and talked to him for a moment, then returned to the car, and they headed south to the ranch.

Brooke was eager to meet everyone at the Christmas party and officially be welcomed to the pack.

She hoped she could remember names. She had brought the Santa suit and Natalie Wood's coat and hat in garment bags to showcase, and when they arrived at the ranch, Cassie Wildhaven placed them in a special place of honor on a table for display, along with the black-and-white version of the movie and a colorized version.

Cassie was a redhead with pretty green eyes. Leidolf was also a redhead with green eyes. They made a handsome couple.

Maverick had brought some reindeer to the party, and everyone was having fun petting them and taking pictures with them.

Then Cassie and Leidolf welcomed Brooke to the pack and Cassie said, "Besides the classic cars they found hidden in a barn where our very own Randy Winters has been taking care of them all these years, we hear you've made another fantastic find, and we'd love it if you'd share what you do with everyone in the pack."

Brooke hadn't thought she'd be put on the spot like that, but with everyone looking on, she told the gathered crowd of partygoers about the Chinese royal-family vases she'd just sold for $40 million each.

If the wolves hadn't been interested in what she had to say before this, they were now.

Everyone congratulated her.

She offered, "I will be happy to help anyone have their antiques appraised and help to sell them. You might not have anything worth selling—or I should say, that collectors are interested in paying money for—but you never know. You might have something worth a little or a lot collecting dust in your attic. If the items have a sentimental value and you don't want to part with them or believe that in a few more years, they'll be worth even more, continue to treasure them. If you want to rehome them and maybe make some money, I've got contacts, and I'm happy to help."

She realized how much the antique business was part of her life, not just her family's. It truly was in the genes.

Josh was standing with his brother, arms folded across his chest, smiling at her from some distance away, letting her have her space for the moment. She appreciated that, because she needed to meet the pack members, and she knew if he was standing beside her, her attention would be divided between him and the others.

"I could even carry items in my shop on consignment, if anyone would like to do that."

Meeting all the pack members was overwhelming. Everyone was thrilled that she and Josh were mated. She was glad to see Maverick and Adam because she knew them. And she was glad to see Sierra and Lucas too. Leidolf and Cassie, the pack leaders, welcomed her to the pack as if she were an old friend returning to the family. If she'd had any reservation about joining the pack, she didn't now.

"I've got to organize a game." Cassie smiled and gave her a hug. "Josh was the sneaky one, keeping quiet about you being in town."

Brooke laughed. She loved it here.

Cassie started playing Christmas songs, and everyone had to guess what the song titles were.

While others were guessing, Lucas came over to talk to Brooke. "I need to set up a way for your customers to buy stuff from your shop without having to actually go to the shop to pay for them. Josh told me how you had it set up."

"That would be great. How are you liking it here so far?"

"I love it." Lucas beamed. "I'm staying with a family that has a set of twins, a boy and a girl. Jessie showed me how to ride a horse."

"That's wonderful. I'll have to learn how to ride one

of these days." Though when she visited the ranch in the future, she'd be more interested in running as a wolf.

"We could teach you! Her boyfriend doesn't like that she's teaching me." Lucas smiled again like he was glad he was able to spend more time with her. Then he lost the smile. "Two of the women here are twins, and they just found each other. Do you think I might have a twin?"

"Not all of us have twins. Sometimes our human genes take over. Other times, the wolf genes do. Besides, your parents were alive until you were seven, right? So you would remember having a twin, and I'm certain they wouldn't have had any reason to separate the two of you."

"Yeah." Lucas shoved his hands in his pockets. "I guess I wished I had some real family."

"You do. In all of us."

"Thanks. I'm going to start working on your website tomorrow first thing if it is all right with you. Do you want me to come over in the morning before the shop opens so you can show me the setup? I can begin working on it then."

"We're closed tomorrow, so you can stay at the house and work on it. You should be safe enough. No answering the door to strangers though. Josh and I will be in and out of the house while we are going through the boxes of merchandise."

"I could help with that too. I can't believe a couple of old vases from China sold for that much."

"It's rare art and was owned by an emperor of China. That's what made them more valuable."

"Okay. I want to earn some extra money so I can buy presents for the family I'm living with. I mean, they said not to buy them anything, but they're going all out to make me feel like part of the family, and I want to do something for them."

"That will be great."

Lucas glanced around at the others eating and drinking and playing the Christmas song game. "The only job here for me is to muck out the horses' stalls. I figure I'll have plenty of that work to do at the reindeer ranch when I do my community service time with Ty. I'd rather work on the computers for you. For Josh too." He looked beyond her. "Your mate is coming. You should hear all the bachelors grousing about Josh keeping you secret and then mating you before they had a chance to meet you."

She smiled. "He's helping protect me." And much, much more.

Josh walked toward her, his expression turning from serious to a smile. "Want to dance?" he asked, taking hold of her hand.

She realized the musicians had started to play music for dancing. "Yes. I do. Lucas wants to work on my website at the house tomorrow. We'll be closed and working back and forth between the house and shop, unpacking boxes and pricing the merchandise. Do you think it will be safe enough for him? He wants to earn some Christmas money for gifts for his new family."

"If we're not going to be tied up with the shop being open, sure."

"Can I help you solve the mystery of your great-aunt's list of treasures? Josh said that you were trying to unravel where everything is located and why they're valuable," Lucas said.

"You sure can," Brooke said.

Josh pulled her close to dance, and they began the waltz.

"Before we return home tonight, I want to run as a wolf," she said.

"We'll sure do that."

# CHAPTER 23

Josh had tried not to show how possessive he felt about Brooke at the party, wanting her to meet with the pack members and enjoy herself without him hovering over her the whole time. She didn't need his protection here, but he couldn't help that he'd continued to watch her, letting the other bachelor males know that he was observing them. The way they'd been smiling at him, he knew they'd been amused and getting him back for keeping her secret from them.

Once Josh held her in his arms to dance, everything and everyone else faded away. "How are you liking the pack so far?" he asked, pressing a kiss against her ear, hoping she was happy to be with them, since he wanted her to feel at home here with the pack and with him.

She wrapped her arms around his neck. "Everyone has been so welcoming, and I'm glad I have a greater value to the pack, other than just being an eligible female for mating. Or needy, requiring pack members to shop at my store to keep me in business."

He smiled down at her. "I'm glad. After hearing about some of the finds you've made among your great-aunt's items, they realize you're financially set, if you weren't already. It took every ounce of my strength not to chase away the bachelor males speaking to you though."

She chuckled. "We're mated, Josh. I love when you're being honest with me, particularly when I can see you making sure they're behaving themselves, yet letting me do this on my own for a while. But you could have joined me sooner." She danced nice and close to him, her body snug against his. "You don't have to worry, you know. You're the one I wanted to keep around, even after the danger has passed."

"I couldn't be gladder for that." The way Brooke was holding him close stirred his blood and other things, and he was damn glad they had mated already. He kissed her cheek, her jaw, her other cheek, his eyes gazing into hers. "You needed full-time protection and a full-time assistant." She parted her luscious lips to say something, but he quickly added, "In addition to a mate."

She sighed. "I agree." She kissed his chin. "We'll work in the most pleasurable mating business anytime we can"—she slipped her hands down to his buttocks and pulled his groin even tighter against her—"but I'm really glad to get a...partner in all things. Still, having a career you love is something to consider. And it's important for our kind to have police detectives who are wolves who can protect us when we're in our wolf coats. It's not about just me. It's necessary for all of our kind, so I don't want you to feel you have to retire right after the case is solved."

"A mating is forever. A police job is not. I don't need to be there for everyone. You are the one I need to be there for. Finding the she-wolf for me is more important than any temporary job I might be working. I put my twenty years in. I'll work as long as it takes to take these men down, and then I'm retiring. You need me, sure, but I need you even more. You said so yourself. I'm the perfect wolf for the job."

"Oh yeah." She kissed him on the mouth as they

continued to dance, their bodies working up the heat, and he knew if anyone was watching them dance, they'd realize no other bachelor males had stood a chance. "I just wanted you to be sure."

He chuckled and kissed her again. "Are you kidding? I am."

Brooke laughed. Josh loved her laughter. It made him feel lighthearted, and he would always remember this pack Christmas party above all others. His first with his lovely mate.

She rubbed up against him in her pretty red sweater dress. "This has been the perfect day, and you're making me hot and needy."

Josh smiled down at the vixen. "You're the one who's making me rise to the occasion."

Trying to get his mind off what her body was doing to his, since they couldn't do anything about it right this minute, he glanced around at everyone else who was dancing. One of the older wolves was playing Santa, sitting on a throne while the reindeer were nibbling carrots on either side of him and the kids were standing in line to sit on Santa's lap to tell him what they wanted for Christmas.

Someday, Josh figured, he and Brooke would have kids of their own standing in that line to sit with Santa. He couldn't believe they were mated already, but he sure was glad about it. When he retired, he could be there with her day and night and always protect her.

He thought of Christmas Day and what he could get for her. He knew she said she didn't want anything, but what would be the fun in that? Then he thought of the perfect gift. She'd mentioned she needed to renovate the kitchen.

The pack had a cabinetmaker, plumbers, and electricians. He'd make up a gift certificate for her for one completely overhauled kitchen, and he'd take her all over to find just the right tile, appliances, and cabinet styles to create the kitchen she'd love. He'd get a book on different styles of kitchens to give her some ideas of what might work in addition to the gift certificate, and she could have a new kitchen after the holidays.

"Hey, did you want to get something to eat?" she asked after dancing a few dances.

"Sure." He took her to one of the tables filled with platters of turkey, ham, and cheeses, potato salad, green salad, and pumpkin pie, cherry pie, pecan pie, and chocolate cake topped with a snowman decoration, with wolves on either side of him and trees behind them, perfect for a wolf Christmas party.

They filled their plates and picked up cups of mulled wine and sat at one of the tables at one end of the barn. The tables were covered in red tablecloths, and each had a poinsettia bouquet in the center, making them perfectly festive.

Adam and Sierra joined them, and then Maverick did too. Josh noticed Lucas was dancing with a teen girl, the one he was living with now. He was glad to see Lucas having fun.

"He's enjoying himself," Brooke said. "I didn't think I'd ever say this, but I'm glad he stole the reindeer before he got into any other trouble and you were able to catch him at it."

"I agree," Josh said.

"Some of the male teens in the pack don't." Sierra sipped some of her mulled wine.

Josh noticed two teens watching Lucas dancing, their arms folded across their chests, their expressions dour.

"Maybe one of them is the old boyfriend," Adam said.

"As bachelor males in a pack, they have to learn only one gets the girl and gets her for keeps," Maverick said, saluting Josh. "It's good they learn that early on and how to process it. From one who knows."

Josh chuckled.

Adam saluted Maverick with his drink. "That goes for me too."

Then they saw Ethan heading their way with a plate full of food.

Josh was glad he could join them.

---

"You've heard Brooke and Josh are mated, haven't you, Ethan?" Adam asked.

"Aw, hell, that's the end of me trying to win you over," Ethan said to Brooke.

"Once Josh accused Brooke of stealing our reindeer, I knew he was after her, and not for the aforementioned crime," Maverick said.

"You guys gave up too easily," Brooke said.

"They knew it was a lost cause." Josh kissed her.

Ethan gave her and Josh hugs, congratulating the two of them.

"Hey, are you ready to run?" Brooke asked when everyone had finished eating.

"We might have even more pack members running with us, if that's okay with you," Maverick said. "Everyone usually finishes off the party with a wolf run."

"Oh, do we need to wait until Cassie or Leidolf say it's

time to run as wolves? I don't want to mess up their party. I never even thought anyone else would want to," Brooke said.

"No, not at all. Everyone does their own thing, so you can run when you want to," Josh said. "Come on. Let's go find a place to strip and shift."

Josh and Brooke hurried to strip off their clothes behind a barn. And then they shifted.

God, he loved her. This time, running as wolves was different because they were mated. He nuzzled her face, nipped her ear, and licked her cheek. She nuzzled him back and rubbed her whole body against him, telling him she had claimed him too. He couldn't wait to take her home and make love to her. But he loved this time with her as a wolf too. She was beautiful and all his.

Adam, Ethan, and Maverick soon joined them in their wolf coats and greeted them. Then they all took off running. They were having a ball. Josh was glad she could set the business of the armed robbers aside for the moment and just enjoy being a wolf. He was having the time of his life, racing alongside her. He'd always enjoyed running as a wolf, running with his brother, Ethan, and Adam, but running with his mate was the best thing ever—with her licking and nipping at him in playful fun, chasing his tail around, teeth ready to bite.

He swore the other guys would have been laughing up a storm if they could have while in their wolf coats.

They ran down to a river, and she stood watching the trout swimming in the water. She suddenly woofed. She wanted to fish. They could certainly do that and have a fish fry some other time. He couldn't wait to do everything with her, this season and every other.

Then they ran through the woods across the river and heard wolves howl. Other pack members were now taking a run. Josh howled back, and Brooke howled with him, her wolf's voice melodious and enchanting. He would know it always now, just as she would recognize his howl if she heard it again. Adam, Ethan, and Maverick took up the chorus of howls.

Then they continued exploring, racing, Adam and Maverick tackling each other, something Josh would normally have taken part in. This time, he was sticking with Brooke. He wanted to enjoy every wolf moment with her.

He thought of Lucas being at the house tomorrow, when Josh would have spent the day in bed with his mate. He sighed. Lucas wanted to earn some extra money for Christmas presents, and if Josh and Brooke really wanted to spend some time alone with each other during the day—like he was certain they would—they could send Lucas out to get lunch or something.

Brooke finally nipped at Josh and turned to head back to the ranch. He hoped that meant she was ready to go home, but they needed to drop by his and Maverick's ranch so Josh could pack some of his things. Adam, Ethan, and Maverick followed them back to the ranch house. When they reached the barn, Josh and Brooke quickly shifted and dressed. Maverick, Ethan, and Adam had disappeared but soon joined them, already dressed.

"We'll head to the ranch so I can pack some more clothes and personal items," Josh said.

"I'm going to relieve the other officer watching over the store," Adam said. "I'll see you in a little bit."

"Yes, and you have to join us for breakfast," Brooke

reminded him. "Lucas will be joining us to help with my website and online store."

The idea of Josh moving in with Brooke permanently and having her to love on anytime they could get away hadn't sunk in yet. But he was certainly ready for that.

# CHAPTER 24

JOSH AND BROOKE SAID THEIR GOODBYES TO THE REST
of the pack, carefully put the Santa suit and Natalie Wood's
coat set in the car, and then Josh drove them to the reindeer
ranch. Maverick followed behind them in his truck, pulling
the trailer carrying the reindeer, but they lost him somewhere along the way.

"What are you going to do about the clothes from
*Miracle on 34th Street*?" Josh asked.

"I could sell them, offer them to a museum, or make a
special display for them at the store to bring in more business," Brooke said.

"I'd display them in the shop. Make up a poster with a
picture of the movie cover and some particulars about the
story since it's your favorite one."

"That's what I'll do." That was what she was leaning
toward in the first place. "I love the pack. I just hope the
bachelor males aren't mad at both of us for not giving them
a chance with me."

Josh chuckled. "They'll get over it. Besides, the pack still
has two eligible she-wolves to date. Who knows? Maybe
others will join us unexpectedly like you did. I'm surprised
we never saw you when you visited your great-aunt."

"Except for during the summers, I rarely was able to
come here, with helping to run the shop back home. My
great-aunt didn't attend a lot of pack functions here either
because she was busy running her shop. You know how that

is if you don't have anyone to help. She didn't hire anyone to work for her, even near the end, because she had her way of doing things. When I visited, I'd want to help her organize things, and she'd tell me not to because she wouldn't be able to find anything after I left. I still can't believe she had so much valuable stuff she hadn't tried to sell."

"She was probably like you and unable to keep up with all of it. She might not have had the contacts like you do to sell the really rare items to collectors either."

"That's true. When I visited with her, she knew the value of antiques, but a lot of her connections had died. You know how it is with human connections. They don't have half the life expectancy that we do. And she wouldn't get the internet, which is the way I make a lot of my connections for the big stuff now."

When they reached the ranch, she took in the size of the ranch house and the Christmas lights on the house and the big red barn and several other buildings, but the red barn was what caught her attention. She stood in awe of the whole place: forested land, a river meandering through the meadows down below, even a small Christmas tree farm. She loved it.

A hand-carved, gilded sign hung over the entrance to the barn: WILDING REINDEER RANCH. Nearby was a corral with another engraved sign: REINDEER MAKE DREAMS COME TRUE.

Another smaller corral was near that: WHERE THE MAGIC BEGINS.

"That's the corral for the reindeer calves when tour groups come out to see the reindeer. We'll let the kids go in and pet them," Josh said. "Come on inside and meet the reindeer." He turned on the lights inside the barn, and it was just like Christmas. Little colorful lights twinkled over each of the stalls, and each had a hand-carved sign with gilded letters proclaiming the name of the reindeer. Each stall was trimmed in gold, and the whole barn was painted red inside, including the siding and stall gates. Up above, the ceiling was blue, covered in stars and the moon.

"This is beautiful. I expected a working barn, not a showcase work of art."

"We have tour groups come here year-round, actually. So we wanted to make their trip truly special. We considered just making it all natural, but reindeer are part of the magic of Christmas, so we opted for a more magical setting."

"I love it. Who made the signs for the reindeer?"

"Maverick. Woodworking is his hobby. He made them for the corrals too."

"Oh wow. I'm hiring him to make some display signs for me."

"I'm sure he'd love to do that. Just tell him what you want, and he'll do it."

"You know, he could make signs to sell in the shop too. Whatever sold would be his own money. I wouldn't charge him to put them in the shop. I love hand-carved and painted signs. They sell well. Created just like he does, too, with a vintage look. I won't have to buy them to stock my shop."

"That sounds like a good deal."

"Do you do anything creative?"

Josh smiled. "No. I hope that doesn't change our status."

She laughed. "No. I can set up fun displays, but when it comes to creating arts and crafts? No talent whatsoever."

"No time either, I imagine."

"You're right. Sierra says she does artwork other than police sketches. Maybe she'd liked to display some of her art in the shop. In fact, anyone who creates arts and crafts in the pack could have an outlet for their work. My mother was big on embroidery, but after she made so many pictures and pillowcases and gave away so much of it, she didn't have anyone else to give her artwork to. She finally started selling it in their store. Maybe others have crafts they do like that." She realized how much she could offer to the pack, and she felt really good about it.

"That would be great."

Brooke walked through the barn, seeing each of the adult reindeer and the calves, petting the ones that greeted her. They all had their own personalities, nudging her for more petting, licking in greeting, more aggressive or shyer.

Then Josh brought Brooke into his arms and kissed her. "I love you, Brooke. I can't believe my good fortune that I met you before any of the other wolves did. And that you fell in love with me and no one else."

"Oh, you are so right about that," Brooke said, then kissed him back. "I thought there was something wrong with me. Here I'd met both you and Maverick, and he was being really sweet to me, and you weren't, yet who could I not quit thinking of?"

"Are you kidding? After all the harassment over the reindeer? That was just a ploy to get your attention and to have a reason to keep seeing you. Even Maverick told me that."

They heard Maverick's truck pull up outside.

"He must have stopped for gas. I'll go help him unload the reindeer." Josh headed outside, and Brooke followed him out.

She smiled and waved at Maverick. Then Josh helped him unload the reindeer and put them up for the night.

"I love the signs you made. Can you make some for me? I'd pay for them." Brooke didn't want Maverick to think he had to do a lot of work for her for free. She explained about showcasing his work at the shop so he could earn some extra money.

"I'd like that. I'll get on it when I have free time."

"Okay. Since you have such a showcase here with the reindeer, the big red barn, and the Christmas tree farm, I think the vintage truck will work well as part of your displays, don't you? You could decorate it for all the seasons, for the special holidays. Just have fun with it. You could paint the name of your ranch on the side. That will be my Christmas present to both of you."

"Who gets to drive it first?" Josh asked his brother.

Maverick laughed. "Thanks, Brooke. I can't tell you how much that means to us."

"You're so welcome. You don't mind that we're mated, do you?" She knew it would be a big adjustment when the brothers were close and lived and worked on the ranch together.

"I should be upset you and I didn't tie the wolf knot, but I'm glad that if it was going to be someone other than me, it was my brother." Maverick gave her a big hug. "Welcome to the family, Brooke. I can't think of a nicer and more fun person to have as a sister-in-law."

She hugged him back. "Thanks, Maverick. I'm so glad to be part of the family."

"I'm going to head on inside and pack some bags," Josh said.

"I'll help you." Brooke hurried after him.

Maverick followed them to the ranch. "Do you need some boxes?"

"Yeah. We can haul more stuff over later in the truck. I just want to get most of my clothes."

"The ranch is nice and spacious. You won't miss living here, will you?" Brooke started to pull clothes out of Josh's drawers while he began to grab the clothes hanging in the closet.

"No. We have four thousand acres—"

"And my thousand acres bordering your land," Brooke added.

"Uh, right." Josh smiled. "If we ever decide to, we can build our own ranch house out here. Otherwise, I'm fine with living in town. We might come out to the ranch to enjoy the wide-open spaces during the days when the shop is closed, once we deal with whoever is trying to steal from you. Or at night to go running as wolves. The land and everything on it is ours, too, even though I'm moving in with you. There's a guesthouse on the ranch we can use if you don't want to build a larger home of our own. That way, when Maverick finds a mate of his own, he can have the house."

"That sounds like a good deal. I'm so thrilled we'll be able to run at either ranch. I love the river running through your property and the forested land. It's perfect for exploring as wolves. Do you harvest the Christmas trees?"

"We lease the land to another wolf who grows the Christmas trees and sells them. It's the perfect setup for all of us. We use the Christmas trees for a backdrop for promotional pictures of the reindeer, and for tour groups, we have a photo op with visitors petting a reindeer while standing in front of the Christmas trees."

Maverick brought in some boxes and began packing them with clothes.

"That's really neat."

"Whatever we can't fit in the car, we can get later," Josh said. "When we have time, I can't wait to take you all over the property, running as wolves to see the sights, Brooke. Anytime you want to go running with us, you can, too, Maverick."

"Thanks, I'd like that," Brooke said, and Maverick agreed.

They began loading the bags and boxes into the car, and when the trunk and back seat were filled to capacity, they said good night to Maverick. "I'll send you a list of signs I'd like made."

"Sounds good to me. Congratulations, you two. We'll have to have a celebration for your mating. The other was really for your selling the vases."

"I was thinking we could do it with you and Adam one night. I'll fix a prime-rib dinner for all of you," Brooke said.

"That's a deal," Maverick said. "Let me know if I need to do anything to help out, either with the business or with the protection."

"We sure will," Josh said. "Hopefully, we'll be okay. Adam's going to continue to stay with us at night, sleeping at the shop until we know for sure who's behind the men trying to rob her."

They each gave Maverick a hug, then got into the loaded-down car.

———————

They finally reached home and drove into the garage. They thanked the police officer for watching the place. He was the same cop who had hung up on Brooke when she'd called about the reindeer calf, so she figured he was trying to make it up to her.

"'Night, folks," he said. "It's been quiet."

"Thanks so much," Brooke said. "I really appreciate it."

Then they said good night to the officer, and when he drove off, Josh lifted Brooke in his arms and carried her across the threshold into the house, locked the door, and hurried to the security alarm to turn it off.

A knock on the back door sounded. "It must be Adam," Josh said, sighing. He deposited Brooke on the bed in the master bedroom. "I'll be right back." Josh was certain it had to be important, or Adam wouldn't be bothering them.

"Take your gun, just in case."

"I've got it." Josh headed for the back door, peeked out, and shook his head. He opened the door. "You know what you're interrupting, right?"

"Sorry. I talked with the patrol officer who was watching the shop on his rounds, and he said everything was fine. I'm retiring for the night, but I want to interrogate the robbers at the station in the morning," Adam said.

"I agree. 'Night, Adam, and thanks."

"No problem. See you in the morning."

Josh went into the house and locked the door, then strode to the bedroom. Brooke was reading text messages on her phone, sitting on the bed, waiting for him. She smiled at him.

He was ready to finish the moves they'd started while dancing at the Christmas party.

"What did Adam want?" She set her phone on the bed-side table.

Josh crouched down to pull off her black boots. "He wants me to help him interrogate the armed robbers who threatened you again in the morning."

"Good idea. But for now…"

"This is all that's important to us." He ran his hands up her legs covered in pantyhose. She was such a dream come true. He kissed her legs, pushing her sweater dress up. "Hmm."

He reached up to pull off her pantyhose, peeling her out of them, kissing down each leg, one at a time, until he had removed the hose and tossed them aside. Then he helped her to stand and wrapped his arms around her, loving the feel of her soft curves enveloped in the soft sweater dress. "I didn't want to let you go when I saw you wearing this dress before the party."

She smiled and hugged him close. "I know. If you'd had your way, we would have stayed here and been naked in bed again."

He chuckled. "Yeah."

She pulled his red sweater up and over his head and tossed it aside. Underneath, he had a soft, black knit shirt, and she ran her hands over his chest. "This is like opening a Christmas present, only I have to keep peeling away the wrapping paper."

He laughed. "At least you don't rip away the wrapping paper."

"Wait until I see my presents." She made him sit down on the bed so she could remove his boots and socks. Then she pulled the bottom edge of his shirt up, kissing his abdomen, his chest, his nipples, neck, jaw, and finally his mouth as she continued to draw his shirt up. He lifted his arms, and she removed his shirt the rest of the way. She placed her warm hands on his waist and nuzzled her face against his chest. "Hmm, you smell so good—all wolf and mine."

He nuzzled his face in her hair. "Your fragrance is a turn-on for me." He swept his hands over her breasts, then down her dress until he reached the hemline and tugged the dress up to dispense with it, enjoying the sight of her in her white bikini panties and bra. "So beautiful."

"So in love with you."

"Uh, me too with you." He kissed her breasts while she tackled his belt and was soon pulling his zipper down and yanking his jeans down his hips. He finished removing them.

"You are ready for me," she said, kissing his straining arousal in his boxer briefs.

His cock jumped. "Always." He unfastened her bra and pulled the straps down her arms and dropped the bra on the carpeted floor. He kissed her soft shoulders, cupping her breasts in his hands. He still couldn't believe the treasure he had in her, glad she was his mate.

She kissed his neck and jaw, then licked his mouth. "You taste so good."

"So do *you*." Then he removed her panties, and she pulled his boxer briefs down, freeing him. He was so ready to finish off the night in the best possible way, making love to his mate.

He climbed into bed with her, then kissed her eager mouth and lost himself in the sweet taste of her. She combed her fingers through his hair, the sensual assault stirring his cock. She gently bit his lip, making him so hot with need. He wanted to infuse himself with her strength, beauty, kindness, and cleverness.

Brooke was his fantasy mate—the woman and wolf who was making his dreams come true.

As her hands moved to his nipples and stroked, he felt his groin tighten. He moved his mouth from hers to her jaw, pressing light kisses to her cheek, her throat, her collarbone. Working his way down, he took a nipple in his mouth and tongued it, then switched to the other breast and lathed it too.

Heat coursed through his veins, and she said his name in a sensuous way, telling him she needed this just as much as he did. She slid her hand down his buttocks and squeezed. A rush of arousal raced through his body. Her pheromones were enticing him to mate.

He turned her over on her side, her back to him, moving her leg so he could access her slick sheath, and stroked her nub. He kissed her shoulder and her spine. She tensed under his strokes, and he pulled her hair away from her cheek and kissed her neck. She sighed.

She was barely breathing, tense again, and he licked her shoulder. She pressed her mound against his questing fingers, demanding more.

He inserted a finger into her, swirling it as deep as he could go, then pulling out, and she moaned in protest. Smiling, he inserted two fingers this time and eased into her, using his thumb to stroke her feminine nub at the same time. She was wet for him, writhing with his touch, begging for more.

Eager to make her come, he intensified the pressure until she cried out. He kissed her neck. "Are you ready for me?"

"Oh yeah," she said, her voice sexy and sultry.

Glad to bring her pleasure, he pushed his cock into her, seating deeply.

He ran his hand over her thigh, his body throbbing with unspent need, and thrust.

———————————

Brooke had never imagined that being with a wolf, her mate, would be this hot, this fulfilling, this magical. Josh was everything to her and more, the way he touched her, made her feel exquisitely sexy and needy. Until he had mated with her, she couldn't know how good it could get. In the position they were in, his hand was free to roam all over her body with whisper-soft touches. He massaged her breast, the palm of his hand rubbing against the nipple while he kissed her neck with tenderness and continued to thrust.

She relished the way he touched her with his hands, his mouth, his cock. She absorbed the rugged feel of him, the spicy scent of him, the sweet taste of him.

He rocked into her, his hand sliding down her hip, moving to where they were joined. He began stroking her again, but she didn't think she could come again that soon. He was relentless and stirred primal needs that were buried deep, bringing them to the surface and making her want to howl.

Her adrenaline surged, his pheromones tantalizing hers as he drew her up in a swirl of sexual pleasure.

She was caught up in the maelstrom of emotions from raw joy to deep need. The second climax stole her breath, rocketing her to the moon in an explosion of fireworks that lit her world on fire.

This time, she howled, and he exploded in her, thrusting and kissing her shoulder before he finally finished. He wrapped his arms around her, still connected, not disengaging.

"God, I love you," he said breathlessly against her hair and kissed her ear.

"No more than I love you, you wickedly sexy wolf." She thought he would pull out and snuggle with her until they fell asleep, but he was semihard, and he wasn't going anywhere. She smiled. He was one hot wolf.

# CHAPTER 25

THE NEXT MORNING AFTER BROOKE AND JOSH MADE love in the shower—she'd never thought she could get that much pleasure out of cleaning up—and dressed, Adam and Lucas arrived at the house right before they all had breakfast. Brooke was amused Lucas had made it just in time to eat. Boy, did he eat! A double serving of hash browns, five sausage patties, two servings of scrambled eggs, and four slices of toast.

"You're sure you're all right to stay here with just two of the guys from the pack?" Josh asked Brooke.

"She's got me too." Lucas spread butter and blackberry jam on another piece of white toast.

Brooke reached over and squeezed Josh's hand. "I'll be fine. One of the guys will stay mostly in the shop and the other here. No matter where I am, I'll be protected. The same with Lucas."

"Hey, I've taken martial arts. If push comes to shove, I can shift," Lucas said.

"No shifting to bite anyone," Brooke said.

"If someone will give me a gun, I can shoot. My foster dad taught me. It was the only thing he wanted to do with me. Take me to the gun range."

"No guns," Brooke said. "Maverick and Sierra's brother offered to help sort out stuff from the boxes, too, so we'll all keep busy."

"Okay." Josh picked up his mug of coffee and pointed

it at Lucas. "You do what everyone says if anyone should break into the house or shop."

"Yeah, yeah."

Brooke suspected Lucas would try to protect her or take out the bad guys if they showed up.

They finished breakfast, and then Josh hugged and kissed Brooke as Brad and Maverick arrived. Brooke hadn't been surprised when Josh had asked a mated wolf to watch over her, even though the bachelor males wouldn't have hit on her now that she was mated. She thanked both for coming.

"We'll keep her and Lucas safe," Maverick promised Josh. "Go, learn what you can about the men who broke into her shop and who orchestrated it. We need to stop these guys."

"We will. Then we'll return here." Josh hugged her again, and she loved the heat of his body pressed against hers in the chilly outdoors, and then he kissed her soundly. "See you in a bit."

"Don't worry about us." But she knew his worried expression meant he would.

Then he and Adam drove to the police bureau.

"Okay," Brooke said to the others when she returned to the house, eager to begin working. "I'll show Lucas my website, and then we'll get started on the boxes." She showed Lucas what she wanted for the website and online store.

He offered her some options for taking money on her website, and she picked the one she wanted. Then he began to work his magic. She was glad he could focus his attention on something positive instead of getting himself into trouble.

"What do you want me to do?" Brad asked.

"Josh usually checks the security videos in the morning to see if anyone was hanging around observing the house or shop, if you wouldn't mind checking the one in the house." She figured that was a good job for a Navy SEAL. "I can give you a box of vintage replica merchandise to tag. Lucas can add them to the online store too. I usually don't have time to add faux vintage items, just the real thing."

"I can do that," Lucas said.

"Okay. I'll check the video while you're over at the shop," Brad said.

"Thanks, Brad. I so appreciate it. Maverick can haul over a couple of boxes so you don't get too bored. And I can get caught up." By the time the new year rolled around, she should have the shop in tip-top shape.

Then she and Maverick headed over to the shop.

"You know, it's my fault you saw Josh first," he said.

"How's that?" She went inside and turned off the security alarm.

Maverick followed her inside. "I saw the news about the reindeer calf showing up at your shop. It was on Twitter and other social network sites. I'd been watching for any news about a reindeer calf in Oregon, somewhere close by. When I saw the calf, I knew it was Jingles from the collar he was wearing, and I told Josh. He said he was on his way to check it out."

"So if you had come to see for yourself instead?"

"Teaches me to send my brother instead of going myself. He was just closer, and being a police detective, he knew he had to do the investigation. I knew for sure he was hooked on you when he wanted me to bring the reindeer to your place again."

Smiling, she took him upstairs to one of the storage rooms. "That was so much fun. I really appreciated both of you for doing that." She motioned to some of the boxes. "These are new merchandise. I have their original prices on an invoice inside the boxes. If Brad can mark it up by 100 percent, that would be good. If they don't sell, I can put a discounted sale price on them later."

"All right." Maverick carried the first of the boxes over to the house.

Brooke put on Christmas music to enjoy while they worked. Then she looked for another safe in her great-aunt's shop, something she'd been meaning to do.

The very annoying sound of a smoke detector suddenly went off in the shop's kitchen, telling her it needed a new battery. She headed for the kitchen just as Maverick returned to get the other box for Brad.

"Brad said the security video didn't show any trouble. I'll look at the one for the—" Maverick paused as the smoke detector beeped again. "I'll change that if you have a battery, once I drop off another box of merchandise at the house for Brad."

"I do. And thanks. Great on the security video. I imagine it's too much to hope that whoever is in charge of the attempted thefts has given up."

"I doubt it, if that thumb drive is worth enough." Maverick carried the other box over to the house while Brooke found the batteries and a stepladder. When he returned, he changed out the battery on the smoke detector.

"Smoke detectors are a necessary evil. I hate when they go off. Ivy has about ten of them, five in the shop and five in the house, and they all keep going off periodically, letting me know to change their batteries. She must have had them installed all around the same time. With our enhanced hearing? The shrieking nearly kills me."

"Now you have a smoke-detector battery changer at your disposal. If one goes off in the middle of the night, you can get Josh to change it."

She laughed. "I will. I need my beauty sleep."

"I'm going to check out the video security."

"Great. I'm on a safe hunt."

"I'll help you look once I'm done with this."

She started in the office where Maverick was looking at the security video. "I see a couple of pickup trucks driving by when everything is closed."

"But they're not stopping?" She looked behind a painting of a mother and her child sitting on her lap. There was nothing but a wall behind it.

"No. I'm watching to make sure no one's sneaking around the place." Maverick continued to scan for anything that looked like trouble.

Brooke looked behind three other oil paintings, one of them a vintage painting of a pack of wolves playing with little ones. It was one of her favorites, and she wanted to move it to the house to showcase. She wondered if the painter was one of their kind, since his name was Graythorn.

She looked behind furniture, then checked the floor to see if there was a floor safe, but no luck. "If someone is watching the shop, it will probably be when postal deliveries arrive. What about the bakery? They have tables inside where people can eat baked goods: pies, breads, cakes, sandwiches. Someone could sit there and watch the shop around the time the mail carrier comes."

"I'll check the video to see who's coming in and out of the shop then. When does the mail carrier usually come?"

"Between half past eight and ten. He usually gets here before I open the shop. Sometimes he comes later, depending on the number of packages he's delivering, especially during the holidays. Sometimes I have an afternoon delivery."

"I'll look at those time periods. Josh could ask at the bakery to see if they have noticed anyone who has frequented their shop more regularly lately."

"Right."

"No luck finding the safe?" Maverick asked.

"Not in here. I would think my great-aunt would have placed it in the office where she could watch things while the shop was open or somewhere in the house."

"You haven't checked the house yet?"

"Off and on. I've been busy. Every time it seems I have a moment, something else goes wrong, and I have to fix it." Or she and Josh were making time for each other.

"We'll find it. Did you want me to help you look for that now? Or unpack boxes?"

"I really need to work on the boxes with you at the *same* time so I can learn how much the items are worth. So why don't you help me find a safe, if there's one in the shop."

"Will do."

Another smoke detector started beeping. He smiled.

"I think that's in the hallway outside the bedrooms on the second floor."

"I'll get it. Got more batteries?"

"I stocked up on them the last time I had to change out one of the batteries. They're in the third drawer in that chest on the right."

Maverick grabbed a battery and the footstool and headed up the stairs.

"You sure are handy to have around."

"Thanks. I'm glad to have a sister-in-law. By the way, will the two of you be getting married?"

"Yeah. I haven't talked to Josh about it, but I think it would be nice to have a wedding with the pack. I've been trying to decide if I should keep Cerise as the name for the shop or change it to Wilding."

"It's been here for how many years?"

"Seventy-five."

"An icon then. I have a question. When Ivy mated your great-uncle, she didn't give up her surname, right?"

"Yeah. So I'll probably keep the name the same in honor of my great-aunt and great-uncle. My great-aunt was a feminist early on. Cerise means a bright or deep red color. We're red wolves and she wanted to keep the name. My great-uncle didn't have any problem with it." Brooke moved to the counter to see if maybe her aunt had a safe hidden near the cash register.

"It sounds like a good idea. I think Josh would agree."

She looked in the drawers for anything important and found an RFID card that would open a security lock. "I found something," she called out to Maverick.

He came down the stairs and looked it over. "Hmm, maybe she had a safe that this unlocks? It would have to be something newer. Not something that's been around for years. What about that shelf? It looks really new." He took the card and ran it over the shelf next to the check-out counter. The bottom of the shelf opened to reveal two handguns and several rounds of ammunition.

"Ohmigod, that's not what I was expecting. If I had

known she had these guns here, I could have pulled one out to stop those men and not used a frying pan," Brooke said.

Maverick chuckled and checked both guns. "Locked and loaded. Do you know how to use them?"

"My parents made sure I knew how to use a gun. I guess my great-aunt did too."

"Good. Do you want to leave these here?"

"Yeah." She slipped the security card back in the drawer. "We'll have to let Josh know about it too. I'm thinking the safe my great-aunt was talking about is probably in the house. Do you want to go to the house for a while, and we can look for the safe over there? We don't need to split up to watch the shop, just make sure Lucas and I are protected if we're not in the same place."

"We can all stay at the house."

"I'm so glad I have you and Josh in my life. He said we'd spend Christmas together."

"If you want to be alone—"

"No way. He invited me to share Christmas with the two of you. Now that I'm with him, we're still doing Christmas with you." She started to head for the house when she got a knock on the front door. "It's probably the mail carrier."

She could see her favorite mail carrier outlined in the beveled-glass door. When she opened it, he smiled and had her sign for a couple of boxes. "No reindeer here today, I take it."

"No, just one of the owners of the reindeer farm. Thanks. Hope your holidays are great."

"Same to you." Then he hurried off to his truck to deliver a million more packages, she was certain. When she looked at the address for the two boxes, she realized they were from Phoenix, and she gasped.

Maverick looked at them. "These are the ones the robbers were after?"

"Yeah. Five boxes are coming from Gulliver's estate. These are the first two. I began to wonder if they were coming at all—if Mr. Lee hadn't really sent them."

"I'd wondered about that too. Let's get them inside and begin going through them." Before Maverick could help her move them into the shop, a souped-up Camaro tore up to the door, and a ski-masked guy jumped out, waving a gun at them.

"Where are they from?" the masked man called out.

In the worst way, Brooke wanted to lie, but not when the guy was waving a gun at her and Maverick. "Phoenix."

"Load them in the car."

Brooke recognized the man's scent as that of the man who had been in her attic shooting at her. No way did she want to hand over the boxes, but Maverick told her, "It's not worth it."

She wanted to scream, she was so angry. But she didn't want to be shot or be the reason for the robber to shoot Maverick. She and Maverick loaded the boxes in the car, and after the man jumped into the back seat of the car and the driver tore off, she took pictures of the car and its license tag.

Maverick was on his phone to Brad at the same time, giving him a description of the vehicle. "Brad's jumping in his car and going after them."

"It could be too dangerous," Brooke said, calling Josh right away to tell him what had happened.

"He's not going to try to apprehend them, just tail them until the police can catch—" Maverick's phone rang, and he answered it. "On our way." He ended the call. "The car stopped and dumped the boxes of stuff on the sidewalk and tore off."

"So they got the thumb drive."

"Or they didn't."

They locked up the shop and hurried through the courtyard to the house. Excited, Lucas wanted to go with them. "I can help. Let me help."

"We're picking up what they dumped. Some of the stuff could be valuable," Brooke said, even if it wasn't the thumb drive. They climbed into Maverick's truck and headed down the street to where Brad was pulled over, putting stuff back into one of the boxes.

They were soon helping gather all the stuff together into the two boxes. Brooke called Josh back. "We've got the stuff. They dumped it on the side of the road. No thumb drive."

"I've called an APB out on the vehicle, though they don't have the stolen goods now. Unless they got the drive. If one of the men is Ackerson, at least we'll have him in custody, if we can catch him."

"Thanks. We're headed back to the house."

At the house, Brad and Maverick moved the boxes into the dining room and set them on the table.

They emptied the stuff out on the table, glad nothing breakable had been in the boxes. "Old keys," she said. "Silverware. Some tintype photos. Lace. Nothing extremely valuable. And no thumb drives that I can find. Nothing they could be hidden in."

Maverick shook his head. "Some old books, more old lace, vintage pictures."

"You never know about pictures. They could be

unimportant or pictures of someone famous. Books could be first editions, signed by an author, rare copies. The same with the tintypes." She looked over all the items and shook her head. "I hope the thumb drive wasn't in either of these boxes."

"If it was, they'll leave you alone." Lucas pushed around the items on the table.

"Do you get your money out of this stuff?" Maverick picked up a picture and looked at the back of it.

"Yes. Always. But not always right away. Sometimes it can take years. In the meantime, I move things around so I don't have the same merchandise sitting in the shop all the time. Though this was all free, so it will be all profit," Brooke said.

"Now the question is, did they get the thumb drive or not?" Maverick said.

"How did they know the boxes were delivered right then?" Brooke asked.

"They could be watching the store to see if any deliveries are made," Brad said.

"Yeah. Maybe Sarah has them on video, sitting in her shop watching the place."

"I'm headed over to the bakery to ask her if she'd let me see the video, and I'll take pictures of the patrons." Brad headed out of the store.

"It would have been so easy if we'd found a bloodied knife or a gun in one of these boxes."

Maverick pointed to the butter knives with the rest of the set of silverware.

"A little longer and sharper than that." Brooke called Josh and told him the news.

"Make sure you stay with the guys." Josh sounded worried, and she suspected he wanted to stop what he was doing and head straight home.

"I am. Brad went to the bakery across the street to see if anyone's been watching the shop from there and they've been caught on video."

"Good idea. We're going in to interrogate the first of the attempted robbers now. I'll let you know how it goes. And keep Maverick close. I'll return as soon as I can."

"He's right here with me. Good luck." Then she called Brad. "Do you see anyone who looks suspicious at the bakery?"

"I'm taking some selfies with all the delicious foods the bakery has."

She assumed he was taking picture of the customers, pretending to take selfies.

Brad finally returned to the house and said, "Sarah was too busy with customers to ask about the security video. I figure Josh can drop by and check on it." He showed some pictures of the patrons at the bakery shop to Brooke.

"No one who looks suspicious to me. A woman and her kids. An older couple. Two women friends. A single woman." Brooke halfway expected to see the guy who shot her sitting in there having a piece of pie, though she suspected he wouldn't get near her place again. Certainly not in broad daylight. "Wait." She peered closer at the single woman. A blond in a black, fluffy angora sweater, black skinny jeans, and high heels that would kill Brooke's arches. "She looks... familiar. I can't place her. She might have just been in my shop recently. You know what? I'll run over there and take a closer look at her. If I can have someone come with me."

"I'll go," Brad said.

Brooke and Brad took off through the courtyard to check out the woman at the bakery. She figured she could start up a conversation with her, asking her if she still needed a particular Santa, or was it a teacup she'd been looking for? If the woman said she was mistaken and hadn't been in her shop, Brooke would at least have a chance to see her close up.

As soon as Brooke and Brad entered the bakery, she noticed the woman in the picture Brad had shared with her wasn't there, but Sarah frantically waved them over.

Brooke had a bad feeling about this. She already could smell a man's scent in the bakery—the same man who had shot her in the attic. She quickly looked at the patrons there, but he wasn't among them.

"You've got to check out my security video," Sarah said. "This woman was having coffee and pie, and then this guy comes in, and she's angry, having a fit that he joined her here. It caught my attention, and a couple of my customers' also. Anyway, I was about to ask them to take it outside, but I grabbed a tray to clean a couple of tables instead, in case they settled down, so I could better make out what they were saying.

"When I got close, she motioned to your shop and said to the man, 'No thumb drive after stealing the boxes in front of God and everyone?' That worried me because you've had so much trouble lately. He said, 'How did you expect me to try to grab the boxes? And no. It wasn't in the two boxes. Do you know if Lee really put the thumb drive in one of them?'"

"That's the man who broke into my place and shot me," Brooke said, chills running up her spine. "He just stole my boxes of merchandise and dumped them down the street."

"He needs to be arrested. I've seen the woman in here before. The man, too, but he was with some other guy. I didn't think much of it because they always got coffee and baked goods. They took their time eating though. One time, I noticed one of the men going into your shop. I was busy after that. The woman said to the man, 'Your dead partner swore Lee dropped it into one of the boxes, but Pinky didn't tell me until *after* they were shipped off,'" Sarah told Brooke and Brad. "I left out the swear words.

"I never thought they'd be sitting over here watching your place. I'm so sorry. He sounded surly when he said, 'What do you want me to do about it?' I moved to the next table and slowly picked up the used pie plates and coffee mugs. 'Not bungle it like the last time,' she said. 'If I go down, you go down.' He cast her an evil smirk and glanced at me. I hurried to move to a table farther away to clean. The two of them gave me goose bumps. I was going to call you, or your detective, but then they left, and here you are."

"Thanks for all your help with this, though I hadn't meant for you to get involved."

"They involved me when they started coming here as part of their clandestine operation." Sarah glanced back at the door leading into the kitchen. "Don't tell Mr. Burns, or he'll try to arrest them himself."

Brooke gave her a hug and immediately called Josh with an update.

# CHAPTER 26

WHILE AT THE POLICE BUREAU, JOSH GOT ANOTHER call from Brooke. She was excited, telling him what Sarah, the owner of the bakery, had told her and shown her on the security video.

"They're gone now, but I recognized the man who shot me by sight and by his scent," she said. "I thought the woman seemed familiar. I'm sure now it was the woman I saw arguing with Mr. Lee at Gulliver's auction, though she had to be wearing a wig this time or had dyed her hair and cut it short."

"Adam and I are on our way. The Camaro they were driving was stolen and ditched about a half mile down the road. They must have had a getaway car there, just like the night they broke into your shop and shot you." Josh had already headed for his car, Adam hurrying after him. He was glad she hadn't confronted the woman and the man. Who knew how that would have gone down?

"We're headed back to the house. Brad's with me," Brooke said. "Sarah gave me a copy of the security video so you can look at it."

"See you soon."

A short while later, Josh and Adam arrived at the house. He and Adam went through the boxes Brooke had received from Phoenix, making sure no one, crooks included, had missed a thumb drive. Brooke folded her arms across her waist, head tilted to the side, looking very much like when he'd first met her and was questioning her about Jingles. Josh smiled at her and gave her a hug.

Then he and Adam reviewed the security video from the bakery. "That's the guy I saw running away from the shop," Josh said. "The woman confirmed that one of her henchman saw the murdered Mr. Lee hide the drive in one of the boxes. Since the other Mr. Lee sent them to you, we need to learn what his involvement is in all this. Do you have the business card from him, Brooke?"

"I kept it with me, planning to call him again when I thought about it." Brooke handed Josh the card.

"I'll use your phone in case he'll answer a call from you."

"Sure." Brooke handed her phone to Josh, and he called the number.

"Ms. Cerise," Mr. Lee said.

Josh was a little surprised when he got an answer, since Brooke's calls to Mr. Lee hadn't reached him.

"This is her mate, Josh Wilding, a police detective with the local police bureau. She says you're a wolf and someone she trusts, but I need to know what the hell is going on. You told her that her great-aunt had been involved with someone shady in Colombia. Then Brooke gets a delivery of clay sculptures filled with cocaine."

"Cocaine?" Mr. Lee sounded surprised.

"How did you know about it? Are you the one responsible for it?"

"A rogue wolf? No. I'm with the FBI, but I had been working undercover on this one. I learned about the cocaine shipment from my brother and diverted it, and we confiscated it."

"Well, apparently, not all of it." Josh was really irritated with the FBI over that.

"Is Brooke all right?"

"Hell no. Now we've got armed men looking for some thumb drive a Mr. Lee hid in one of the boxes you gave her. But we've discovered Mr. Lee was murdered before the auction."

There was a long pause.

"The boxes," Mr. Lee said.

"Hell yeah, the boxes," Josh said.

"The boxes haven't arrived yet at the shop?" Mr. Lee asked.

"Two of them finally did, but a man grabbed them and took off with them, then dumped the boxes on the side of the road. We have reason to believe the thumb drive wasn't in those two boxes. The other three boxes haven't come yet, but I suspect they'll be here any day. What about the woman who was berating you at the auction?"

"Daisy Gulliver. She's at the root of all this."

"So who are you really? Brooke was shot twice already over this business with the thumb drive."

"She's all right, isn't she?" Mr. Lee sounded shaken up.

"Luckily. What the hell is going on? Did you even know her family? The cashier wasn't even the cashier. The sales of the statues never went through."

"Listen, I'm on my way to catch a plane out to Portland. I'm in Eugene right now about another case I was wrapping up. It'll take me about an hour to reach your location. Just for your information, the Mr. Lee who was murdered was my identical twin brother. He was Mr. Gulliver's assistant, but he began learning about all the illegal stuff Gulliver was involved in. Murder, cocaine smuggling, you name it. I told my brother to quit the job, but he said it was too late. He knew too much. Through spy cameras, he was videotaping what was going on—some of the drug sales, including the cocaine shipment that was supposed to go to the antique store, some of the murders. My brother had the run of the mansion, and no one suspected him of anything."

"Yet he was murdered," Josh reminded him.

"I guess I should say until the end. I didn't know he had been murdered. Not until the day of the auction when he didn't show up. I was worried about him, but no amount of telling him to leave this business to law-enforcement agencies made an impact. Yes, I knew Brooke's family. My brother had sent her the invitation to come get the boxes of stuff for free and the wolf statues at a huge discount, but only for her. Gulliver was dead, and my brother was leaving the estate to move in with our sister. Though I suspect he would have ended up in the Witness Protection Program once the details of what went on came out. He was supposed to hand over the thumb drive to me at the auction. I had no idea he might have hidden it in one of the boxes. No one knew my brother had an identical twin."

"He would have given it to you, had he been alive, and it would never have gone to Brooke, I suspect," Josh said. "Maybe he was afraid that when he showed up at the auction, they might be on to him and search him for it. So he hid it in one of the boxes to retrieve when he met up with you before Brooke took possession of them."

"I'm thinking the same thing now. I searched his whole place, along with other members of the FBI, but we couldn't find it. We thought Daisy Gulliver had found it and destroyed it. Apparently not."

"Why would she be behind all this?" Josh asked.

"I suspect something on the thumb drive incriminates her. I'm boarding the plane now. I'll see you soon. At the shop?"

"Yes. Adam Holmes is here also, another wolf, and police detective. The DEA special agent running the cocaine investigation, Ethan Masterson, also a wolf, will probably join us. And my mate, who has been affected by all this."

"If I had known... I never intended for her to be involved in any of this."

"She tried calling you."

"I've been undercover. Be there soon."

---

Brooke was relieved that Mr. Lee was one of the good guys. She was a little surprised he was on the case when his brother had been murdered though.

"Are you all right?" Josh asked her, taking hold of her shoulders and rubbing them in a compassionate way.

"Yeah, and I'm hoping this will be resolved soon."

"Hell, me too."

"I reached Ethan," Adam said. "He's on his way."

"Good. He needs to be here for this," Josh said, "since he was involved in the cocaine bust."

"I called the local FBI, and they said they've talked to Mr. Lee," Adam said.

"That's good. That was going to be my next step," Josh said.

"Should we look for the safe?" Lucas asked Brad.

"Why don't you do that," Brooke said. "I would have thought the FBI would take Mr. Lee off the case because this is personal with him."

"True, just like it is for me though," Josh said.

"And me," Adam said. "These people can't do this to one of our kind without some payback."

"I, for one, am glad you guys are on my side." Normally, Brooke would be busy doing something with the merchandise in the shop, but knowing the person behind all this was most likely close by and still after the thumb drive they hadn't secured meant she couldn't stop thinking about it. She fixed everyone cups of coffee in the meantime.

Ethan showed up about a half hour later and wanted to see the boxes.

Smiling, Brooke shook her head.

"Hey, the more eyes on this, the better," Ethan said, smiling just as broadly. "Since no one's found the thumb drive." He looked over all the items but didn't find anything either.

"I was thinking of making everyone lunch once Mr. Lee gets here." She realized she needed to learn his first name.

"That works for me," Josh said, the others all agreeing.

When Mr. Lee did arrive, Josh got the door for him. Ethan snapped his fingers as soon as he saw him and said, "FBI. Special Agent Ben Lee. I remember a case you were on when I'd just joined the DEA. Hell, why didn't I remember that?"

Mr. Lee smiled. "You have a good memory. Can I see the boxes?"

Brooke sighed.

Mr. Lee began to sort through the stuff in the boxes. "I want to take down the woman who killed my brother."

"You said she was Mr. Gulliver's daughter. Ethan discovered she was in Paris at the time. But he had another daughter—" Brooke said.

"His stepdaughter, but she was adopted by him so she has his last name. Her biological father's name was Fern," Mr. Lee said. "She looked like she'd seen a ghost when she saw me at the auction. I knew she had my brother killed, but I was trying to find the evidence to put her away."

"That's the woman one of the perps we've taken into custody said hired them to get the thumb drive. Daisy Fern," Josh said.

"That's her," Mr. Lee said.

"So you were working undercover, assuming your twin's identity while you were at the auction," Brooke said.

"I wouldn't have done so if my brother had shown up, but I just knew something was wrong, and considering the information he was going to hand over to me, my concerns were valid. My brother wanted in the worst way to help me take Gulliver down for his criminal activities once he learned about them. Because Gulliver was targeting Ms. Ivy Cerise, I told him I'd handle it. But my brother was stubborn. They must have realized what he was up to and killed him."

"But who killed Gulliver?" Brooke asked.

"Possibly a man by the name of Ackerson," Mr. Lee said. "I suspect he killed my brother too. But Daisy Gulliver is the one behind all this."

"I still can't believe you knew a shipment of cocaine was in those boxes and you didn't alert us," Josh said, sounding furious.

She didn't blame Josh. They could have all been murdered over it.

"I warned Ms. Cerise that her great-aunt had been dealing with unsavory types in case she had any contact from these men. When Ivy died, my brother warned me that Gulliver had the shipment diverted from the antique shop to a different location. Gulliver was afraid whoever took over Cerise's Antique and Gift Shop could be a problem. We intercepted the shipment before it reached a warehouse. Apparently, they *hadn't* diverted all of the shipment and some of it ended up at the shop. We hadn't known about that.

"When Gulliver died, my brother told me he was afraid Daisy knew the feds were going to take her stepdad down. She was afraid she'd lose any inheritance if he went to prison and lost his estate over it. But I couldn't prove it. My brother told me he wanted to sell you the statues because your family had been so good to ours. And that there were five boxes of items you could sell for a goodly sum. I went to meet him at the auction, and everyone thought I was my brother. Daisy was shocked to see me. Everyone else was upset I had gotten to the auction late. Because I was involved in selling and giving the items to you, the culprits must have wrongly believed I—pretending to be my brother—had shipped the incriminating information to you. I would never have done that."

"Maybe the thumb drive is not in one of the boxes but in one of the wolf statues," Brooke said.

They all headed out to the courtyard and began searching the three statues for hidden compartments.

"Here!" Ethan said, opening a little compartment in the wolf leaning up against a light pole. "Well, no, nothing, but it is a secret hiding place."

Brooke looked over the wolf couple sitting on a park bench. "Ohmigod, this one has a hidden compartment underneath the bench. And…there's nothing in there either."

"This one has a hiding spot too," Josh said as he and Adam searched the wolf drinking out of the fountain sculpture. "It looks like they were made to conceal a house key. But no thumb drive is hidden here at the base of the wolf's paw."

They were all disappointed.

Trying to cheer everyone up, Brooke announced, "Let's have lunch at the house."

"Then I need to get with the local FBI agents and talk to them about what's going on. The DEA too," Mr. Lee said to Ethan.

"I'll drive you over, and we can meet with some folks," Ethan said.

"I'm going to hang out with you and Brooke, unless I get called in on a case," Adam said.

They all headed over to Brooke's house. She made introductions for Brad and Lucas and Maverick and Mr. Lee.

Lucas looked like he was about to burst with news. "I found it! A hidden safe behind a panel in the bookshelf."

For a second, Brooke thought he meant the thumb drive.

Everyone joined him in the living room, and Brooke shook her head. "I would never have figured that out."

"I was pulling out books and tapping on the wooden panels until I found one that sounded different."

"You're a genius," Brooke said.

"What's the combination?" Lucas tried to guess the combination as he twisted the knob.

"Now that I don't know. Use your wolf's sense of hearing." What Brooke really wanted to do was send everyone on their way and enjoy the rest of the day and night with Josh before the shop opened tomorrow. "There's a shelf by the checkout counter that has a secret compartment that conceals guns," she told Josh.

"Your great-aunt put that in?" he asked.

"She had to have. Anyway, the card that opens it is in the drawer of the checkout counter."

"That sounds good if you have any trouble while you're at the counter," Josh said.

"Right, since the police confiscated my frying pan."

Josh smiled at her.

Brooke went into the kitchen to make sandwiches for everyone. "Do corned beef sandwiches sound good to everyone?"

"Sounds good to me," Josh said.

Everyone agreed.

"I'll help you make lunch," Josh said.

"I'm going to crack open the safe." Lucas put his ear next to the combination dial and began spinning it. That was one thing about their exceptional hearing. They could even crack safes.

Brooke was getting ready to spread mayonnaise on the bread when Josh pulled her into his arms and kissed her.

She kissed him back. "Hmm, after lunch, I was thinking we don't need anyone to be here, since you're my protection."

He smiled. "I was thinking the same thing."

"I got it!" Lucas opened the safe.

They all went to see what was inside the safe.

Inside, they found diamonds and gold jewelry. It was a small safe, so nothing big was inside it, but it looked like the items could be worth some money. And she found Ivy's inventory lists.

"Wow," Lucas said.

"Nice find," Josh said.

"Did you write down the combination?" Brooke asked.

Lucas gave her the number and she made a note of it. Then Lucas closed the safe back up, and they finished making the sandwiches and sat down to eat.

When they were about finished, Adam got a call. "Hell, I'll be right in."

Everyone was waiting to hear what it was all about.

Adam smiled. "Who wants to interrogate Ackerson? He was just arrested after speeding near here, driving yet another stolen car, and the police officer recognized the police sketch we have of him."

"The guy at the bakery who was talking to Daisy and who shot me in the attic," Brooke said.

"Yep. He's the one." Adam smiled at Josh. "This couldn't have been better timing. Let's go see what he has to say."

"It's about damn time," Josh said, and Brooke hoped they could end this guy's crime spree and convict him for shooting her and for the other crimes he was involved in. And maybe, if they got lucky, he'd squeal on Daisy.

# CHAPTER 27

Brad, Lucas, and Maverick stayed with Brooke at the house while Josh, Adam, Ethan, and Mr. Lee went to the station to question Ackerman. Josh was hoping they'd finally get somewhere with the case, but he was glad Ackerman was now in custody.

Mr. Lee and Ethan watched the proceedings through the one-way mirror.

Cold blue eyes stared back at them, and like the sales-clerk had said at the one jewelry-store robbery, Ackerson had a dark-brown beard and mustache, his hair dark brown. He was wearing blue jeans, heavy black boots, and a dark-gray parka, just as he had in the robberies and in Brooke's shop.

Josh recognized Ackerson's scent from the two armed jewelry-store robberies.

Josh stood near the wall, a cup of coffee in hand. Adam had a file in his hand and stood near the table, both towering over Ackerson.

"I didn't do nothing." Ackerson leaned back in his chair, his arms folded across his chest.

"We know you robbed two jewelry stores." Adam started out with those charges they were filing against Ackerson. "Your cohorts both named you as the guy who set it all up."

"Hell, I don't know what you're talking about."

"In addition to that, you were identified by witnesses at both scenes," Adam said.

"Did Daisy hire you for both those jobs? Besides the one where you shot the owner of Cerise's Antique and Gift Shop twice?" Josh asked.

Ackerson's eyes widened. At least that got the reaction Josh was looking for. He was sure Ackerson wanted to deny he'd been shooting at a woman and had been trying to kill a big, angry guard dog instead.

"She was wounded, twice. You and Pinky both attempted to kill her," Josh said.

"We have all the evidence. The casings. The photos of her injuries. The weapons used in the crime," Adam said.

Josh didn't glance at Adam, even though he wanted to see if Adam had made it up or had some news he'd forgotten to tell Josh.

"No way in hell," Ackerson said.

"No? She was trying to hide behind the crates and boxes so you couldn't shoot her again," Josh said.

"It was a big damn dog, and he knocked me down. He was trying to kill me."

"There wasn't any dog in the attic. She doesn't own one. You shot the owner of the shop, and she gave your description to the police sketch artist." Adam showed him the sketch.

"That could be one of any number of men."

"What were you looking for in the attic?" Josh asked.

Ackerson frowned and didn't say anything.

"Let me help you out. You were looking for a box from Gulliver's estate," Adam said. "You mentioned it when you and Pinky were looking for it. While you were in the shop."

Not exactly, but if it helped to move the interrogation along…

Ackerson remained mum. He must have realized he shouldn't have said anything about being in Brooke's attic in the first place.

"She recognized you as the man who carried in the box the mail carrier delivered earlier in the day. She saw you casing the shop, entering all the off-limits rooms, but you couldn't get into the attic because it was locked," Josh said. "She thought you'd been chivalrous when you carried the box for her. Then she discovered you'd trespassed in all the rooms where you shouldn't have been, and she had another impression of you. A potential thief.

"When she heard you and Pinky in the shop, destroying her property, she called the police from the attic. You told Pinky you should have checked that room first since the light was on and the door was open. She heard everything you said. She told the police you broke the window with a brass lamp after you couldn't get the window open."

Ackerson tapped his fingers on the table.

"You grabbed a couple of boxes at the antique shop in a stolen Camaro and ditched the boxes, their contents, and the stolen car, then went to see Daisy Gulliver at the bakery across the street from the antique shop. We have video of you speaking with the woman who hired you," Adam said. "You didn't find the thumb drive in either of the boxes from the Gulliver estate."

Ackerson flinched, then looked down at the table.

"You didn't take Pinky to the hospital," Josh said.

"He bled out."

"Not for a while. You dumped him in an alley. If you'd taken him to a hospital or even called 911 so someone could give him emergency medical care, he could have survived.

We found your prints in the abandoned car and his blood. It's all over for you," Josh said. "Unless you can give us something on the woman who orchestrated this, and we can press charges against her."

"Immunity?"

Josh shook his head. No way would they offer him a deal like that after he'd shot Brooke and fired shots in one of the jewelry stores. The guy was bad news. "Maybe a lesser sentence. But we need the person behind all this. The mastermind."

"Hell. She goes by the name of Daisy Fern because Fern was her biological father's name and most people don't know that. Randolph Gulliver adopted her, so she's Daisy Gulliver. A thumb drive's in one of those boxes shipped to the antique shop."

Josh frowned at him. "What's on the thumb drive?"

"Something incriminating, she figures. She was ready to shoot me herself when we didn't get the job done. It wasn't my fault Pinky was so clumsy he cut himself badly on the broken window."

"How do you know her?" Adam asked.

"I did a lot of work for her rich daddy. If you ask me"—Ackerson leaned into the table, pressing his arms against it—"she killed her daddy for the money and for the power." He sat back in his chair and stretched his legs out and crossed them at the ankles. "They didn't get along. She was always saying she wanted to kill him for some reason or another."

"Did she? Kill him? Or hire someone to do it?" Josh asked.

"I'd say she had it in her to kill him, personal vendetta because she wanted to run the business and he wouldn't let her, but she likes to hire us to do her dirty work."

"What about his assistant, Mr. Lee?" Josh hoped they could catch Daisy and put her in jail before she hired any more thugs to go after Brooke and her store, or anyone else.

"She said Lee was gathering damning evidence against her daddy and he had to go. But I think Lee gathered evidence against her, and that's why she's so anxious to get the drive."

"Who killed Lee?" Josh asked.

Ackerson shrugged. "You got 'em locked up, don't you? Howie and that other joker? They might have even killed her daddy. They're both from Phoenix."

"And you?" Adam asked.

"Me too, but I didn't do them."

"What about the jewelry stores?" Adam asked.

"What about them?"

"Did she hire you for those too?" Josh asked.

"Nah. Those were my idea. I'll testify she hired me for the job at the antique shop. Once you catch her, she said she'd give me up to you, if I hadn't been caught already, so I might as well do it first and get something out of it. Hell, those other yahoos got themselves arrested right away. You really ought to look at their alibis for the times of Gulliver's and Lee's murders."

"What about yours?" Josh asked.

Ackerson smiled. "I was in jail both times."

Josh made a note of it. He was damn glad they had Ackerson in custody, and the other men too. Now they had to get that thumb drive and arrest Daisy.

When they were done interrogating Ackerson, they went in to see Howie again.

"Your partner, Matson, says you were the one who was supposed to kill Ms. Cerise."

Howie didn't say anything, his arms folded across his chest, his gaze on the floor.

"We know you killed another man, and charges are pending on that." Adam gave him the date Randall Gulliver was murdered, without context, and asked, "Where were you that day?"

Howie frowned. "In Phoenix. I wasn't anywhere near here."

"Where in Phoenix?" Josh asked.

"Hell, that particular day, I don't know. I didn't get up here until about two weeks ago though."

"On this job for Daisy Fern."

"Yeah."

Adam gave him the date of the day before the auction and asked him where he was that day.

"In Phoenix still. I told you I didn't come up here any earlier than that. Yeah, I was incarcerated here before, but that's been several months back."

"Where in Phoenix?"

"How would I know?"

"So no alibis for the date and time of the murders of Mr. Gulliver or Mr. Lee, his assistant?" Josh asked.

Howie's eyes widened.

"We have word you were hired by this same woman to kill them," Adam said.

"I want a lawyer."

"That's your right, but we found the murder weapon used in both murders, and your fingerprints were all over it," Josh said. "If you want to tell us why Daisy wanted you to murder the two men, then maybe we can ask for a lesser sentence. But we want the one who hired you for the jobs."

Howie ran his hands through his hair. "I still want a lawyer."

Unable to get any further with him, they interrogated Matson again.

He was stony-faced and said, "I'm not talking to you without my lawyer."

"That's your right," Adam said, and they left the interview room.

"Did they find the weapons discharged in Brooke's shop?" Josh asked Adam.

"Did they find the weapons used in the murders of Gulliver and Lee?" Adam asked him.

Josh smiled.

Adam's expression matched his. "We make a great pair of detectives. I'll miss you when you retire." He let out his breath. "I've got to get back to work."

"We can handle everything now. Maybe tomorrow around the time the mail carrier comes, you can drop by and give us some backup in case we have trouble," Josh said.

Ethan and Mr. Lee joined them. "You call all of us and we'll be there. I'm going to take Ben to meet with my boss," Ethan said.

"I'm headed home," Josh said, then he shook Mr. Lee's hand. "Good to meet you and hope we wrap this up soon."

"Same here," Mr. Lee said.

When Josh returned home, Lucas greeted him. "Did you get the truth out of him?"

"Some of it. We just need to arrest Daisy and find that thumb drive."

"Can I return tomorrow and help some more?" Lucas asked.

"Yes," Brooke said. "The shop will be open, and you can help organize more merchandise."

"If you need me again, don't hesitate to call on me," Brad said.

"We will, thanks," Josh said.

Lucas said, "Same time tomorrow?"

"For breakfast?" Brooke asked.

"That would be great."

Brooke would have to get more food soon. "See you tomorrow, Lucas."

After Brad and Lucas left, Brooke was going to check out the value of more of the jewelry, but Josh had other ideas. He grabbed her up, tossed her over his shoulder, and headed back to the bedroom. It was past time to make love to his mate, and she was all for it.

# CHAPTER 28

EARLY THE NEXT MORNING, THE ALARM WENT OFF, AND both Josh and Brooke groaned. No way did he want to open the shop today. All he wanted to do was stay in bed with Brooke.

Josh kissed her. "It's going to be a long week before the shop is closed for two days after we're off for Christmas, but with all the help we've had, we're going to spend more time just…doing this."

"I'm all for it. Shoot." Brooke released Josh and scrambled to get out of bed. "Lucas is coming for breakfast and Adam, too, and then he's back to his real work. We're wearing Christmas sweaters today at the shop."

"I don't have one. I've never worn a Christmas sweater." Josh supposed he could wear the red sweater his brother had picked up for him.

"Hold on." Brooke grabbed a package from under the tree, returned to the bedroom, and handed it to Josh.

He was already wearing a pair of jeans, and he smiled. "Then I need to give you a Christmas present early."

"Sounds like a great idea."

He opened his present while she pulled on her own sweater of a Christmas tree with lights that said: *Get lit*. His was blue and white, with a picture of a reindeer skiing down a slope wearing ski glasses.

"I love this." Anything reindeer was perfect. Why hadn't he thought of that before? He gave her a hug.

"Are you sure? We could always give it to Maverick as a Christmas present."

"No way." Josh pulled the sweater over his head and sat down to put on his socks and boots. "I'll get your present in a minute."

She had just put on her boots when Josh returned to the bedroom with a present for her. She eagerly opened it and laughed. The sweater of a reindeer had a big red nose and Christmas lights tangled in his antlers. "I. Love. This."

"You're part of a reindeer family now, besides being part of a wolf family."

She switched sweaters and hugged and kissed him. "I love my sweater, and I'm so thrilled to be part of the reindeer family."

"We need to get one for Maverick too."

"I did. I just didn't expect you to get me one. I love it."

---

After they had an early breakfast of pancakes and sausage with Lucas and Adam, Josh and Brooke headed over to the shop while Adam went to work and Lucas updated Brooke's website at the house. She was so excited because she'd received a text saying the men were coming to pick up the imperial vases. Having that done would be such a relief. Once the money cleared, she and Josh would be well off—secure if the shop didn't do well or the reindeer ranch fell on hard times.

She'd barely opened the shop when the men arrived to pay for the Chinese vases and take possession of them.

"I've got to handle this transaction," she told Josh.

"Do you need my help?" He looked like he wanted to be her bodyguard detail, which, after all that had happened, she totally understood.

"Yes, if you'll watch the shop while I do this."

"I'll sure do that."

"Thanks." She led the men to her house and served them wassail and tea cakes, then retrieved the imperial vases for them to see. She couldn't believe this was really happening, and she was thrilled.

Lucas seemed fascinated while he enjoyed the wassail and tea cakes too.

The Chinese antiquities expert verified they were authentic. Yes! Then he paid Brooke the funds in a wire transfer. She was glad to have had the vases for a short while and gladder still to give them to someone who would share them with the world instead of keeping them sealed in a steamer trunk in a dusty attic. And to have all that money! She wanted to dance around the room and howl.

She couldn't be happier to thank the men and see them leave with the vases in hand. All smiles, she escorted them back through the shop and out through the front door where they strode off with their treasure. She joined Josh behind the counter and hugged him, not caring that he was trying to check out a couple of ladies' merchandise.

"All done?" he asked, smiling down at her.

"Yeah. I'll cancel the insurance on them. The buyer will have to insure them now." That was what she was doing when the door to the shop opened. It was the mail carrier with three boxes.

"I'll get them," Josh said, handing over the register to Brooke.

As soon as he signed for them, he nodded to Brooke. They were the ones Daisy had to be after.

Her customers left the shop with their packages in hand.

Josh and Brooke moved the boxes to the office, and Josh immediately called Adam. "The boxes are here. Okay. See you soon."

She was already opening the first of the boxes and was going through the stuff as quickly as she could. "Ohmigod." She smiled to see the Steiff mohair Christmas reindeer, the tag saying its name was Renny. He was just adorable.

Josh glanced over at her.

"Nothing. Just...don't look." She slipped it into a sack and set it aside for Josh for Christmas. "Looks like all kinds of fun little trinkets to sell. Vintage Christmas ornaments, some new ones, old keys, just a mixture. No thumb drive."

"Same here. Just more stuff," Josh said about the box he'd opened.

Brooke frowned at him. "Some of which might be valuable."

"Of course. Until then?"

"It's just stuff. You're right."

Josh was cutting open the last box when they heard someone come into the shop. He pulled his gun out.

She stilled his hand. "It might be a customer."

He hid his gun but went out with her to see it was indeed a couple of ladies visiting her shop. She smiled at them. "Is there anything you're looking for in particular?"

"No, just browsing for now. You don't have your reindeer calves here today, do you?" one of the ladies asked. "We saw them on the news."

"No." Brooke smiled again. "Not today." She was

beginning to think they needed a permanent reindeer resident here.

Then Ethan walked into the shop, to her surprise, but she was glad to see him. "I was in the area, and Adam called and said the boxes had come in. I thought you could use my help if you had any more trouble," Ethan said.

"Thanks. I'm glad you're here, just in case."

The door jingled again, and Brooke looked up, expecting more customers, but it was Adam. "Did you find anything in the last boxes?" he asked.

Josh had just finished with the last one.

"Nothing in them. I'm closing early for Christmas Eve. Most everyone doing last-minute shopping is at the mall or other big stores," Brooke said.

"Once we get this wrapped up, we need to celebrate," Adam said.

"I'm with you there." Brooke hoped they'd catch Daisy before long.

"You call us if you have any trouble," Adam said.

Ethan agreed. "All of us. Mr. Lee included."

When the men left the shop, Josh pulled her over to the arch where she'd hung mistletoe, having forgotten it was up there, and then he kissed her. "I've wanted to do that since I first saw the mistletoe hanging over the archway."

She eagerly kissed him back when they didn't have any customers to watch them. "It's past lunchtime. Did you want to get something to eat? Something light because we'll be having baked pomegranate-glazed salmon for Christmas Eve dinner with Maverick."

"Sure. Do you want me to order something?"

"No, that's okay. Why don't we just grab a sandwich at

the bakery across the street? I could never do it when it was just me here, but I've always wanted to try her holiday sandwiches. She's closing her shop early too. She's got braised short rib with melted mozzarella and roasted red pepper sandwiches that I want to have."

Josh smiled down at her, rubbing her arms. "And you had me go out and get you regular meals for lunch?"

"Sure, because I'd have lunch and dinner on you that way."

He laughed. "You got it. Why don't you come with me? You don't have any customers right now. We'll get our sandwiches and bring them right back. Or we can just order them, and I'll run over and pick them up."

"Order them, and we can run over to get them. I can wish Sarah and her husband a Merry Christmas before we both close our shops."

Josh got on the phone and placed the order.

They didn't have any more customers, and they still had two hours before the shop closed. She might close earlier next year, if business was this dead. The bakery had at least a few customers, probably getting lunches or treats to go.

Brooke began to really sort through the last of the boxes Mr. Lee's brother wanted her to have.

"What do you want me to do?" Josh asked.

"Can you move the Christmas items to one of the shelf units? Then when we open after Christmas, I can make that our Christmas sale shelf."

"Sure." Josh got busy on that.

She loved how helpful he could be.

Inside the box, she discovered a smaller box, and when she opened it, she found thirty marbles—vintage and probably worth a fortune. She whooped!

Josh turned and smiled at her. "Good, huh?"

"I'll say. Mr. Lee had told me the items in the box wouldn't be worth much to collectors, but they could be worth something to me. They are worth lots to both collectors and me!"

Josh came over and checked out the box, then kissed her.

She smiled. "I should have asked Mr. Lee about not being charged for the wolf statues when he was here."

"Give him a call now." Josh went back to moving things from one shelf to another.

She called Mr. Lee, and he answered right away. "Any trouble?"

"Uh, no. I just found vintage marbles in one of the boxes. Did your brother know I collected them?"

"Yes. Several times over the years during the summers when you were gone, your parents had him over for dinner. He enjoyed the wolf camaraderie. He didn't join the pack, but he thought the world of your family. They often mentioned you and how proud of you they were."

Brooke wiped away tears.

"Whenever I had a chance to visit with my brother during the summer, they'd have both of us over. As Mr. Gulliver's assistant, my brother didn't have much time to himself, but when he had the opportunity to visit with your parents, he did."

"But I didn't pay for the wolf statues."

"He was cleaning house, knowing when he had enough evidence against Mr. Gulliver, he'd be leaving. He wanted to tell you himself the story behind the treasures he left for you. He wanted you to have them. When I found out he had been murdered, I wanted you to have the statues as a gift from our family to yours."

Josh's phone rang, and he answered it. "Our sandwiches are ready. I'll just run and get them."

Brooke nodded to Josh. "The man who took my credit card number wasn't a real cashier," she said to Mr. Lee.

"No. He was another federal agent, a friend of mine, there as backup."

"I wish I could have given your brother a hug for his kindness. Thanks for carrying out his wishes. If you don't have any plans, would you like to have Christmas Eve dinner with us?"

"I would be delighted."

"We'll have dinner at—" She noticed that the mechanic, Randy Winters, who had been taking care of her great-uncle's cars and truck had parked the Ferrari in front of the shop. She'd meant for him to drive it around to the house and hide it in the garage. She hoped she could reach Randy in time and tell him to move it to the garage before Josh saw it. Then Maverick pulled into the parking space next to it. Smiling, he looked thrilled to be driving the vintage Corvette.

The door jingled open, and Brooke saw the woman from the auction, her hair long and black, her spiky heels clicking on the wooden floor, her gaze shifting from Brooke to the boxes from the Gulliver estate. It was Daisy Gulliver.

"She's here," Brooke whispered to Mr. Lee on the phone. "Where's Josh?"

"Across the street getting our sandwiches."

"Do you have a gun you can easily get to without arousing suspicion?"

The shelf! "Yes." She loved her great-aunt for being pre-pared. Brooke knew how to shoot a gun at cans. People were a different story.

"If you can safely get to it, do so. We're headed back to your place. Don't hang up! Adam's calling Josh to tell him the trouble you're in. He's closest to your location for now."

Daisy pulled out a gun and pointed it at Brooke. "Hand over the thumb drive."

"I have the FBI on the line, and they've just notified the police detective across the street you're here. The thumb drive wasn't in any of the boxes."

Keeping her eye on the woman, Brooke set her phone on the counter and pulled the security card out of the drawer and stuck it in the porcelain bowl on top. Then she slid the bowl across the top, and the shelf opened. Before she could grab the gun, Daisy glanced back out the glass door and cursed. She raced out the door. She couldn't get away!

Brooke ran after her, gun in hand, not sure what she was going to do about it. She couldn't shoot the woman in the back. Then Daisy grabbed the keys from a startled-looking Randy, jumped into the Ferrari, and nearly ran over Josh, who was running across the street to stop her.

As soon as Daisy peeled out of there, Josh jumped into the passenger's side of the Corvette, and Maverick and he sped off after Daisy.

Police sirens were wailing in the distance. Brooke stood on the sidewalk, gun in hand, watching as Josh and Maverick chased after Josh's Christmas present. She prayed no one would be injured or killed and the vintage cars wouldn't be damaged. And that Daisy would be arrested and jailed this time!

"Hell," Josh said, his heart racing, Maverick's too, as they turned down another street, trying to keep up with his Ferrari. "If she destroys my Christmas present, she'd better get life."

Maverick smiled darkly.

Josh asked, "What were you and Randy doing here with the cars anyway?"

"We were delivering your Christmas present. I was going to give Randy a ride to the mall for some last-minute Christmas shopping afterward. His wife was picking him up after that."

"On Christmas Eve?"

"Yeah. Randy says that's when the best early sales are." Maverick took another hairpin turn to keep up with Daisy. Thankfully, traffic hadn't been too bad, with a lot of the shops in the area closing early.

Then they saw a roadblock ahead.

Hell, would the woman give up or plow through the roadblock? They saw Adam and Ethan's vehicles, along with three police cars, and three more were following Maverick.

"I hope they know you're with me," Maverick said. "I can see me getting tickets for speeding, reckless driving, failure to stop at stop signs, and half a dozen other reasons."

"Adam will tell them we're in the Corvette in pursuit of Daisy." They had her blocked in, but would she wreck Josh's car in one last senseless act of revenge?

Josh's hands were fisted, his muscles tense as she slammed on her brakes—*his* car's brakes, technically—and spun the car around. *Hell.* Then she stopped the car and fled on foot.

Josh knew he had to take chase, though he wanted to check out his car.

Maverick pulled the Corvette next to Josh's car. "I'll take care of the Ferrari. Go get her, Josh."

Josh jumped out of the car and took off running. Adam soon joined him, other police officers in pursuit.

Daisy had disappeared into one of the shops, Josh figured. At least with their wolves' sense of smell, they'd locate her before the officers did.

"In there," Josh said and ran toward a stationery store. A sign said it was closing in fifteen minutes. He and Adam barged inside.

Wearing a green apron and a red Santa's hat, the clerk was wringing her hands and said, "We're closing in fifteen minutes." She motioned with her head in the direction they thought Daisy had gone.

Josh and Adam had their guns out. "Leave the store," Josh ordered the clerk, showing his badge.

The woman hurried out, and they began to search the premises for Daisy. It was easy to find her trail, using their sense of smell, and it led them to the women's restroom.

Adam motioned for Josh to go first.

Josh sure the hell hoped he wasn't going to take some bullets on this one when he was planning to have a lovely Christmas Eve and Christmas Day with Brooke.

He pushed open the door. There were no windows in the restroom, thankfully. He began shoving stall doors open and found one that was locked.

"You can come out now. You're not going anywhere," Josh said, he and Adam waiting for her to comply before he kicked in the door.

The lock clicked, and the door opened.

"Put the gun on the floor," Josh said.

Red-faced, Daisy put the 9mm gun on the floor.

"Kick it away from yourself," Josh said.

She did, and Adam retrieved it.

Then the police joined them while Adam was tying Daisy's hands behind her back with a plastic tie. Josh read her rights to her, which reminded him of Brooke telling him what her rights were when he'd questioned her about Jingles.

Then they took Daisy away in one of the patrol cars. Josh immediately called Brooke while he and Adam headed back to where the Ferrari and Maverick were waiting for them.

Adam looked over the two cars, the Corvette and the Ferrari, while more of the officers joined them to admire them.

"You have all the luck," Adam said and slapped Josh on the back.

Josh had to admit Adam was right.

On the phone, Brooke said to Josh, "Tell Adam he has to come for Christmas Eve dinner. Mr. Lee and Ethan are here babysitting me, and they have no other plans for tonight."

"All right, honey. Are you okay?"

"Yeah, are you? Maverick said he rescued your Christmas present."

Josh laughed. "Yeah, and Daisy's now in custody. See you in a minute." He turned to Adam, "We want you to join all of us for a salmon dinner."

"I guess that means you're retiring for good now," Adam said to Josh. "The upside of all this is we caught all the bad guys, but the downside is—"

"We might not be working on cases together at the department, but you know I'll always be there to consult for you. You're free to visit us anytime you want to get together, wolf runs and otherwise," Josh said.

"You're right. I'll certainly take you up on it."

Josh got a call from Jefferson, and he put it on speaker-phone. "What have you got for us?"

"We've got the guns from Ackerson's luggage in his car. Ballistics prove the bullets he used are the same as some of the rounds fired in Ms. Cerise's attic and some of the rounds fired in the jewelry-store robbery."

"We need to find out if it was also used in Michael Lee's murder," Adam said.

"Yes, sir. The gun they confiscated from Ms. Gulliver will also be tested against the shell casings and rounds that killed her stepfather."

"Thanks, Jefferson. Is there anything else?"

"Nothing at the moment, but I thought you'd want to know."

"We sure did. Thanks again. And Merry Christmas to you."

"You too, sir."

When they ended the call, Josh told Adam they'd meet him for dinner at Brooke's place.

"I'll grab some more salmon steaks for dinner before I come," Maverick said and drove off in his Corvette. Classy.

Josh headed home in his Ferrari. Brooke was waiting for him outside her shop, and he parked, jumped out of his car, and hurried to pull her into his arms to give her a hug. "I swear this better be the last time I'm away from you when you are in trouble."

"Where are our sandwiches?"

Josh chuckled. "Sarah said she'd save them for us. She'd deliver them, but it's kind of dangerous at your shop."

"Not any longer."

# CHAPTER 29

THAT NIGHT, BROOKE AND JOSH PREPARED THE Christmas Eve salmon dinner, and after everyone ate, they had a special cake Sarah's husband baked for Brooke as thanks for sending all the traffic their way when the reindeer visited and for buying so many treats from Sarah for her customers. After the meal, Brooke, Josh, and their guests watched *A Christmas Story*, which had Ethan, Mr. Lee, Josh, Maverick, and Adam all commenting on the "shoot your eye out" part because they'd all had BB guns growing up.

Then they took a run in Forest Park later that night as wolves: red wolves and a Tibetan. That made for the best Christmas Eve ever—a celebration everyone would always remember. The culmination of solving some of the recent crimes they'd been investigating. Making a new wolf friend who was a Tibetan wolf from Maryland. Finding some closure in the case involving Brooke. Her neighbors would be happy about that. Since Ben Lee was from out of town and because the other guys were bachelors and had no real plans for Christmas lunch, Brooke invited them to eat with them, with the provision that they watch *It's a Wonderful Life* with her.

Once everyone had finished their brandy eggnog and had left the house, it was Brooke and Josh's time, and she was ready to make the most of it. "Ready for some Christmas Eve loving?" She pulled Josh into her arms and kissed his mouth, tonguing him. Even that simple action sparked a deeper need to possess, to claim him, to have him filling her wet, feminine sheath with his growing cock.

With the lights sparkling on the tree and the fire blazing in the fireplace, she was eager to enjoy her mate in every way possible.

"We had fun, didn't we?" Josh slid his hands over her shoulders and gently massaged them, kissing her mouth again, hot passion igniting her blood as his hard body grew harder and pressed against her softness.

"Yeah," she said. "I had to invite the guys for Christmas Eve for all their help and because they didn't have anywhere to really be."

He nuzzled her jaw, his eyes closed, breathing in her scent. "We're wolves. A pack. It was great. And we have time for this. Tomorrow will be fun, and once everyone leaves, we'll be back to this again." He smiled. "I can guarantee it."

"Good. That's that I wanted to hear." She thought they were going to the bedroom until Josh pulled the wolf blanket off the couch. Individual wolf squares bordered the main wolf couple in the center—the alpha pair—and he turned it over on the carpet near the fireplace, facedown so they wouldn't see the wolves watching them. She smiled.

He slid his hands up her sweater and over her breasts, his face slanting over hers to capture her lips. The twinkling Christmas lights and fire reflecting off their skin made the setting feel fairylike, magical. His dark-brown eyes gazed down into her green ones before he gave her another searing kiss. Her heart—and his—were pounding furiously. Aroused. Excited.

Their lips still pressing together, he pulled her black lace bra down, exposing her breasts to the inside of her sweater, the fabric soft and caressing, his touch on her breasts tantalizing.

She breathed in the heavenly scent of him, all man and wolf, raw and primal, and she was ready to give in to the lust consuming her. She ached for him in all the sensitive, feminine places.

He tasted sweet and creamy from the brandy eggnog they'd had, almost floral, lively, delicious.

"Hmm, you taste so good," he murmured against her mouth.

"So do you." And then she tasted him again, rubbing her body against his, ready to strip and do this, finish off the night with a hot-blooded climax, climb into bed, snuggle with her loving mate, and listen for Santa and his reindeer high above the rooftops.

He moved his hands to her jeans skirt and unfastened it, pulling it down her hips and letting it slide the rest of the way to puddle at her feet. "Have I ever told you I love your lace undergarments?" He ran his hands over her breasts, his palms doing a teasing number on her sensitive nipples.

"Hmm, no, but I suspected so." She ran her hand over his arousal pressing against the zipper of his jeans, and he groaned. "Did I ever tell you I love the way you fill out your boxer briefs?"

He chuckled. She smiled, then unfastened his jeans and pulled them down over his lean hips.

Before they tackled their boots, he slid her sweater over her head, her breasts exposed, her bra still fastened. He leaned down and kissed a breast, his hands cupping both of them under her bra, and she was in heaven.

"Beautiful," he said.

"Hmm, so are you." She pulled his sweater over his head, dropped it next to hers on the floor near the blanket, and ran her hands up his abs, loving the feel of his hard chest and soft skin against the palms of her hands.

He sat down on the chair, intending to remove his boots, but she did it for him while he combed his fingers through her hair. It felt good, and she wanted him to keep it up, but she wanted them naked even more. She slid his pants off the rest of the way.

Then he pulled her onto his lap and removed her boots and unfastened her bra. His hands on her breasts, he kissed her neck and shoulder, sliding one of his hands down her panties. He found her clit and began to stroke. She leaned back against him and spread her legs. He kept up the strokes, kissing her neck, her ear, his free hand caressing her breast. She felt exposed and sexy and loved.

"Oh, Josh," she moaned as her blood heated and she craved completion. A euphoric jolt coursed through her, and she moaned with ecstasy, the climax hitting her with a rush of exquisite contractions.

Her breathing ragged, she arched her back against him. He kissed her shoulder, her neck, her ear. His erection nudged at her buttocks, provocative and clearly ready for more action. She was on top of the world and then falling in a cloak of warmth and serenity.

---

Josh moved her off his lap and rose to his feet, pulling off her wet black lace panties as she pulled off his boxer briefs. And then they were on the blanket by the fire. She spread her legs for him. He centered himself between her legs, his cock throbbing with need. He kissed her with deliberate, measured kisses, wanting the moment to last, their first Christmas together.

Her teeth grazed his lips, and he licked hers back, tasting, teasing, and then devouring them. Desire welled up in him, the need to claim her as strong as it was the first time they'd mated, as if the wolf connection they made would never get old. Hungry for her, he pushed into her, joining her, mate to mate.

His breathing husky, he began to thrust. He lifted her buttocks so she was pressed against him, and he drove in deeper. She incited him to take his fill and to pleasure her just as much. She was soft, willing; he was hard, eager.

Their pheromones were at an all-time high, and he felt the ending coming. He tried to stop it, tried to control it, but there was no stopping the intensity of the orgasm that hit, filling her. He continued to thrust, and her body milked him dry. For a moment, he rested on her, not believing their initial meeting would have led to this.

"You are exquisite." He kissed her nose and then her mouth.

"Hmm, so are you."

He smiled and helped her up, intending to take her to the bedroom, when she glanced at the clock and smiled. "It's time for bed."

"Then you'll be ready for some more of this." She kissed his nipples before she pulled away to grab their clothes.

"I am always ready for more of this." He kissed her nipples, licking and sucking. "Always." A promise he meant to keep.

Christmas morning arrived way too soon. They woke late and scrambled to get showers and dress because Maverick would be arriving momentarily.

The doorbell rang, and Josh gave Brooke a hug and a kiss. "Merry Christmas, honey."

"Merry Christmas." She gave him a big hug back.

Then he hurried to open the door for his brother. "Merry Christmas, Brother. The Corvette looks good."

"All revved up and raring to go," Maverick told Josh, then saw Brooke and gave her a hug.

"I'd say we found our own treasure in Brooke joining our family," Josh said.

Brooke smiled and fixed everyone eggnog. "The cars will win the guys over every time." She handed Maverick a big Christmas card.

When he opened it, he found the title to the car. He couldn't have looked any more thrilled and gave her another hug.

Brooke handed a Christmas card to Josh, and he found the title to the Ferrari inside.

"Hot damn, honey. Thanks so much." He gave her a hot, steamy kiss, and she wanted to take this to the bedroom.

"I'm glad Daisy didn't wreck it before you got to enjoy driving it." She gave him another present.

"I haven't given you yours yet."

"This goes with the car."

He opened the package and found a vintage-washed baseball cap with a Ferrari embroidered on it. He quickly put it on and smiled at her, and she led him into the garage so she could take a picture of him at the steering wheel, looking as though he was ready to take it for a spin.

"You can take me for a ride in it later to see the Christmas lights."

"You've got a deal."

They went back into the house, and Maverick handed her a package. Inside was a sign for her shop, beautifully hand-carved with two wolves sitting together, and another: SOME OF MY BEST FRIENDS ARE WOLVES.

"*I love this.* Thanks so much! You're going to have to make some of the *best friends are wolves* signs for other wolves, because any who visit the shop are sure to want one. They're not getting mine." She gave Maverick a hug and pointed to a red and green package under the tree. "That's yours. You need to open it now."

Maverick did and found his very own reindeer sweater.

"You've got to put it on."

"I'm glad to." Maverick pulled off his sweatshirt and pulled on his sweater.

She snapped a shot of him. "Looks great on you."

Maverick laughed and handed her a reindeer Christmas card, naturally. Inside it had a gift certificate for any and all reindeer she wanted to showcase at her place anytime of the year.

She laughed. "This is precious. I will be taking you up on it."

"I sure hope so. You have been the best thing yet for business."

Then Josh gave her gifts: a beautiful scarf in blues, a cashmere cardigan poncho, slipper boots, and a blanket for the couch to wrap themselves in on cold nights while they cuddled and watched a movie with a fire crackling in the fireplace. He even got them travel thermoses engraved with His/Hers and red wolves.

She showed him a Weber charcoal grill she'd bought for him, grill equipment, and an apron that said: *Mr. Good Lookin' is Cookin'.*

He chuckled. "I love it. What's this?"

Inside one of the big pockets, he found the Steiff Christmas reindeer.

"That was what I found in one of the boxes I opened, but I didn't want you to see it."

"Vintage and worth a fortune."

"Could be."

"I love it, so it's worth lots to me." He set it on the garland on the fireplace mantel.

"Now that you're part of the household, I expect you to grill meals," Brooke told him.

"Gladly."

Brooke gave Maverick another gift, a hat like Josh's, except it had a vintage Corvette on it. "I'll have to take a picture of you in your car a little later." Then she motioned to a taller package by the tree. "For both of you."

Maverick and Josh opened it and laughed when they found a reindeer statue, a heated birdbath, a starter kit of birdseed, and birdseed hangers resting in the dish.

Brooke started making ham-and-cheese omelets but saw a big snowman Christmas card for her sitting near the fridge. She opened it and found a gift certificate for one completely redesigned kitchen. "Yes! I was so afraid the stove would go out on me before long, and since it's set in and an odd size, I'd never find one that would fit and have to redo the counters and everything." Then she opened the item below it that she was sure was a book. She pulled off the gold paper and found a book showing the most beautiful kitchens she could imagine.

She turned to see Josh and Maverick smiling at her. "You don't know how much this means to me." She gave Josh a hug and kiss and then Maverick.

"We're so glad you're happy with it, and we'll start on it as soon as you decide on the kitchen of your dreams," Maverick said.

"I'd love that." She served the omelets while Maverick poured cups of coffee for them and Josh made some mimosas. "I had initially planned on selling the house and antique shop and starting all over when my three-year contractual obligation was through."

"You planned to move to another location and set up another antique shop?" Josh asked, sounding surprised.

"No, doing something completely different." She sat down and raised her glass of mimosa to the guys. "Merry Christmas."

"Merry Christmas," the brothers said, taking their seats at the dining table and raising their glasses to her before they drank their mimosas.

"What had you thought of doing?" Maverick asked.

"Nothing I could think of. Then something magical happened. A little reindeer calf came to visit. And I met both of you. This is exactly where I was meant to be."

"Despite all the trouble you've had," Josh said.

She reached over and grasped his hand. "Absolutely."

"I'm glad." Josh took a relieved breath. "I didn't think working in an antique shop would be as rewarding as it is, but the kind of treasures your great-aunt and great-uncle accumulated sure changed my mind. And working with you makes all the difference in the world."

"That's exactly how I feel about you and Maverick."

---

After breakfast, Maverick brought out board games, and they played until it was time to start the turkey. Once lunch was ready, Adam, Ethan, and Mr. Lee dropped in to eat with them and watch the movie, all three of them bearing gifts—pumpkin pie, pecan pie, and white wine.

This was the best Christmas with family and friends Brooke could have hoped for. The last three Christmases she'd been alone, since her parents had died. She had suspected she would be this Christmas too. She'd never believed she'd be laughing at the table, eating with a whole group of wolves, and then watching her favorite movie with them afterward.

She might never have left Phoenix to come to Portland if her great-aunt hadn't stipulated in her will that Brooke had to keep the shop for three years. It hadn't taken that long to convince Brooke she was right where she needed to be—with her mate, a new pack, and her new family and friends.

---

The meal was perfect and the company great, everyone having a grand time talking about the new year and their new year's goals. Before Brooke had come into his life, Josh really hadn't had any new year's goals. Every year was about the same. Same work. Same living arrangements. Same people to hang out with. In a heartbeat, she'd changed all that for him.

First on the agenda was making sure she had a new kitchen. And renovating anything else she needed to have done. He wanted to make a special corral for the reindeer when they came to visit so they'd be secure for visitors, because now they had two places to showcase the reindeer—the ranch and her place, when she wanted them there.

But he also wanted to arrange to have others taking care of the shop while they took trips. He hadn't gone anywhere in eons, too busy with work. In fact, the emergency leave he took to be with her, to protect her, was the first leave he'd taken in years.

"So when are you going to have a wedding?" Maverick asked.

Josh looked at Brooke. She reached over and took ahold of his hand. "In the summer? I want it to be warm."

"Sounds good to me."

"A honeymoon?" Maverick asked. "We'll have to watch the shop for you, but you deserve to go somewhere for your honeymoon."

"Fiji? I've always wanted to go there," Brooke said.

"That's where we'll go then."

"We'll have you covered," Maverick said, Adam agreeing.

Then it was time to watch *It's a Wonderful Life*. The guys all took seats on sofas and chairs. Josh smiled at her and pulled her into his arms, and the guys were quiet until the scene where Uncle Billy lost the money he was supposed to take to the bank.

"That was $8,000, worth $100,000 today," Mr. Lee said.

"Now that's a lot of cash to be carrying around in an envelope," Adam said.

"Hell, you know that $242 that the bank loan customer took out? That would be the equivalent of $3,500 dollars," Ethan said, figuring it out on his phone.

"The $17.50 would be worth $250 today," Maverick said.

Brooke started to laugh. "I will never watch this movie again without thinking about the inflated value of money."

The guys all laughed.

"Totally different perspective for me." She snuggled against Josh and got all teary-eyed when George wanted to end his life because he was worth more money dead than alive. Some things never changed for her, and she loved that she could watch a movie that moved her and cuddle with her mate at the same time.

At the end of the movie, everyone agreed it was great, and then Maverick said, "Hey, want to watch *Jingle All the Way*?"

---

Josh deferred to Brooke because, even though he'd love to watch the movie and he knew they'd all be commenting on that one, too, and they were all having a good time, he was just as ready to make love to his mate on Christmas Day.

Brooke smiled. "That would be fun. I'd love to see how you guys react to *that* movie."

"If I had a kid who asked for something for Christmas, I wouldn't forget," Ethan said.

"Ha! You get so caught up in your drug busts, you'd be just like the dad," Adam said.

Mr. Lee admitted, "That was me when my kids were young."

"I won't be. I'll be retired," Josh said.

Everyone looked at him.

Brooke blushed.

He chuckled. He'd sort of walked into that one. But making beautiful babies with Brooke? That was next on the agenda, once the guys took off.

Mr. Lee eyed the Steiff reindeer on the mantel that Brooke had given Josh for Christmas. "That's from my brother, isn't it?"

"Yeah, from one of the boxes of stuff he gave me," she said.

Suddenly, Mr. Lee and Josh were headed for the reindeer.

"I didn't see that in any of the boxes," Ethan said.

"Me neither," Adam said.

"Not me either," Josh said.

"I didn't want Josh to see it because it was a Christmas surprise," Brooke said, sounding guilty, like she'd done the wrong thing.

Josh smiled as Mr. Lee pulled a thread loose from the belly of the little reindeer and out popped a thumb drive.

# CHAPTER 30

BROOKE PULLED OUT HER LAPTOP, AND EVERYONE gathered around to see what was on the thumb drive. It showed videos of the men who had broken into Brooke's shop talking to Mr. Gulliver about drug shipments. And his stepdaughter, Daisy, arguing about where they should be sent.

"They shouldn't be sent to a stupid antique shop. Sure, the lady's old and she'd probably never figure out what's in the pottery, but what if she puts them out to sell?" Daisy said.

"Have you got another location to ship them to that would be more secure?" Gulliver asked Ackerson.

"A warehouse."

"Which we raided and took possession of the cocaine," Mr. Lee said for everyone's information.

"Not all of it," Josh reminded him.

Another video revealed the stepdaughter arguing with her stepfather. "Your daughter lives in Paris. She's not interested in running the family business. Neither of your sons are interested either. They're in Geneva. Let me run part of the business to show you how well I can do. You know I can be as ruthless and cunning as you."

"You're only my stepdaughter," Gulliver said. "My sons will tire of Geneva, and when they do, they'll return home to run the business."

Daisy laughed. "You always said I was like one of your own kids, but when it comes to business, I'm not. Fine.

Have it your way. Not." She pulled out a gun. He raised his hands in a pleading way, but she shot him in the chest with a bang, and he crumpled to the floor.

Brooke gasped, not expecting that. She thought... Well, she didn't know what she thought. That Mr. Gulliver would reconsider? He probably would have had her terminated after threatening him. "Your brother caught all this on video?"

"Yeah. He always wanted to be like me—catching the bad guys, putting them in jail where they belong. He turned out to be the best undercover agent he could have been. At least he didn't die in vain."

"I'm sorry I never got to meet your brother," Brooke said. "He was a true hero."

"He was," Mr. Lee said.

Brooke said, "I can't believe I hid the reindeer from Josh for a Christmas present when it had the thumb drive concealed inside it."

"You protected Jingles, and now this little reindeer is going to protect you, once the evidence on the drive puts Daisy and the others away for a very long time," Josh said.

Ethan, Adam, and Mr. Lee were going to the police bureau to sort out the files on the thumb drive and get with the local FBI and DEA, too, since the Gullivers had been involved in drugs, murder, and other criminal activities across state lines.

"If you want to go with them, you can, Josh," Brooke encouraged. "These are your cases too."

"Hell no. I'm retiring, and my place is here with you," Josh said while the other guys waited to hear the verdict.

Brooke had found her own hero in Josh, who would set aside this other important business to be with her.

When the guys left, Maverick gave Brooke and Josh a hug. "Merry Christmas. I've got to get home to the reindeer since the ranch hands have Christmas off and Adam and the others are coming over later to watch movies and have dinner there. Thanks for all my gifts. It makes up for me not getting the girl." He winked at Brooke, and she smiled.

They wished him a Merry Christmas and saw him off, and then Brooke and Josh returned to the warm house, Christmas lights sparkling on the tree, the fire crackling in the fireplace. It was time to enjoy their Christmas as mated wolves. Though she wanted to repair the poor little Steiff reindeer.

Josh had only one notion in mind. He kissed her, scooped her up, and hauled her back to the bedroom. Christmas would never be the same for her. And she was glad about that!

# EPILOGUE

AFTER CHRISTMAS, BOTH LUCAS AND HIS FRIEND TY helped to work off their community service debt to Josh and Maverick by mucking out reindeer stalls, but Josh also had them demonstrate how they hacked into the security video. What they loved best was they got to show off the reindeer to visiting tour groups. His friend Ty was glad Lucas had finally been adopted into a family and had his own girl-friend so Ty could continue to see Sandy as his own.

Josh and Brooke managed to free up two of the second-floor rooms at the shop. They decorated the first with seasonal merchandise, and the second contained consign-ments from the wolves in the pack. Maverick's beautiful signs were on display all over the shop. Almost daily, a wolf would come in to have Brooke appraise some item's value or bring arts and crafts to consign. She loved it because she felt really connected to the wolf pack members.

All the men and the one woman charged with the crimes against Brooke were in custody, awaiting trial. Ethan was still working on the Colombian cocaine case. And Mr. Lee had to return to Florida where he was based, but he had already wished them a happy new year, and Brooke and Josh wanted to keep in touch with him.

Come spring, she, Josh, and Maverick intended to go through the old homestead and its storage places to look for treasures they no longer wanted.

The guys would soon put in her dream kitchen, and she couldn't have been more pleased. And she'd found her great-aunt's diaries. Ivy had been to China and traded some other merchandise for the vases, way back when they must not have been valued at much. As for the Santa Claus suit and Natalie's clothes from the movie? A friend who'd worked on the set had given them to her because the movie had been Ivy's favorite Christmas story from way back then.

Now Brooke and Josh were getting ready to celebrate the new year with the pack, and she was wearing the red gown after it had been professionally cleaned. It was beautifully vintage, and she felt sexy and unique wearing it.

Josh smiled and raised his brows. "I told you that you'd look great in that dress. I just couldn't envision how much so." He took her hands and leaned down and kissed her mouth. "You are beautiful. When I first met you, I was hoping I could convince you to spend New Year's Eve with me."

She smiled up at him. "When you still thought I was guilty of stealing your reindeer? Or after you cleared me?"

He chuckled. "Before. I really didn't think you had stolen the calf."

"I had an accomplice, right?"

"Hell, I wanted to see more of you."

She wrapped her arms around his neck. "You got your wish. So did I."

Nothing could make the new year better than being mated to the wolf she loved. "You were meant to be my partner in all things."

"I agree with you about that. You know what made it happen?"

"One adorable little reindeer calf named Jingles. Well, and one teen wolf on a lark."

Josh loved Brooke with all his heart. She was the only wolf for him. He would never forget the way they'd met. The way she'd been so annoyed with him for not searching for any other suspects in Jingles's case. How could he when he'd already found the wolf he wished to be with?

She was truly beautiful in her vintage red dress, and he wanted to ring in the new year as soon as possible so he could peel her right out of that dress and make love to her to bring in the new year right.

He was still thankful that Lucas had borrowed Jingles, that Brooke had taken care of him and her customers had shared the news with the world, and that he was the first one who met the she-wolf, got to know her, and fell in love.

His new year had begun in that moment. "I love you, Brooke, with all my heart."

"I love you too. Let's go celebrate with the pack and return home to show each other just how much."

He took her out to the Ferrari, and they drove to the pack leaders' ranch in style, everyone cheering them when they got there, several of the guys wanting to check out the car.

Josh was ready to make the hot moves with Brooke while they were dancing.

"You know we're here now at the ranch," she told him. She held him close, dancing with her hot little body tight against his.

"Yeah?"

"We should ring in the new year the way only wolves can."

He groaned.

She kissed his mouth, spearing his tongue, caressing, rubbing against him.

"At home after midnight."

"After we run as wolves."

He sighed. "You know you're killing me, don't you?"

She laughed. "Yeah, but you love it."

And so they did just that. Danced, toasted to the new year, and ran as wolves, howling to the new year in the way only wolves could, and then made love back home that night under a full and glorious moon.

# ACKNOWLEDGMENTS

Thanks to Donna Fournier who is always looking up unique sayings for clothes, or fun little details to add, or reminding me in snowy stories when I'm writing during the heat of the Houston summer, when it's 107 degrees Fahrenheit, that the characters in the story need some hats, gloves, and warm winter parkas, and the ground and lakes and rivers might be frozen. And thanks to Darla Taylor and Donna for beta reading for me at the last hour and catching so many of my typos and other mistakes. I appreciate Deb Werksman for believing in me from the very beginning over a decade ago and giving me the opportunity to share with my readers from all over the world. And thanks to the fantastic cover artists who give my characters a visual appeal—both human and wolf—and combine that with a setting that makes them world-class covers.

**Read on for a sneak peek at
Terry Spear's long awaited
next Highland Wolf**

THE WOLF Wore Plaid

**Coming soon from
Sourcebooks Casablanca**

# CHAPTER 1

"We've got trouble," Lana Cameron, the baker, said to Heather MacNeill, motioning with her head to the big glass windows of the Ye Olde Highland Pie Shoppe, located in the quaint village near the MacNeill's Argent Castle.

Heather glanced out the window and saw Lana was right. Heather had been hoping the rumors about having more problems with the Kilpatrick brothers wouldn't prove true. But redheaded Robert and his equally redheaded brother, Patrick, were climbing out of their truck, looking around to see who was eating at the café tables outside, and then speaking to each other before they entered. They looked like wary gray wolves.

They should be wary. After Patrick had killed the wolf Heather was going to mate, she wanted to end Patrick herself. The only thing stopping her was that the fight had been her mate-to-be's fault.

Lana joined Heather behind the counter. "Did I tell you Enrick MacQuarrie came in when you were gone yesterday afternoon?" Lana raised a brow and gave her a smile.

Heather frowned. "On purpose?"

"Of course he came in on purpose."

Heather let out her breath in annoyance and folded her arms. "He came into the shop when he knew I wasn't going to be here?" As owner, manager, and general hand-on-deck, Heather was nearly always there, though she was training Lana to take over whenever Heather had to be away.

Lana let out a long-suffering sigh, placing her hands on her chest and looking heavenward. "Aye, if 'twere up to me, I would chase the hunky Highlander all through the heather until I had him pinned down to a mating. But alas, he sees not me as a prospective mate."

Heather continued to frown. "Me then? Why come when I wasn't here? On purpose."

"He is a hardy warrior but with feelings running deep for ye." Lana was keeping in character with her role here at the shop. The medieval Highland theme of the shop and the food was what brought in customers locally and from around the world for a unique dining experience. Who wouldn't want to try something both different and authentic?

"'Tis you he wished to see, but he fears you're still in mourning over Timothy and doesn't want to approach you too soon for a courtship."

Heather didn't lose the frown. Lana couldn't be serious. Was she up to a bit of matchmaking where none would be possible? "He has never had time for me...ever. He's a workaholic, he doesn't believe in having fun. He's a...stick-in-the-mud." With her. Not with others. She let her breath out in a huff. "Okay, so then what did he do?"

"He asked me how you were feeling."

"And you said?"

"Good." Lana laughed.

Heather curbed the urge to sock her.

Lana sighed again. "That you were ready to date if he would get on with it and start making an overture. Don't expect too much at first. I'm not sure he took me at my word." Lana smiled, then frowned. "Just think if he were your mate." She motioned to the windows where the Kilpatricks still looked unsure about coming inside or not. "He would toss them out on their ear if they came in. Or at least Enrick would make them shake a bit in their boots. They wouldn't be so cocky then."

But Enrick wasn't here to serve and protect, so she was on her own.

Protective, oh, yes. Enrick and his two brothers were protective of her when Heather chanced to go to the MacQuarrie castle. But the brothers thought she was too wild, too impetuous. And that irritated her. She'd overheard them talking to her brothers about it, how difficult it was to keep her in check. She sure didn't need a mate who felt that way about her.

She was seriously surprised Enrick had come to talk to her friend and feel her out about how Heather felt about dating again. As much as she'd had a crush on the wolf forever, he wasn't the one for her. She'd figured that out a long time ago.

What was wrong with wanting to do things on the spur of the moment? To take a chance and do something fun and whimsical? That was who she was, and she wasn't changing who she was to fit some concept a male wolf had of the perfect she-wolf.

Take her business here. It had been a risk to start something like this and a few said she couldn't do it. Well, she had proved she could. She'd worked hard to make her dream come true. And it was her dream, no one else's.

"Oh, I've got to tend to the bread." Lana hurried off to check on it while Heather glanced back at the glass door.

She'd heard the Kilpatricks and their McKinley cousins

had been furious they hadn't gotten the film contract to have a new fantasy film shot at the McKinley's castle in the Highlands. They would be even madder once they learned the MacQuarries had gotten the contract to have it filmed at their castle and grounds instead. Since some of the MacNeill wolves, her own clan, would be participating with the MacQuarries as extras in the film, and the MacNeills were McKinley rivals, there was bound to be trouble. Had the Kilpatricks already learned where the shoot was going to be held and that's why they were here? She knew they weren't here to apologize for Patrick killing Timothy. Patrick had felt perfectly justified, and truthfully, he had been.

The MacQuarrie pack leaders were keeping quiet about the film location for now, except they'd told Heather's pack leaders because they needed some of the MacNeill clan to sign up as extras. Heather knew because she was going to be in charge of the MacNeill female extras during the filming. She hoped the McKinley wolf pack would leave the pie shop out of their quarrels. The Kilpatricks—members of that pack—had been passive-aggressive of late with both the MacQuarries and MacNeills at pubs or wherever they chanced to meet. It was sure to escalate once the word reached the world where the film production would actually be shot.

She had her cell phone out, just in case she needed to text her pack leaders for some Highland wolf muscle. The shop was busy and she couldn't afford a disruption.

The aroma of fresh bread baking, of hearty beef stew bubbling in a cooker, and of sweet pastries filled the air as Lana brought out another loaf of Scottish soda bread from the oven. In full view of the customers, Lana made buttermilk bread and soda bread in a brick oven, just like in the old days. Originating in Scotland, the bannock bread made of oatmeal dough was cooked in a skillet, so they were making it in their kitchen. The ladies working in the shop were all wearing long dresses with narrow sleeves, long tartan overskirts, boots, and wimples for an old-world charm. Lana's kilt was the Cameron tartan of red, green, and blue, while Heather's was the blue and green tartan of the MacNeill clan.

Heather's pack leaders—gray wolf cousin Ian MacNeill and his red wolf mate, Julia—had assisted Heather in establishing the shop a year ago to help some of their wolves remain gainfully employed and Heather achieve her dream. Julia had loved the idea of Heather sharing the clan's old-time recipes with the world. Julia was American with Scottish roots and had fallen in love with all things Scottish when she joined them a couple of years back. Since the wolves lived such long lives, aging a year for every thirty, many of them had been around for a very long time. Heather was always cooking for Ian and his brothers so she had wanted to own a shop like this to share the old-world charm of the recipes she'd personally prepared. She just hadn't had the means to do it on her own without the pack leaders' assistance.

Heather manned the cash register as a man and his wife paid for two venison and cranberry pies.

The woman said, "We've been wanting to come here since the shop opened. It's so fun and best of all, the food is great. I love your costumes too."

Heather smiled. "Thanks, I'm so glad you enjoyed the visit."

Agreeing with his wife, the man nodded to her and carried out the pies as the couple left.

No one could accuse her staff of wearing costumes that weren't true to the period. Though about that time, some of the women were casting their wimples aside.

Ironically, many of the clansmen who cooked and served in the shop had sworn they never wanted to work under medieval conditions again, but those who did make the food and helped run the shop had gotten a kick out of the nostalgia. Conditions were much harder back then. Now they had modern ovens and stoves and fridges in the back to keep up with the growing business, and, of course, fresh running water instead of having to carry the water from a well like they did in the old days.

She glanced outside and noticed a family taking seats at one of the tables before they came in to order, perfect for nice weather like today—sunny, warm, breezy.

Everything was going fine, busy as usual, when the two men of the enemy wolf clan finally walked into the shop, making her feel as if they were turning her sunny day into something dark and dangerous. The brothers glanced around at the customers eating and visiting there. Were they checking to see if any of the men of her clan were there, ready to stop them in whatever they were up to?

The *lupus garous* attempted to look nice and easygoing, when she knew they were anything but. Their clan had been fighting with her people through the ages. They'd been pirates in the old days, and were still trying to cheat or steal from others in this day and age. Robert epitomized cunning and deviousness. He was a cutthroat who wouldn't hesitate to kill someone who got in his way. His brother went along with everything he did.

She wanted to tell them they weren't welcome here, but

she didn't want to cause a scene in front of her customers. As long as they were behaving themselves and had only come in to shop, she just had to deal with it and leave her feelings out of it.

The wolves dealt with their own kind if they were involved in criminal acts. They didn't want a wolf incarcerated long-term, even if the rogue wolf could control his shifting during the full moon phase. So if the Kilpatricks caused any trouble, she couldn't call anyone other than her own wolf pack leaders to handle it.

A chill ran up her spine as she eyed them with a wolf's wariness. Sometimes there were MacNeill clansmen working in the shop, but not right this minute.

There were three women in the back cooking, and Lana was still baking bread, while another two servers were in the back filling trays with the meals. Another was handling takeout orders in the back.

Robert Kilpatrick, the older of the two brothers, gave her a tight smile. It wasn't warm or friendly or reassuring in the least. More calculating. She didn't trust him or his brother.

Robert had never forgiven the MacNeill clan for the time Heather's cousin Cearnach MacNeill had rescued the Kilpatrick's cousin, Elaine Hawthorn, and her Highland properties from their greedy grasp. *Too* bad.

Cearnach had given Elaine a good home with the pack and loved her with all his heart. All the pack did. Her relatives had only cared about the properties she'd owned and wanted her mated to someone loyal to their clan.

To their way of thinking, Elaine had mated with the enemy. Cearnach and his brothers had to kill a couple of

Robert's cousins, as there was no stopping them in the fight the MacNeills had wanted to avoid. A grudge between the clans would go on forever because of it.

Another couple of customers entered the shop, two men, all smiles, wearing T-shirts from the Big Apple, jeans, and sneakers. Americans? Maybe.

The Kilpatrick brothers glanced at them, but the Americans ignored them and continued to the counter. "We'll take two of the steak pies," one of the men said.

She knew that face. He looked suspiciously like Guy McNab, the star of the movie they would be filming at the MacQuarries' castle. Heather smiled brightly at him. "Aye, sure." She rang up their orders and noticed that when Lana glanced at the two men, her jaw dropped.

*Don't burn the bread or drop it,* Heather wanted to tell her.

She wanted to ask if they were here because of the film, but she couldn't in front of the Kilpatricks. She was dying to know if the man was Guy—or maybe it was his stunt double.

The Kilpatrick brothers were reading the sign listing all the meat pies. Realizing she was watching them, Robert smiled at her a little again. It still wasn't a friendly smile. Patrick didn't bother. They sauntered over to the glass case filled with sweet desserts on display: clooties, black buns—Scotland's version of a fruitcake—shortbread cookies, empire biscuits—shortbread filled with jam, with a bit of icing and a cherry—and Heather's favorite, millionaire's shortbread, filled with caramel and chocolate, with a shortbread base.

A Canadian customer was taking pictures of the

medieval décor: brass lanterns and swords and shields, and a bow and quiver of arrows, and was sharing them with friends and family, which always helped Heather's business. Paintings of Highlanders in ancient kilts and even wolves and Irish wolfhounds standing with them in full color, with a textured look to give them an aged appearance, hung on the stone walls. Of course, it seemed like a paradox since wolfhounds took down wolves in the old days, but with the wolf packs, the *lupus garous* raised wolfhounds as pets and hunting dogs from early on. Of course *their* dogs hadn't hunted the wolf kind.

Heather smiled at a lady from Wales who came up to the counter to get a sweet dumpling to go. She chose a clootie dumpling filled with sultanas and currants, made with breadcrumbs, sugar, spice, milk and golden syrup all mixed into a dough, boiled in water, then dried in the oven. Heather boxed it up for her and set it on the counter, then took the money for it and thanked the woman before she left.

No one in the pack had envisioned the shop would be such a success when it first began, though Julia, a well-known romance author, had written about it in some of her stories and had intrigued visitors who read her books to check out the pie shop while on vacation to the area. Even the locals who lived nearby loved it.

The shop had started to get party requests for medieval meals, and it looked like they were going to be expanding their staff and building to accommodate the orders. Not only that, but her shop was contracted to help cater the main meals during the shoot. Heather was thrilled at the opportunity.

"We've heard so much about your shop, we had to come and check it out," Robert said, leaning against her counter.

She didn't believe him for an instant. Her phone was sitting on the ledge below the high counter and out of his sight, so she started to text Ian to see if he could send some backup—other than her three brothers, Oran, Jaime, and Callum, who would just as soon kill the Kilpatricks and ask questions afterward—if she needed help keeping the peace.

The doorbell jingled again, and she looked up, afraid it would be more of the Kilpatrick's kin. Instead, Enrick MacQuarrie pulled the door closed behind him and a bit of relief washed over her. Now he was a welcome sight. Not for his supposed interest in dating her. That was so far-fetched, she couldn't believe Lana would even think that. But Heather knew he was protective when it came to her or any other she-wolf of the MacNeill wolf pack.

She didn't send the text message to Ian, figuring Enrick could deal with the clansmen if they gave her any trouble.

Enrick looked so much like the man with the New York T-shirt sitting with the other at a table, waiting for their steak pies, that he could have been his double. Ever since Guy McNab had made it big as a film star in America, Enrick had been mistaken for him whenever he ventured out of the area.

He was the middle triplet brother of Grant and Lachlan MacQuarrie, tawny-haired and good-natured—except if he was defending the pack members or his friends, then watch out. He had a warrior's heart, yet she'd seen a real softy side to him too—playing tug-of-war with the Irish wolfhound pups, chasing the kids around the inner bailey in a game of tag, growling as if he were a wolf in his fur coat, making the kids squeal in delight. She'd seen him playing with his brothers as wolves and he was totally aggressive, not wanting either of his brothers to win the battle between them. And in a snowball fight, he was the fastest snowball maker and thrower she'd ever seen. If they played on teams, she wanted him on hers.

So he did let his hair down, so to speak, with the kids and with his brothers and others. With her? He clearly thought she was trouble.

But he was a wolf with a pack friendly to her own and she smiled brightly at him, glad he was here in case she needed him.

There was no smile for her; his look instead was dark and imposing as he glanced from her to the Kilpatrick brothers, who were apparently still trying to figure out what they wanted to buy. They hadn't noticed Enrick's arrival and she hoped he wouldn't start a fight when the other men were behaving...for the moment. There were so many customers in the shop, she didn't want to see a brawl break out in front of them. It surely wouldn't help business.

Robert pointed to the sign on the wall listing the kind of pies they sold. "We'll take a couple of the steak and kidney pies to go."

Okay, so they weren't causing trouble. Yet. Enrick was observing them with a do-anything-I-don't-like-and-you'll-die look.

Robert leaned against the oak countertop. "We hear there's supposed to be a movie filmed at one of the castles nearby."

Her heartbeat quickening, Heather's gaze darted to Enrick's and he raised his brows at her. Man, she really wasn't supposed to give away the secret yet. She knew he would question her next, once the Kilpatricks had left. He could probably hear her heart suddenly beating way too fast.

"We had that movie filmed at our castle a few years back, but that's it." Heather placed their order with RUSH stamped on it. She'd never used the stamp before, but this was certainly one of those times it came in handy.

"Not *that* film. A new one. More of a...*fantasy*," Patrick said. "Featuring wolves, even."

"At the MacNeill's castle? No," she said, shaking her head. She wasn't lying. Ian MacNeill swore they would never have another film shot at their castle. At the time they'd been in dire straits financially, and the only way to keep the castle solvent was to do the film. Wolf packs had to keep their identity secret. Having tons of non-wolves traipsing through Argent Castle and the grounds could be problematic. They had had to send a couple of newly turned wolves to stay with the MacQuarries, just so they would have no surprise shifting during the full moon.

Several female members of her wolf pack would really love a chance to playact in another film, though. She was waiting on a call from Colleen MacQuarrie, confirming how many would get a chance to be in the new film at the MacQuarrie's Farraige Castle. Heather was excited to take part also. Maybe she'd even get to see Enrick fighting in good form on the battlefield.

The MacNeill leaders and Enrick's pack leaders had talked about having the movie filmed at the MacQuarrie castle this time because the MacNeills would need to send reinforcements for the battle scenes and as extras around the keep. But it was all hush-hush so she didn't know if

Enrick was aware of it yet. And Robert and Patrick could very well have served as a couple of the extras who got into a fight with her people during that earlier film and were looking to stir up trouble again.

In just a few minutes, one of the MacNeill women brought out two steak and kidney pies in a box. Heather thanked her and began ringing up the sale, wanting to get the brothers out of there quickly without making it appear she was trying to rush them.

"I think you know more than you're saying," Robert said, glancing over his shoulder at Enrick, finally noticing she had a wolf warrior watching over things, standing off to the side, arms folded across his chest.

Stiffening a little, Robert sneered at Enrick, who didn't move a muscle, just stared him and his brother down in a wolf-to-wolf kind of confrontation like he was ready for the fight, come and get it. They didn't need whiskey to make them cantankerous. All they needed was their clan pride, and in this case, their wolf pack pride too. The battle between the clans had been going on forever. Stealing cattle, horses, brides, land, and fighting for more power in the beginning. The quest for more land and power was always an ongoing condition.

Robert paid for the pies, while Patrick grabbed the box with a jerk. "We know the film is being set in Scotland at one of the castles. You better not have lied to us." And then the two stalked out the door.

At least they hadn't fought with Enrick, and they did buy something. Miracles did happen sometimes.

"Hi, Enrick, did you need something?" she asked, relieved beyond words that the men had left without causing any real issues.

"Are you okay?" Enrick asked, looking genuinely concerned.

Enrick had seen everything that had gone on, so Heather didn't believe he thought the Kilpatrick brothers had done anything to her. Perhaps Enrick was worried about how she felt coming face-to-face with Timothy's killer today, even if he couldn't just come out and say so.

Though she had loved Timothy's wild manner and decisiveness, he couldn't or wouldn't control that darker wolf side of him that was always ready to battle the enemy wolf clans, no matter who else it might hurt. The pack leaders had met after the killing and determined Timothy had been at fault, but it didn't lessen the hurt she'd felt at losing him. It just made her angry with him for starting the physical fight and getting himself killed.

She tried to tell herself it was better she hadn't mated a wolf who was so reckless and might have left her to raise a couple of kids on her own at some point later in their lives. And she did appreciated Enrick's asking if she was okay. He might be as growly as all the other wolves combined, but he knew when to fight and when to leave it for another day. He never drank too much, so he always had a clear head, unlike Timothy. She'd loved Timothy, sure, but he'd had his faults. Enrick did too. Everyone did. So it wasn't like she would ever end up with Mr. Perfect Wolf, nor was she looking for that.

No one had shown any interest in courting her after Timothy died. It had happened two years ago, and she couldn't help but feel as though she was being judged for Timothy's actions, that selecting him for her mate said something about her. She'd considered leaving Scotland

and going somewhere else, hating to live with the stigma of what he'd done, though everyone said she was not to blame.

But she couldn't leave her friends and family behind. Argyle Castle was her home and always had been and always would be. She felt connected to it, to her family, and without it, she would be less than whole.

"I'm fine." She shrugged. "They didn't do anything or say anything hurtful."

"I was just…making sure." Enrick frowned. "So, a movie is being filmed at your castle again? I thought Ian would never agree to that." Enrick studied her expression, breathing in her scent. It wasn't that he was trying to catch her in a lie, but it was just a natural condition of being a part-time wolf.

She was sure she was giving him a ton of mixed messages—concern, anxiety, relief—and he wouldn't know it wasn't just because of the Kilpatricks being here "Uh, I'm sure Ian wouldn't agree to that after the last time. So what did you come in for?"

Enrick looked at the sign featuring the variety of savory meat pies, bridies—Scottish hot pockets smothered in brown sauce—soups, burgers, and baguettes.

"I'll get the Scotch pie. You know how my pack leader is. Colleen has wanted to try it—beans and chips, smothered in brown sauce. She has been talking about it ever since she heard about them and no one has made them at the castle since she's been there. Since I happened to be in the area…"

Right. He just happened to be in the area, checking up on her for her brothers. She might suspect someone from her own clan of doing the same thing.

"Good choice. It's fresh out of the oven." She sent the

order back with a note it was for Enrick MacQuarrie, and a couple of minutes later one of the MacNeill ladies brought it out, boxed up for him, all smiles. All the ladies were interested in the two unmated MacQuarrie brothers, so Heather wasn't surprised, even though she hadn't put a RUSH stamp on the order.

Enrick smiled at the lady and she smiled back, blushing furiously, then headed back into the kitchen.

"I'm surprised to see you in here," Heather said.

"I was surprised to see the *Kilpatricks* in here."

"So you came in to protect me."

"If I hadn't, Colleen would have had my head."

"Thank you."

Enrick paid for the pie but hesitated to leave. "Are you sure a sequel to the film isn't being made at Argent Castle? After the film came out, the reviews said the scenery and costuming and battle scenes were better than anything they'd ever seen. I always suspected they would make another film there, maybe not a sequel, but another Highland period piece. Or at least try."

"They had great reviews for good reason. The 'costumes' were ours and perfectly authentic. Anyway, no, Ian's not allowing another movie to be filmed at the castle. Why? If he did, would you want to fight in it?" The MacQuarrie brothers had been having trouble with another clan last time and hadn't been able to join them. The guys were all about fighting. They hadn't had a good battle in a while— even if it was just film-making magic—and she was sure the need to fight was in their blood.

He gave her a smirk.

"I thought so." She chose her words carefully. "You know

if it's in the works, the ones in charge probably wouldn't want anyone to leak the details until they're ready to share it with the rest of the pack."

"Then he is. *Great.*" Enrick smiled, then frowned. "So how come these guys had some idea it was happening when no one else does?"

She sighed. "I didn't say it *was* happening, but if it did, would you sign up to be an extra?"

"If the film is at the MacNeill's castle? Sure. See you around. And thanks for the pie."

See you around? To check on her? Make sure she was behaving herself? He was more interested in being in the next movie. "You're welcome." She sighed as Enrick left the pie shop.

Lana immediately came over and punched her lightly in the shoulder. "You didn't say *anything* that would indicate you wanted to go out with him."

"He wasn't here for that."

"Aye, he was here to protect you. And he asked how you were feeling. It helps to have wolf hearing. His coming here has to mean he wants to have something more to do with you. But since he's a man, he's cautious and afraid of rejection. Oh, and what's this business about a movie being filmed at Argent Castle?"

Heather sighed again and shook her head. "There isn't going to be a movie shot there. Ian wouldn't hear of it. Trust me."

Enrick wouldn't be happy with her when he learned she had known all along the film was set at his castle, not hers, and she hadn't told him. And she even had a role in the film. She glanced at the New York men eating their pies. The star of the film could be sitting here right this minute, but Enrick hadn't even acknowledged if he'd seen him. She was glad he hadn't, or the man could have given it all away.

——————————————————

Enrick had been fuming when he saw the Kilpatricks had parked their red truck at the MacNeill's pie shop and he suspected they were up to no good. He hadn't planned to be anywhere near the shop today, yet he'd driven in that direction, not even realizing where he was going until he was there. Subconsciously, he'd wanted to see Heather for himself. Her brothers were concerned that if she was ready to start dating, she would date the wrong wolf. He didn't want to be insensitive to her feelings, though.

Her dark hair and eyes had always captivated him. Even now. She'd always caught his attention. But she was not the she-wolf for him, he reminded himself. He envisioned someone who was a lot less…spontaneous. More predictable. Less out of control.

When he saw the Kilpatrick's vehicle there, any notion of approaching her about a date had flown out the window. Protecting Heather after what Patrick had put her through was all he could think about. Enrick still wasn't sure what to make of what had just transpired. She had put on a brave face in front of the Kilpatricks, but he'd smelled the tension she'd been feeling, too. He had wanted to throw the two men out of the shop bodily, but he didn't want to react to them the way Timothy had done and get himself in the same predicament.

Since Timothy had been a wolf of the MacQuarrie clan,

that had also kept Enrick from approaching her. He didn't want her or anyone else thinking badly of him for not giving her the proper time to grieve, while her brothers were worried she could just start dating a rogue wolf at any moment.

Enrick had been so been busy helping Grant run the estate, he hadn't had time to find a female to court. What with the trouble Grant's mate, Colleen, had from the Kilpatricks and their cousins, and being second in command, he'd had his hands full. Yet he had seen Heather was making a mistake with Timothy and had tried to stop her from courting the wolf in the first place. Though, from what her brothers had said, if they told her not to do something, she was sure to do it.

Enrick let out his breath. Now she was free and could be hurt all over again, if he and the others didn't watch out for her.

# ABOUT THE AUTHOR

*USA Today* bestselling author Terry Spear has written over sixty paranormal and medieval Highland romances. In 2008, *Heart of the Wolf* was named a *Publishers Weekly* Best Book of the Year. She has received a PNR Top Pick, a Best Book of the Month nomination by Long and Short Reviews, numerous Night Owl Romance Top Picks, and two Paranormal Excellence Awards for Romantic Literature (Finalist & Honorable Mention). In 2016, *Billionaire in Wolf's Clothing* was an RT Book Reviews top pick. A retired officer of the U.S. Army Reserves, Terry also creates award-winning teddy bears that have found homes all over the world, helps out with her grandbaby, and is raising two Havanese puppies. She lives in Spring, Texas.

# SEASON OF THE WOLF

Next in Maria Vale's extraordinary
series: The Legend of All Wolves

For the Alpha, things are never easy. The Great North Pack
has just survived a deadly attack, and Evie Kitwanasdottir is
dealing with new challenges, including the four hazardous
Shifters taken into custody. Constantine, the most dangerous,
is assigned to Evie's own 7th echelon.

Constantine lost his parents and his humanity on the same
devastating day. He has been a thoughtless killer ever since.
When Constantine moves under Evie's watchful eye, he discov-
ers that taking orders is not the same as having a purpose. In
Evie, he finds a purpose, but there is no room for small loves in
the Pack and Constantine must discover whether he is capable
of a love big enough for the Great North.

**"Prepare to be rendered speechless."**
—*Kirkus Reviews*, starred review for *Forever Wolf*

For more Maria Vale, visit:
**sourcebooks.com**

# WOLF UNDER FIRE

New from *New York Times* and *USA Today* bestselling author Paige Tyler is the action-packed, international series STAT: Special Threat Assessment Team

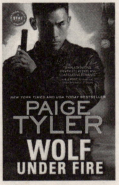

Supernatural creatures are no longer keeping their existence secret from humans, causing panic around the globe. To monitor and, when necessary, take down dangerous supernatural offenders, a joint international task force has been established: the Special Threat Assessment Team.

STAT agent Jestina Ridley has been teamed with former Navy SEAL and alpha werewolf Jake Huang. Jes doesn't trust werewolves. But if they're going to survive, she'll need Jake's help.

**"Unputdownable... Whiplash pacing, breathless action, and scintillating romance."**
—K. J. Howe, international bestselling author

For more info about Sourcebooks's books and authors, visit:
**sourcebooks.com**

# WICKED COWBOY WOLF

Cowboys by day, wolf shifters by night—don't
miss the thrilling Seven Range Shifters series
from acclaimed author Kait Ballenger

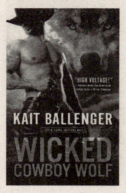

Years ago, Grey Wolf Jared Black was cast from the pack for a
crime he didn't commit. Now, he's the mysterious criminal wolf
known only as the Rogue, a name his former packmates won't
soon forget. But when a vampire threat endangers the lives of
their entire species, Jared must confront his former packmates
again, even if that means betraying the only woman he's ever
loved...

**"This story has it all—a heroine with grit and a hero
who backs up his tough talk with action."**

—*Fresh Fiction* for *Cowboy Wolf Trouble*

For more info about Sourcebooks's
books and authors, visit:
**sourcebooks.com**

# BEARS BEHAVING BADLY

An extraordinary new series from bestselling author
MaryJanice Davidson featuring a foster care system
for orphaned shifter kids (and kits, and cubs)

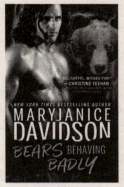

Annette Garsea is the fiercest bear shifter the interspecies foster care system has ever seen. She fights hard for the safety and happiness of the at-risk shifter teens and babies in her charge—and you do not want to get on the wrong side of a mama werebear.

Handsome, growly bear shifter PI David Auberon has secretly been in love with Annette since forever but he's too shy to make a move. All he can do is offer her an unlimited supply of Skittles and hope she'll notice him. She's noticed the appealingly scruffy PI, all right, but the man's barely ever said more than five words to her... Until they encounter an unexpected threat from within and put everything aside to fight for their charges. Dodging unidentified enemies puts them in a tight spot. Very tight. Together. Tonight...

**"Davidson is in peak form in this hilarious, sexy, and heartfelt paranormal romance."**

—*Booklist* starred review

For more info about Sourcebooks visit:
**sourcebooks.com**

# Also by Terry Spear